VOICES 1

ISSUES 1 - 6

1972 - 1975

VOICES 1

THE MANCHESTER BASED MAGAZINE
OF WORKING CLASS WRITING

ISSUES 1 – 6

1972 – 1975

PENNILESS PRESS PUBLICATIONS

Website: www.pennilesspress.co.uk

Published in original format 1972-75

First collected edition November 2008

This edition February 2019

ISBN 978-1-913144-01-2

CONTENTS

INTRODUCTION   7

ISSUE 1   9

ISSUE 2   44

ISSUE 3   89

ISSUE 4   151

ISSUE 5   199

ISSUE 6   272

CONTRIBUTOR INDEX   314

INTRODUCTION

The first issue of *Voices* appeared in 1972. Its founder, Ben Ainley, an academic teaching English in Manchester was diffident, almost apologetic, in his introduction:

> "I can make no great claims for these pieces, except that they are, it seems to me, varied, interesting, freshly written, and in most cases the work of men and women taking up a pen late in life; with some qualms, though with real curiosity as to how it will turn out."

But it flourished; Ben had struck gold. Over the next 12 years 300 contributors produced nearly half a million words. It became a national phenomenon; there was nothing quite like it before – and there hasn't been since. When asked for financial support the Arts Council scratched its head, squirmed and pronounced worker writing: 'successful in a social, therapeutic sense, but not by literary standards'.

Ben was a Communist Party activist - without his energy, commitment and contacts *Voices* would have died an early death. His banner under the title from issue 6 onwards became "working class poetry and prose with a socialist appeal". Politics and aesthetics remained tangled right up to the end.

This volume reprints everything in issues 1 to 6. By May 75 the eighteen foundation writers had been joined by another sixty. The tone was becoming more confident and the treatment more artistic – though those early accounts of the Glass Works, the General Strike and radical activism were fascinating as social documents.

Voices ran for 31 issues until 1984 with contributions from Manchester, London, Liverpool, Glasgow and Newcastle. Original sets are now impossible to find – there are some in Universities and one in the Working Class Movement Library at Salford.

A web site at *www.mancvoices.co.uk* contains everything which appeared in the magazine.This paper incarnation is for those who prefer books. The five volumes are available from *www.lulu.com/uk* and can also be accessed via the Voices website or the Penniless Press website at *www.pennilesspress.co.uk*. This is a non-profit making project and each volume, at approximately £10, is sold at cost price. There are five volumes altogether which contain the entire contents, graphics and text, of the original 31 issues.

I was an early contributor to *Voices* and met Ben Ainley a couple of times. I was not, however, involved in any of the *Voices* committees or those of the later Federation of Worker Writers into which *Voices* merged.

The background to *Voices* is well covered in the excellent papers of Tom Woodin, extracts of which appear on the *Voices* website. A more synoptic overview of British proletarian writing, which also touches on *Voices,* can be found in Ken Worpole's classic *Dockers and Detectives.*

I'd like, finally, to acknowledge the invaluable help of Tom Woodin who supplied copies of issues 28 to 31 which were missing from my own set and thank Rick Gwilt, Ken Worpole and Penniless Press editor Alan Dent for their encouragement and support.

Ken Clay – November 2008

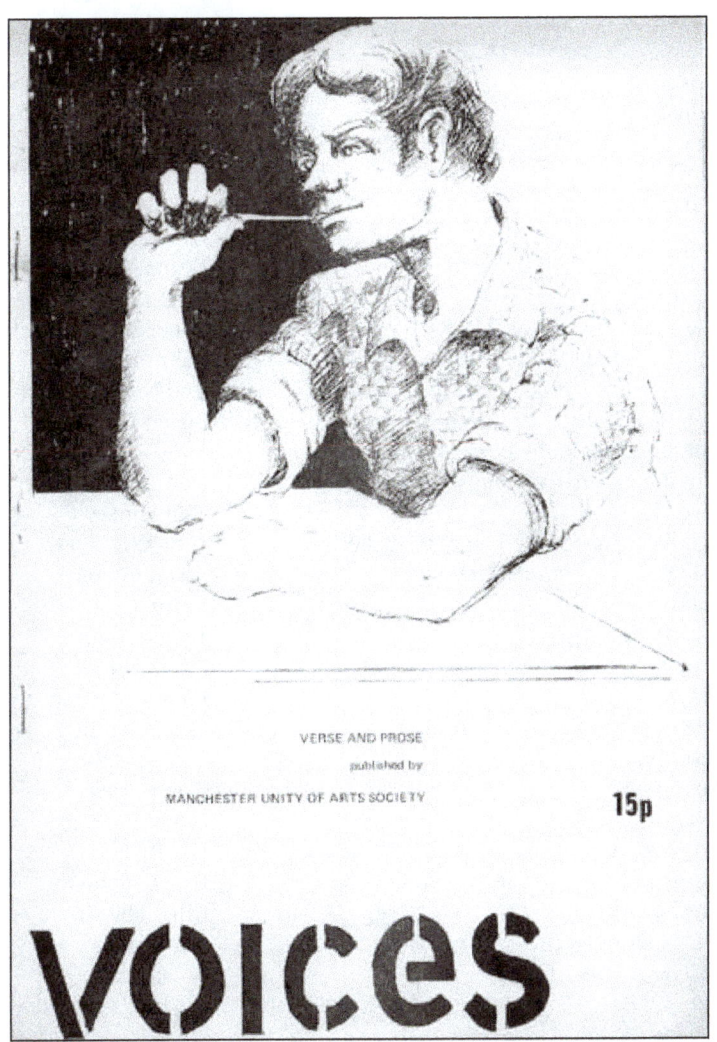

VERSE AND PROSE

published by

MANCHESTER UNITY OF ARTS SOCIETY

15p

voices

cover size 330 x 200 mms

CONTENTS

11.	Introductory	Ben Ainley
12.	Poem	Angela Tuckett
12.	Action	Frances Moore
13.	Industrial Strife	Frances Moore
14.	The Glass Works.	Frank Morgan
16.	1967	Frank Parker
16.	The Silent Bird	Ted Morrison
16.	Home	Denis Maher
17.	A Tribute to Jack Coward	Denis Maher
17.	Poem	Denis Maher
18.	The Freedom of Reason	Vincent O'Donnell
19.	Further Education	Fanny Morgan
20.	The Violent Universe	Ted Morrison
20.	Opening Stanza "In Death's Dream Kingdom"	Susan Cole
21.	Autobiographical Chapter	Syd Booth
25.	Moving and Bright Days	Ben Ainley
27.	Parting	Ben Ainley
28.	Recollections of the General Strike	Joe Day
30.	A Sonnet: With Sufficiency	Anonymous
31.	Dawn	Susan Cole
32.	Two Poems	Jim Leavers
34.	Brown Eyes Such an Honest Stare	Frank Smith
34.	O.T.M.S.	Fanny Morgan
34.	What Gentle Saviour With Love in His Heart	Frank Smith
35.	Suburban Automatism	Ted Morrison
38.	An Appeal	Robert Fletcher
37.	Pete	Frank Parker
38.	A Dying Art	Joe Bishop
39.	An Auld Man Cam to Heaven's Gate	Bob Cooney
40.	Our Neighbours	Ethel Hatton
41.	Why I Don't Write	Sol Garson
42.	At The Popular Cafe	Sol Garson

INTRODUCTORY

During the Autumn and Winter of 1971-1972, an English class met at New Cross Ward Labour Club, which I conducted. Its purpose was twofold: to discuss literature on the basis of a Marxist analysis, and to encourage free and original expression by the class members. These aims are distinct, and are not easily brought into one focus in a series of class meetings. The collection of writings by 20 contributors contains the work of 15 contributors who attended the class, including me. Six other contributions have been included because we knew them as the work of worker-.writers.

I can make no great claims for these pieces, except that they are, it seems to me, varied, interesting, freshly written, and in most cases the work of men and women taking up a pen late in life; with some qualms, though with real curiosity as to how it will turn out. We offer this collection to the Labour movement at large, but especially of Manchester and district. We hope to produce another collection towards the end of 1972, and will welcome any contribution from anyone in the Labour and T.U. movement and we would also welcome criticisms and comments from all who may feel able to make them.

A word about our title, "Voices". We felt that at this stage we had not achieved a single purpose; our writing was not yet a manifesto, or a call to action, but a series of individual utterances. Later perhaps a more unified and. challenging character may emerge in future collections.

Our thanks go to Brian Ridgway, for the front-page design, to New Cross Ward Labour Club for their hospitality, to Pauline Maher, Jean Schofield, Beryl Richardson and Maureen Druker who did the typing and duplicating. We are also grateful to Angela Tuckett, Frances Moore and Bob Cooney for their contributions. Robert Fletcher has been dead. many years; his "Appeal" is plainly dated: but we thought it witty and interesting and we have no fears of infringing copyright. "Anonymous" is genuinely unknown to us. Many years ago a schoolgirl of nine at Denton brought me this and some other poems of a boy friend to read. Shortly afterwards I lost contact with the schoolgirl, and never met the writer. If by a miraculous chance the schoolgirl of more than 30 years ago, or the writer of the sonnet should read this, we hope they'll forgive the liberty we have taken in printing it here, and will get in touch with us.

Ben Ainley.

Please send comments and criticisms or contributions to a further collection to me at 13 Victoria Way, Bramhall, Stockport. 8K7 lDE

A POEM

There will be no time
For me,
And there will be
Not one
To call my own.
Within my lifetime the dry bread,
The cold hearth and the narrow bed,
The trudge along the rain-swept street
Past those who stay with lagging feet,
The mushroom cloud and the storm-sky;
We'll not go dancing, you and I.
Will there be no time
For me ?
And will there be
No song
Carried along ?
Within my time the unpicked fruit,
Verses unwritten, voices mute ?
Always the human heart's brave beat
Still keeps in time with marching feet;
Although I never write a line
Yet every marching song is mine.
There will be a time
(Maybe,
Even for me ?)
When here
As everywhere,
The last to march join in the throng,
Their drum-beat heard before their song.
Joyous, upon the plinth you stand
Applauding.
I stretch out my hand;
Unseen, I clap our all-triumphant host
And shout - with every other happy ghost.

Angela Tuckett

ACTION

Finished! said the masters.
Broke! said the bosses.
Sack all the workmen and cut our losses.

No! said our lads and they stayed in the yard.
We learned from our fathers Union manners
are more than a matter of dues and banners:
It's stand all together when the boss plays hard.
Shorter hours and better pay
are won by workers the bitter way:
tighten our belts and strike if we must
or the boss will bargain us into the dust.
But we're not on strike said the U.C.S!
It's human nature and human right
not to give in without a fight.
and U.C.S. at Clydebank stands
for the Hand's right to use his hands:
for the right to work as a human right.

INDUSTRIAL STRIFE

A man has only his two hands,
only his mother wit
against these conquerors of lands
these rich men and their State.
They crush him if he tries to stand
and never notice it.
Odd workers are expendable
but they need a working class.
Our hands are indispensable
so when our interests clash
where they'd crush an individual
they have to heed our mass.
Our interests being opposite
create industrial strife
the boss invests for profit
but the worker works for life.
Which ever side may benefit
the other feels the knife.
The battle of the factory floor
expressed in politics
is the master's aim to contain by law
the worker's fight to exist.
But production Needs the worker more
than it needs the capitalist.

Frances Moore

THE GLASS WORKS

The Glass Works was now owned by the Co-op, purchased to meet the ever growing demand for milk, jam and sauce containers. It had previously been owned in the old glass blowing days, by Mr. Jones an important figure in the town, and a City magistrate, who sold it for a sum reputed to be around £50,000 The co-op had immediately installed three large, second-hand automatic bottle-making machines, made in Cincinatti. So, whilst mountains of silver sand and soda-ash went into the factory at one end, an endless stream of bottles and jars came out at the other, an average of 20 a minute, off each machine, 24 hours a day, millions of jars a year.

Johnny wondered, "who could eat all this jam? Even the Co-op couldn't surely be selling all that much sauce." He had never worked in a place like this glass works. The loud clatter of the machines, the oil and dust, the pungent smell of burning lubricant liberally used to regularly swab the hot machines; the intense heat of the large furnace operating at more than 12500 centigrade, with large annealing ovens in close proximity to the machines. All made for almost intolerable conditions in the heat of the summer but in winter it was warm and pleasant. Above all the character of the men fascinated Johnny. They appeared to be moulded by the conditions of manufacturing within the factory. He had found that all the machine men and helpers were rogues, liars and thieves. He found to his cost that anything of value, tools or materials mysteriously disappeared if he turned his back or misplaced them. Nothing was sacred. There was no respect for authority, no discipline, except that imposed by the machines, their speed determining the bonus earnings. The supervisors and foremen were regarded contemptuously as supernumeraries as far as the men were concerned, except when the machines broke down or were held up for reasons outside the men's control who as a result, lost their bonus. Earnings were high for 1936, in the region, a consistent wage of £7 to £8 a week for 37.5 hours when generally a skilled engineering craftsman received £3.12. per week for 44 hours. Thus any stoppages were violently dealt with by the men and the foreman was suitably abused.

It appeared that when Jones the previous owner was a magistrate on the bench during the First World War the culprits before him were given a choice of either a sentence in the army in the mud and blood of the Flanders fields or to work in his Glass Works. Most of those who thus appeared, being sensible men, preferred the Glass-works to the Glass-house, especially as the slaughter in France was at its height.

Jones died just after the sale of his factory to the Co-op but he left all his money to his secretary - not a penny piece to his wife. The lads told Johnny 'he did it to spite his wife because she made scenes at the factory about his secretary. He got on well with his secretary they said. 'Cow Elsie we called her'. She did most of her secretarial work on the new couch in the office that Jones had bought specially. We used to watch 'em from the stairs and she knew we were watching. They were the rummest crowd that Johnny had ever seen or worked with in his job as a skilled maintenance engineer.

There was 'Mad Alf', a scrawny wisp of a man who had been in trouble with the law more than once. On drawing his wage of £7.10/- he would separate £2 to give his wife. 'Is that all you are giving your wife out of that packet and you are keeping all the rest for yourself?" "Course I am" said Alf, 'Don't forget, I buy my own clothes out of it'

Then there were the two brothers who had a tremendous reputation as lady killers. Many a time a husband arrived at the factory enquiring with violence in his voice as to the where-abouts of Dickie. Dickie was never around of course, but unfortunately had his love life ruined later when somebody, either by accident or design, dropped a blob of hot glass down his trousers.

After a while Johnny came to realise that he had no longer to face hostility in his relations with the men. They even returned his tools or materials that he had inadvertently left on the machine floor. He had been accepted 'on all fours' with the rest of the shop.

There was nothing these men would not do to help you once you had been accepted. Their comradeship which was so tightly knit, was in fact Johnny came to realise, directed against authority. This was their common denominator.

An example of this was the occasion when a foreman nicknamed 'Knocker', (he was a joiner by trade) had the gall to sit outside the main exit to prevent the men leaving before their recognised meal-break at 12-30 Somebody, by arrangement, from an upstairs window conveniently placed, poured a full bucket of water on to Knocker. It was said by an eye witness that he received every drop in the bucket. Every worker in the factory knew who had tipped the water. The management however does not know to this day who the culprit was.

Alas, the old glass works is no more. Its inadequate lay out and out of date machines proved unable to cope with the expanding demands of new generations of bottled-food eaters. Its workers scattered with their specialist skills to the four winds of industry. New gigantic factories have been built to serve Co-op customers, but where-ever the bottles were made, it's quite certain that the workers in those factories will have the same disregard for authority as those employed in the old Glass Works.

Frank Morgan.

1967

I want to be as a dream, to have no substance
To be consciousness looking in, life is hard and the
soul wreaks much pain.
Remove the nerve and retain the interest –
And yet when we were young with unarmoured mind
How blue the sky!
And music, colours, how bright!
Then was pain delight, and uninformed love urges liquid light
Now at 40 how I feel sere and yellow and wanting to give up the fight
To die, yet live a little and feel no more.

Frank Parker

THE SILENT BIRD

Wandering on a wooded fell
I tried and stopped to sleep a spell,
And dreaming there I saw a bird
Sun-silvered in a tulip tree.
No song nor bird-like sound I heard
As silver-eyed it gazed on me.

And though I tried I could not rise
And to my lips rose soundless cries
And in my heart a growing dread
And my eyes on the dumb-bird lock'd.
Slow-winged it flew then tow'rds my head
Its glittering orbs my panic mock'd.
O, endless dark with silence wed!

Edward Morrison

HOME

House made of stone, brick and cement.
You give me shelter –
You protect the people from the cold, snow and rain.
But much more than that - you're part of living life,
You're the dwelling place where human beings, love hope and
dream.
You're part of their feelings, conflicts and happiness.

You're the pride in the heart of the people ,
You're home, home.

Denis Maher.

To a man I did not know

The common bond of Communism in each man - I recognise and understand.

TRIBUTE TO JACK COWARD.

A heart is only so big, and can only beat so long for the people, then it
must stop.
You were a communist man, with a communist mind.
A mind that has felt the pangs of hunger and want, the cold. prejudice and
injustices.
And yet, a mind that deeply heard the tears of pain of other people.

Struggle makes the man.
You struggled all your life for the highest principles possible,
that of man himself, in freedom, liberty and dignity.

Your class will always be proud of you,
Your memory will be a golden glow of courage for us all to follow

Your manhood was a beauty -- a real deep beauty in action.
Action where you put your life on the line for what you felt was right.
And that is the most that can be given by a human being, his life.

Comrade your principles were high, your courage deep.
The world was that much better off, for you being on it.

Denis Maher

POEM

We are born,
We die.
The in between we call life –

Hoping, desiring, thinking, reasoning the world about us.
Truth is nothing unless shared by others..
Prejudice, injustice obsessed by hate,
love of what could be.
Death is something we can -never experience, it is the unknown,
that can never be known.
We are part of the process of nature –
Millions before us - millions afterwards will follow this process
History is living men in action, struggling out of the age of darkness
Into the light of progress.
Martyr's scream out for vengeance - for the suffocating misery of
people.
Human beings are not vegetables that grow unaware –
But become conscious of life - death and living people and the per-
sonal honour of being one.

Denis Maher

THE REASON FOR FREEDOM & THE FREEDOM OF REASON

If reason in revolt now thunders and emotion becomes
its-pupil in self control and clear expression.
This is not a subject for wonder.
Have we not all shared in the material plunder.
From countries near and far stolen from those who
have known exploitation, humiliation and fear.
Dictated by military laws conceived in power and greed still
we are denied the right to heed the calls of reason and freedom
from those
Whose greedy hands are ever stretched to rob the living and the dead.
In many ways this has been said in the hills, valley and the plains.
In the gaols and the concentration camps of Spain.
In Africa, Buchenwald and Ulster too.
And still we must unite the Black the Yellow and the White, the he
the she and the in between in our graduation from confusion to
enlightened reason.
We must rid ourselves of inhilation and inferiority if Unity
and Reason is to win for all our overwhelming majority –
So essential to human freedom.

Vincent O Donnell

FURTHER EDUCATION

Joining the metal-work class at our local night school opened a new and interesting world for me,

The choice of subject was limited, and the normal classes for ladies already had enrolled their full quota of students, and I thought it wasn't too late in life to learn new skills, so I found myself a middle-aged (well, elderly) lady in a class of boys and men learning something entirely new.

Up till then, my acquaintance with machinery had been limited to a sewing machine and a washing machine, and now here I was in a world of lathes, borers, grinders, saws, etc.

I soon learnt that forging had nothing to do with getting rich quick, a jig was not a dance, and brazing had nothing at all to do with cookery.

The teacher was a kindly jolly man who welcomed me most sincerely; it was as much a novelty to him as to me to have an elderly lady in his class. My class mates were most interesting. The boys were mostly working for their O levels, and the men were nearly always mending some household gadget or doing something for their cars,

I suppose that previously I would have regarded most of these boys as yo-bos, but in this situation I found them very well mannered and quite likea-ble, and I looked forward to my weekly two hours in their company. I know that when they offered to help me saw through a piece of iron 14" x they regarded me as they would their misguided grandmother, but they were very nice about it, and later when they asked me 'what are you mak-ing, Mrs, ?' they had almost accepted me as a fellow worker,

After two hours in this new environment I would walk home in the sharp evening air in a state of elation, with a blister on every finger and my rheumaticky shoulder playing me up something awful and thinking poeti-cally 'I too will something make, and job in the making,'

My masterpiece turned out to be a wrought iron coffee table. Its full of faults that I know about, and probably many that I don't know about, but it stands squarely on its legs, and the glass top doesn't wobble and its in regu-lar use. But my best moment is when my husband points out 'the wife made that.

Fanny Morgan

THE VIOLENT UNIVERSE

From the mountains of our hurtling globe
The telescopes of science probe
And radio-ears to earth reverse
The secrets of the universe
Behold:
A myriad silent stars we see
Are ghosts of long-dead galaxy;
Those silver lamps by lovers treasured
Mere spirit-beams in 'light years' measured.
This land on which we yearn to linger:
A cooling piece of solar cinder,
The sun itself a fragment from
A vast exploding cosmic bomb.
And all life-forms, including man,
have no more point or purpose than
Bacteria on a ball of earth
Perpetuating birth on birth.

Edward Morrison.

IN DEATH'S DREAM KINGDOM.
(The 1st. stanza of a poem about 300 lines long)

Travelling back and forth and I heralding
another day's existence with silence
screaming through my eyes like tortured vehicles of misused
faith;
Skies collapsing within
the framework of my mind
Trees felled by
demon hands
Skeleton fingers aching round the bark.
Drift past motionless hours carry the testament of dying eclipses
through melting oceans
of sandpapered guilt.
I climbed past the raven's nest on
Macbeth's sanguine castle. Edging over
unlit rainbows, bathed in charcoal darkness,
Night was like a tombstone; the horizon,
a graveyard in the fleeting glimpse,
of a seagull's rain-chant eyes.

Transparencies, traces of unlit moments enmeshed on feverish
indifferences.
Forests of wordless confusions....
void....
Living moments
In starship cathedrals
Find a zone
of non-realisation.
A silver second
In a timeless non-consciousness
Earthbound amongst cannon-songs
Incantating irrelevancies
Drawing shop-window conversations
Through steel barriers and mindless tripods
To a desert scene
Where loaded insignifia
is the plenteous cactus plant.

Susan Cole

AUTOBIOGRAPHICAL CHAPTER.

My two brothers were so much older than I that they were demobilised
from the army two years before I even left school, which was 1922. Frank
was ten years older than I, John two years younger. Frank had been caught
up with the propaganda of the time and had joined the army two years under age at 16 and left just after his 21st birthday. Now free, he threw himself into everything, sports, girls, his union and the Clarion. Cycling Club,
and through the latter, his first real socialist ideas.

A French Polisher like my father, he had made a friend of another in his
Union Branch named Jack Calder. The latter was a foundation member of
the Communist Party and a C.C.C. enthusiast. Frank kept his socialist convictions to himself, for although his athletics were with Salford Harriers,
his swimming, dancing and the Irish Clubs were all connected in some way
with the Church. Deep down he developed a growing hatred of religion
which persisted through life. He was learning for the first time how God
was used by the clergy on both sides in the war, no laughing matter to a
man who had seen his comrades killed only too often. I was quite unaware
of his convictions. I saw him as tall, gay and intelligent with a string of
girls chasing him.

Our mother had come from Irish parents which was why we all considered
ourselves Irish "rebels" and it was natural on leaving school I would gravi-

21

tate to St. Patrick's, joining the scouts and the swimming clubs, and making my pals there.

John was a much quieter personality than Frank, but he also was mixed up with the swimming, scouts (as a scoutmaster) and his Union. He was an upholsterer, in a different Union than Frank and I followed him into the upholstery trade. It was John who first followed me into the Party, for an unbroken membership through life.

Learning the upholstery trade was a hazardous business for the only shops open were the small ones and this often meant losing a job in the summer months, I couldn't get into the Union either, one had to be a bound apprentice or in continuous work in the same factory from 14.

I remember little of my Father. Older than my Mother, he died when I was 20, and in his last years spent most of his time in a pub. He found it difficult to acclimatise himself when the much older sons came home. My mother told me he was for a period a Chairman of his Union branch and helped in getting his own shop organised.

When the General Strike broke in 1926 I was working for a small boss on Stretford Road in the Sale district. He didn't sack me for the summer and paid me wages even if there was no work. A former worker himself, he put on his letter paper "Late of Kendal Milnes" and it was very effective. He told me to stay at home while the strike was on, and paid me arrears of wages when I came back.

My father and Frank were both on strike, but I have only a few memories of it: a huge meeting in Platt Fields made up of many platforms and of a speaker holding up a small leaflet and saying "Behold the "Daily Mail!, one million circulation", of a traffic jam in Piccadilly at the corner of Mosley Street that nearly crushed the student "controlling" it and lanes of stilled traffic, and on the second Sunday of the strike a leaflet handed to us as we left the Church. It stated this was not a strike in the ordinary sense of the term, it was a strike against the State, the State was the mouthpiece of God, thus it was a strike against God himself and to take part was a mortal sin; it bore the name of the British R.C. Cardinal. Like all similar propaganda, it never got off the ground.

On the morning of the return to work I stood dreamily at the tram stop. On the opposite side of the road were the usual newsagents placards: "T.U.C. Surrender" "Government Victory," and only the Daily Herald's "T.U.C. Victory".

I sneered, the capitalist liars were up to their tricks again. Certainly I had a long, long road to travel.

Twelve months later found me working in my first large factory, Wood-houses. Its entrance was opposite the huge side entrance of Strangeways Prison. I came to work one morning and the workers were still outside, an execution was to take place, eventually the prison bell tolled rather loudly and the stunned workers quickly removed-- their hats, two warders- came out, pinned up a notice and went back. The bell continued to toll at inter-vals, It seemed to me aimed at striking terror into the thousands of people who could hear it and I wondered how the prisoners felt. I felt appalled and it was a miserable day in the shop afterwards.

Woodhouses was a piecework shop, and piecework was not recognised by the Manchester branch of the Union. I was daywork, as all under 21s were. This firm had another factory in London, and the E. C. and branches in London had a much more progressive approach, where piecework shops were organised. The General Secretary came down, a likeable person named Wilsden with whom I came on very good terms a few years later. He was firm, either the new branch could change its policy towards piece-work or a new branch would be formed by the E.C., the shop could not remain unorganised. In the event, a new Branch was formed called Man-chester No.2. I joined the old one then, I was daywork and my brother was in it. I have pleasant memories of some the older generation in it but one stands out, a woman well into her fifties, she came on her own. sat erect throughout the meeting without ever speaking, and going home again. Her name was Miss Hough.

A year after the war we called a "fraction" of upholstery boys of the two branches in connection with some election we were preparing for, Imagine my feelings when she turned up, she had joined the Party and was now nearly seventy

After joining the Union I came out of the library with a book on Trade Un-ions by G. D. H Cole, probably a short history. At the bottom it read, "A W.E.A. Textbook". Frank picked it up and read it. He had once had a brief association with the N.C.L.C. (Labour Colleges), who hated their "state-granted" rival, the Workers' Educational Association, he told me if I felt that way I ought to take the N.C.L.C. correspondence courses which were free to Union members, he suggested starting with Economics and I did.

I had no idea then that I was taking a small path that would lead me to a main road leading to an adult, better life. In fact early on I had some small misgivings. I had taken a second subject called European History. The third or fourth lesson dealt with the power of the Church in medieval times, amassing its riches and being a ruling power in feudalism. I had been to a catholic school but had never known this. I had some minor doubts, but the subject was dealt with quite factually, and the remainder so interesting that I did not want to drop it. The text book was by Maurice Dobb, and even today it is so interesting that it remains in my bookcase, old and tattered, but the one that was "never lent"!

I stuck at it, taking one subject after another for about two years. When I was about half way through Frank asked me if I would like to go with him to some Irish Club in Hulme. It was a dance, I hadn't learned to dance, - but when it was over about five or six of us went into a parlour of a small house in Rusholme Road, at (the Oxford Road end, where we could have cups of tea in a small parlour and a talk. A chap named Atkinson was more or less dominating the discussion and at one stage mentioned Marxism. I chewed the bait and talked with him about the Labour theory of value.

I would have forgotten the incident except that I didn't go again and Frank once asked me to but I refused with some excuse. Atkinson was tall enough to be a policeman and had a very English name and accent. I had a suspicion that the Irish Clubs teemed with spies and there were frequent police raids for drinking after hours. Many years later I walked, into the Party rooms in Fountain Street and Bill Rust was talking to - Atkinson he didn't recognise me and we did not speak; but for my romantic ideas .I might have been in the party much earlier.

I had continued in the scout movement, we were in the senior section called Rovers, mainly because it was the centre that kept us together, I kept dropping out and was appealed to to come back. Three years later I had a letter printed in the' Manchester Evening News, at that time a very "Liberal" paper, attacking the scout movement as being anything but peaceful, printing my name but, customary at the time, not my address. A number of people replied, for and against, one a "Scoutmaster" who thought it plain I didn't know what I was talking about. It stung me into replying about games like "stalking the enemy" and other examples. The Editor conveniently wrote underneath "This correspondence is now closed." I was quite thrilled about this first incursion into the press, the inspiration coming from one course on English and Article writing.

This was the last Course I took, the remaining subjects, like Esperanto, having no appeal. This tutor had never put name or initials on any lesson and I asked him his name in the last lesson. The final subject had been an essay on some aspect of Marx and Engels, finishing half way down the page and he wrote underneath, "Glad you have discovered Marx and Engels Now get on to Lenin Then you won't need a tutor (only don't shout about it !) T. A. Jackson." Marx and Engels were underlined, but Lenin three times ! I didn't shout about it.

Just before this Course ended the NCLC wrote me asking if I would like to train as a tutor with the local College. I was unaware one existed and agreed. The Course was in the Organiser's house, in Winton, Eccles, and lasted two years except the summer months, involving weekly visits, "home work" and considerable practice as tutors. Finally we were tutors and could take classes, an easy thing after our experience, single lectures even easier, I can't remember all the classes, but Irlam, Rawtenstall, Bolton and Levenshulme come easily to mind. I cant remember my first, certainly Levenshulme was my last.

Within twelve or eighteen months of the Strike my father died and John married and when I was 21 my brother Frank married too. My mother and I lived with them for a brief period in Tipping Street, Ardwick. It is all now covered by the Mancunian Way. A small communist meeting took place thirty yards away from us at the corner of Union Street. The speaker was young and clearly dressed, spoke eloquently and with a deep sincerity. I don't remember what he said and was not impressed - - except that he was a decent type. Years later I caught a glimpse of him at some meeting, but never saw him again. My mother moved to Harpurhey with me, leaving behind Frank and his wife, and it was mainly from Harpurhey that I began to function as a tutor.

Joe Day.

MOVING AND BRIGHT DAYS.

Moving and bright days.
Days that sing themselves.
Through sunshine into lengthened shadow. Happily,
happily I live through them taking now
the whole sweet taste of them into my mouth,
Like grapes, the skins sucked dry, and then outspat.
Boys comrades. girls, friendship that gives me gladness,
Friendship that stabs me with its sudden daggers,
Failed friendships. realised joys, realised sorrows,
Neither ideal joy with bronze sun smiling,
Neither ideal sorrow, glassy-eyed, trembling,
But grand reality, incorporate, grasped,
And joyed in, and enthralling, being grasped.
I face my life. It stretches out before me,
Glad days and bad mad days. Tension and looseness.
My mind tomorrow a fine white wire of purpose;
My mind next week a dull brown stretch of country;
My mind this instant a coloured Japanese lantern;
My mind some day haply, a smoking extinguished candle,
Smelly, stuffy, with only a red spark to it
My friends; and some will be not true to me

My friends, and some will go away from me,
My friends, and some will come, knowing me, to hate me,
Because I am what I am, neither a wise man,
Nor yet a fool, but both by turns, both gladly.
Always, and I made part of it, revolt.
My fellows, my comrades, the workers, shaking from them,
As suddenly conscious of being strained by them,
Their chains and links of servitude ...
How many things are happening? Tomorrow ?
Today is eternity being realised
And I shall go to bed tonight alone,
Inviolate, virginal, a boy, a baby,
Philosopher, communist, a thinking engine,
And a dreamer of tender dreams. In bed alone,
Thoughts will be moonbeams in my darkened room,
Cold moon, my mind with silver light will burn,
And tomorrow, after warm body is sunk in sleep,
Tomorrow, awakeness, joy, rebirth, the rendezvous
with every day's eternity. And hedged about
with much that's not significant, by thoughts,
Aches, penny troubles, newspapers, torn boots
Letters not written, trivial stupid worries,
Sometimes a luminous thought, sometimes realisation,
Sometimes sheer gladness in a girl's caress,
Sometimes great pride in work for the revolution,
In the thought that in slight ways, one man in millions,
I have taken my conscious part with comrades in the fight.
Sometimes a starry night, and long long talk
And the urge and emotion of struggle our heritage.
Comrades this me, unmoralist, this me,
Baby I said, philosopher, nay soldier,
Worker-soldier for communism, this me
Unsurrendered, a person, a protoplasmic
Complete determined entity, this me
Loving poetry, loving life, loving a gay girl,
This me faces existence. Sees these things,
Blinks not, forgets not, emptiness, recurrence
Knows man a little, knowing myself a little, -
Knows children much, seeing them, knows their weakness
Their link, my own, with our humanity.
Unsurprised by passions, emotions, jealousies, littlenesses,
Taking them, embracing into myself, and laughing
Even at contemptible self, grovelling yesterday,
Because a gay girl didn't write a letter.

Thus at the beginning of February
Month purficatory, so the old Latins styled it,
Facing endeavours, struggles, trials, movements,
Most glad, most glad to be alive.

Ben Ainley,. 1925

PARTING

The moon came up the sky that very night,
And all the while we quarrelled, yellow rays
Fell on her hair, her dress, and on her face,
And passed around slowly from left to right.
All this I noticed with especial care,
Though her small face was flushed with anger, pain;
"You must not come, you must not come again;
You shall not come to me; you would not dare."
I listened never speaking: On the road
behind me, a tram passed, and passing clattered,
stopped near us, then went on. A Shelley ode
Came to my head, and "When the lamp is shattered"
I murmured to myself, and for a second,
Black night around, this passionate angry girl
Once intimately my friend, a far past beckoned,
And parting was great sorrow In a whirl
of thoughts thus warm and tender, a strange thought
Move icycold came to me, and I said:
"Spare all your tears, for if we both were dead
your anger and my indifference would be nought.
But as it is, since you live, and I too,
It needs no words to tell me not to do
What, for weeks I have had no impulse for."
Then she spoke, wept, grew angry, stamped her foot,
For many minutes she spoke, her voice was shrill,
Subdued yet shrill, her face was drawn. I cut
Across her angry speech with cold cold words,
And when the dawn came up, the sky, grey, leaden,
Sharpened the treeshapes round us and it met
Her face , pale cold, and filled with ashes, yet
Not colder, than my own mind's emptiness

Ben Ainley 1922

RECOLLECTIONS OF THE GENERAL STRIKE.

In another 4 years and a few months, 50 years will have passed since the General Strike of 1926.My memory is not the best in the World. In fact I have a struggle remembering what happened last week, yet some of the happenings that took place during and shortly after the General Strike are as clear to me as if they had happened yesterday.

I was 16 years old at the time and worked for the L.M.S. Railway Company, and I was considered to be fortunate in having a job that brought in regular wages and holidays with pay. Very few people had holidays with pay in those days.

The General Strike itself only lasted. a few days, and during that time every town and City in the land had it's march and demonstration. The march that took place in Manchester culminating in a huge meeting held in Platt Fields, seemed and still seems to me to be the greatest march ever held. Never have I had the feeling of excitement that I had that day. Maybe it was because I was very young and this was my first march and everything was very new to me.

I walked along with my young workmates and felt as proud as Punch. It seemed to me that all the world was marching that day.

There were policemen everywhere, almost one policeman to each row of marchers and their normal duties such as traffic control etc. were taken over by the Special Constabulary.

We saw many of these Specials on the march to Platt Fields and booed and catcalled every one of them with great enthusiasm. We, the young ones really enjoyed it all.

Finally we reached Platt Fields, where platforms had been erected and speakers were already addressing the huge crowds round each platform.

At the particular platform we arrived at the speaker was describing how God had made the world. Eventually he reached the point in his speech of the last and lowest form of life God had made - a jelly fish. He paused and then apologised to his audience, "I am sorry," he said, "there was something he made that was lower than a jellyfish, he made a scab." This got a great cheer from the crowd. and a man standing near where I and my workmates were standing, shouted in a loud but most beautiful Oxford accent, "Hear, hear, Oh hear, hear." We had never heard this form of applause before, and we nearly died. - it bowled us over completely.

It was a huge source of fun to us on our walk home, each of us every few minutes would mimic the man in our best cut glass accents.

That march was my first industrial and political commitment and it made a great and lasting impression upon me,

After the Strike was ended, partly because of the disorganisation to industry, and partly I think for punishment revenge not all the strikers were taken 'hack immediately, Each day a list of names was placed in the window of the lodge naming the men who had to start back the next day and I was out of work for 5 weeks before I started back This long wait to start back was the cause of some concern to my mother, who badly missed my wages and was convinced that I would never start back again.

The hatred, anger and bitterness of the men after this Strike was really astounding to me. I have never encountered it in such a widespread manner since.

You must remember that I was only 16 at the time and all this was new to me and I didn't fully understand what was happening around me. It was impossible not to overhear the men talking and arguing and you couldn't avoid this intense anger, it rubbed off on one.

One man, who, it was said had been a warder at Strangeways sometime in his life and who had been a blackleg during the Strike, was given regular work, whilst many of the strikers still remained unemployed. Although this man had. never worked on the railway before the strike. The men felt that this was another way of rubbing their noses in it, and were not prepared to stand it.

It was with great difficulty that the Union Officials at the station prevented them from going out on strike again.

They gave this man a terrible time, he was constantly in arguments and fights until one day he never came back. I don't think the Management sacked him, I think he left of his own accord.

During the Strike our strike headquarters were in a room over a coal yard To reach this room it was necessary to climb several steep wooden stairs which finished with small platform surrounded by a handrail. This led to the door of the room where the strike committee met every day and all day,

It was the habit of the Chairman of the Union branch, who was also the Strike Committee Chairman, to come out of this room, stand on this platform and give us the news of the strike or read out a telegram to us, This he did several times a day.

One day when we were all standing about in the yard waiting for news of the progress of the strike, he came out of the room and stood on the platform We all looked up expectantly and immediately it was obvious that he was drunk. he stood there for a couple of minutes swaying and then shouted down to us "Stand firm and solidarity", and then fell from the top of the stairs to the bottom and lay there sleeping.

He was a big man this Chairman, and was popular and well liked by the men.

Some 12 months or so after the strike, he was offered a Foreman's job by the Management and he took it. The. anger and bitterness of the men hadn't abated very much and they took this appointment very badly. he was a traitor and they did everything possible to make his life a misery.. This attitude of his old comrades was too much for him.

We watched him shrink visibly and after about 13 months as a Foreman, he died. "They" said it was with a broken heart, whatever that may mean.

For many years afterwards, you would hear the men talk about others who had played a bad role in the General. Strike, with the same viciousness and contempt that Irishmen are able to put into their voices when they talk about the "Black & Tans".

Looking back I think that 1926 was the nearest thing to Revolution this country has been in my lifetime and I can't help wondering how different the situation would have been if the Government hadn't had the foresight to imprison some of the Left Wing leaders in 1925 and to keep them in prison during this confrontation of 1926.

And so I could go on with many more memories of the 1926 Strike, but that would make a book and that is not what was asked for.

Syd Booth.

A SONNET WITH SELF-SUFFICIENCY.

You say you would be different. I can see
You will not say what other people say,
Nor wend your life along the common way.
And yet your goal is theirs; that you agree.
Think not I understand not. You are free
Your head's dictation to obey, until
Your heart shall vindicate me; as it will
Some day when you read this and think of me.
I will attempt not now, then, to dissuade.
Yet you, whom things material cannot mar,
(You disregard them) must see what you do
Is less important; always it must fade
Into a shadow beside what you are:

Rare, fresh, unchangeable. And you are You.

Anonymous

DAWN

Satin words of purity
I see
In the midst of decay
In the golden sunrise
I see
The light of a dawning day.
My eyes alight with passion
As forgotten dreams of freedom
Are blazing in my mind
I collide with my memories
I jump to the sky
As the clans of insanity
Are lost in the tide.
Exultantly I run
Into the glittering sea
And I see my reflection
Forming in the waters
Of past glory
And future promise
As a bird flying freely
I laugh in the wind
I float to the sun
And my heart opens to sing.
No man is free
Till the chains of his wrath
Are buried
In the fury of the ocean deep
Where the sea
Pounds and beats
At his lost sadness
Till the peace of night
Buries the storm of hatred
And is lost forever
In the fathoms of the deep.

Susan Cole

POEM:

A distance from me
You are saying
Some thing
Dreamy priests drift
In between
Punctuating silences
With smiles and gentle nodding
While I sit
Thick summer hangs
The dust a slow car swirls
As fingers wave
A weariness away
Your lips are moving
Making faces
On a hot day.

J. Leavers.

POEM.

A door
brown and indifferently painted
Opens and a child
Carrying a cat
Appears a tall man
Follows with an umbrella
They pause and close
The door. The man
Smiles
The moon balled cat
Mews and leaps
The child watches
But the man continues
In the direction
Of a tree lined avenue
Shadows formed by trees
Dapple the pavement grey
It is afternoon
The boy sits
And rolls with the cat
Ahead the tall man
Turns concerned and shouts
The boy to come
What does he want
The boy thinks and catches
At the cat who claws
his face the man impatient
To continue grows angry
But the boy cries
And goes to the door
The man turns
And walks the door
Opens and the boy
disappears the cat
stretches in a patch of sunlight
And sleeps.

J Leavers

WHAT GENTLE SAVIOUR WITH LOVE IN HIS HEART,

What gentle saviour with love in his heart,
For his creatures could plan such a road,
There disease, earthquakes and fangs rip apart,
With suffering's terrible loads.
The wonder is how through all this gore,
Can emerge a heart that is kind,
Like a Snowdrop peeping through winter's floor,
Blooms this jewel, the reasoning mind.

BROWN EYES, SUCH AN HONEST STARE,

Brown eyes, such an honest stare,
Shines warmer on me than any sun,
When they peep 'neath auburn hair,
At me when day is done.
However dreary the toil of mine,
How many times at some behest,
More sure to you at evening time,
I hurry and feel refreshed.
Strange when in mood I think,
That one can cause such joy in me,
Strange that worlds apart distinct,
Dwell behind the lockturned key.
And strange that through the passing years,
A freshness from you never fades,
Some say Youth's gone as time measures,
Yet still you're sweetest, maid.

Frank Smith.

O.T.M.S.

I've said it before, I like going to night school. At this point, however, my rheumaticky shoulder persuaded me against embarking on some new hand-icraft, but there was nothing wrong with my feet, so I joined the dancing class -Old Time-Modern Sequence. I had discovered what must be the most delightful, varied, friendly, egalitarian form of exercise there is. That so many different combinations of movements and rhythms can be made during the course of sixteen bars of music never fails to amaze me.

Before very long you realise you have acquired a considerable repertoire, and almost learnt a new language:- chassis, step-through, scissors, lock, turn and lock, chassis step through scissors, lock, turn and lock, lady under to centre, balance, quick, quick, quick, tap to wall, quick, quick, quick, tap to centre, swing out and lock, feet together, there; you've done the Balmoral Blues, and added one more dance to a seemingly endless list of tangos, waltzes, blues, saunters, quicksteps, ad almost infinitum.

My two favourite lady partners will have saved me a seat. There's Clara, rising 80, a born dancer and a stickler for getting it just right, - "I'd be quite happy to die dancing" she says. And Bertha, 74, "It keeps me nimble; besides, if it wasn't for this class we'd never have met" she says, and Bill, "Let's get in't middle o't floor where there's plenty o' room and put a bit o'style in it!"

Being a CLASS you see, it's alright for anyone to ask anyone to dance, and a lady can ask a gent without losing face and it's very sociable. It's grand to see so many of our senior citizens, who comprise about half of the class, merrily negotiating a new sequence, but the teachers are working hard, and before very long we can all do it, some quicker than others of course, but that's what's egalitarian about it, vie all start together. And the names of the dances are so delightful, Forget-me-not Waltz, Midnight Tango, Tango Solair, Mail Swing, Esso Blues (popularly referred to as 'paraffin dance'), Waltz Katrine, Dawn Waltz, I could fill a page and not mention them all, and all different.

I'm looking forward to my 60th birthday, when all night school fees will be waived. Come on, it's th'last Waltz.

Fanny Morgan.

SUBURBAN AUTOMATISM

Get rid of your depression, man
go clockwork like I am.
Mow the lawn once a week
Get your 'aircut on Saturday.
Regularity, that's the key, boy,
Get regular!
Now, take my bowels
Well, all right, don't take them.
But you've got to listen to me, son,
I've got things to tell you
About life, an' all that.

Did I ever show you my wounds?
Got'em in the war, you know.
Here, look at this
Copped that at Dunkirk.
Retreat? Well, we went back
And sorted the bastards,
Didn't we? A land fit for 'eroes to live in
That's what we were promised, lad.
You wouldn't know that, of course,
But you ask your Dad.
Fools? Yes, we were to swallow that guff,
A land for the young to be arrogant in,
Would be nearer the mark.
Yes, we were fools right enough!
We should have known that one
Has to lie and to lie to get on,
And the higher you get,
Why, the more you've to lie!
Even God has 'is tongue in His cheek
Half the time.
It's Him that shows you the world from the hill
"All this I will give you, young man"
Says the Lord.
And there's hope in your soul for a week.
If you'll only be good
All the world will be yours.
What's the use of the world
when you're too old to care?
Death's a friend when you're worn,
But, meanwhile, there's the lawn
To be mowed, oh, aye and me 'air
To be cut;
Today's Saturday, you see.

Edward Morrison

PETE

Sam and Norman were talking - "How did you get on last night?" Norman asked. How d'ye mean?' replied Sam. "With the Bird", "All right", said Sam. "All right!', exploded Norman. "Did you, or didn't you?" "Course I did", said Sam. "All right, eh", giggled Norman. "Not bad", said Sam - weakly, I thought. I carried on straightening a pillar that carried the hand rail round the boiler. "Love 'em and leave 'em, I do", said Norman. "I'll ditch this one", said Sam. "She' s a widow you know, got a seven year old boy. I got what I wanted." Sam is about 40, very thin. I was shocked. I liked Joan. She was a welder about 35, matronly and handsome. Sam, I always thought of as a nice fellow. He had a pencil moustache, and dark, but oily wavy hair.

I was just past 16 and feeling very mature I warned Joan off. A couple of hours later Sam confronted me - "A great mate, you", he hissed, "You really put the spoke in." He was bitter, hurt and angry. Myself? I have never experienced this before. It was like a melting of my very core, and such an ache. I could not answer him, and I felt shame too for I realised then that his words to Norman were just bravado. Sam was a nice fellow. Next morning crossing the loco shed Sam glared at me, balefully. "She won't even talk to me", he said and passed on. I went to the welding bay resolved. "Hello Joan", I said. "Hello Pete, how's Sam?" "Oh, he's O.K." I answered. "Joan, I have to tell you what I said is untrue. I made it up. I was jealous of Sam, because I couldn't have you - didn't see why he should, but it was wrong of me and I'm sorry." She smiled beatifically, "How do you know, you never tried?" I left her. I was sweating a good deal. It had been a terrific strain on my nerves. I was watching the locomotive being pulled out of the erection shop by the capstan when Sam came along. Before he could say anything I said "Sorry Sam, over what happened." "That's all right", he said "congratulate me, we marry in July"

Frank Parker

'AN APPEAL"

Men are attacked for stating facts
In all climes and religions:
Tho' no Palme Dutt, I well may put
The cat among the pigeons.
Who is to judge, far less begrudge
What joy's derived from drinking,
Yet one pint less per month I stress
Can save our Fund from shrinking.

This must be said, the' on my head
Descend a thousand furies,
More must be given to Barbara Niven
And less to local brew'ries.
Not mine to spoil for those who toil
Some slight relief from tedium
But please forego one cinema show
Or the price of ten Players' Medium.
And those who lay a bob each way
Avoid this snare of Satan
Let Conscience' voice dictate your choice:
"Get thee behind me, Cayton".
If this my verse make some folk curse,
Set trigger fingers jerking,
Shoot, if you must, my half-bred crust.
But keep "The Daily" working.

Robert Fletcher

A DYING ART

Late February, a cold, damp morning and a colleague was to pick me up in his car to attend the funeral in Wilmslow of one of our workmates, a nice and well respected bloke.

At any time, and particularly on such a wild day, these are not the kinds of functions one likes to attend, but a compensatory factor was three hours paid leave from work, a warming thought even on such a day. Promptly at 10.50 a.m. my companion called for me, and it was decided to take the longest but nicest way into Wilmslow and on the journey after a few per-functory remarks on the coming event conversation soon changed to a much happier theme; like the merits or demerits of City and United.

On arrival at the cemetery with about fifteen minutes to spare, we met several other friends from the various offices in and around Manchester whom we had not seen for some considerable time, and although the conversation was 'sotto' voice, it was animated and full of anecdotes and the few minutes left at our disposal were soon dissipated in a happy and jocular fashion.

Then the cortege arrived and a respectful silence fell upon us all, and as we followed the mourners to the graveside we fell in dutiful line, the senior execs at the front and the minnows in the rear. The sermon was most de-pressing. Weeping, heartbroken relatives clustered around the grave and as the mournful incantations of the professional preacher broke on the still air, and the body lowered into the wet earth, a feeling of revulsion swept through me at the added suffering of the bereaved caused by the prolongation of this pagan practice.

When the relatives had left, several of us broke up into small groups, ours to adjourn for sustenance, and away from the commitments of respect and duty, and, under the warmth and conviviality of food, drink and companionship a new atmosphere was engendered, and our departed friend was forgotten, as we all recounted incidents involving characters and humorous situations connected with work. The time passed quickly, and as more barleycorn was imbibed, so did the company expand, and I began to wonder if I had been to a funeral or a wedding, but whatever it was, it was a good do.

Work for the rest of the day was out, so I decided I would walk the few miles home, and as I wandered through the lanes I meditated on all that had (gone on that day, starting out to pay respect to a friend and workmate, finishing up slightly inebriated with not a thought of Bill, and in between all this the grief and sadness of the close Relatives, the hypocrisy of the prayer man, spouting sermons with as much feeling as the girl at the airport announcing the next flight up there. What a cruel and barbaric act is the Christian burial: surely something more decent and humane can replace this outmoded, painful and expensive charade. The real and deep sorrow must be when the beloved takes his last breath and the eyes have ceased to see, the lips will smile no more, and the farewell can be taken in private.

At present even intelligent people and advanced Socialist States are all subject to the never dying of the dying industry and it is from these people a lead should be given to ensure that something much better should be found when we have played out time.

Please, for me, anything but this hocus pocus, and if my friends are still around, dispose to the knacker yard my decaying flesh, and then away for a good jug up and a laugh. These would be the best farewells.

J. Bishop.

AN AULD MAN CAM' TAE HEAVEN'S GATE

An auld man cam' tae Heaven's gate
An' loudly tirled the bell
"Come let me in" he tauld St. Pete,
Pete answered "Gang tae Hell".
"It's plain you don't know who I am,
The auld man cried in pique."I ken ye fine wi' that cigar
An' a' that brandy reek.
"Then you should know I won the war

And saved Humanity".
"Man hauld your tongue-ye're gaun too far
Wi' sic profanity".
"Wars, ye should know are NEVER won
Except by profiteers
An' politicians like yoursel',
Demagogoes an' Leears.
"Let's tak this war o' which ye spoke
How came about this war?
Let's just consult the minute-book
For 1924." That year in Rome ye did abide
Consortin wi' the deil.
Wi' Mussolini by your side
Ye gied a little spiel."
"Ye there addressed the serried ranks
O' Blackshirts - coarse and vile,
An' publicly ye geid them thanks
For crampin' Lenin's style.
"The chicks then hatched cam' hame to roost in 1939.
This war that gied thy fame a boost
was caused by thee and thine."
"At Dunkirk time, we thought perhaps
You'd dropped your knavish tricks
But then ye lapsed tae wicked ways
At Fulton, '46."
The wicked ranks, ye chose yoursel',
So now I must command ye,
Henceforth ye must in hades dwell
- That's if wild Nick can stand ye".

Bob Cooney

OUR NEIGHBOURS

My childhood, was spent in a two-up and two-down terraced house with my father, mother, younger sister and three brothers. We played most of our games in the dirt street we lived in and when we were tired we used to sit on the low garden wall in front of our house.

Our next door neighbours were a family called Roberts, who seemed to have their front door open most of the time when weather permitted. The living conditions in these houses were so cramped that the front door opened directly onto the living room, which was also the dining room and my sister and I saw a lot of little comedies and dramas as we sat on the garden wall.

I remember on one occasion Mr. Roberts, who was a night watchman, decided that he would have porridge for his tea before going to work. A plate of porridge so thick that it resembled castle ramparts was placed before him, flanked by a dish of treacle and water and a dish of milk and water. He would scoop up a spoonful of porridge, dip it into the treacle and water and then into the milk and water mixture. This fascinating performance was always enhanced for us when he put the spoon into his mouth and his Adam's apple would bob down and than come up like a lift.

This family was unusual in the sense that the mother was the irresponsible member of the family. In particular she was a heavy drinker and a poor domestic organiser. But although she never failed to spend some time in the pub she would practice strict economy in the matter of food. It was not unusual for her to rush home from the pub at dinnertime with threepenny-worth of pie pieces she had bought on the way home. These would be boiled in a pan on the open coal fire with a few potatoes and a pastry crust put on top of the lot. This was called Sea pie and was always decorated with specks of soot from, the chimney.

The eldest daughter was a star-crossed girl who always seemed to be in the throes of a broken love affair. On one occasion she was breaking a slice of bread into cheese dip at teatime and weeping copiously about her latest letdown.

"She wants to give over skriking into that cheese dip", said my Mother, knowledgeably, "It's watery enough." Mrs. Roberts always made her cheese dip with water instead of milk.

We have had many neighbours since those days who have been steadier and more worthy people. But, perhaps because there was no garden to place an artificial barrier between us, perhaps because the economic conditions drew us more closely together or perhaps because I saw them through the uncritical eyes of a child, I remember the Roberts, with warmth and affection.

Ethel Hatton.

WHY I DON'T WRITE

Words are dangerous. Commit your ideas to paper and you stand committed - condemned. How can I after 50 years of silence expose to all and sundry my loves and hates ? Ideas that have for so long been personal and private and secret ? Things to play with in oblivion, like the little smooth stone in your pocket. Nobody can see when you hold it in your hand in the dark. Judging by my output they are going to remain secret

I have wonderful ideas for a 'good' story when it is practically impossible to sit down and write. At work with wet sharp heavy glass in my hands I can see in detail every phrase of the most important work on the lack of dignity of labour. The complete absence of dignity in labour when it is not of one's own choice and how few of us are lucky enough to do what we enjoy for a living ?

It's easy to write but it's easier to talk oneself out of doing it.

Sol Garson.

AT THE POPULAR CAFE

I remember clearly how I sidled up to the long green Counter of the Popular Cafe. I felt a complete stranger there and all eyes seemed to be staring at my dirty and torn dust coat (well-named). God knows why I should have felt so. That's the other side to my character. Now it's my home. I go there three times a day and know a goodly share of the names of the regulars - Harry, Arthur, John and so on. On the other side of the counter are Andrew, Eileen and Liz. I know a lot about them all because not only do I talk a great deal, but ask many personal questions like "How much do you get?" and "Why did you leave your first wife then?".

Sometimes, because the 4-seater tables are quite small, I cannot but fail to hear what the two opposites are saying. Even before Ben Ainley's evenings I wanted to commit to paper all these stories, but having heard these four you can understand my hesitation in doing so.

I go there at 10, 12.30 and 3.30, and it always tickles my imagination why some people are eating their breakfast or dinner at 10 in the morning - likewise dinner at 3.30 and so I ask ! There is a betting shop next door and several pubs within spitting distance and I'm sure these produce many of the flamboyant, grotesque, wonderful, and saddeningly belligerent clients of our Cafe.

"Fascist, Fascist - you're calling me a Fascist ? I'll stick this bloody knife in yer", said the man who had been going on about Jews running the country. Mind you I must have provoked him by saying "Shit and nonsense - that's Fascist talk-talk brother". Oh yes – and I did start by saying "I'm a bloody Jew. And that's a good one because I'd shed my last drop of blood to defend Atheism".

"She's going to leave me. I'm sure of it", the young man opposite said to his friend beside him. They were both clean, and Burton-dressed-office workers. Try as he might the good sympathetic ear could not smooth away the wrinkles that should not have been on that sweet young brow. He was going to lose his young wife and he did not know why. How he had tried to please her. For a year - all their married life - he had been her slave. He was going to cry. I looked at my dinner. He got up and went to the door. My eyes followed. His shorter leg was slightly bowed. He opened the door and went out.

Arthur is a surly-faced bastard. Had many a good row with this one. After all the Popular Cafe is my stomping ground. This is where I propagate the faith. They know I'm a Communist and still talk to me. In two years I've had dinners, teas and toast and one recruit, but that's another story. Today was no different and neither was Arthur. This mealy mouthed manager, self-styled and really a fucking foreman - or perhaps not. He looked so sour I had to ask once again why didn't you get married ? "I did have a girl for six years once" he replied. "She tried to run my life for me. Made a list of people I could not see and have a beer with - and my brother was on the list. So I said put your name on the list darling and walked out". Arthur's stiff face began to crack. "I heard she married a Scot who didn't know the difference between the toilet and the front room carpet. He was drunk most of the time and kicked her out once or twice, I believe she's divorcing him". Arthur laughed - loud and long. I've never seen him even smile before.

Sol Garson.

VOICES

Verse and Prose
Published by

Manchester Unity of Arts Society

The Second Publication of the Series

Hon President :

BEN AINLEY, 13 VICTORIA WAY, BRAMHALL, STOCKPORT, SK7 1DE, CHESHIRE
from whom copies can be obtained,
and to whom all communications should be addressed.

PRICE 20p

cover size 253 x 204 mm

CONTENTS

46. Introduction — Ben Ainley
47. Tribute to George Jackson — Denis Maher
47. An Idol Without Feet of Clay — Joe Bishop
49. Three Poems — James Leaver
50. A Meeting in the Night — F.G. Walker
52. Committee — Ben Ainley
Three Pieces:- — Sol Garson
53. 1. On Seeing the Pithead at Aberfan
54. 2. 1 Million Plus 1
56. 3. The Magindovid
57. If you Want to Get Ahead Get a Hat — Ethel Hatton
59. The Engine Room — Kin Willey
59. Sans Almost Everything — Fanny Morgan
60. Book Collecting — Edmund&Ruth Frow
61. Industrial Worker — Frances Moore
63. The Ragged Trousered Philanthropists — Edward Morrison
67. Desire — Ben Ainley
68. On Returning Home After a Long Absence — Rick Gwilt
72. The Boy — Frank Parker
74. Woman — Rick Gwilt
75. Moon Laughter — Edward Morrison
76. If Oo Could Oo Would — Frank Smith
79. Missin' The Clubman — Alfred Edwards
80. Rockabye Statesman — Angela Tuckett
81. Wartime in Ford's — Joe Day
87. Communication — Frank Parker
88. Stranger in Vietnam — Denis Maher

INTRODUCTION

This is the second issue of 'Voices'. Whether it marks an improvement on the first, the reader must be the judge. There is more prose here, and I think that an advance, though there must be poetry or there will be no vision. The political content is clearer, as more writers write and those who have written before mature. We welcome contributors: poetry, prose, fiction, reportage; we exercise no censorship except such as the limitations of our space dictate. We would like to appear four times a year but this depends on the support we receive. We would welcome reviews in Union journals, the progressive press. If a score of Unions would circulate 20 to 50 copies among their members, to bring 'Voices' to their notice they would help. Is a publication like 'Voices' worth keeping alive?
You must decide. Send contributions, orders, queries and maybe donations to me at 13, Victoria Way, Bramhall, Stockport SK7 IDE, Cheshire

Ben Ainley.

TRIBUTE TO GEORGE JACKSON

Hurt me, imprison me, shoot me, kill me,
Only the best of men fight and die for the wrongs they
see around them.
George Jackson the prison walls could not stop your
developing mind - a freedom of mind your guards or
oppressors would never know or understand.
They tried to dehumanise you with filth and dirt, in
pain and hurt - till at last they shot you from this earth.
Involvement made you, involvement graved you.
In death as in life you gave meaning to be free -
In mind
In pride
In courage
In dignity and honour of-
being a man.
Your bones and feelings have gone out of this existence yet your
courage lingers on.
You have helped us all George Jackson to be that much more free

Denis Maher

AN IDOL WITHOUT FEET OF CLAY

Lenin, Stalin, Pollitt and Robeson, these men I placed on a pedestal, but another idol of mine is a man of much smaller stature who brought a lot of happiness to hundreds of youngsters.

As a boy of 10 or 11 years I had a deep passion (no, not a dame, that came later). My passion was sport.

In the poor, rough district of Hulme there was no running track, no river for rowing, not even a park, so our games were played in the street. Cricket, a piece of old wood fashioned into a bat, the lamp post for the wickets, so your offside strokes were limited, and a rubber ball, likely as not nicked from Woolleys or collected for with odd farthings or halfpennies we had managed to acquire. Football was played between two entries for goals, there were no bounds, and only throw-ins if the pill went up someone's lobby or down a grid. If no ball was available one was made of rag tied with string and if the street was wet the rag became a soggy mass, covering us with damp and dirt.

Another pastime indulged in was to march down Foster Street that linked St. Wilfs and City Road where gangs from each school would engage in a battle royal, "Cathy Dogs v Proddy Dogs".

This was 1920 and some of the younger teachers from both schools were returning from the Army, and, unknown to us had got cracking to form the Hulme Schools' League for football and cricket, the games to be played on the Barracks, City Road; this was being evacuated by the Army and taken over by the corporation, with the lovely title of "St. George's Park";, a mass of shale and chippings. The league was to consist of all the Hulme schools, two Catholic, three Church of England, and three Elementary schools, and when the news filtered through excitement knew no bounds.

Our teacher, who was one of the moving spirits, was young, tall and well built, and the forerunner of Cary Grant. They were dead ringers for each other; he had been wounded in the war and to add to all this he could crack a ball with both feet. He had been an amateur with 'Spurs whilst at Winchester, at cricket he could sling a nifty leg break and could bat a bit so he was a natural for our adulation.

His enthusiasm knew no bounds and our first match was against St. Wilfs, Saturday morning, kick off 9.30. At 8.30 he and Pop Doyle, of Wilfs, brought a bag of sawdust from a nearby saw mill and with the aid of kids marked out a pitch, and pitched some wickets for goal posts.

He had scrounged a strip of black end white shirts, some of us had football boots, but others only had one on his best foot with a shoe or-clog on the other and as the shirts came over our wrists and up to our kees we must have looked a pretty rum bunch, but boy! we were proud.

Charley, that was the Christian name of our idol, taught in 6B, and most of us hoped we would duck the exams and be sent to B not 6A, for not only was he tolerant but helpful and thoughtful. He encouraged us and in some cases drove the backward and lazy, and showed no favouritism to any.

When I was 12 I played for Manchester Boys Juniors and we won the Lancashire Cup. He was chuffed that two boys from Hulme were on the team and just before the next season started the boys considered likely for Manchester Boys Seniors went to a weekend camp at Strines. Twentyfour boys and eight teachers all from various schools around Manchester. And during a trial game some chaps from the village came and claimed the pitch. The teachers reasoned with them and the upshot was a challenge between us and them, our team consisting of five teachers and six boys.

They were duff, we hammered them 7-2, and Charley got four.

As we were leaving the pitch a big lout of about 20 gave me a dig for something I said to him and immediately Charley was over remonstrating with him. The local took a swing, this was parried and my hero flattened him. You can guess by playtime on Monday morning he had scored six and seen three louts off.

That year I was lucky enough to be selected for the North v South of England trials and it was Charley who brought me the news and for the first time he pulled my hair and I could see he was proud of me. I felt great! Years later he was given a headship at a school in Levenshulme, and I heard that on his retirement not only pupils but parents subscribed and gave him a great send off.

He is not around any more but it is never too late to say "Thanks for everything". An idol without feet of clay.

Joe Bishop

THREE POEMS

The unknowing victims
the old men
who are pursued by no hunter
sit in tight circle vision
and sigh memories
personal things and happy
to tell a meander
of once people
we cripple we maim
because we are afraid
of age
and of the aged
he dies
degraded.

The rain comes
across the roofs
disturbing the waking birds
the window limits the world
and encloses reality
how fragile
the rain marks the window
distorts the view

the last of the birds
listlessly circles and falls
and the rain comes.

Out in the sunshine. Whispers.
Run. Along the roofs
and walls. Whispers Archimedes
rain.

James Leaver

A MEETING IN THE NIGHT

The building was old; it stood back off the road. It had once been an inn. I walked towards the door, conscious of the low rumble of thunder and the leaden clouds. I pushed at the door; it swung loose on its one hinge and almost collapsed. I paused while my eyes became orientated to the gloom. Remnants of twilight, filtering through the doorway, revealed one large room that ran its length from where, I stood to some impenetrable region of darkness. The low ceiling was heavily timbered, and the floor, although solid, gave off a musty, unhealthy smell of rotting wood. I stood a moment, wondering if I should stay. Then, a louder peal of thunder erupted into the silence, and whiplashes of rain, like the patter of a thousand feet, began beating a furious dance upon the tiles.

I moved further into the room and paused as I heard something. A rat disturbed by the rain? Some other creature? Or a...? A match hissed into life on my right. I turned. Framed in the rugged circle of light was a man. He was standing behind what appeared to be a long bar-counter. He was tall and angular, with a narrow face as pale as a butter bean. He must have been hidden in the shadows, watching me. He applied the match to the stub of candle and came towards me,

"Who are you? What do you want?" His tone bit like acid.

"Shelter....from the storm" I said, startled. "I've been here before".

"Ah!" He thrust the candle forward, so near my face that I shielded my eyes. "You're one of them tramps that keep coming in here then -"
"No.....I'm not a tramp, I'm a traveller"

He laughed in his throat. His voice edged with sarcasm, he said - "That's a new name for a vagrant.....where you from then?"

"Woodhallow" I said

He moved the candle aside. Our eyes met. His were black and unfathomable, like pools of darkness. He rubbed at his chin with long, bony fingers. "Woodhallow" he mused. "I know everyone there. I haven't seen you before."

"And I've never seen you" I remarked.

There was a little silence as he screwed up his eyes in thought. Then he said "You say you've been here before?"

I nodded. "Several times".

He laughed, sending fingers of breath towards the flickering flame of the candle. He said, almost choking, "Well, you won't be able to come here again".

"Why not?"

"Because it's being opened up again. Then the likes of you won't be welcome here".

His words stunned me. It was some moments before I could make comment. Then with some difficulty I said, "You mean that there will be people here, and lights and music?"

He gazed at me for several seconds. A superior smile sat upon his lips. He said with some shade of malice, "That's right, and that'll keep the likes of you out of here."

"But I'm not a -"

"-tramp" he finished for me. "Then what are you....dressed that?"

I looked down at my clothes. They were old and thread-bare. I tried to think of something to say.

He grunted in triumph at my obvious discomfort. Then he said "I'm surprised at you wanting to stay here anyway.... seeing that the place is supposed to be haunted."

I said nothing.

He gazed at me with the meditative stare of a butcher weighing meat. He said "I suppose you know about it don't you?"

I nodded.

"And it doesn't frighten you, that right here someone was stabbed to death a hundred years ago?"

I shrugged. I said "I know all about it. Everybody does where I come from. I don't mind staying here."

He looked disappointed. His face seemed to come to pieces for a moment. Then he said viciously "Well you can just clear off. I don't think you're! from Woodhallow at all."

"But I am" I protested.

He reached out and grabbed my shirt. He seemed to go rigid. His face contorted into a grimace. He let out a horrible, unearthly sound; it was a strangled moan that began in his throat and lingered on his breath, until it became intermingled with the varied utterances of the wind. He withdrew his hand. We both stared at it. It was covered in blood.

I said helpfully "I'm from Woodhallow cemetery".

He drew back and dropped the candle. And, with a scream as excruciating as a knife drawn across glass, he ran crying into the night.

Frederick G. Walker

COMMITTEE

In moments when the routine of Committee
Circles, and idle comrades, pencil in hand,
Propose, Amend, Adopt, or sketch their witty,
Amusing cartoons on agendas, and the bland,
Somnolent air is filled with drone and chatter,
Reports of sub-committees, delegates, fractions.....
The secretary reads a circular letter
Giving instructions to Labour Party factions......
In moments such as these I have sensed a grim
Tension in twenty faces - the Committee
Becomes a sacramental pact, and dim,
Almost unheard, a voice speaks, without pity,
Without emotion, telling of great events,
In Germany, of Lenin dead, the new need
For proletarian leadership; my sense
Of all that's noble in us being freed -
Lenin is dead, draw closer, closer, comrades,
Tomorrow in Germany ten thousand comrades
Wait with white lips and stiff chins certain death,
Tomorrow, we, maybe, idle and wearied,
Will draw quick breath, sensing a sudden zest,
A sudden peril joining us in endeavour.
It comes, flickers, goes, and the minute after,
We hold up our hands, negating a resolution,

Making a feeble joke to rouse fleet laughter,
Holding the passion of our minds in thin solution.

Ben Ainley (1924)

ON SEEING THE PITHEAD AT ABERFAN
Working for Arthur Jones. April 1972 - Rhonda Valley.

Miners married to old hills of rubble
Tied to the filthy holes in the ground.
Tired from the toil of tearing but treasure,
Made move mountains of wealth for the wealthy.
Lost their health making wealth beyond measure.
Young miners married to, the whore with deep pit.
The old men know her well.
They've paid their price in sweat and blood.
Lived on their knees, crawled in the mud,
Tearing black babies out of her womb,
Matching her hiss with a cry and a groan,
Choked with her gas and left all alone,
To die.
Their lungs full of dust,
The old prostitute's still full,
Of lust.

Sol Garson

ONE MILLION PLUS ONE

Chapter 1

As is my wont, day by day since 6.45 on Tuesday morning, I had been putting off the ugly moment.

It is Friday now and I must procrastinate no longer. Get into your best suit Sam, I have heard tales! But first you must try your last gambit. Bang me knuckles on Boss-Brother's door.

"What do you want?"

"I want some money, I need..."

"Get your body out of here or I'll call the Police!"

So I went to the office, took my cards and P.45 and went. Now for the real test. The Labour Exchange - or is it the Department of Social Security? I was here fifteen years ago with my friend Terry Ward. Took a snotty bastard clerk to task to no avail. Couldn't get his money, so I had gone to speak on his behalf

Nobody with me today.

"I am without a job, unemployed."

"What did you do?"

"I managed a glass factory."

And that was a lie. For the last few years I had managed nobody but myself - a one-man band. Cut the glass to shape, bevel, polish the edge and then put on the fancy design.

"A manager, will you please go..."

I was removed from the long straggling line of saddened workless workers to a much nicer place upstairs, with chairs.

"Good morning, sir, how can I help you?"

I'm glad I am clean shaven and in my best suit.

"I am unemployed, without a job."

"Have you been here before?"

"No."
"When did you start this job?"

"1937"

54

I had worked out this by starting at my birth in 1923 and adding 14. My eyes filled and my face screwed up by itself and I filled out a form, wiped my eyes and went out.

Because pay day is Wednesday at this place, and because I had asked for money, I was given a sealed envelope to hand in at the local office in Chorlton.

Because my queue was twenty strong; because at the rate they were being processed I would be there for the rest of the day, and because the toilets were locked and I would have to ask for the key at the desk, and because my wife was working, I stood up and walked out. I think I said "Shit on the bastards, I'd rather starve."

Chapter 2.

"Have you filled out the dependents' allowance form?"

I looked blank.

"It's a little white form."

"I'll see if it's here" and I began to look through my little file of papers; put ever so recently by my wife in this folder with 'Israeli Discount Bank Ltd,' in gold on the front. Where the hell did she get it from? Anyway, for some obscure reason I cut the 'Israeli' out.

"There it is - fill it out now".

I could see a space for the date of birth of my children. Perhaps I am too ready to be ashamed, but shame was on me now and I covered myself with anger.

"I don't know the exact date" I nearly shouted

"Kathy is eighteen and David sixteen. I can give you the year."

"It must state the day and month"

'Why' I said to myself - "three times I've been here and I've not had a bleeding penny". I was aware I was swearing - even though I had promised myself not to do so.

"It's not my fault; if you fill in the form you can post it."

"I will post it then"

There were tears in my eyes; again I turned away quickly.

This asking for money.

Akin to begging.

I hate it.

Bad enough when I have worked for it -but when I have done nothing? I can't stand with my hand out. No hand-outs!

No money! No need for it. Thus token of exchange. Back to exchange and barter. I will give my labour for food and clothes and a little warmth. This shame - this guilt has been a long time with me. I can remember the guilt I felt when I asked my mother for a penny. I can remember my mother. See her on her knees, gripping brush and soap. I can remember the smell of the hot soapy water in the galvanized bucket and I can't remember the birth-days of my children - what's wrong with me?

I can remember - standing at the iron railings of the concrete veranda of the 'buildings' in Knowsley Street. High up, too high up this prison faced block - too high. Fear, flight. I wet my dark pantaloons and stand there till they grow cold. My mother - her hand touches the wet and she is not re-pelled. "Oy" - and I am stripped and changed and warm again. At the railings of Greengate Elementary School I stand and watch and smell the toast that the other boys' mothers bring at playtime. Where is my mother? Where is my toast? Where is my dole? Where is my job? When I was in work, this and that little shitty shop-owner would say to me "Sam - how would you like to run my place for me eh? It would be a good job - and well paid!"

A good job hmm?

More than you're getting now

So now I say to them "Well?" - and all I get is a million 'ums' and 'ers' and no job.

Hell, I wouldn't work for them if they got on their hands and knees, like my mother scrubbing the floor, and begged me.

Sol Garson

THE MAGINDOVID

All I could see was the little golden magindovid. This shiny Hebrew sym-bol. This shield of David - one triangle set on another - this Jewish cross. Say something! for Christ's sake say something!

She did say "I'm very pleased to meet you" and it did sound as if she meant it.

Say something!

"What a small smooth hand she has" said my big rough worker's hand - and it was warm, like mine.

If only Tchaikovski had been here. I bet he'd have clapped his little hands off when he heard her play his violin concerto.

Say something!

"I'm Sam Cohen". Sam - that's Jewish enough. Like her. She looks Jewish. Well - she does have that magindovid hanging on its thin gold chain from her neck.

Simpatico - I'm like her. She's good. Did you hear her play? Maybe she didn't hear, "I'm Sam Cohen - a sculptor - I would like..." God, I would like to see her face. Look up man, look! She is beautiful. Damn that glittering gold sign. It's blinding me. It's noisy down here, underneath a thousand people; standing at her dressing room door and all I can see "Sculptor - and I would like to make your head". Make your head! What a bloody awful way to say "I want to be famous like you". No - I want to be good at making heads. No, not that either. I want to be a sculptor - a famous sculptor, skilful, wanted; people should say "You're good, do me, do me!" "I will pay you - you won't go hungry whilst you're doing it".

It matters not now, A wasted favour Ron the manager had done. Sent me round to the stage door. Who to ask for, taken underground to this Sylvia - this wearer of a little golden magindovid that shone. Sylvia Markovici - I bet it was Markovitch! She wasn't going to be here long enough; off in the morning, this twenty-year-old beauty. And one day the whole world will know her and love her because she is good and skilful and they will say to her "Come and play - for me - for me -for me!

Sol Garson

IF YOU WANT TO GET AHEAD, GET A HAT

This slogan was better known in Denton during the years between the wars than the town motto.

Felt-hatting was the principle industry of this small Lancashire town where I was born. In particular the production of high quality fur-felt hats. The wearing of the local product was taken so seriously by hat-masters and workers alike that although I was never employed in the industry, it would have been unthinkable for me to go out dressed up without a hat. My father would have considered me to be indecently dressed. Many a Denton man has been seen walking along Blackpool prom, during a heatwave in grey flannels and shirt-sleeves with his fur-felt trilby or bowler hat clamped to his head like a limpet.

Of course the workers in the industry could buy slightly imperfect hats at a very cheap price because the employers were well aware that the best advertisement for their hats was that they should be seen to be worn. This fetishism led to some incongruities. When I was a teenager I have gone out at night wearing a peach-bloom fur hat that Royalty would have been proud to wear, but with hardly enough money in my purse to scrape admittance to the local cinema. And I have seen men queuing for the dole wearing Anthony Eden hats of a quality and shape like works of art.

When I think about what happened in the industry I feel sure that this deep craft pride was one of the factors which led to the decline of hatting in Denton. Unionism was very strong especially amongst the journeymen. But it was a craft Union first and foremost with all the weaknesses which that implies. For instance, hatting was considered to be a seasonal trade and the Union seemed to accept the principle of a fair day's wage for a fair day's work for only part of the time. With the general slump conditions and a rapidly shrinking market a situation was reached where short time working and unemployment far exceeded the seasonal boom. But when one of the bigger manufacturers bowed to the inevitable and began to produce the cheaper, poorer quality wool felt hat, many craftsmen felt that a canker was eating into the heart of the industry. When Luton began large-scale wool hat production the death knell was sounded for the fur-felt industry. The advent of the last war delivered the final blow from which the industry has never recovered. Small pockets of the craft still exist in Denton, but the former glory has gone. This is not entirely a bad thing. No community should have to be so dependent on one industry.

But sometimes I can't help feeling saddened when I realise that generations are growing up with no knowledge of the skill and craftsmanship with which their forebears were so well endowed and I hope that some day when we have a stable socialist society and the dictatorship of commercialised fashion has been removed, we may see a little resurgence of this old craft in my home town. Surely then there can be no objection to the production of a thing of beauty just because it is also long-lasting, hard-wearing and useful?

Ethel Hatton

THE ENGINE ROOM

The hiss of steam as pistons pound
The rumble down the tunnel as golden blades
churn the sea
The engine dances merrily away
Auxiliaries sing in an appropriate way
The warm air kisses the engine man's cheek -
The sweet smell of warm burnt oil
The slumber up above as crewmen sleep -
Gauge glass brass gleams with brilliant lustre
Dials and faces peer down to say
The moment's news at that hour and day
"Pressure up as oil is down"
Pistons pound and rumble on

Ken Lilley

SANS ALMOST EVERYTHING

While in the Health Food shop the other day, I saw something that I hadn't seen since some time during the war - Soya Flour. I tried to remember what I had done with it or used it for but I couldn't.

I knew it was packed full of goodness, and recently I had heard on the radio and seen on the tele, that some very clever food manufacturers/chemists were doing something with it to make it into mock steaks or what the Americans call Perky-Jerky; Anyway, I thought, I am sure to have a recipe somewhere, so I bought a pound.

I searched through all my post-war cookery books, but there was nothing on soya beans, so I looked up some wartime cookery books that I had saved. There was nothing on soya beans there either, but turning the pages I came across a recipe headed "Chicken sans Poulet".

One had to be resourceful in those days of dried egg and household milk (what was that?), but "Chicken sans Poulet" - the mind boggled; it had a kind of genteel euphemism with a hidden threat.

I don't know any French, but I know a bit of Shakespeare and all those sans's, - sans eyes, sans teeth, sans taste, sans everything. It didn't take me long - chicken without chicken. It had been broadcast by the B.B.C. on the 3rd of August 1943.

Nearly thirty years ago, and wartime, but was it really necessary to kid us to that extent? Surely, if there was no chicken we could have faced the fact and gone on living. Or was it kindly meant like those hearty jokes to help us through with a bit of self-delusion?

Actually the dish can be made with sausage or rabbit.. Now I remembered what I had used the Soya bean flour for -Almond Paste - Almond Paste sans Almonds.

Fanny Morgan

BOOK COLLECTING

It's not a hobby, it's a disease. Once the tendrils of absorbing interest have gripped you there is no escape. Your house becomes a cross between a public library and a museum. Decorating assumes monstrous proportions and even a relatively simple matter, such as catching a mouse, is fraught with danger. You learn to live a sedate life stepping gingerly round the precariously perched pamphlets and controlling your instinct, to throw things in case you hit a bookcase.

Mind you, there are compensations. Holidays take on a hew meaning when each visit to a bookshop might bring a find of real value; a forgotten text or little-known item that throws light on one of the dark ages of our history. The occasional telephone call may be a stalwart, anxious to unload his collection of priceless ephemera, painstakingly gathered throughout a lifetime of service to the movement. The postman's knock may bring a catalogue which has an item of rare and absorbing interest Every moment of every day can be filled with the demands of the books and before you know where you are you are hooked. Your life is forfeit. You are diseased.

Having admitted our weakness, we ask in all innocence, can you think of a better way of killing yourself? Think of the joy of being buried beneath the weight of several tons of rare volumes when the floor finally collapses. Think of the pleasure to be had from breathing in the dust and dirt of ages while grubbing through the dark corners of a bookshop. Think of the bread and cheese eaten for breakfast, dinner and tea, because you have spent up on buying some costly item too good to miss. Think of having no television because you have no wall left to put it against.

Before you become too sorry for us, we must in all fairness point out that book collecting is one of the most rapidly expanding growth industries. It used to be said that diamonds were a girl's best friend, but today, the careful father invests in a library or two in the certain knowledge that when his daughter reaches years of indiscretion there will be a greatly enhanced nest-egg to deal with the inevitable crises. The price of books has increased by leaps and bounds in the past twenty years. The education explosion, while it may have had dubious effects on the recipient has certainly provided grist for the booksellers' mill. So much so, in fact, that today's bookseller is rarely the rheumy-eyed, gnarled scholar of absent-minded aspect which is the traditional picture in fiction. He is far more likely to be a bright young man with a large overdraft who expects and sees that he gets a high percentage profit on each deal. He does not live on the shop premises among the damp and faintly musty books. He shuts the shop on the hour and drives to his modern semi in suburbia the same as other shop-keepers.

Although some of the uncertainty has been taken out of the business by the modern methods of the bright new boys, one can still spend many happy hours browsing round a remote shop, find a bargain at the end, wake the proprietor to pay your ten pence and be home in time for a wash and late tea.

"But what is the use of all those books?" you may well ask. It's all part of the class war really. If you know your past and use the knowledge intelligently, you can chart the future. That is basically what Marx and Engels did. They read the works of the economists, the philosophers, the historians and the idealists and from their reading, compiled s blue-print from which the workers can build a society suited to each country's particular conditions. Lenin did just that for Czarist Russia. We have to get down to the job of building.

If anyone would care to try, the theory is all here in our house. It only needs someone to translate it into practice.

Edmund and Ruth Frow

INDUSTRIAL WORKER

In the hurrying workshops
where men and women sweat
harder and faster
under taskmaster
harsher than winter weather
our characters are set.
The urgencies temper,
the hurry and worry and fret

bond us together.

In this lies our strength.

Alone each is nothing
except as of use
to help create value
which sold could produce
profit perhaps -
profit for bosses!
If not, cut their losses
and labour is scrap.

Nothing but hands.

But many together
to work or to stop
we are lords of the shop.
Let the boss go play
To another place -
who misses his face?
But let us go away
and everything stands.

Lesson by lesson
life hammers it home,
each is nothing alone,
but working as ONE
we are essential
to all that is done.

We who are makers
of city and farm
maintainers and takers
from hither and yon -
not the graspers who squat
spiders in office
accounting the lot
in language of profit -
we whom they manage as
blinkered asses
dulling with carrots and blows
our senses,
WE are the not to be done without
and we are beginning
to fathom it out!

Frances Moore

THE RAGGED TROUSERED PHILANTHROPISTS?

Who are the Ragged Trousered Philanthropists? This question tantalized me for years whenever I considered the bizarre possible answers to it. I was aware that The Ragged Trousered Philanthropists was the title of a book, but that was all I knew; the question remained: who are they? It was only very recently that I discovered that the Ragged Trousered Philanthropists - far from being, as I'd speculated they might be, a band of altruistic tramps or a society for hard-up humanitarians - far from being any of these things, were well known to me. So well known in fact that in a very real sense, I'm one of them!

Robert Tressel coins his novel's title "The Ragged Trousered Philanthropists" to describe the working class who "sweat and toil at their noble and unselfish task of making money for their employers." More particularly though he is talking about the workers of his day (at the beginning of the century) and especially those employed in the building trade.

The story is set in the town of Mugsborough (another sly, ironic dig at the Ragged Trousered Philanthropists) and centres on the lives of a group of painters and decorators, property repairers and their families. Also taken into account in the story are the notorious "sweat shops", corruption in local Councils and the rottenness generally in the structure of the town. Mugsborough can and should be taken as a microcosm of the whole of Britain at that time.

I don't intend here going into detail about the unscrupulously mercenary and merciless employers that live in the book and doubtless existed in real life. Let the names Tressel gave to them suffice: Rushton, Grinder, Sweater, Makehaste and Sloggit, Bluffem and Doem-down, Snatcher and Graball, Smeeriton end Leovit, Pushem and Sloggem, Doger end Scampit, and so on. Nor am I going to use much of his description of the neat-starvation which existed among their employees as a consequence of their ruthlessness, for there will be plenty of my readers who have experienced conditions as horrifying as those that Tressel describes (I use the word "describes" rather than "writes of" because Tressel says in his preface that he "invented nothing"; everything he speaks of - he witnessed.) For my own part, I can corroborate much of what he says about near-starvation from my own experience in the thirties. I remember for example, the "shopping" expeditions I went on with my grandmother to Smithfield market, where, instead of purchasing, we picked up from the gutter where they'd been tossed to await the refuse collector, bruised and faded fruit and scabby-looking vegetables. Memories, such as that of our school teacher dividing her lunch sandwiches among the half-starved children in the class - a practical example of the loaves and fishes feeding the multitude, but without the miracle of multiplication. Memories of the joy we felt on pay days after father had managed to get temporary work as a labourer on a council building site. Apart from the penny chocolate bars he always brought home on these occasions, it also meant that we'd have something more substantial, for the weekend, at least, than the bread and dripping or the bread and diluted milk pottage. For those readers too young to have such beautiful memories, The Ragged Trousered Philanthropists is essential reading and I urge them to read it at once.

Rather than mull over these atrocities I would prefer here to examine the causes of this heinous poverty, causes which are pin-pointed and scathingly analysed in this novel. It is important to say right away that although Tressel expresses hatred for the employers and all those instrumental in upholding such a brutal society, he did not blame them: "They (his employees) all hated and blamed Rushton. Yet if they had been in Rushton's place they would been compelled to adopt the same methods, or become bankrupt: for it is obvious that the only way to compete successfully against other employers who are sweaters is to be a sweater yourself. Therefore there is no upholder of the present system who can consistently blame any of these men. Blame the system."

But an inanimate thing such as is a system of running society cannot really bear the responsibility for its own being. So Tressel's thesis of blame becomes twinfold. Whenever he speaks about those with whom the real responsibility lies, at, any rate the great bulk of the blame, his language contains words like "imbecility", "contemptuous", "stupidity", and "degraded". Words which most people would think much worse if applied to themselves than "hateful", "wicked", "cunning", or "aggressive". Who then are the people who inspire such feelings of contempt in the writer? Who then, are these contemptibles who are responsible for the iniquities of the Capitalist system? The high ranking Tories? The pastors and masters? The Capitalists themselves? Well, judge for yourself from this extract from the book -

"As for these people (the workers), they vote for what they want, they get what they vote for; and by God they deserve nothing better! They are being beaten with the whips of their own choosing and if I had my way they would be chastised with scorpions! For them the present system means semi-starvation, rags and premature death. They vote for it all and uphold it. Well let them have what they vote for. let them drudge - let them starve!"

Although this is from the lips of a disenchanted Socialist, one who had his head almost, stoved in by a rock thrown by one of the jeering crowd of workers as he tries to address them; although this is out of the mouth of a bitter man who has just witnessed the same crowd cheer him as he spoke to them (disguised with a beard) as a paid orator for the Tory candidate, in essence and in tone it is the same kind of statement that Tressel makes himself through the narrator of the story or through Owen and Barrington, two active Socialists. He does not of course conclude with the same sentiments but there often appears to be a kind of self-struggle to remain committed to the Socialist cause. Barrington undergoes this struggle, this revulsion of feeling following the scenes he witnesses at the elections.

"The blind, stupid, enthusiastic admiration displayed by the philanthropists for those who exploited and robbed them.., their callous indifference to the fate of their children, and the savage hatred they exhibited towards any one who dared to suggest the possibility of better things, forced upon him the thought that the hopes he cherished were impossible of realisation."

But his anguished feelings toward the children of the workers, "his younger brethren", save him from total disillusionment.

"He felt like a criminal because he was warmly clad and well fed in the midst of all this want and unhappiness, and he flushed with shame because he had momentarily faltered in his devotion to the noblest cause that any man could be privileged to fight for - the upholding of the disconsolate and the oppressed."

The same kind of see-sawing of feelings is witnessed in Owen, the chief character in the novel. Articulate, clear-thinking, and level-headed - if angry - Owen expresses most of Tressel's views, experiencing a curious love-hatred, of more accurately a compassion-contempt as he looked on these "little children in men's bodies", the same paradoxical feelings that Tressel must have felt, for he, like Owen, worked all of his life among them. "Thousands of (these) people like himself dragged out a wretched existence on the very verge of starvation...yet practically none of these people knew or even troubled themselves to enquire why they were in that condition! and for anyone else to try to explain to them was a ridiculous waste of time, for they did not want to know".

They did not want to know; yet this did not stop Owen from spending most of his spare time and money (on pamphlets) in doggedly trying to force them to become aware" of their condition. As also, we can surmise, Tressel must have done. In Owen we constantly witness the struggle between these two antipathetic states of mind and of feeling towards his fellow workers; feelings that we can be sure the author also fought with. But with Owen, as with Tressel, compassion and reason always triumph over revulsion and contempt. He knew the reason for this despicable lack of self-respect, for their abysmal ignorance and for their servility. He understood what made them roar with admiration as their betters fed them rhetoric, and what made them hoot with rage whenever anyone tried to show them the causes and the cure for their poverty, for their degradation. For the chains Karl Marx spoke of bound, not their wrists or their ankles, but their minds. "From their very infancy" says Owen, "they had drilled into them the doctrine of their own mental and social inferiority, and their conviction of this doctrine was voiced in the degraded expression that fell from their lips so frequently when speaking of themselves and each other . The likes of US!"

It is, I think, worth repeating here the same statement of fact, but more fully developed, as spoken by Barrington to the renegade socialist, towards the end of the book:-

> "From their infancy most of them have been taught by priests and parents to regard themselves and their own class with contempt - a sort of lower animal - and to regard them who possess wealth with veneration, as superior beings. The idea that they are really human creatures, naturally absolutely the same as their so-called "betters, naturally equal in every way, naturally different from them only in those ways that their so-called superiors differ from each other, and inferior to them only because they have been deprived of education, culture and opportunity - you know as well as I do that they all have been taught to regard that idea as preposterous".

It is worthwhile also to listen to the renegade's answer, in order to see how once again Tressel balances one thought against another so that the facts of the situation continue to see-saw relentlessly in objectivity and truth.- "Go and undeceive them...go and try to tell them that the Supreme Being made the earth in all its fullness for the use and benefit of all his children. Go and explain to them that they are poor in body and mind and social condition not because of any natural inferiority, but because they have been robbed of their inheritance. Go and try to show them how to secure that inheritance for themselves and their children and see how grateful they'll be to you".

Of course the constant repetition of these two facts: the infamous treatment of the majority, the working class, by a minority, the established rulers, and the insane way that majority will insist on the privilege of being so treated, these two facts are not intended to be taken merely as a diatribe either against the working classes or against the rest of society. In the "loafer" classes, Tressel no doubt wanted to sow the seed of their guilt, and perhaps (but he hasn't much faith in this happening), spontaneously cause them to restructure Society more fairly. But most of all it is clear that his prime object was to stir the workers into awareness of their own shameful mental stultification; to show them themselves, as in a mirror, so that they might stiffen with horror at the sickening apparition that they perceive. And then, realising it is indeed their own image reflected there, be shaken to their roots with self-revulsion that will compel them to stiffen the sinews, summon the blood, disguise ugly nature with hard-favoured rage (to paraphrase Shakespeare^ Henry V) and then do something about their "heritage".

The "pull" of these two facts: an intolerable system and the paradox of the people who incredibly (to Owen and the socially aware), and degradingly tolerate that system is felt throughout the book, and provides the extraordinary force of the message. And although Tressel may play upon the emotions of the reader like an inspired musician plays upon his instrument, he never indulges in sentimentality! he is always scrupulously fair in his judgement and in his apportionment of the blame, and scathingly, almost brutally frank about the character of the people whose rights ,he champions. It is this determination on the part of the author not to let his political bias cloud his judgement that gives his assessment of the state of society at that time its ring of truth, its powerful impact and its claim to greatness both as a political indictment and as a novel.

Edward Morrison

DESIRE

Desire that troubled me, that harried me, pricked
My body with pins, and made my mind a fire,
How you have wronged my thought austere and strict,
Which asked for beauty cleansed from vain desire.
I have passed girls at night, my heart has ached,
Little red flower faces nestled on glistening furs,
I have groaned in an anguish of urgency unslaked,
And goaded my futile passion with cruel spurs.
Factory girls, shawled laughing girls that passed,
Arm in arm, down the street, and girls more prim,
Looks of desire furtively, I have cast
Out on you as I walked down town streets dim.
How many times in sweat and strain I have spent
In passionate thought for girls I have not known,
I have loved you all as silently past I went,
Possessing you in secret though I walked alone.
Yet in calm moments and glad I love you truly,
Dear comrade girls, to walk with you and play,
O because I am washed in water of vision newly,
I ask your forgiveness, comrades, I ask you to stay
By me: I am wise too, for I plainly see,

You too are troubled by that same which troubles me.

Ben Ainley

ON RETURNING HOME AFTER A LONG ABSENCE

The lights of New York City and the luminous chains of cars on the Long Island expressways ore far below and behind me now, fading into the past. Beacons of America, now claimed by the darkness, I watch them disappearing, until my 747 is itself swallowed by cloud. No friendly, floppy-eared jumbo this, but a cold, impersonal juggernaut. It's only a couple of hours since I was saying 'goodbye' to a beautiful lady with dark, sad eyes. Now I feel only the emptiness, and perhaps a dull pain, which could be just fatigue - or maybe the birth pains of hope?

I am awakened as the plane lands at Heathrow on a dull, rainy English morning. Walking stiff-legged through Customs and corridors, bustling and lonely, and finally out into the rain. Catch a red bus and on underground train, Through a long, long tunnel and out again. That's London, that was.

I call to see a stranger who is my brother. He talks about football, and I realise he means soccer. Something I used to be interested in. His accent belongs to London now; mine lost its allegiance somewhere between Manchester, England, and California; our conversation is trite. We do not touch, or show any warmth we are very polite.

Hitch a ride to the edge of the countryside, make a phone call and walk down a road. A small, family car slows to a halt beside me and a strangely familiar man, plump and ageing, opens the door for me. He is making an effort not to be too solicitous. I am making an effort not to be too casual. There is no doubt that this man is my father.

He shows me round his house. Impressions of rooms, clean and tidy, register momentarily, while psychologically we are jockeying for position: we are trying to get on the same side as one another, but first we must find out which side this is.

Meanwhile, back in the little market town, a middle-aged woman, wearing brown-rimmed glasses that make her look strangely severe, is waiting on the pavement. She peers short-sightedly and sees us, but is not sure that she has seen us, until after we have passed and turned around. She runs up excitedly and climbs into the back seat, rushing in mental circles around the main question, fastidiously trying not to appear fussy. This woman is my mother.

So Dad goes off to buy the bacon. He always was the one who brought home the bacon. Mum hopes she has time to run to the library, heels clacking anxiously on the flagstones, anxious in case he should return first and be annoyed, anxious as always.

Tea-time is for lighting a fire and crooking a meal. Evening is for sitting talking. Building little bridges across great oceans, like jetties on distant shores that never look like meeting.

And tomorrow it is time to move on. Afternoon sees me in Manchester, back at my grandmother's. Where I came to when I left home - a long time ago now. She's my best friend, really, but the generation gap seems to be wider now, I start to collect her aphorisms, as if they are the most accessible part of that wrinkled exterior. Kind old lady, rather settled in her ways now, probably forgotten more than I ever knew, and no way to explain it to me, except in bits and pieces. And now she looks so much older, as though she is slowly turning into a gargoyle on the church that is humanity, and I who am only concerned with the theology of the matter, I am powerless to reach out and save her.

Monday means looking for a job. Going round the sites, trying for a start. Most have "No Vacancies" signs up if you're lucky you can fill a form in. On to the Labour Exchange; "Listen son, there's 6,000 men looking for a job in Manchester right now, and 250 of them have been in before you today". So it looks like the old story again - queue up and sign on. Don't know why they don't call it the Department of Unemployment. A man runs into the building, holding his prick in his hand, heading straight for the toilets. If you're on the dole long enough, you stop caring about yourself, you can't even be bothered to go for a piss until you've left it too late. I've no regrets about going abroad to seek my fortune, even if I never did find a rainbow's end.

Monday also means looking for a place to live. Walking round Moss Side, looking for the cheapest bedsitters. Watching the people who have lived for so long under dirty Manchester skies: white women with their pallid faces, almost anaemic; West Indian women, growing plump as they lose their youth, but seemingly never losing their cheerfulness. And all around them, so many demolition sites; a little, children's playground, empty now, looking incongruous at the corner of one great block that has been razed to the ground to form a playground of rubble, a playground by default. So much demolition; how long before it starts to breed derelict people? Questions, that still hang in the smoky sky, as once again I move into an English slum district, this time in Rusholme. Just a city street, a street for kids to smash bottles on, and for dogs to shit on.

A couple of weeks and I've got a start - only a mile or so away. Heaving and hammering until six o'clock in the evening all for 42.1/2 p an hour. And a man who is earning a lot more than me says, "We're all part of a team here", and gives me a copy of the Company booklet, which bears a photograph of someone else who is in the team and earning more in a fortnight than I will in a year. But having sold myself, I know I have to knuckle down to it. When your body is vibrating to the rhythm of a concrete-breaker you don't do too much thinking. But when you're digging a trench in a remote corner of a building site in some forgotten port of the city, you become very conscious of the sky. You leave your shirt off in the hope that the weak sunshine will preserve the brownness of your skin. You look up sometimes and to the east is Japan and to the west is California, and beyond that the sky goes on forever.

At lunch-time you can walk around the city, but it seems that here in Manchester nothing moves in freedom. Car doors swing open, but always remain on their hinges. Buses ply the thoroughfares, but always return to the garage at night. Lorries deliver, salesmen travel, housewives shop, but by evening all have returned home. Young people emerge from boutiques with the latest trendy clothes and unisex hairstyles, and for lack of the real thing to measure against this is mistaken for progress. Except for momentary aberrations, the faces are expressionless, like the faces of pawns in a game of chess. Maybe that's why I feel like the only living boy in Manchester - I seem to be the only pawn who doesn't accept the rules of the game, and I'll do my best to change them. Failing this, I shall show that I am not a flat-bottomed piece controlled by some alien power - I shall fly away. Would that make me an emancipated pawn or just a flying zero? Perhaps life should be a balance between, on the one hand, trying to enlist the aid of the other prisoners in breaking the encircling walls of that zero, and, in expressing ourselves, ceasing to be mere pawns, and becoming human, and, on the other hand, making sure that one's own wings do not become weak from disuse. And the people who have never fought or have given up fighting for either of these things, they are the zombies I see around me, thronging the streets of Manchester.

One evening I bumped into Ted, a close friend from the old days of playing football and going to watch United. We sat talking for a few hours without communicating. He seemed to be playing the role of a rock, pretending that individualism is his fortress, when deep inside he must know that loneliness is his prison. Ted, who is adamant about the necessity of winning every game, irrespective of why it is being played. Ted, who concentrates his attention fiercely upon each trick, never looking beyond the edge of the tables Ted, who went off into the night, returning to University to be the ambitious Law student. Ted - someone else I used to know.

Another evening, I called to see a friend working at the local Youth Club. He was having a spot of trouble with a few of his young members who had been trying to wreck the place. Afterwards, someone asked if it didn't make him feel like giving up. His answer was "No - these kids are the product of a society that is itself destructive, and so they try to hurt those who are most vulnerable - those who are trying to help them. And the people who control this society think that all we need is more 'law and order.!" They feed us on violence and when we shit they wonder why it isn't love that comes out!

A week or two after starting work, I heard about a Building Workers Conference in Birmingham and decided to hitch-hike down there. Although I had neither credentials nor Union card I was welcomed into the hall, where there was a tremendous atmosphere of unity. Those speakers who were less certain of their way were helped onwards by the men on the floor.

If they stumbled, we were there ready to help them get their ideas out. We were there to understand each other's meaning, not put each other on trial, for all of us, there was the knowledge of strong solidarity to take from that hall. And for me there was the knowledge that I am not the only pawn who does not accept the rules of the game.

On the way back a driver commented "I bet half of them were Communists where you've been to". I wondered if that was supposed to be good or bad. In the weeks that followed several people at work told me that I was a Communist, I was always unsure whether or not to argue, until I solved the problem - by joining those pawns who are fighting to change the rules of the game.

Sometimes an older worker - a joiner or a steel-fixer, will say to me, out of the blue "You're wasting your life away, young man". But after a while things become clearer to me, and I no longer feel so powerless at work. I start to realise that a lot of orders are given by a foreman just for the sake of asserting his authority, and that, if you have the confidence, you can make a job much more satisfying by taking the initiative yourself. And a lot of the mystification is removed. And when a worker ceases to believe in his own inferiority, when he ceases to believe what he reads about himself, he can start writing his own story. Amilcar Cabral, some of Whose thoughts on the liberation of Africa could not but find their way into an article on the liberation of Manchester, England, has been assassinated since I wrote this piece. And so I am dedicating it to him, as a way of saying that "you can kill a revolutionary but you can't kill the revolution."

Rick Gwilt

THE BOY

The boy, tall and slender, with grave face, had hurt his foot. Vigour had gone, with pains coming. He sat on the green form, amidst the cacophony of shouts and screams from the crowded swings; alone.

At nine, we are afraid, of many things. Not of the dark, but of the shadows from stray rays of light. Of bigger boys; bully boys. Exuberant, in their assertion of their rights, won by trial of strength. Of adults, clumsy, capricious, improvements of our mind or manners. Of lack of love.

Unhappy when bored. Mischievous and a devil. An angel, when sitting now, brooding in a flood of pain. His mate, solicitous, has been and gone, swinging high on the bright, mauve plastic seat. A few words. "Are you alright?" No reply. Not able to cope with an adult's field of assurance and re-assurance. He wanted his Mam. She would have scolded him for being clumsy. Rubbed his foot, Kissed him, and said "Go on now, don't be a baby. You're a big boy now."

The day was spoilt. Only healing balms of sleep would help. He sat on. At one, with bruised grass and broken twigs. Just barely into consciousness, but new sensations, new knowledge, etching in the mind.

He tried the foot out. Gained confidence. Went homeward bound. Slowly, through the wicket gate. Along the path, between park, and school playing field. Kicked stones. Picked them up, and shied at pigeons, sparrows, pecking in the grass. Found a stick, and machine-gunned the air with vibrations from the railings. His hurt forgot, but his spirit still dampened.

His mate, comes running up; hard; to emphasise the difference, The boy, races him, to show there is no change.

At the road, between cemetery and school, large hoppers form collecting points for rubbish outside the Council Parks' Committee yards.

They delve. Wondering at engine parts. Broken pans, A once super toy. The sad remains of a doll. Down the quiet road, a hop, short run, a stone to shy. Thinking. Of food. What's on tele? Tired. For it's been a long day. The road they ran along before seeming endless. Plodding now. Steps slow and slower. Reaching Manor Road. Turn left.

The pace quicker here. Cars whizz past. A motor bike, a bus. Clinging to railings on low wall. Progressing hand over hand. Jump down. The slow plod to horticultural hall. Past the little new-built houses, faced by the newly crested garden on the opposite side of the road. Roses against the crumbling, former old mill wall. The new placed turf showing the lines, separating one piece from another. Looking over the canal bridge. Underneath - a road. The water gone five years past, and mountains of rubble. Around the pharmaceutical works, always smelling of vinegar. Up High Street, over Hart Street, and home.

He had many charges levelled at him. He was dirty. He was late. His mate's mother was looking for him. He had missed his tea. Everyone worried to death. Water off a duck's back. He had heard it all before. Look at those hands. Wash before you eat. All that off. Better have a bath. Go on, while I make your tea. Orders. Instructions. A clatter across the head. Even a dig in the ribs. A flip across the bottom. What is it all about? Adults. For no apparent reason being angry. So often upset.

Moods. They have moods the little girl said as they swung, aide by side. "Can you do this?" standing on one leg. "Course" he said. "My Mam's having a baby. I heard her and my uncle talking when I was in bed." "Isn't that lovely?" "I hope it's a boy like you". "Why?" "So he can live with me, Mum's always leaving me. I don't like being on my own. Doesn't your uncle live with you?" "Oh no. He visits. Mum says I'm hearing things. She says there is only her and me. But I've seen him through the window." "Where does he live then?" "I don't know" "Does she shout at you?" "Who?" "Your mum". "Sometimes when I'm naughty". "My mum's always shouting at me. You shouldn't be naughty. She shouts at me for nothing." "Mine doesn't. I like your mum" "I like yours." "You don't know her". "I like her because I like you". "Girls are all the same always talking that way." "What way?" "About liking people" "I like liking people". "It's soppy". "What's that?" "It's daft". "It's not". "It is". "It's not'.

Eating, in front of the tele. Sitting on the rug. Hardly stirred by the guns, and drawling threats. Interested in the fist fight. Amused by the adverts. Frightened by the proximity of death, ad adults, twelve inches high, kill one another away from the romantic confines of the west. In a room like this one. In clothes like these. Going up the stairs, in the little room. Still aware of the tiger who might still roam the landing as he did only a few years ago. But more sophisticated now. There are ghosts. There are monsters. Tyrannosaurus Rex is in the garden. You can see him. Lurking near the fence. Under the tree. I won't sleep. I never go to sleep. Not for a hundred years.

Holidays in summer are a generation long. Unpunctuated by the ritual stops and starts of school term. Are as one day, in their continuity. To the boy, one day became as another spent in killing time. In dream. In play. Eating and sleeping and continuous complaint of having nothing to do. Halfway through; boredom; as insidious as asbestosis, turns all the boys to paired and gang fights. Mostly with stones. And great arguments. A noise as of starlings, twittering. There is hurt. There is anger. Tears flow. Children are just like adults. They feel. They have hopes. They need love, warmth, companionship. They know misery. Can feel ignored and forgotten. Can almost hope to die from hurt pride. And can burn with shame at the mocking laugh and ill-considered word.

The childhood game is fast. Torrential. Played on a cliff edge. With minute experience, every day now. The hurts, exquisite pains on so raw nerves. And social pressure, parental prejudice, teachers imparted knowledge; shapes the clay. To make the future man and woman, leaving derelicts - it's failures. Rejects. Piled high along the way.

Frank Parker.

WOMAN

She is a descendant of Eve
Half-contesting Adam's property rights.
Sometimes, with a borrowed sense of importance
I try to stand her up,
But she always seems to lie down again,
And I wonder,
Does the doll's house
With the endless Punch and Judy show
Exist outside my mind?

She's my arena;
She's where I battle and wait
For opponents yet to arrive.
But my shadow gives me a hard fight;
I always emerge bruised and bloody,
Extract wild eulogies
From the spectators of my mind
While marking time
And awaiting a challenger

Last night's bout was rough,
Its dialectics skilful,
Until midway through the third
(With my shadow ahead on points)
A strange thing happened.
The arena stood up and the ring tilted
Toward the sky. I spun,

Endlessly, clawing for the ropes,
Searching for my shadow in the darkness.

And the arena spoke and accused me
Of scuffing and skipping upon her
And a lot of other things
That were true. Now my doll's house
Is in revolt. I have lost
My rhythm and the white canvas that
I always cast my shadow on,
And the championship series
Is threatened with cancellation
On grounds of absurdity.

Rick Gwilt

MOON LAUGHTER

The city's continual roar
eases to an occasional croak
massed on rubbish dumps
hoarse gulls sleep fitfully
night
is an undertaker's parlour
but the moon
refusing to be a corpse
slips its tattered shroud
appears
leers
deathly white
and on a graveyard world
pours rivulets of sickly light.

Presently dawn comes
sublunar bones stir
rattling around their coffin houses
knowing not how dead they are
rattle rattle rattle and ring
flock to the charnel ball
watch as they rattle, rattle and fail
cadavers dancing on profit's string
dance rattle and fall

No God will tell them
no God will say
that they could be here tomorrow
that they're gone today
wake then wake!
discover how
your freedom beckons
here
now.

Edward Morrison

IF OO COULD, OO WOULD

No gracious house was this
An old black-leaded fireplace glistened
Its own light cascading
From the great sideboard's mirrors
The gas light half turned on
Whether from hatred of the post
Or fear of the future
Hissed
Beneath at a table sat an old man
One that a soft wind could blow
Reaching high he pulled the chain still lower
Till only the flickering fire
Lit his crevassed face
Sitting up he swelled his chest
Like threatening man, as if it gave him greater authority
And began to speak

"Nar Ellen" he said "tha's bin gone some time
And a miss thi sommat terrible
Tha were a spiritualist all thi life
And wi often argued
Thee saying tha were a Lord
An a life hereafter
Me tha were nowt, if oo could let
Little childer suffer
Tha often prayed
Fu one thing at tother

Which I thought seemed daft!
Fu he already knows what tha wants
Better than tha does thisell
And anyway tha never had so much
If ar childer kept asking us for summat
Like some do to him above
A'd think we wernt bringin them up reet
Tha often said tha'd come back
And prove me all wrong
A wish tha would
A hope thaft reet
A'm waiting nar
But one thing A do know
If anybody can come
Thor would if tha could

Again he sat down and mustering all
His feeble energies
"Fa the last time Elin!" he shouted
That made him cough and splutter
To crack like a suffering tenor.
He waited a little, his hands
Pressed over his eyes as if
To blot out this most certain of all plagues
So near him.

His beliefs were false
There was another world
Another life he wanted to believe
Where truth justice
The love of fellow men
Where the real jewels
Not the money-lending muck heap
This midden
Where greed, gain, selfishness
Is rewarded, nay worshipped.
In loud guffaws, Virtue scorned,
From gold-plated mouths,
Hollow laughter

He wanted to see his mate again
Everyone, his brother Richard
Drowned in a Haslingden lodge
Last century, a speck of light

Snuffed, choked, throttled
Mother in factory
Big door key round his neck
On a string
Suffer little children
To come unto me.

Then there was silence
The ticking clock
Seemed to emphasise its depth
Tick, tock, tick, tock, it seemed endless
On the walls in the flitting firelight
Patterns seemed to appear to merge
Farming pictures of all
The previous occupants; some I knew
Who grimaced, gesticulated, gibbering,
With beckoning fingers for me
To come and join them
In their silent nebulous world,
I shook my head wildly
Gripping the chair arms
Shouting "no, no, no, never"
Which must have stirred the old man.
To come to him I'm sure he meant
And I wondered with not a little awe
As to how men o f his day
Mostly undernourished, undersized
Could lord it o'er their women
With such a confidence,
"Thi father's coming" she would say
"Canta hear his clogs" as if the Lord Almighty was approaching.
Perhaps it was the many children
Almost yearly wives had then to bear
This normal sequence of the wild
Became their bondage
To their breadwinner
"Nar am gooing to shout three times,
Perchance tha't walking somewhere
For a have heard nowt yet
So a hope tha't listening"
He summoned what was for him a deep breath
And nodding his head as a beat
Shouted "Elin can ta hear me?"
It sounded and was a long lost cry

Of a man wandering in the wilderness.
He waited a little, then,
Slowly raised his eyes towards the ceiling.
They circled the room,
With his hands he cupped his ears,
Cocked his head on one side
Adjusting like a miniature Jodrell Bank,
But there was nothing, only silence, a deadly silence.
Again he braced himself,
"Elin" he shouted "this is second time."
Just then a newspaper placed near the door
Protecting some mopping lifted
Glided a little, rasping
As it settled on the oilcloth.
"Is that thee?" he cried
Defying his age he ran to the door
Snatched it open, into the kitchen.
The outer door was ajar
As if someone had fled
Into the- yard he hurried
Then into the lamplit street
Peering up then down Into the swirling gloom
Returning he was shaking his head
Mumbling "It was nobbut wind, nobbut wind.
A should a known better
Fa it allus does that when't wind
Blows fra yon chimney"

He got to his feet
And like the housewife
Palms her crumpled tablecloth exclaimed
"Tha's nowt, tha's nowt, tha's bugger all
For if oo could a come, oo would a come, if oo could".

Frank Smith

MISSIN' THE CLUBMAN

Get toft front room winder - keep a sharp luck-out
Try not to miss the clubman, this week 'e's gettin' nowt
Don't move t'bloody curtain – jus' see that yer can see
Wen 'e calls we mus' be sure we're quiet as quiet can be

I've paid th'rent an't telly, an' also't Provident
This week we'll miss th'insurance, 'e can't 'ave wot's bin
spent
'Cepf' my bit fo't Bingo an' a pack o' fags
There's nowt left to give 'im (can't do wi'out me fags)

Ma! 'E's parked 'is car now, down at th'end o't street
Mekin' sur 'E's locked it, 'e mus' wanna keep it neat '
E's called at Mrs. Jones's, 'er that's like a mouse
She don't pay - 'e sheks 'is 'ead an' lux towards our 'ouse

Keep behin' the door clear - 'e may use the flap
I'd rather do it this way than talk a load o' crap
Rat-tat the thin door trembles - Now don't mek any sounds
'E'll soon get tired o' knockin' an' go on, on 'is rounds
Get to't front room winder, tell us wen it's clear
Mek sure 'e doesn't see yer!! - d'yer want some tea m'dear?

Alfred Edwards

ROCKABYE, STATESMAN

I was born under a shooting star,
Within the sound-wave of the smash,
When V-for-Vengeance from afar
Came buzzing with the fly-bomb's crash.
This was my earliest lullabye:
"Rockabye, baby, do not cry!
You're not the only one to die."
My mother rocked me on her arm,
Knee-deep in glass in the market-place,
In time to the wailing siren's alarm,
With shell-shocked eyes and blackened face,
Rockabye mammy, do not cry!
Men of science will tell you why
Some of your children may not die.

My daddy won a Purple Heart,
And H-for-Horror-Bomber's star;
Before his mind went, he was part
Of the crew that bombed Hiroshima:
Rockabye daddy, do not cry!

Nowadays even pigs can fly,
You won't be first nor last to die.

These are some of the reasons that
Today we stand up where we are,
Defiantly wear a funny hat,
Rock'n'roll with n cha-cha-cha;
Rockabye babes with fall-out hair,
Rocking into Trafalgar Square,
Rocking you mad lot out of here.

Angela Tuckett

WARTIME IN FORDS

"A" Site was a very large factory, specially designed and built to make aero-engines for Rolls Royce of Crewe. The plant was more than half a mile in length and half as wide. Inside were four rectangular buildings called A, B, C, and D, with cross roads between as straight as a Roman fort. In addition there were smaller buildings outside, the tool room section previously mentioned, and towards Urmston, the "X" and "Y" sites of assembly.

I had heard and read about Fords. One N.C.L.C. Course had dealt with the American variety of "Fordism", the massive quantities of machinery, breakdown of operations and skills, speed-up and an enormous increase in production. They hated Unions in Britain and would sling out a worker simply for Union membership.

However, this wasn't operating here. The headed paper on all the notice boards announced "Fords" in large letters, while underneath in the smallest print read "(Under the auspices of the Ministry of Aircraft.)" As always, it's the small print that counts, but Fords had the freedom of production management, and they were certainly production-conscious.

I had come into Fords prematurely. The factory was not ready for production and only a skeleton number of (mainly skilled) people were around. I had been grabbed because they wanted to train enough men in preparation for production.

There is a world of difference between a lone trainee and one among hundreds. I was soon accepted, helped by my admission of being one. The Government had agreed with the Unions that Trainees would leave the industry after the 'duration'.

My first friend from the first day was an engineer about 45 years old named Jack Cottriall. A fine trade unionist, he had been a ships' engineer and had the unmistakeable roll of the seaman. Once he found how much we had in common he became a key in popularising me with other engineers. He became a shop steward later and was my first recruit in the factory.

He could tell a fund of stories without repetition. One was about the old-time engineering factories where a man wouldn't be employed if he wore spectacles for fear he would read a micrometer incorrectly. The older ones would look round and if the foreman was out of sight, get out their glasses, adjust the 'mike' and put them back again. This trick was wholesale. He had learned a great deal in his travels. When in a Soviet part he made for the workers' clubs where foreign seamen were welcome. He came back boozed and happy; those chasing women were glum and sour. He got me interested in Shakespeare where no professional teacher could. His quote of Hamlet "Now could I drink hot blood" was frightening! Years later, when the effects of overwork passed, and I was on a train to London, I looked up what was on at the Old Vic. If a Shakespeare play was on which I had not seen, I made the effort.

A few months before I entered Fords, Churchill had ousted Chamberlain, become Prime Minister and formed a sort of Coalition which included people like Bevin and Morrison. The latter had become Home Secretary and only two or three weeks before I started in Fords had banned the 'Daily Worker'. Jim Hewitson, the factory convenor, asked me to lie low for a while on Party activity. I would have done so anyway. The factory was in an embryonic stage, militants could easily be found simply by discussing the need for a 100% union shop, and that time I had my hands full as a Party Secretary in the Platting area.

Around this time I went to a meeting addressed by Pollitt; it was either an aggregate or an 'active' and well-attended. A hurricane of anti-Communist propaganda was having no noticeable effect on the 'public'. The recent pre-war years of anti-fascist work by the Party was now proving what an ally it could be, but the propaganda continued. Pollitt was concerned that some members were almost welcoming an ides of underground work. He gave us an idea of what this meant in reality, concluding with an intimate appeal that was unique to him: "You know comrades, in the middle of war, you are lying on a bed of roses" and added it was our duty to preserve the legality of the Party.

I received an invitation to attend another meeting in June, an Industrial Conference on a Sunday morning. We were already on overtime, and I stayed in bed till the last moment, swallowed some breakfast and dashed out. The meeting was somewhere in Moss Side and I was lucky to be only fifteen minutes late. A number of comrade were leaning over the table which was to serve as a platform. I assumed some factory urgency had arisen. I sat down on a form and waited. A comrade sat beside me and asked what I thought of it. He must have seen a very blank face and explained that the Sunday papers carried the news of the Fascist invasion of the Soviet Union. I realised now that Pat Devine had gathered around him the District Secretariat. It was the Industrial Conference that never was.

The whole day's discussion centred on the complications involved, and decisions could be crystallised in its final slogan: "All Aid to the Soviet Union!" A Party aggregate later in the week found that the Lancashire District had been closest to the line of the Central Committee. I could take no credit, but I felt taller!

That weekend I spoke at a specially organised meeting in Platting on the Albert Croft. I gave it all I could! When it was over the "political 'tec" came over and congratulated me on my speech. I was puzzled and reported it to the Manchester organiser. This had been happening at other meetings too.

In time, the factory began to fill up, at first a trickle, then a flood, people coming from Scotland and the South, though most of course, from the wider Manchester area. Among the first trickle in our department were two girls who started together, Rae Cohen and Jean Taylor. We were not on production and had time to gossip. I told Rae I was an upholsterer and had worked with Jewish people. She asked me if I knew Joss Davidson. When I said he was a close friend she followed up with the casual remark that she had two brothers, Jud and Manc. She knew how to go about it! I could have kicked myself: her face would have convinced anyone she was Manc's sister.

Now we had three party comrades in our building, the other being Charlie Wellard from London, who had started before me, highly skilled and working as an Inspector. He seemed to me to know the interpretation of the A.E.U. Rules to perfection and was later a powerful adviser in our stewards' work.

Shortly after, Rae could tell me that Bella Kline had started in "B" building and that another YCL girl - Gussie Howard - had started higher up in our own. Three YCL girls, none over 24. They were to play a major part first in the recruitment, and later the development of the party in the factory.

Our early party meetings started small and weak. Hewitson, Wellard, three 'shy' YCL girls and myself. We were later joined by Leah Cohen, Rae's sister, in "Y" site, where she was badly needed in later stages. Jim Hewitson almost dominated the first meetings around the subject of a hundred members on paper (he had names and addresses) who were supposed to be in the factory but could never be traced. They were written to but no replies. We never did find them either.

I don't remember why, but Jim Hewitson resigned as group leader. Later he deserted his wife for someone else, left the party and in the end, the factory. I never heard of him again. His wife worked in the factory in the same building as Bella Kline and continued till the war finished. Her son started there and he too joined the party. To this day she retains her membership.

I was elected as a group leader. I felt we were wasting time chasing names on paper and suggested that we start from bottom building a new one. I was relieved to find that all comrades had the same approach.

We had some advantages over most factories; one was a lack of tradition leading to 'sects'? another that the factory, in closing down at the end of the war meant no future, no inhibitions to keep a job (though in fairness, this didn't seem to count so much even in places like M.Vs), but the most important was the inexperience of the Ford management, three of whom had been 'imported' from the U.S.A. A worker could not be sacked for being a trade unionist, a militant or even a communist, and this was the only weapon in Britain they had ever known!

At first they tried to persuade people not to join a union. A rumour was spread that the high wages would cease and drop to the minimum if it became a union shop. The party scotched that one by getting stewards to explain that a strongly organised shop would get better, not worse wages and conditions than a divided one. The management then said they would negotiate with the stewards but not the union. A little later they were willing to negotiate with the union but not the stewards! They didn't know how to turn and must have made many English managements smile.

Their next step was to try 'discipline' in an isolated corner of our building, in the first bay as you entered. During the morning round of the tea trolley a pompous commissionaire came in, stopped someone eating a sandwich, saying they could drink but not eat! If he caught anybody again they would be sacked on the spot. He came in again the same time next morning. Everybody immediately grabbed their sandwiches and began eating. He walked the length of the bay as red as a beetroot and out the other end. He never came again. I found out the sandwich-eating had been organised by a person named Joe Topping, a brother of Dick Topping, and I didn't know he worked there, nor did he know there was a party in the place either, but Joe, a former builder's labourer, didn't stay long.

Perhaps the story passed on to me by Jack Cottriall put the tin hat on the lot. When we started we were given a numbered badge which we ware supposed to wear on entering and leaving the site. Many were reluctant, saying they were human beings and not 'numbered prisoners'. One morning, a doorkeeper called after a man not wearing one, but he blissfully went walking on into the factory. He was chased and turned round. The man gave him a real punch, knocking him to the ground. He was then surrounded, taken into a room and the Police called. When they arrived, and before anyone could speak, the man informed the Police that he had been assaulted and compelled to defend himself, and that he wished to make a charge. They had touched upon a skilled engineer who also understood something about law! The case concluded with the firm giving him a humble apology. As far as I know, that was the last of the pinpricking. It was in this spirit of collective and individual militancy that we set about our party work.

Whether 'under the auspices of the Ministry of Aircraft' someone whispered in the ear of the Ford management - The A.E.U. had been involved in the assault case - or the firm realised their limitations and concentrated on the main aim of production, I don't know, but Fords ceased their provocations until they finally closed down. A wave affected the workers after the June '41 events which was a mixture of patriotism and international class solidarity with the Soviets that lessened the need for an imposed discipline, in spite of nerve-wracking situations created by unceasing overtime and shift work.

Before the first .'trickle' into the factory commenced, we were split up for the coming operations. Jack Cottriall told me one day I was to work with him and he had insisted on this with the departmental manager, Charlie Feeley. The latter was an old Ford staff man with a grim face, but completely fair with the workers, and you liked him the more you knew him, but except when everyone spoke up, as they did in the petitions against Mosley's release later, he kept all his opinions to himself.

I was very well placed for the job of a group leader, right at the end of the line near one end of the bay entrance. Every bay ran across the width of every building with two open ends, each clearly numbered, and as you came out you came into the wide passage way running the length of the building on both sides. Anyone could come and talk to me and go away again. No-one ever complained, we coped with our work and the lower the management, the less they wanted to know as long as the work went through.

I was also helped by Charlie Wellard in a quiet but bold manner. I have mentioned he was highly skilled and an Inspector. Some time after the June events he was called into the main offices and offered the job in charge of inspection for the entire building. The subject of his party membership arose. I'm not sure who raised it though I have the impression it was Charlie himself. I remember that Charlie made two things clear; one - he was patriotic, two - (pointing to his chest) his political beliefs were firm and unalterable. The reply was they were not concerned with his politics; their information was that he was the man for the job - would he take it? In those circumstances, Charlie agreed.

Charlie paid me occasional visits ostensibly to buy party stamps - he could easily have got them elsewhere - and would stand talking to me in his spotlessly white coat for a considerable time. No staff man would offend so highly placed an Inspector. Charlie was demonstrating to whom it may concern that I was a sacred cow not to be touched, as well as his own loyalties. He remained until about twelve months before the war ended, when he went back to London. I met him again at the Battersea Congress in 1956, and by then he had his own small engineering place. That was the last time I saw him. Jack Askins now tells me he has had to give the place up.

Jean Taylor, the girl who started with Rae, also came on our job later. She told us that in the pre-war days, her father bought the Daily Worker whenever he could. Jack got a mate to start and come on our job who later joined the party, so that we could have two on each shift and all reliable and safe for anyone.

Rae Cohen once explained to me the difficult position girls were placed in. A man could move around without hindrance. A girl would be quietly pounced upon by a charge hand.

Imagine the position of Bella Kline in "B" building. All the workers in her bay were women, and she was in the middle unable to move. The party was weak there, the only other being Mrs. Hewitson. The only one able to move around was the bay foreman. Like most of the skilled engineers, he was a good union man. She got to work and a few weeks later I had his registration party card! His name was Arthur Davenport, In no time he was chasing all the left wingers he knew in the building, recruiting and the recruits recruiting others, I could never dare to be without a stock of cards.

This kind of thing was the usual pattern in party building, though it required a party comrade to start it. I suspect there were pockets of left wingers willing to join if someone would take the plunge but in other cases not knowing whom to contact.

One large section where we had no contact whatever was the large polishing shop in our building, until one day a newly arrived comrade introduced himself to me. I deeply regret I forget his name and even his Lancashire town and he had started in polishing. He was a jewel. Not only did the recruits come in, thick and fast, but when November came round, he told me it was no business of mine to enquire how, but he had got bottles of whisky, rum, sherry and port which he wanted raffling in the building for Xmas! These poisons were unobtainable. We had unbelievable success and for once we may have achieved our 'quota' to our party branch.

Gussie Howard did her job in holding and developing comrades at the top end of the building and was the pivot of the organization there, but the strain of overwork hit her hard. She developed T.B. and had to go, but at least she has now recovered and is happily married.

*Recent published papers by the Cabinet of the time now show that Morrison was for banning the Party, but the majority view was a fear of the Party's influence in the factories and unions.

Joe Day

COMMUNICATION

People watching, people listening,
See the crowds, all around, everywhere you go.
Faces viewing other faces,
Looking for the secret of the universe.
Minds like little droplets measured into little boxes of
the same viscosity,
Separated by the boxes, so they cannot flow.
Drop your guard, human man.
You, human women, let me in, let all the world in.
Let us through your portals, climb your ivory stairs,
See your pictures on your cerebral walls.
Hear your music, dance your steps, in mind's fantastic halls.
Hear the old salvation cry, come and join us by and by,
Bring your family and your dreams, in sound or rhyme, or
glowing pictures on a canvas,
Or a scrawl on paper to match mine.
Conquer inhibition. Don't you know, you have inherited the earth?
You are Shakespeare, Michelangelo and Pope, Shelley and De
Quincey.
Robert Tressel's hopes.
You have company distinguished, everywhere you go.

Brave men from Tolpuddle, John Ball and Wat the Tiler,
Galileo, Isaac Newton, Harry Pollitt
Countless past and present, from Christ to Luther King,
Spartacus, and Che Guevara, all the known and unknown soldiers
for the working class.
And, today, we poise, a limitless future, unbounded skies.
A multitude of galaxies to survey from this earth,
And through the empty skies, whole nations can ambassadors be,
Worlds enough for everyone on earth today.
To win for mankind, and its human talents, that unity of arts.

Frank Parker

A STRANGER IN VIETNAM

American man you have eyes - you cannot see.
American man you have ears - you cannot hear.
American man you have feelings - you can not feel the pain,
The suffering, the murder you bring.
American man you came to kill - you die.
American man you came to conquer - you enslave yourself.
American man the war machine sends you - you obey.
You fly, so long, so high, so far.
Your bombs of Freedom kill - we die.
You talk of peace - the strangest lie.
The will of the people can never die.
Oh American man with blood on your hands.
Be part of the solution and understand
The Vietnamese people are in their own land.
Freedom, liberty, will be theirs in the end.

Denis Maher

cover size 296 x 215 mm

CONTENTS

92.	What Voices is all about	Ted Morrison
93.	The Escape	A.M. Horne
93.	Arrival in Bowness	A.M. Horne
94.	Tomorrow was Yesterday Back to Front.	A.M. Horne
94.	Perspective	A.M. Horne
94.	The 7.23 Omnibus	A.M.Horne
95.	A House in the Morning	T.M. Cullen
97.	Ssshh!	Rick Gwilt
98.	Huston, Texas	Rick Gwilt
99.	Note Passed in an Empty Lecture Hall	Rick Gwilt
100.	A Visit to Belle Vue	Ethel Hatton
101.	In December 1923	Ben Ainley
103.	The Day I Heard that Lenin was Dead	Ben Ainley
104.	Black man, White girl.	Sol Garson
108.	Electronics Factory	V.Leslie
111.	A Fable	Ted Morrison
113.	Plain Pain in '73	Frank Parker
114.	Onomatopoeia	F. Morgan
115.	Beasts of Britain	John Smith
118.	A Song of Piggy Banks	John Smith
119.	Cupid	F.G. Walker
122.	Holloway Prison	Julie Murphy
128.	Put to Proof	Angela Tuckett
128.	Joy and Pleasure	Angela Tuckett
128.	Song	Angela Tuckett
129.	A Serenade	Alf. Edwards
130.	Words	Betty Crawford
131.	Legend of Xanadu	Rick Gwilt
132.	Some of our Best Men Went to Spain	Sol Garson
133.	Laking - Yorkshire Holiday	J.I. Allsop
134.	Was it Yesterday?	J.I. Allsop
136.	Epitaph for a Bitch	Frances Moore
136.	Magnolia	Frances Moore
137.	Discrimination	Frances Moore
138.	Celluloid Tears	Colin Frame
139.	Rope and Birch	Jim Garnett
140.	Blaming the Woman	Jim Garnett
140.	A Good Woman	Jim Garnett
141.	Pipe Dream	J.E. Sutton
142.	The Gherkin	D. Hughes

143. The Picket   Ron Hughes
145. Rose and Life   Ron Hughes
147. Life is for Living   Dennis Maher
147. Sounds in the Night   John Brennan
148. On Coming on a Tramp   Frank Smith
150. Three Poems   Colin Frame

WHAT VOICES IS ALL ABOUT

This is the third 'Voices'. It continues to be a vehicle for working class expression. We want more writers. We want more readers. We want criticism and appreciation of this publication.

Voices exists because its publishers, 'Manchester Unity of Arts Society' , recognises that there is a need for magazines in which the literary potential of working people can develop and flourish, unhindered by traditions unrelated to their way of life, or by literary fads and fashions or commercial considerations.

This is in line with the general aim of 'Unity of Arts', which is to encourage interest in art, in all its forms, by organising exhibitions of workers' art, putting on plays either written by or about- working class people, sponsoring musical concerts and whatever other artistic activities our members or affiliated organisations call for at any particular time.

Eventually 'Unity of Arts' hopes to build up, with the assistance of working class organisations and other organisations in (sympathy with our aims, a cultural centre with an 'Arts Workshop', and other facilities for concerted artistic activities (Drama, Poetry, Literature, Painting, Drawing, Sculpture, Music), which will be at the service of working class organisations and the working class generally.

To achieve these aims the Society needs to be broadly based, with a powerfully affiliated membership throughout the Labour Movement. It is the Society's hope therefore, that Trade Unions, particularly, will want- to become affiliated and help us; and in this they could not do better than take a number of copies of 'Voices' to give or to sell to their members. It will cost 28p a copy (20p plus postage)

All enquiries to the Secretary, Mr. E. Morrison, 110 Edge Lane, Stretford. (061.865.5862)

THE ESCAPE

Through the blackberry vines cutting grasp
Erect coarse grass stinging our legs
We ran falling, laughing, jumping, rolling,
Away from the people with tut tutting-faces.
Soft grains cushioning our falls.

As feet were forced from sand-filled shoes
We lay on the highest sand dune
Looking over a bay of flat imitation waves.

Watching the sea creep back
Minutely examining its age-old path.
The sun set creating rivulets of orange quick silver.

We turned for home, the cold fastening coat buttons.
With the soft crushing of shells the only sound
I thought of boiled eggs with brown bread and butter.

ARRIVAL IN BOWNESS

The lake was a grey slate slab slippery with rain,
Hills stood cloth-capped in mist the damp falling stickily,
The steamer shivered rasping against the coarse roped jetty,
Its milk white paint work smudged with black plastic macs,
Cameras ready looking for magic they followed the main road to
the shops.
Scraping moss green marble in search of a poet,
Buying a postcard of a sunny day,
They return with wet knees and foggy lenses,
Warming their bums on the hot steam pipes,
While the lake turned into a biscuit tin bottom shining deep and
dull,
And the boat moved slowly away wrinkling its image with a turn
of its screw.

TOMORROW WAS YESTERDAY BACK TO FRONT

My mind is full of people breaking down its doors,
Shouting, grasping, taunting, wanting to be heard,
Faces, full of faces not one to recognise,
Each -expressing nothing but demanding more than life,
Twisted, crippled, they loom before my eyes,
Crashing, lurching, rupture tender fibre,
Teeth dig into bleeding lips, nails indent my palms,
As pigeons peck, peck and peck incessant,
Crushing their beaks on stark tarmacadam.
Tears roll quickly down my cheeks and the terror subsides.

PERSPECTIVE

Trudging slowly to the summit,
My shoes echoing only silence,
The night softly surrounded me,
As start escaped from the cooling tower,
Enormous trivialities slid away,
Standing alone in true dimension,
Gazing at pin holes in a well worn blind,
I smelled truth and was refreshed.

THE 7.23 OMNIBUS

Puffing, panting, boots splashing in murky mirrors,
Heart pounding, speed astounding, for a dreary morning.,
Grasping, leaping, mind still sleeping, (board the sad-eyed bus.
Coughing, smoking, lungs are choking surrounded by sandstone
faces,
Laughing, smiling, fares a-piling came the large conductress,
Softly speaking, of perfume reeking, changed gargoyles into
people.

A.M. Horne.

94

A HOUSE IN THE MORNING

The three little girls were playing outside the old house in their terraced street.

"Salt...mustard...vinegar...pepper..."

"Mind out of the way Julie!'" The little girl stopped turning her end of the rope, which hung in mid-swing, catching the skipper behind the ear, and she turned to see the old lady standing behind her.

"Sorry, Mrs. Milton..." as she moved aside to let the old lady pass; but Mrs. Milton made no reply. She walked slowly, with her head bent slightly forward, past the children and into the gate of the old house set amid brightly painted other houses. The dark stained brown door opened and swallowed the old lady up. The girls resumed their game.

"Salt...mustard...vinegar...pepper"

"I am - going to - my Aunty – Joan's - today - she has - got a -new - baby", Karen recited in slow, chanting, rhythm, as she skipped.

The postman edged by and grinned as he passed.

"Have you got anything for us? Number seven?"

Annie dropped her end of the rope and ran after him, leaving the rope to finish its swing in a whiplash which wound around Karen's ankles as she stopped skipping.

Annie collected her letters and ran on to her own house, while the other two picked up the rope and began skipping together.

"Salt...mustard...vinegar...pepper,..salt...mustard..."

"Here, you kids! Out of the way". The man stepped from his van, collected the carry-crate from the back, and pushed past the girls. "Why can't you play somewhere else?" he grumbled and entered the gate to the first house.

Annie came back, and, ignoring the milkman, they began again. "Salt...mustard...vinegar..."

"I don't know why they can't paint this 'ouse. Its a bloody disgrace. 'Orrible old brown; can't see why they can't do it a nice blue, or green, even that orange; or even that purple over there; even that's much better. Bloody disgrace!" The milkman climbed back in the float and jangled off, down the road.

"Julie!" A voice rose from three doors down and the little girl stopped skipping, and the rope fell against her ankles.

95

"Oh! I've got to go - me and me mum are going to town to get some shoes"; and with that she left, dragging the rope behind her.

"Hey Julie! Lend us the rope please " . She stopped for a second, and then threw it, calling "O.K. Let me have it back later". The rope fell behind Karen, who turned to pick it up and found herself staring at a well polished pair of shoes, above which towered a priest .

"Do be careful children. That kind of thing can cause accidents". He half-smiled and walked on, entering the gate of the brown painted house with the dark windows. He knocked, and after a while the door opened, and he was gone. "Salt...mustard...vinegar...pepper...salt...mustard.."

"Oh! I'm fed up with this" Annie grumbled. "Let's play hopscotch". Karen thought for a moment, and then dashed off saying "Alright - I'll get the chalk and a stone!" Annie picked up the other end of the rope and skipped alone.

"Salt...mustard...vinegar...pepper...salt...mustard..."

Shortly Karen returned and marked the lines on the pavement.

" 'ere! What you drawrin' in front of our 'ouse for?" Eric had just come back from the baths; his hair was damp and uncombed. The girls invited him to play for a while and he said O.,. As they began, a big black car with darkened windows drew up outside the brown painted house with the dark windows and the half closed curtains. Three men got out and one went to the door and knocked. The other two followed him as the door opened, and they all were gone.

Annie's mother appeared, as if from nowhere, and took her away, saying as he left, "You two had better go home too".

The door outside which they were playing opened and a voice ordered Eric inside. A moment later the door re-opened and a hand reached down to pick up the wet, rolled-up towel from the step, and the same voice announced, "You had better go home now Karen".

As she turned to go, the street seemed suddenly empty and quiet. There was only the car, no other people anywhere to be seen. Mystified, she began to walk towards her own home, past the brown painted house with the dark windows and the half drawn curtains; and as she did so the door opened and the three men were slowly spilled out, carrying between them the long box coffin with the shiny handles. The driver got out, opened the door at the back, and the long box was inserted.. The four men then climbed back into the car and drove slowly off into the just beginning light rain, as the door of the house opened again and the minister appeared. He pulled the door gently shut and left in the direction he had first come, his back catching the lightly driven rain.

Annie stood, watching the car drive slowly down the street, as the quiet sounds of the engine diminished and blended with the returning sounds of distant traffic and the sounds of people; and the world returned to the street where the little girl stood outside the brown painted house with the dark windows and the half closed curtains framing the new shed rain tears.

And the little girl began to skip, slowly away from the scene, into the sounds.

"Salt...mustard...vinegar...pepper..."

T.M. Cullen.

SSSHH!

Tomorrow morning
While the sky still hangs in darkness
And the air is a bromide dissolved in the night
I shall go off to work down the tea-mines of
A nameless land.

Down the tea-mines
In the fearsome ranks of the goblin army
I play the renegade to learn
The secrets of their arcane world
And steal their gold.

Down the tea-mines
Open cast against the sunrise
That lights the dust in eastern shafts
A ghost of dawn with crimson fingers
Insinuates.

Down the tea-mines
Where raindrop never dares to seep
No mid-day sunbeam makes so bold
To break the gloom of powdered chambers
In the house of...

Down the tea-mines
One cannot be too careful, nor
Too reticent about one's purpose
Nor breathe one's thoughts where Echo is a

Goblin girl.

Down the tea-mines
Where the air is drier than any desert
Where sound is duller than any silence
Dark machines are slowly grinding
Neath a hill called....

Down the tea-mines
One cannot be too sure; the soul
must take discretion for a guard
Assume the nature of the crypt
Emtombing her.

Tomorrow morning
When the time has stopped in emptiness
Like a train that cannot start without
A passenger, I shall go off to work
Down the tea-mines.

Rick Gwilt.

HOUSTON, TEXAS

Sometimes in this symmetrical city
There are heart transplants
And when is the body really dead?
It is when...no, listen while I tell you,
It is when a yellow light goes out
In some distant window.
Yes, where appearances are everything
Invisibility is the end.

Look, quickly, over there!
No already faded, a flashing neon sign.
Somewhere there will be sadness,
A sense of loss,
Deep within someone's wallet.

Sometimes you will see me bathing in the darkness.
I am a hermit crab,
I wear my loneliness like a shell.
It is not mine.

I was born to wear a coat of laughter
In kaleidoscopic colours.
Above my mind there flies a scarlet banner,
For I know who has stolen my birthright.

Sometimes, if you look closely,
You will see the sadness behind my eyes
As I ask, lady
Take this poison from me.
And afterwards
If you see the sadness linger on,
Do not feel defeated.
It was the wrong battle, anyway.

Sometimes, as the night grows cold,
You may see me sitting in the wind
Singing softly and out of tune
As the rain drapes itself around me
In melancholy folds.
Do not disturb me,
For I have found my own harmony
With the storm.

Rick Gwilt.

NOTE PASSED IN AN EMPTY LECTURE HALL

So you deny being a brown-noser
When your face is browner than a hundred generations
of coconut oil? well never mind

I like the whiteness of your smile bobbing up to meet me
after a day of swimming through seas of faceless faces
each evening we lie prostrate and breathless on another beach
like waifs cast up together in the desperate freshness
of empty conch and limpet shells
with starfish friends and salty kisses
maybe one day the dream will come true and they will
understand
we are not looking for things to put in our skillet
no, we are looking for another way
we shall come together with the crabs and anemones
to look for another way
like travellers to the wizard of oz

we shall carry them across mountains and desert
we shall bear them safely through the cities
in answer to traitors we shall betray even better and more
nobly

at times we shall be others
we shall be who we please
we shall be invisible
we shall find another way

Rick Gwilt

A VISIT TO BELLE VUE

My childhood was spent in a large family during the pre-war depression.

I only remember one holiday at the seaside and outings of any kind were few and far between.

In those days the local Co-op used to offer cheap tickets to Belle Vue and I remember one of these festive occasions very well.

We all piled on to one of the rickety old trains whose route lay between Hyde and Manchester and which stopped directly outside Belle Vue. This ride was an adventure in itself because we kids would wait with bated breath to see if the trolley would come off the wires when it reached the sharp bend at Reddish Bridge. The conductor used to reach a long hooked pole out from underneath the tram and would spend some time manoeuvring about with it until the trolley was back in place.

Belle Vue was a very different place in those days than the present complex. There was more emphasis on animal houses than the open air enclosures of today.

The lion house was nearest to the entrance and I mainly remember the combined stench of animal urine and Lysol, so overpowering that one would stagger out at the other end literally gasping for breath. I don't know what the King of Beasts thought about his abode, but I remember that on one occasion he lifted up his hind leg and expressed his feelings all over a visitor's shirt front.

The monkey and elephant houses were also popular and pungent places and a very big elephant used to walk about in the grounds giving rides to children. The only place I didn't like was the reptile house because I once saw a snake having a dead rat for its dinner and the sight sickened me.

I seem to remember that there was much more entertainment included in the price of admission, with band concerts and open air dancing. on the wooden floor in front of the boating lake, and although the Bobs and Scenic Railway were running then there seemed to be fewer traps for unwary parents in the form of expensive sweetstuffs and amusements.

A free cup of tea and a bun were also included in the Co-op ticket for which we sat at long wooden tables on forms, and although the tea was served in very thick blue end white cups it tasted a lot better than the plastic cupped beverage of today

The highlight of the day was the evening firework display. As dusk gathered a huge crowd would gather in front of the boating pool and the sky would light up with multi-coloured flashes. On the stage behind the boating lake a glittering spectacle representing a Chinese carnival was presented. The climax was reached when a huge dragon wended its way across the stage. I was so enchanted with the scene that it did not occur to me that men were underneath the dragon to give it mobility. I probably thought that one large inmate of the reptile house had been impressed into service for the occasion.

I wonder if today's over-exploited children get as much real pleasure as I did out of a visit to Belle Vue. And I wonder if the shoppers in today's blue and white emporiums are as conscious as my parents were about the value of the Co-operative Movement to the working class. Somehow I think not.

Ethel Hatton.

IN DECEMBER 1923

> I face the nightsky thoughtfully, I young
> Urgent and anxious, hotfoot, gladly living,
> With earnest scrutiny those stars among,
> To one that red and fitful glow is giving.
> It moves me as I stand here and reflect
> Upon the days and years that make my life
> Spent in a tumult thus where class and sect
> And each and all of us are joined in strife.
> That red star glittering quietly seen afar,
> A globe of light swinging through shadowy blue:
> Why does life move so slowly on a star?
> What life stirs there, breaking out ever new?
> We on this earth are harried day by day.

The tasks of every minute and the fears,
They drive our dull and kindly dreams away;
Each day has tumults that spread on through years.
We face the next few generations' heat
With stressful and determined minds, we face
Toil, pain, despair, joy, victory and defeat,
The birthtime of the young world's lusty race.
A million men in Europe, quick in thought,
And passionate in deed, young, earnest, tense,
Look upon life as chanceful, a strange sport,
Zestful with unknown stakes, hazards immense.
Days of transition, while the whole world waits,
Thousands and thousands suffer, die. We stand,
Uncertain in the breaking down of states,
Whether we too will see the promised land...
Under the canopy of night, when light,
Goes, and the world is quiet, and we commune
Each with the stars as I upon this night,
Thoughts sing themselves in a half-mystic tune,
Much lightness and much love we have given up,
Not ours unhappy to sit with dear girls playing,
Through long adventurous nights. We take our sup
at hasty pleasure, working to bring the day in.
Much we have given up because we love.
Because we love we have seemed to make love lass holy.
We have not dallied, dallied with velvet glove,
Fanned, jewelled girls; nor sighed, been melancholy,
We have faced life, flinched not: looked it in the eyes:
Trembled, been weak, yet stuck out hardily.
Weary, blind, stricken at the edge of enterprise,
We have dared to be bold to make our children free.
Knowing what works in the minds of the sleepless gods,
We have been titans working, and we rest,
Conscious of bitter tumult, heavy odds,
Making the fabric of our lives attest
Our will to win: and Europe shall remain
After our sleepless nights, days of campaign,
Free, classless, a continent of enfranchised,
And confident young demigods; our task
Ended, we shall pass on. And the surmised,
Hoped and awaited children will not ask
How we brought gladness to the young continent,
Their joy will rush from them in flooding song
These things are dreamed; they are not evident,

We wait them. Struggle, hope, bear us along...
Star in the night, I, human, weak, yet brave,
Out of my tumult and the war I wage,
Look to your red and changeful glow, a grave
Luminous silence on the starry stage.
Out of young urge and passionate I seek
Ever unsatisfied, laughter and youth,
Song, kisses, gladness, warmth of eye and cheek,
These things laid wistfully by in our stern truth,
Our purpose, our task. I look on you red star,
Lifted; cold, luminous, passionate as you are.

Ben Ainley.

THE DAY I HEARD THAT LENIN WAS DEAD

The day I heard that Lenin was dead
Was a gently adventurous day to me;
I had studied Russian for two splendid hours,
I had written a letter to a kindly friend,
I had spoken across six miles of wires
To a dear little selfish girl-friend making
Rendezvous for an idle weekend.
At sunset I left the library,
And in the damp glitter of Piccadilly
With lamps above, and puddles reflecting them,
Surrounded by sights and sounds, familiar, friendly,
The clatter and grind of trains, the speed of motors,
The hurry of people, skysigns, the darkling skies,
I saw a poster flamboyant with "Lenin is dead",
And my heart was leaden and my brain was angry.
And "No" I said "it is another of their flaming lies.
Our comrade will live to read the hundredth time his
own obituary in their bestial press .
But my fears belied me, and I was afraid,
I forgot my manhood, and when I saw my comrades,
They spoke that evening with hushed and gentler voices,
Because our comrade Lenin, our leader, was dead.

Ben Ainley.

BLACK MAN, WHITE GIRL

The big man was black. He had a broad nose and a full sensuous mouth. Deep purples and reds showed as the sun shone on the skin of his forehead and cheeks. Straight back and as heavy as Paul Robeson, he looked as strong as. Mohamed Ali and stood somewhere in between them in age at 55. He had drawn strength from both these men, from Du Bois and Baldwin, Marx and Maupassant, Shaw, Shakespeare, but he had always been quick to read of the people of his own race.

A small. white and pink girl in a bright yellow coat walked alongside with her hand inside his elbow. His spare hand covered it. Her black curly hair was covered by a tied head-scarf. She had a thin painted black line following. the edge of her small eyelids, but the rest of her face was untouched by false colour.

Gently, as they walked and talked his big hand would pat,. stroke, caress hers, They looked very happy. Many of the shops they passed were shut, closed, for this was Alexandra Road, Moss Side. The year was 1973. Behind the blind and dirty empty shops and the few remaining still open, worked the demolition men. Tall iron arms swinging half ton metal balls in shaky, rotten houses. Purpose-lit fires licked and. ate all the timber that had not been taken away to be sold and teams of heavy tractors and J.C.Bs pushed, flattened, scattered and lifted the rubble on to tip wagons that raced off when the last shovelful had put the tip .on the little mountain.

The tall man with this small young woman on his arm stopped at the last chemist shop to remain open and looked in the window. She pointed, he smiled, and they both walked in. Two-minutes and twenty pence later, they came out. Holding a neat little parcel in her spare hand "Joe" she said, "let's do the streets like we used". Joe, named Joseph by his Bible-bred and believing dad, nodded. "We shall if you want, baby, and there's not much left. A month ago I was not too happy about going. Now I can't get out of the place too quick. All the fellas have gone, The place is sad baby, sad. We will start at No. 1 Portman Street, where you was born, right? Then we'll do the whole hog. Bishop, Hulton, Bland, Meadow, Stockton, Sowerby, right through to Platt." They stood together at the corner of Great Western and Alec. waiting for the lights to change.

> The soldier ants stir,
> The scouts sent out.
> The thirst for blood is about.

Two white pimply youths with matted hair, pushed past with purpose and aimed a blow, knocking the parcel to the ground. A small smash glass sound. The pavement darkens with oozing, clear liquid. The air becomes thick, sweet. The girl, damn it, dear reader, I can keep the, secret no longer. the girl is Joe's daughter. Now because you have read thus far, I feel I owe you the truth. There must be a bond between us.. But only you and I know. The two boys didn't know.

Joe's daughter is called. Kathy and she looked down sad. Joe looked at Kath. Could not allow himself to look down at the spillage. Then he put himself between her and the wet, cupped her face in his white-faced palms and looked into her eyes. Both his thumbs wiped her eyes. His blood beat hard in his chest, his arms, through the heavy veins on the back of his hands. And through his hands to her, and from her, back to him. They stood there sharing a common fear, anger, hatred of the wanton, wilful destruction of a bottle of scent, a present, a gift.

Eventually Joe made to return to the shop, but was held by Kathy, more firmly this time and they crossed the road towards Portman Street. Soon they were smiling and talking of the gay days long ago when Joe, with his delivery bike, would pedal up and down the streets selling the "Daily Worker", Kath and her young brother securely tied in the basket with woollen scarves. Oh, the excitement, the laughter and all the stares. That made the people look. Joe enjoyed his laughter when he recounted - big black man on a bike, with two kids in a basket. One white little girl and one black little boy. One black little boy that died too soon one Sunday morning. Twelve, and sent for the papers across Princess Road. Joe had bitten his hand hard many times since. What happened, mad bastard driver, or not so careful lad? Too late, too bad, the agony of recall brought tears to Kath and Joe and they walked straight faced for the next few minutes.

> The soldier ants scouts return
> And report to Lustful Queen
> There's fresh meat to burn.

"Oh yes" said the fat woman to her pimply sons "I'll soon stop the black bastard's capers. Young white girl eh?" and without taking off her dirty pinnie, she rushed out of the house and ran towards Portman Street. Now out in the fresh sunshine air she would have noticed that she had left the smell of the house behind, only she carried the smell with her person. It was not difficult to recognise at a distance the linking Kath and Joe. Panting and just out of earshot the fat woman shouted "Leave her alone you black bastard", but it was lost on the air. A ragged dog sniffed and lapped dirty water amongst the rubble. In spite of her slipping., sloppy slippers, she made up some distance and again she hurled her wordy missile. Man and daughter stopped and turned. More ill-chosen invective flowed from the fat woman. Life had hardened Joe. Most people who knew Joe loved him. A quiet man and kind, a good man, but not now. This kind of talk he had heard before, knew why it came and would not get used to it. "Piss off, you fat cow" he shouted, because the fat cow had stopped, many yards off when Joe had turned. He had a fierce face on. The clarity of the loud message struck home. Crushed her aggression.

"Piss off or I'll kick your big fat arse, you filthy cow!" he said and it looked like he meant to do it. The filthy cow did feel like pissing. Did not expect such a clear, precise and threatening reply. Swore, and to herself swore that she would yet have this big black bastard. On her way back she knocked on many doors. "Have you heard? Did you know? Guess what happened to me." Her story grew from door to door. By the time that she had reached her hovel it had grown into a direct and unprovoked physical attack on her person.

> Fat with her rivals blood,
> The vile Queen ant
> Reeks with evil intent
> Pushed and pushes unthinking minions
> Rushes to food.

The fat lady felt much bolder now. She had surrounded herself with some eleven men, women and children and one half-man, pushed along in a cane chair with wheels. It was not the perambulation over cracked flags, but a natural, unnatural motion that made his head shake from side to side. His lips tightened and the lower, pressed hard, would slide upwards and touch his nose. His head would fall back to make many creases in his thin, flab neck. All the while his eyebrows would rise and fall, surprise and worry, surprise, worry. This, God's creature, would make many an atheist yet. "Can't you push Fred faster Alice?" panted the fat lady, pointing, shouting- and urging more speed.

More difficult to find now, Joe and Kath were standing till at the corner of Raby and Talbot; looking at the gaping mouth of Moss Side. The rotten stub's were being pulled out and smashed. The noise' and dust offended little. What wrenched was the disappearance of the brick clothing of part of their history. Sadness and sorrow filled the linked pair. With a deep breath and a big stretch of Joe's fertile imagination he could see the beauty that once was Moss Side. Near on a hundred years ago, he thought. New, clean tidy rows of beautiful houses. Each with its little garden in front; well - most. Alright, so some were bigger than others and had a big garden at the back instead of a small yard. And a room at the top, for a servant, but all had a cellar to store coal and keep food cool - Joe's historic eye focussed on the occupiers. These houses were for the managers. Those for the fore-men, and these for the labourers. Broad shoulders, long strong arms, it was the big labourer that got the smallest house. Studying these houses had in the past been part of Joe's political education. The owner bosses used to live in the grand houses with a drive - in Whalley Range. Then they moved to Didsbury. Then they diffused to Bramhall and Mere, Hale Barns and Prestbury, and further afield to fresh and greener pastures, well away from the working mass; but in Moss Side still, the workers lived and in 1973 they move to Hulme. New Hulme, next door. "God damn Hulme" Joe said aloud. Kath looked up and smiled her own little smile. Only one side of her mouth would lift. Joe knew this would disappear in time, as her self-confidence grew. "Most of the time, she's away at College in Ripon. Get a good education she will, and she doesn't know wrong with Hulme". "I'll tell you love" Joe said, in answer to her smile. "For one thing, they didn't clear the sites of old Hulme properly, and the rats and mice got in the new concrete cavity walls and they are still there. Talk to the tenants. The council won't clear 'em, and they won't clear the streets and the rents are mad high, and they are going up and..." Kath pulled heavily on Joe's arm. When Joe was fluent and in full flow his voice would rise, and his hands would squeeze hard on anything in them. Now he realised he had been pressing Kath's ring-finger - "Sorry love".

"No, it's not that dad, its my knee". Joe looked down; a trickle of blood (was slowly moving down her leg. "Something hit me". Joe heard the din of the little raucous mob, Just a second before he got them in his eye. He saw the fat woman with her mouth wide open, in the middle. He heard everything and saw everything but his eyes kept looking on her face. The wheel chair, the pimply ones, the dog, the wet lower lip touching the nose, dirty pinny, eyebrows up -down, surprise, worry, wagging tail, shouts "Black bastard -black bastard - go home black bastard.."

"Where's Kathy?" - take her hand, she must be frightened. "Kath". Kath was bent low over her knew and he put his hand on her yellow coat back. "Take your-dirty black hand off our white girl" slurred the man in front. Broken braces and collarless shirt, his beer-foul breath made Joe take a step back. Emboldened by what he took to be Joe's fear, he lurched another short step forward. Then Joe saw that the drunk had a bread knife at shoulder height. "Give me that knife, you pig' yelled Joe, and the drunk fell backwards. Heeled heavily. on fat woman's foot. She pushed hard with all her wild hurt strength. The drunk fell forward on to Joe with both his hands out. One had a knife in it.

Paradoxically, everything with Joe was how it should be, and not how it was. He could not feel the hard stone flag bed, nor Kathy's soft hand on his head. Was not aware of the mingling of tears and perspiration. Her first proper tears - his last long sweat. He had left school at barely fourteen. Never heard of relativity physics, but was now unconsciously shattering his basic concept of time and space. Yesterday, today and tomorrow, were neatly interwoven. He could see clearly (the day before he was born. His daddy sweating, begging the doctor to come. "Please, oh please sir, come and see my wife". "Have you any money?" "No? - well then, go away and don't bother me; come on Harry, it's your deal". Joe's mother did not feel the pain of lying on her hard board bed - pushed on a hand cart to the Royal Infirmary. But 'Joe, little wet smooth Joe inside water filled bag belly, felt the pain. "Turn Joe, avoid the pain". "Daddy, dad, help will be here soon" said Kathy, as her dad turned, but did not hear "Daddy"; could feel the pain of his mother's pregnancy. Joe could feel the ants crawling over his body. Their knife sharp cutting edges, tearing his meat. He could see them carrying away their little loads, held high.. "See these pieces of Joe, come on, hurry, get some more, more". The soldier ants are relentless, but Joe is strong - his powerful arms begin to flay, and with each mighty blow he crushes ten, a hundred, a thousand, and more and more.

With all his strength gone, he lies back in-the cool water to rest. To float and rest, happy that he has crushed every ant, all over the world.- Happy, happy, and the dream ends.

The little white girl in the red and yellow coat stands up.

Sol Garson.

ELECTRONICS FACTORY

(scene 3)

The Factory Foreman strikes efficiency
into the hearts of all of us
Omnipotent in dark suit with Biros
he patrols the factory floor, finger on the vital pulses
of a smooth productive process.
Went to night school for ONCs
to construct a springboard of knowledge
from which he leapt to his present heights
Too important to smile at
Too clever to argue with
He is the Factory Foreman, if he has a name
its smaller than the title
that is always thought of in capitals.
He is in his place, we are in ours
and if there's a connection between them
it's dwarfed by the dimensions of the gap.

Incredible that he should arrive as he did.
when we six were working late - rush job.

He enquires - are we warm enough
and suddenly, he becomes Gordon,
married with three kids and a dog named Pudge,
member of the Badminton Club,
having trouble with his carburettor,
He sat with us in his Fair-isle sweater
and graded washers for the job.
He fetched cups of juice from the machine
and took a proffered cigarette.
He laughed at the jokes - even told one
all the time grading washers inexpertly.
Come eight o'clock, he offered lifts
a mile out of his way, and he sang
with the radio as we rode home with him.

Incredible that next day, he became
The Factory Foreman again
Without the Fair-isle sweater he was again
his title - the great man - The Boss
Lord over us five hundred women,
and if he remembered the previous night
the memory was shut behind his professional face
and the dark suit with Biros

(scene 4)

Time is money - ask the T & M man
The reason why they don't explain
the why of the operations to girls
of supple minds, -
is that it would take time
And that is the reason why
a girl may scan her operation
with its fifteen wires
families of components
solder joints and panel scans,
with little interest
in what should go where

Time is money - ask the T & M man
The reason why training is minimal
is that it takes time
And that is the reason why
for every fresh operator on the line

there is a fed-up repair girl
doing the job over again.

Time is money - ask the T & M man
The reason why we work too fast
and make our inevitable blunders
is that to do it properly would take time.
It is also the reason why each week
there's overtime for all
repairing, re-wiring, re-making
the results of all the haste.

Time is money - ask the T. & M man
Ask him the reason for his work
and he will tell you;
To save time and money
no matter what the cost
because, Time is money.

(scene 5)

They are unusually honest at work
They wear no make-up, no fashions
Their language is unfiltered
by social consciousness
The jokes are obscene and
the laughter full blooded
Their legs are comfortably open
as they sprawl naturally
And the girls with freckles
or spots are not hiding them.

If the young executive arrives
nothing changes.
They are well versed in the knowledge
that his soul is sold for the next eight hours.
He is dead from the neck downwards
He is deep in thought, considering the possibilities of
a three-handed operator.
And though he moves in a sea of limbs
he does not stir physically.
Rather, he is responding to the joys
of a mathematical calculation in his head.
He has solved the problem of a left-handed operator.

The barrow-boy appreciates the sights,
He leers and whistles at the girls
Cracking a suggestive joke and grinning.
Still nothing changes.
They are immune from rejection.
Their value here is theft efficiency.
They have adapted to the requirements
and in that respect,
each one of them is desirable.

The situation is therapeutic
to the unlovely.
Where else might they find
themselves wanted, even coveted
 than in this communal love affair.
No chance of being usurped in a place
where agility is the prime asset
And the ideal of being wanted wholly
is too far gone down the trail
of disappointments in love
of exercise more than a tug.
They embrace the substitute warmly
and their fingers fly ever faster.

Vivien Leslie

A FABLE

He was an old man and his dream was old, born when through the eyes of a young man the world shone with the promise of a wonderful future, an ideal future. Now he was no longer young and no shining future lay ahead of him, yet he could not relinquish his youth-born dream. He would speak with a fire that long ago should have left his heart of a better world, of the future that was the heritage of his people, the future that he and his generation had fought for with their minds, with their collective strength, with their blood.

For as long as he could remember he could remember he had lived with the vision, vividly recalled when he was alone in the quiet places, that he sought when the need to think weighed upon him, of that future time when every man and woman would be blessed with the dignity of freedom. Not just freedom from oppression, though that was part of the dream, but freedom from ignorance, from the chains that bind the unthinking, whether their ignorance is due to lack of opportunity to learn or some inadequacy in their intelligence. For those who had not had the opportunity to learn, to know the truths that come only to the thinking mind, he burned with sympathy and strove with all his skill as a teacher of men to make them see. To those who no teaching that he or his fellow teachers could devise could free from the appalling burden of ignorance, his pity ran deeper than tears; for tears help only the weeper. Nor was he ostentatiously kind, as some men are with the weak-minded, but he never failed to treat them as equals, bearing their foolish talk and their shallow behaviour with that stoic patience which is common to men who have glimpsed Truth but not the face of God in truth He could not believe in God. Indeed part of his dignity stemmed from his atheism. For if there is no God there is no One to Whom the blame can be attached for the existence of those who can never learn to see the Truth. Thus he was never given to bitterness.

Being without knowledge of God he could not properly be called a saint yet by sheer force of goodness and benignity, he had attracted a group of acolytes around him who shared his dream, quoted his speeches and drew from the well of his inspiration. Among these he had a favourite, although he would not have admitted oven to himself that this was so. Nevertheless, being a very human old man, he was touched by the devotion of one of his followers and took to referring to him as "my friend"

He knew also that this man above all who looked to him for guidance, had the greatest need of his sympathy and help. For this man, he knew had feelings as fierce as his own for his follow men. yet, because he carried the pain and suffering which was woven through his life, compressed tightly inside himself he could not express this feeling in a way that might help both himself and his fellows. Whenever he tried to speak about something which he felt deeply, his inner pain rose up and defeated his intention, so that his words seemed to deny themselves by the violence with which they were delivered. And so nobody believed that he was a man of compassion, though they pretended to be so to his face.

All this the old man knew, though he never communicated his knowledge to anyone. Often when they were gathered together in debate this deep-rooted pain would pour out a torrent of heated words, jeopardising not only his own argument, but, by its disturbing influence, the effect of the old man's teaching. .At such times, the teacher of men would wait until there came a pause in his friend's turbulent outpouring, then, quickly, often with sorrow in his voice, ask a question that seemed relevant to the speaker's argument. As soon as he received an answer the old man would put another question, then another, all seemingly relevant questions, yet each one taking the perturbed man further from the source of his agitation until he had recollected himself. After these outbursts he would lapse into brooding silence, as if reflecting on the conflict within himself. Sometimes he would catch the teacher's glance and embarrassment would pass fleetingly across his face, as if he believed that he had earned his master's displeasure. But the old man never by even a stern glance, confirmed that this was so.

The old man died. His dream of universal light lived on in the minds of his followers, but it was still only a dream. His friend sat by his master's deathbed and couldn't control his emotions; tears ran freely down his cheeks as he remembered how they had shared a noble dream. For two evening hours he sat and looked and remembered. Then the tears abated and he felt a calmness melt through his body, clearing his mind and lifting his sorrow. He thought he heard the old man's voice quietly repeating the words that he had spoken to his friend only a few days before his death: "Tears help only him that sheds them, yet it is sometimes right to shed them; we all need to rid ourselves of troublesome emotion in this way, sometimes. Likewise the pain of living should be shed - but not by tears". "In what way, then?" he had asked, "Can we rid ourselves of such pain?". After a long silence the old man spoke: "Never fight your grief; to do so will merely increase it. Think of it this way - the more pain and grief we experience, the more joy we are capable of experiencing. We must learn to look at both sides of our experience

The old man's advice had not made much sense to him. Now as he sat in the profound stillness of death, understanding touched the edges of his mind and he became aware of a new sense of peace growing within him, pressing out the pain of his past life. Vision arose in him too, and he glimpsed a world in which his master's dream was fulfilled, and he knew that at last compassion would live without conflict, within him.

Ted Morrison

PLAIN PAIN IN '73

If could put on paper
what is in my heart
it would burn
or turn into a shroud
to wrap my shrivelled soul.
I die,
in the quagmire of my mind,
the hot mud,
the lava flow of thought
burns me up,

113

I disappear in flames,
slowly.
Yet; if my body was a perfect mirror of my mind
the agony of Christus could be seen,
the caricatured misery of a medieval hell;
the torment of tortured souls.
pain enough to fill a universe with groans,
and madness incipient, makes the very air surrounding moan.
And never, can I think, has suffering been so deep and long.
A man could endure, and should, for an exalted cause,
for humanity, or for his God;
but me?
Small man: Gigantic pain.
I love, but she loves not me.

Frank Parker

ONOMATOPOEIA

A few days after the first big Manchester blitz found us settling down in this little 140 year old dilapidated hovel about 8 miles south of Manchester lacking gas and electricity, but luckily equipped with flush lavatory and mains water.

We felt safer and our baby could be put to bed at nights whereas previously most nights were spent in the air-raid shelter.

It did not take long before eager gossipy neighbours put me in the picture as to the "goings on" in the Dale.

Many of the men folk in the Dale were away in the services, but Mrs. A. had run away with Mr. B. and left her child with its putative father - but that's another story.

I was flanked by Mrs. Y. and Mrs. Z. Mrs. Z's mother-in-law soon let me know that her son had married beneath him only because "he had to". Personally I thought he had done better than he deserved, because young as she was, his wife managed very well on his very low earnings. At that point there were two children and shortly after he was called up to the Army.

Mrs. Y. had two children and her husband was already in the Army. Both women were determined to fill the role of both father and mother to their children, and these kids could do no wrong.

Whenever the kids had a row the mothers would join in, and at the end of every bout of abuse, Mrs. Y. would have the last word with "You bloody fornicating bugger - you're nowt else".

And so the war years passed, seeming to alternate between the fluctuating gains and losses on the military front, and the squabbles and makings-up on the domestic front.

Makings-up between the neighbours seemed to follow some little relaxation of tensions. The word would go around that the Co-op had had a delivery of biscuits or oranges or suet, and on one occasion the word came that white bristled scrubbing brushes were to be had. That was good news in those days, before washing machines were common place, and everything had to be scrubbed.

Shortly before the end of the war, an agitated Mrs. Y. came to speak to me. "Eh!" she said "Do you know what fornicating is"? "Yes, of course" I said. "Well" she said just found out what it means. You know when I call Mrs. Z. a bloody fornicating bugger - I didn't mean that at all". She hadn't wanted to give me the wrong impression. She hesitated a split second, then with a smile and a wink she said "but it sounds right".

F Morgan

BEASTS OF BRITAIN

A Heathen's in heaven
All hells here on earth.
But green lights glow
Down the line in the gloom,
and twinkle their greetings,
On back to back meetings
Where scarecrows and beggars
Cough blood by the embers
And count up the members
Of fish and chip families,
Bottles of ale,
And spit out their scorn
For express, sun and mail.
While the telegraph's rest isn't
Pestered by pictures of
Festering sores and dirty diseases
From soot-soggy sneezes
Down dark dirty murky dark mines.

115

Do the Downing Street dodos not know
That the mine is a mine
Of unmined minds, and a pit
Of wits decaying?
Yet wave a wand and
Whisk those wits to the
Waltzing chintz and whiskey stints
Of country mansions, chandeliers,
Of E-type tooting cavaliers,
And unearned tears of wives of peers
And sterling fears of racketeers -
Then light would fight those
Bones of stones and coal-dust mingled minds;
Those slag-heap humans, mighty moles.
Would see the cage of light
Descended shafts of countless
Slinking, shivering, Sweat-soaked,
Quivering, Scuffling, shuffling,
Shuddering, shovelling shifts.

And they'd drop their picks
And lift the sticks of blood-red banners,
March in mass through Fleet street fog
Down mansion mews where bloated bellies
Bulge and simper, cringe and fawn
And with a whimper give them newsprint- Papers mooing,
Proving greed is man's undoing.

And they'd kiss those vile and
Violent villains -Twisting, tweedy, ball-point villains,
Oxbridge, ogres, city rogues,
Harrowing parasites, poor eaten appetites
Gobbling gold and gourmet pheasant,
Trampling servants and spitting on
Peasants who don't answer back - why?
They're scared of the sack,
Which is waiting for those few
Debating the weighting of wealth
On the social scales.

Now first-class cigar smoke
Is sneaking from pink champagne
Reeking from financial times,

Compartmented city to city;
And rising mists mingle in magical swathes,
Revealing the stealing, the hate
And the reeling of junkies
And vice squads; the pawn shops
And porn shops where
Shameless debauchery revels and gambols
While prostitutes shamble
Down Wardour Street weeping
For what might have been.

Do they weep for their young ones?
Unsanctified young ones?
Those giggling, gurgling,
Dimple-faced, dumpling faced
Lullaby babies are doomed
From the first to the landlord
Town tenements - cash-raking
Muck-raking, rat-ridden,
Horn-honking houses
Where flick-knives flash faster
Than bleary eyes blink over peelings,
And feelings are stifled while
Men mortgage muscles to entrepreneurs
Making millions from donkey's years
Man hours of misery -Selling their donkey dirt souls
For the sake of some surplus value..

And is your life for this?
That a lifetime of labour
Spent licking the boots
Of a millionaire neighbour -
A tender pretender to airs and
To graces, is finally stopped
By a gold watch and chain
(if you're lucky) and handshake
That says you're consigned
To the scrapheap of has been
Humanity - humbled, rejected,
Forgotten, neglected, to die
In your soul-shrinking, free-thinking,
World of calamitous vanity,
Pensioned and dying a dog's death
Of senile insanity?

Workers of Britain
You're being had; you're being done;
You're being rationalised;
You're being bamboozled
And fiddled and diddled
And done and undone
By handfuls of men
While you sweat through the day
And each night brings you
Nearer to penniless death, -You're being exploited!

You're being exploited
While deep in your hearts
In your tick-ticking hearts,
In your quick-ticking, clock ticking,
Clock-working, hard-working
Slave-working hearts,
You know what to do.
And you know how to do it.

John Smith

A SONG OF PIGGY BANKS

Sing a song of piggy banks,
Buckets full of beer,
Dogs and cats and guns and tanks
And stinging salty tears.

A face, a place, a rendezvous,
A match, a flame, and glow,
A plastic raincoat, hasty kiss,
And boot-prints in the snow.

A door-way, stone steps worn away,
An iron grate, a hole;
Pigs trotters trotting through the hay,
Two hedgehogs and a mole.

There's no romance upon the sea,
There's little on the land,
No happiness for you and me,
Just hard skin on the hands..

No peace, no rest, no fireside calm,
No candlelight and tea,
Just empty bottles, paper bags,
And stifling memories.

When will it wilt, this wicked whirl,
This dance of death and shooting?
When will the smoke of ruins
Swirl away from vultures looting?

When piggy banks are smashed and broke?
And human pigs abolished?
When wealth belongs to simple folk?
And no gun barrel polished?

John Smith

CUPID

"Leave me alone....I don't want to talk to you" said the blonde girl in the blue suit. She began walking away along the embankment.

The young man in the sports jacket followed her, uncertainly. "B-but Mabel...let me explain" he stammered.

She stopped, turned and gazed at him as if he was something that had just come out of a drainpipe. "Pah!' she said then.

The young man chewed at his bottom lip. "It wasn't what you think" he said tentatively. "Her shoe got stuck in a grating and..."

"I don't believe you".

"It's true and I..."

"And what's more were finished. Here..." She struggled savagely with something on her finger. Then she threw an engagement ring at his feet. "Take your ring". Her voice was strident, but throaty.

The young man's jaw went slack, his mouth dropped open. He bent down, picked up the ring. For a few moments he watched how the diamonds winked in the afternoon sunshine. Then he said abruptly "Mabel, be reasonable."

She sniffed; turned her back on him. She stood there, arms folded, one foot tapping rhythmically on the footpath.

As the young man opened his mouth to protest he saw the cop standing on the other side of the road. He came slowly across. He eyed the girl before querying "Is this man bothering you miss?"

The girl stopped tapping her foot; glanced sharply at the young man. In a voice like chipped ice she said "Yes, he is Then she stalked away and stood near the embankment wall.

"Now look here officer..." The young man's voice trembled. "It's alright, we're engaged".

"Oh" The cop smiled mysteriously, then he winked. In a knowledgeable tone he said "I understand sir, just a lovers' tiff".

The girl wheeled round. Her eyes blazed with a green fire. "It is not".

The young man took a pace towards her. He held the ring at arm's length. "Oh, come on Mabel, take the ring back" he pleaded.

She twisted sideways as he tried to take her hand. The ring fell to the ground and bounced near the cop's feet. He picked it up and advanced on the girl. "Come on miss, you can't throw a thing like this away" he said.

The girl pouted her bottom lip, looked at the man, flickering her eyes up and down. In a tight, petulant voice she said "Give it to him then the cop shrugged, turned to the young man. "Perhaps you'd better take it then sir" he said hopefully

"No constable, it's not mine. It's hers".

The girl let go a quick exhalation of breath.. "It is not and I don't want it and I'm off" she panted. With that she tossed her head and began walking away along the path.

The cop looked at the ring; frowned. In a small, uncertain voice, he said "What about this sir?"

The young man shrugged his shoulders. "I don't know" he said perplexed-ly. Then he turned on his heel and hurried after the girl. He caught her up and took her arm.

She tensed. Without stopping she said "What now?"

The young man bit his lip, then he said coaxingly "Look Mabel, let's go somewhere and talk".

"What about?" The girl paused and looked up at him.

He grinned sheepishly; his fingers tightened on her arm. "I don't know...about how much I love you, I suppose

"wha..at?" .

He saw the anger fading from her face. On a sudden impulse he slid an arm round her shoulders and pulled her towards him. "Tom! Not here" she cried. A blush the size of a small forest fire burned in her cheeks.

He laughed.. "We'll take a taxi then". He turned, looked up the road and signalled. A taxi came purring up and rolled to a stop.

The girl said "Where are you taking me?"

"Does it matter?" he threw an anxious glance at her. "Not really,..as long as we're together".

The taxi driver rested one arm on the steering wheel, made a clucking sound and raised his eyes in a gesture.

"Where to sir?" he asked in dry tones.

The young man ignored him. To the girl he said "Then everything's alright Mabel?"

Her face became a little dreamy. "Of course, darling" she began. Then she looked down at her left hand. In an awed whisper she said "Tom... the ring".

There was a strained silence between them. Then all at once they saw the cop coming along the pavement. When he drew level the young man said "Constable, Mabel and I have got engaged".

The taxi driver leaned forward; laughed throatily. "Blimey" he said.

The cop smiled indulgently. He dived a hand into his pocket; brought out the engagement ring. "Allow me madam" he said.

The taxi driver sat up straight. His mouth opened and stayed' open.

The girl held out her left hand. The cop slipped the ring on her finger. He saluted and sauntered off along the path.

Swallowing painfully, the taxi driver murmured: "Blimey, bloomin' Eros."

Frederick G. Walker.

HOLLOWAY PRISON

Four weeks! Ann couldn't grasp it. Four weeks! How could her appeal have failed?

Bitterness and self pity mingled in her thoughts. In a nightmare she was propelled into the prison van. A month! And she had been certain of release. Her knees pressed hard against the cubicle wall. She felt entombed. The dim light from the small translucent pane only heightened her misery. To have to return! She wanted to scream out to the scurrying figures in her path. What did they care for her world, as they bustled deafly like beetles with their eyes fixed on the scattered oblongs of the pavement. The van bumped to a stop. Holloway!

Robot-like, she followed the warder took the proffered cape and undressed in the cold brick cubicle. She bathed mechanically and put on the prison clothes.

"Doctor next" said a voice, and she followed it to the tiny sick room.

Her anguish was suddenly shattered. She reddened; perhaps she had not heard correctly.

"Have you got V.D.?" the doctor spoke irritably.

"Why, have you?" she retaliated coldly.

The fury broke.

"Any more of that and you'll go straight to the punishment cells. Get on to the couch and let me see"

So the humiliation was to be carried on to the end. On reflection she felt that the doctor was being degraded, not herself; perhaps that accounted for the nasty temper.

The examination was followed by finger-printing. The form said "Take an imprint of the prisoner's right thumb before and after she has signed her name". The first right print was taken, Ann signed her name with her left hand and the warder mechanically took another print of her right thumb. Ann chuckled inwardly and felt a slight vindictive satisfaction. She felt less tense and began to look about. Everything seemed calculated to depress - whitewashed brick walls without the usual veneer of plaster; high-barred windows which seemed to diffuse everything with a grey light. Everywhere the jangle of keys proclaimed where she was, smirking rhythmically that the only way out was through time.

She followed the jangle at the warder's waist, past groups of women ferociously scrubbing as they came and relaxing as they went, or others arrogantly leaning on their hands and staring challengingly at the warder. Few looked at the prisoner with curiosity for it was a scene with which they were well acquainted. Only one, with more cynicism than compassion, shouted, "Cheer up, luv, it's not that bad".

The warder, wisely ignoring all round, marched stolidly on to the Governor's office. She tapped on the door and entered with Ann. The Governor, expecting her, looked up slowly.

"I'm sorry your appeal failed; I didn't think it could. However, I can't treat you any differently from the rest of the prisoners whilst you are here, but you will go into the block for first offenders and your work can be in the warders' hostel.

The block to which she was taken consisted on three sides of three tiers of doors bound in by landings. Access was gained by steel stairways, so that the whole differed very little from the mental picture Ann had gained from American films. Stretching from side to side, and halfway down the well that was formed in the middle, was a tough wire netting, which the prison authorities had thoughtfully provided to prevent would be suicides from escaping from their lawful punishment. The only thing missing was the bars with the tough, criminal characters chewing languorously and turning a sneering shoulder on the gaoler. Each cell was in fact, the very essence of compactness, being neatly enclosed, with only a tiny peep-hole in its heavy steel door by which Authority could ascertain that the prisoner was not embarrassing it by hanging herself or doing something equally drastic.

In the cell Ann looked about her and a blanket of claustrophobic panic swathed her lungs. Putting heel to toe she paced the room - thirteen by fourteen. The furnishings, though sparse, made it seem much smaller;- a bed, small scrubbed table and chair, and a corner fitting with basin on top and bucket underneath. A tiny barred window shone out near the ceiling, and Ann, moving the table underneath, climbed up to stare into the courtyard by which she had entered. The sight of space revived her mind a little, though this did not improve its state.

"What if there was a war? What if a bomb dropped? How would she get out?"

She laughed at herself to regain her calm. "Being melodramatic again".

Her fight was interrupted by a key in the lock and as she jumped quickly from the light the parson entered. He smiled quietly and asked her to sit down.

"I'm afraid there's not much I can say. I really didn't think I'd see you again. However, if I can help you in any way, just ask to see me. Politically, I don't agree with you, but in the matter of Peace there is a lot we should all do'.

Ann was up long before the morning began. She stared at the walls and thought. If only she had been a moron, she could just sit and think of nothing. Prison was not equal in its punishment. A day in gaol could be just boring for one person, and purgatory -for another. Some people could accept philosophically or without any thought, but to her it was torture of the finest degree. She felt she must cease to think or succumb to madness.

The prison woke with the daylight. A jangling began in the corridor; doors slammed and voices began to mingle with the noise. Her door suddenly flung itself open and a peremptory voice told her to empty her slops and get water. Friendly prisoners told her the procedure, and she felt relief in the gregariousness. After tidying her cell she joined the file of women in the breakfast queue. She refused the slop of porridge, took the two slices of bread and pint of tea and returned to eat in solitude.

Work came as a relief. The warders' hostel was clean and light and the housework easy. The woman in charge, motherly and sympathetic, gave mild endless lectures on the folly of attending political meetings. Her sympathy didn't end there however. Mysterious, well-wrapped parcels of cakes and boiled eggs were placed regularly on top of the dustbins. She worried sincerely over her charges, and grim was the day when her concern caused her to hand in her resignation.

Dinner from day to day was unvaried, and eaten only as a starving man might eat a cat - telling himself it was chicken. Tea was the same as breakfast, minus the porridge. Ann wondered how the pregnant women survived on such a diet, For their only addition was a pint of milk. The babies, which they saw on their walk to the hostel, looked pale and sad. They too, suffered for their mothers' crimes. For them their cell was a cot from which Ann never saw them emerge, and their gaoler the oldest, most decrepit prisoner of all, an old granny who could scarcely wheeze, let alone attend to each tiny cry. The brightest child was blind: she spent the whole cry whooping up and down inside her bars, making a mockery of the macabre spectacle.

"You'll be able to go to the library" said her friend on Monday.

"That's good! How many books can you have?"

"Two a week"

"Only two, and locked in for twenty hours a day!" Ann was amazed.

"Yes, and you don't half get it if you're caught swapping with another prisoner!"

The library in the first offenders' block turned out to be a converted cell with two cupboards on the walls. The books were jumbled together, un-classified and uncared for. Ann picked up one and read the title - "The Murdered Blonde". She put it down and looked at another - "Confessions of a Bride".

"Come on there, you haven't got all day".

Ann sighed, ignored the speaker and turned over a few more spines. At last, in desperation, she picked up the two thickest, signed her name and returned to her bed. If I can't have quality I'll have to plump for quantity - it might make the time pass, anyway" she philosophised, gamely trying to sound convincing to herself.

Bathtime was the hangman of all modesty. True, each bath had its own cubicle, but the doors appeared to have been put up as the survival of an old custom, as each was only waist high and terminated at the ankles. The water was controlled from the corridor, so that it was either scalding hot or reminiscent of the Antarctic. Fresh clothes were distributed by a fellow prisoner, who, being used to abuse and neither caring nor heeding, looked neither at size nor fit, so that one week one's dress would gaily wrap itself around the ankles and the next would terminate abruptly just below the thighs.

Ann was particularly interested in the other sufferers. She noticed that mo-rale was high in spite of everything, and that a great effort was made to "keep up appearances". Make-up was a cherished possession, and could be bought once a week at the prison shop, although the sevenpence received in payment for work was hardly likely to buy very much. Ann felt most sorry for the women who smoked. They must have suffered agonies. Every morning, on the way to work, there was a mad scramble for discarded "dog ends". An inveterate smoker would trade anything for them, the barter usu-ally being food. As soon as it became known that Ann was a non-smoker and also demanded no payment for the drug, an endless stream of tobacco beggars seemed to drift past her cell in the nightly recreation periods plead-ing their craving. Ann rationed them out painfully, then greeted each sub-sequent plea with a useless shrug - impotence meeting misery.

All was not gloom, however, and for one glorious evening she managed to get out for a lecture. A lecture never experienced in the outside world. Women - hungry for news of normality. Questions came thick and fast - "Describe the latest fashions" "What was the price of eggs?" - Ordinary everyday things that sickened the mind with their simplicity, and showed her how far removed from life was this citadel in the centre of the largest city in the world.

The women jokingly referred to Ann's sentence as "Bed and breakfast" and although questions were rarely asked they seemed to know the details of each case. All crimes, with one exception, were cheerfully tolerated. "The only difference between us and them outside is that we got caught" was the way one old lag aptly put it. The exception mystified Ann for to her it seemed the one excusable case, and the one that called for most pity. She felt deeply for the ostracised woman, who in sheer desperation had abandoned her children on a step. It mattered not to the stern prison code, that the poor woman was emaciated and ill with nerves, that she had been turned from her flat and that her one thought had been to have her children received into some comfortable home. It was obvious that she had had her share of civilisation and now prison was turning into anything but a haven. Her rightful place was obviously in some rest home, where she could be awakened to life and its responsibilities, but Civilisation had decided otherwise; the Law must be upheld; weakness must be crushed ruthlessly; the individual must fit into Society or suffer for her shortcomings.

"Only a week now" said Ann to her friend one day. "You'll be going before the Panel soon then".

"What's that?"

"Oh, they ask you if you need any clothes or money on your discharge, and find a job for you.

A few days later her friend's words materialised.

Ann was led to a small room and found herself the focus of six or seven pairs of eyes. Feeling mildly embarrassed she sat down in the proffered chair. She had decided in the back of her mind that she deserved paying for her ordeal and that if money was forthcoming she would take everything she could get.

"We see here", said the chairman looking at his notes, "that you don't need any clothes, but how about your job?"

"The Union's dealing with that at the moment".

"Oh, well, we can't do much to help there, then. Now, how about money? Is your husband coming to meet you? We see you had nothing when you were admitted".

Ann could not bring herself to lie outright. "I don't really know".

"Well how much would you need to get home, if he doesn't come?" Again she lied - "I don't know"

"Well we'll see into that, and there'll be something for you on Thursday, so don't worry".

Thursday started long before dawn. The hours before the warder's keys seemed interminable, but at last their familiar jingle swung towards her door. Breathlessly she followed the few other dischargees towards the cubicles and received her bundle of clothes with emotion. Everything felt so soft and luxurious, and her shoes were gossamer - like after the prison brogues. Coming out of their privacy the women bubbled with talk and smiles. How different they all looked! Surely, this wasn't Mrs. Grey, and look at Pat over there!

Their guide led them on to a small office overlooking the gate. "Can't let you out til eight, y'know. Oh, this envelope's for you but if your husband comes you must give it me back". Ann took it and tried to feel the coins inside.

"How much?" she thought.

"You'd better stand upon that chair near the window and see if he's waiting".

Ann got on to the chair and saw Jack at the gate.

She jumped down quickly before he noticed her. "No, he's not there" she said determinedly, her heart thumping.

"Well, you'd better stay up there til its time to go. There's another five minutes yet".

Obediently she remounted per perch and gazed down upon her husband. As if willed by her eyes he looked up, gave a start, and then waved vigorously. Ann jumped down again quickly without replying. She was determined not to weaken, and felt as if a battle of wits was going on between her and the Authorities. The clock suddenly struck her reprieve and the prisoners moved towards the door joking with the warder.

They stepped into the yard and waited whilst a small door was unlocked in the great gate. As they stepped one by one into the world, four men who had been brought from Brixton to repair a roof looked longingly at the freedom beyond. As Ann stepped out, two hands grasped hers. Jack looked pale. For a minute neither could speak as tears came to the surface.

"You did have me worried. What were you doing at that window?"

Ann laughed through the mist in her eyes. "Oh, I just thought I'd get something out of them. I can open the envelope now".

She slit the packet at the top and the coins tumbled out into her hand - two shillings!

Julia Murphy

PUT TO PROOF

So how to tell what's true
From what is vain?
The old will yield to the new,
Dark become plain?
All struggle puts to proof
Each heart and brain:
The hard got seam of truth
Begins with pain.

No other proof than Spring
Will come again,
Returning birds will sing,
Frost melt in rain;
Plough deep the ice-bound earth
To harvest grain:
Who bring new worlds to birth
Begin with pain

JOY AND PLEASURE

A pleasure is like ice
Held in burning fingers
You may grasp it boldly
For a while it lingers.

Like quicksilver is joy,
You may grasp it never,
But you may hold it lightly
On your palm for ever.

SONG

As falls the rose,
As the stars set,
As ebbs the tide,
So we forget.

Dawn follows stars,

Tides make the sea,
New rosebuds spring,
How then should we

Stand still unchanged
And let life pass,
Waxwork dummies
Behind the glass?

Live, change, forget!
Somewhere I'll be
Alive in you,
And you in me.

Angela Tuckett

A SERENADE
(to be sung to Toselli's serenade)

You, you're my delight, giving such pleasure
I know you're the one to end the loneliness that I have known.
Take the hand I give gladly, my treasure,
Let me lead you to the wonderland we'll make our very own.
All my love I'll give to you,
All I ask is your love true,
And then we'll know that bliss of a love beyond compare,
It's our paradise
That we will always share that none can make compare
Must take especial care to be so very fair,
And we will have that oneness we seek so eagerly.
You must know as I now feel
That this love can be quite real
And so we must betroth our hearts in such loving trust
It's our rainbow's end,
You know this is a must we'll not betray this trust
We'll love till we are dust with such a loving trust,
And we will share that oneness we seek so eagerly.
Whisper you'll be mine light as a zephyr
Reassure me so I'll know I'll never be again alone,
This is our serenade.

Alfred Edwards

WORDS

 People use words in various ways, each newspaper can't mean what
it says,
yet, daily they sell, and daily you buy, then workmates all
argue which told the lie,
your paper said this, my paper said that, the editor sits
back, and purrs, like a cat,
you've paid his price, he's snarled up your brain, the
Press Lords are happy; they publish for gain.

People use words in various ways, stage, screen, or radio,
and television plays.
the working class are lazy, boorish, greedy, vulgar, crude,
the upper class are cultured, clever, generous and good,
yet, they tell us we're one nation, and their favourite word is Fair,
but, they legislate our wages, while they keep the lion's share.
Don't you ponder as you view this, can't you recognise yourself?
Its you who are the simpleton, producing all their wealth.

People use words in various ways, verbal acrobats in Parliament,
merely serve to fill their days,
there's a vicious wages spiral so the whole damn lot agrees,
there's one way to teach the workers, impose a wages freeze'.
But the words they use are clever;
Say 'the future can be bright, and we're all in it together;
till they put the matter right.
So you shrink your family budget, though you grumble more and
more,
but you won't do aught about them, till the wolf is at your door.

Will people like us ever learn how to say
these are our words, and this is our way ?
Our old folk are hungry, our children in need,
so share out, or clear out, enough of your greed.
Speculations and corruption, sordid details by the score,
the ugly face of Capitalism must go - for ever-more
People use words in various ways - Democracy isn't what Capital
says.

Betty Crawford

LEGEND OF XANADU

When the Sphinx was a young girl, she was very popular with everyone, being gay and carefree and yet managing to remain unspoilt. But as she grew older, being Sphinx gradually became a full time job, and she found she had less and less time to spare for friends. Almost imperceptibly the prettiness of her face began to change into a cold contemptuous beauty. Old friends would be turned away by her stony gaze, and yet deep inside she longed to burst out from behind the facade. And so she found a compromise of sorts. Under cover of night she would take the young men of the village to her bed. She never slept with the same young man twice. Love was a luxury she could not afford, but orgasm offered her relief for weeks, sometimes months, at a time.

Then one day a stranger came, a young man from a foreign land. He looked rather fierce, and he took her by surprise with his gentleness. For the first time since the Sphinx's childhood, something troubled the waters of those deep brown eyes. A tear rolled down her bronzed cheek. He spoke to her softly, telling her of his travels through storms and blizzards, over mountains and sea. And they lay a while in silence until in the cold light of dawn, she remembered who she was.

She tried to command him not to come again, but his eyes just smiled. She started to plead, but she read something in his face that told her it was futile. He said simply "You know I'm not going to leave, don't you, love?" I want to free you from the name you are 'carrying". He' disappeared quickly lest the morning catch thenr together. And she knew there was no longer any room for compromise if she were to remain a Sphinx. And so s he made her decision.

The following night the stranger returned. Uncertainly, he knelt before her, scarcely blinking as he stared at (her, his face struck with disbelief that slowly gave way to sadness. All night long he knelt there, sunk deep within himself. There was already a trace of dawn in the eastern sky when he rose abruptly and, slinging his bag over his shoulder, walked away the way he had first come, leaving only his footprints in the sand. The Sphinx showed no trace of emotion, for she had already turned into stone.

Rick Gwilt.

SOME OF OUR BEST MEN WENT TO SPAIN

Some of our best men went to Spain
And some of our best men died
And some of our best men never went,
Oh Comrades, how they lied
About the pros and cons and politics
Of why some stayed and gently prayed
That they were there.
Smash my leg, turn white my hair
And posthumously praise
My heroic deeds
Whilst Fascist Franco's needs
Were gained
As were razed
The white-washed sunny
Walls of Spanish town.

When they came back
Our heroes tall
With limp and legless badge
Joined in the fight
But faced a war,
A war within
Their war-torn minds
More savage than before.

Some of our best men left behind
Were left in Burgos jail to rot
And some were shot
And others since garrotted
And Garcia Lorca should have wrote
God help you freedom fighter
When you stand up from below'.
They'll wire your testicles for sound
And shock the world to make a good example
For other gentle gentlemen to follow.
Like the Vorsters and the Rhees
And nameless Colonels who rape split Greece
And gentle Thieu,
To name a few.

And the dead shall lie together
Side by side from Viet Nam

To Derry and to Sharpsville
Like the keys in a piano.
George Jackson and the Rosenbergs
Lumumba and Cabral
And Che Guevara with his death

Brought Glory from the horror.
I wonder what the price is
Of insurance for Angela Davies?
Will she as a wife
Enjoy a life with children
Or draw an old-age pension.
She yet may sing
With Martin Luther King
And be angels together.

Forty years of time has marched
The young troops now turned old
Find difficult to comprehend
When they are told
It's right and proper
Now to trade
With Franco's Fascist Spain.
If we did not
And left the field, wide open,
How would it gain
The proletarian struggle?

Neither sad, nor cynical be,
The times they are a changing,
The rules are not so simple now
The space men that you see
Are Yank and Ruski
In Sputnik and Apollo joined
And soon we'll find
Its all done by co-operation
Like in Ireland.

Sol Garson

LAKING -- YORKSHIRE HOLIDAY

To where do you go when laking?
The highways, skyways or railways taking.

For to find that peace of mind,
With life's pressures far behind.

By some sunny beach of tropic clime
Inner cooled with Lemon and Lime,
Evening dances on a palmed veranda
Exotically dressed like Carmen Miranda.

Or away to the Isles, Lochs and burns,
Highland slopes with their pines, heather and ferns,
That ere time passed this way,
Left little to remind of a busier day.

Oh, where do you go when laking?
Without any of these pathways taking,
You will come to no harm,
Stuffing your guts on a farm.

But, don't get caught like me,
As a cat high up on a tree.
For to please the loving, spouse,
You decorate the whole bloody house.

WAS IT YESTERDAY?

The stillness, eerie quiet before a storm,
The peace, tranquillity that brings the dawn,
Was suddenly broken by a human scream,
A cry of "Fire " awoke my dream.

Twas not a time of deepest sleep,
Twas not either a shepherd with his sheep,
But a "limber gunner" on dawn standby,
As oft before, in hissing rain, but now in desert dry.

Shatteringly came the splitting crack,
Our own twenty five recoiling back,
And for miles along the line,
Shells spewed out with menacing whine.

The day wore on, barrage unabated,
Our thoughts cried out to our related,
That the enemy had not yet replied,

Lifted our morale, so sorely tried.

The sun grew hot, then began to fade,
The tanks came through, our point was made,
Orders given to increase our range,
Load, fire, repeat, or barrels change.

Now in front the battle high,
The armoured Seventh and the P.B.I.
Through the night, and following day,
Then "Limber Up" were on our way.

Word went round that Jerry's cracked,
The chase was on and we were backed,
The R.A.F. this time, up aloft,
Support from behind was far from soft.

However sweet may victory sound,
The sickening, nauseating smells of death abound,
Now the living, as one, thank God aloud,
For life to be lived and not a desert shroud.

Our comrades fallen, we now lament,
Sour turns the wine of victory, for our descent,
To be human butchers, like our foe,
The inner voice calling, yet on and on we go.

Long after the sand has stilled,
Soddened by the blood that spilled,
That the time will forever fly,
Like the skite hawks in the sky.

We look back on those days and say,
Did we ever pass that way,
That our sons be never sent,
Nor the world stay forever Bent?

EPITAPH FOR A BITCH

Grant she was sour and sharp
-bitter lemon
Life is no tune on the harp
For a working woman.

Monotonous drudging at mill
At bench or sewing machine,
Come home to drudgery still,
To cook, wash, tidy, clean.

The honey of courting done,
Comes the drag of children,
The lonely stint at home,
A work-worn husband.

Tele and football pool,
Happen some bingo,
Daughter from work or school,
Resentful and spiteful

Not even in old age
Reprieve from worry,
Hunger and a cold grate,
Not enough money.

Put by her bitter tongue,
But all these things recall,
Which warped her since she was young,
As they cripple us all.

Frances Moore

MAGNOLIA

Lament, lament the victim's pain,
The broken flesh, the twisted mind,
But shall lamenting bring again,
The dead, or make the killer kind?

The wailing of the mourner. keens
The wailers when the next bombs fall.

Vietnam today - and New Orleans -
And Hiroshima. yesterday,
And shall tomorrow burn us all?

Frances Moore

DISCRIMINATION

Black man or white, all you want woman for
is bare in bed; not mates
co-operating in the human race.
No more than colour can we dodge our sex
and its attendant pressures, nor
the insults due to the uncircumspect;
when cerebration or emotion draw
consciousness clear of outer accident.

Daily exposure in the common streets
or in the daily press
of lush young woman flesh
lures the consumer to expense
on purges, booze or what other sweets
outside of relevance
even to human coupling; but heats
male sexuality in excess
and scales the female partner down as cheap.

Just as fast transport sets
those who break barriers of distance frets
of black-white, day-night metaphor-,
and whets
weapons to complicate division for
those who have vested interest in more
occasions of internal war
-race hatred or
the genocidal enmity of sex.

Never allowing us not to remember
we never can qualify as equal member
of a man's world; a white man's world; a world
where Male White Money talks; and all our right
is to drudge up another's gaudy night.

Frances Moore.

CELLULOID TEARS

I was standing in a movie queue with my girl friend. There were lots of other couples too; all hanging around in the cold waiting to see Diana Ross sing the blues.

Two small boys were enjoying themselves playing football around the crowd; weaving swiftly in and out of the people. It had been raining all that day so the ball was wet and dirty. We all stood like plaster statues, only our eyes moved, following the moving ball, ready to jump aside quickly to avoid being hit by it. We did not want our clean Saturday clothes messed up by a shitty ball.

No-one thought to tell the boys to go and play elsewhere. We just stood and watched them in a kind of silence, of each others discomfort.

The boys sensed our unease, this was their victory. They swelled in arrogant pride; call it bravado. They became more daring, they raced up and down the waiting people -faster and faster weaving faster and faster. Then something happened. One of the little boys tripped and fell headlong on the hard pavement.   I think that he broke one of his teeth, blood bubbled out of his mouth. He stood up quickly and ran away to hide his pain and humiliation. His friend, quiet, looked at us, then went after him.

The crowd stood in silence for a few moments then someone laughed. The laughter was infectious, others joined in. Soon the entire crowd was rocking with laughter. They obviously enjoyed the boy's accident. Someone said that it served the bastard right, he had no right to be playing football there.

The movie hall opened and we all filtered in to weep for Diana Ross. Celluloid tears.

Colin Frame

ROPE AND BIRCH

We are a backward people
We come from "Down the Vale"
Live quite near the tall Church steeple
Now listen to our tale.

We never think to buy a book
And read it in some quite nook,
Wed sooner buy the Sunday "Dope"
That s why we're shouting for the Rope.

And when we go to cast our vote,
It's still the same old story,
We'd gladly give it to a goat,
If they labelled it a Tory.

Although we sometimes go to Church,
We're firm believers in the Birch,
We'd make wrongdoers squirm and squeal,
The flesh from off their backs we'd peel.

We don't sit down to read and think,
We'd rather have a drop of drink,
And neither do we care a damn,
How many die in poor Vietnam.

And what goes on in Ireland,
We do not care a jot,
As long as it's not Englishmen,
We don't care who gets shot.

So all we do is live and hope,
That some poor scoundrel gets the rope,
With evil hearts we go to Church,
And pray; Oh God, bring back the birch!

The above poem was written by me in the Mill after two young married women had been round the mill and the village getting signatures on a petition sheet calling upon the Government to bring back hanging.

Jim Garnett

BLAMING THE WOMAN

Adam was the only man,
This tale you must believe,
And Adam was a lonely man,
Until he courted Eve.

Poor Adam felt ashamed,
Because he's nothing on,.
But Eve, she was a Weaver famed,
She wove two figleaves strong.

Soon they felt they'd like some food,
So to the Orchard went,
They both felt in a merry mood,
He had no bad intent.

Eve took him to an apple tree,
And spun a yarn so well,
Her story stung him like a Bee
Twas then poor Adam fell.

So this is how the story's told,
It comes to us from days of old,
I think it is a dirty shame,
To make the Woman take the blame.

Jim Garnett

A GOOD WOMAN

She ever was so blithe and gay,
Full of joy and childlike play,
Angel like, your hearts she'd sway,
With smiles just like the Sun's bright rays.

But when she's laid beneath the clay,
And flesh and blood are in decay,
The "Soul" has gone its "Heavenly Way",
No more to fight this earthly fray.

And time has come for "Judgement Day"
The lord will turn to her and say,
You have no Sins to wash away,

140

Pass on my dear, be on your way.

Friends left behind you need not pray,
Wreaths and Flowers you need not lay,
Bow your heads not in dismay,
She never had a debt to pay.

Jim Garnett

PIPE DREAM

Step on my cloud
enjoy with me my
land of love and liberty.
Peaceful days
and no tomorrows.
filled with weeping
filled with sorrows.
No more bombs
no class distinction.
No more fears of
world extinction.
No-one there to make the law,
one for rich and one for poor.
Black and white go hand in hand
all are equal in this land.
This land of love and liberty
should not be just a fantasy.

J.E. Sutton

(Translated from La Nouvelle Critique) (Anon:)

A Typical story
- THE GHERKIN -
A true Story by Dominique-Hughes

In a factory not far from Paris a trade unionist is having a petition signed to support the claims of the staff.

A personnel manager calls him "Have you got the permission of the manager?" The argument warms up. They refer to the manager. The personnel manager holds his hand in the direction of the telephone. The union delegate becomes impatient - "Pass me the gherkin" he says.

"The gherkin?"

"The gherkin!"

The personnel manager chokes himself on the telephone. "Sir, you have just been seriously insulted". The manager chokes himself in turn - "Three days suspension". The union delegate does not understand; to him gherkin is a popular word for telephone. This is what he explains to the personnel manager who demands that he stops making fun of him so openly. Neither he nor the manager nor anybody else knows this meaning of the word 'gherkin'

The delegate is sure of his facts but how to establish the truth? He enquires of the District Secretary of the C.G.T.. how to prove that he is right? A few minutes thinking, then an idea; I know a lecturer of Nanterre University, he should be able to find the reference of the word 'gherkin'. Little cucumber, clot, nothing to do with the telephone. But I will make enquiries.

Feverish enquiries and exchanges of phone calls between linguists of Nanterre; at last a lecturer rushes towards the library, flips through the reference books, finds the word and the equivalent "Telephone - Pop." Three hours later the Union delegate presents himself to the personnel manager with the photocopy. A gherkin is really a telephone. There has not been any insult.

If the story stopped here it would be a very nice one. But there is more to it. While the gherkins of Nanterre were ringing indefinitely, the workers of the factory, hearing of the delegate's suspension, had immediately threatened to go out on strike. The manager had given up, lifted the sanction and besides given satisfaction to the claims, without having consulted the dictionary.

This story is exemplary in more than one way and could introduce long developments on the following topics:

LINGUISTICS AND CLASS STRUGGLE. The Industrial relations being what they are, the word "gherkin" in the manager's head could only mean "Imbecile". See "The Exception and -the Rule" by Bertoldt Brecht.

ALLIANCE OF THE WORKING CLASS AND THE INTELLECTU-ALS, OR THE UNIVERSITY IN THE SERVICE OF THE WORKERS. Imagine the fever of the academics who are at last able to put directly their science (their knowledge) as they say) in the service of the workers. It is not everyday a true feast.

THE RULING ROLE OF THE WORKING CLASS. Imagine the disappointment of the academics when they hear that a little threat of strike is stronger than big dictionaries.

There remains the most important question and the thickest mystery of all. What meaning of the word 'gherkin' did the delegate have in mind when he said "Pass me the gherkin"?

THE PICKET

Cold this morning,
everything,
quiet,
crane overhead
slowly rusting;
seven weeks now
it has stood idle,
shiftless and listless,
will be seven more,
if Thirty's not paid.
Canteen's not changed,
it's as dirty as ever,
flies from the bog
cover the tables.
Cement's all wet,
rained hard yesterday,
agents too lazy
pull over the tarp;
would not have happened;
that's one job,
when this is over.
Here comes the first

Pat from Belfast,
up early this morning;
Did you shit the bed?"
I'd like to shit,
on this bloody agent"
Not a bad lad,
first time on strike,
just joined the club.
Who's that singing?"
Big Joe Jones,
the calypso king,
worth ten on a picket
when the pigs
do their duty.
They pick on Joe
It's the colour of skin
black as the heart
of building employers.
Here's the I.R.A..
Dublin Branch,
Top of the morning Pat;
how went last night?"
Better than home,
your mates were active".
I've told them mate,
should be over here,
they'll find the culprits,
waxing fat on profits".
Here come the last,
get us a bad name
just come from mass,
prayed to the Lord, .
take the employers
to heaven,
or to hell,
but off this earth,
for workers to begin,
all of them together
to build the houses,
hospitals,
schools,
roads and docks,
and in the process,
build the workers' Republic.

They've a lot to learn,
God's with the Employer,
it's his creation:
He's the employers' property.
We create the wealth,
of this prosperous country.
Let's claim our property,
dispense with employers;
then we'll start to build
Socialism,
and emancipate our lives.
It is a long hard struggle
to reach our goal,
but every strike won
is a nail in the coffin
of the employing class.
So stand firm lads,
when this nail
reaches its mark,
we are one step nearer.
Now at the blacklegs
and re-educate them brothers,
We'll need them with us
in' the final battle.

ROSE AND LIFE

Red, white, fragrant,
gentle petals, tempting bees,
sucking honey, food for life.

Who? How? Where?
are the enemies
that you have faced

Greenfly, rust, mildew,
these from time immemorial
won as much as lost

But
today
face
the new
enemy

Computerised
Mechanised
Sterilised
Progress

Clean your shirts whiter
progress
Drive your car faster
progress
Nervous breakdowns quicker
progress
Once fed CO_2
returned to us
lift support substance

Now choked on
gastrostomic exploitations
such delights

Strontium ninety
Carbon monoxide
Sulphur dioxide
Radio-active fall-in

Free
from
progress
declining
gifts

to
mother-nature
aids
to her
destruction

So arise
you slaves
of bastard progress

Break your chains
put back the fragrance
in rose and life.

Ron Hughes

LIFE IS FOR THE LIVING

Young once - with spirit for love
-generosity for life
-need for people

You give so much - received so little.
Life is for living.

Old and grey, lined face, struggled bones,
varicose veins, weary heart,
you have lived.

You lived the filth and dirt, the
wrong in every act,
You lived the small truth in
life with the understanding fact
that you give yourself to life.

Life is for living.

My contempt, my familiarity.
My conflict, my experience.
Look up not down -
Real beauty is in men's' action.
Self is lonely being.
Together is the being of living.
Conflict is oneself as well as other things.
To smile is the first chance of happiness.
Laughter has no language.
Life is living, it goes on.

Dennis Maher

SOUNDS IN THE NIGHT

When mantle of night has fallen
and people lie abed,
Strange notions, thoughts and fantasies
Completely fill one's head.
The breeze that by day is a whisper

Can at night seem forlorn and long
Moaning its way through telegraph wire,
as though singing some ghostly song.
Rain beats on the window,
can that be the roar of the sea.?
Cold dark sky hurries on by
With not one star to see.
Now! was that the cry of midnight owl?
Or sound of lonely, wandering ghoul.
Then another sound the night assails
be feline species' plaintive wails
But secure and safe, within my own four walls
I meander slowly, into misty hall,
There to seek out Morpheus' charms,
Then at last succumb to her welcome arms.

Maximilian
(John Brennan)

ON COMING ON A TRAMP

I found him squat where a dog affirmed its beat
Unconcerned with shoppers as they buy
And they with him reminding me of sheep
That go on grazing while another dies.
Sticky tape holds his second eyes in place
Beneath smashed lenses was cottonwool to blind
He's squinting, sly, one moment searched my face
Then returned to the deserts of his mind.

But is not the eye the window of the soul?
And in it I saw no love that binds
Man to man, for love's sap had turned to gall
And the withered branches to the light were blind.

Bowed and stunted not much more than dwarf
How they had savaged their race
Their grinding jaws wore their legs in half
Till scarce he peeps o'er backyard place

Perhaps one day some scourge
Or in him life's tuningfork was stale
Despised, degraded when he needed love
In every heart men had driven nails

148

Yet here perhaps from ambitions domes
Was poet, explored where the ice winds whirl
Or scholar gowned, statesman famous known
For the oyster must be coaxed to bloom its pearl.

When man walks so constant in a groove
His footsteps wear it to the deepest rut
There like the tapeworm never known to move
Scavenging the tubes in society's guts.

So helpless now he should be revered
The wing of clucking hen spread over him tight
At the sound of danger or imagined fears
To glide him towards his longest sleep.

It seems that childishness swifter comes
To some untaught whose minds have never flown
The skies of learning where dwells countless sums
That should sting to flight the cerebrums drones

Yet perhaps there is compensation there
When winter comes to those who meagre drink
For pity the erudite who is aware
His mind may arise to see his body sink.

Can you not hear the death hounds baying?
Soon they'll be slavering you cannot flee
So merciless think hangsman laying
Your diabolical trap, there's one for thee.

Now he rises like a new-born foal.
Lurching, staggering to find his feet
And parts the sea of faces as he crawls
Like a leper in an Eastern street.

Once he must have sucked a mother's breast
Some say they hover over us, ever involved
But if she is, and sees such distress
Her eyes must, have bled till they're long since dissolved.

You poor little aged waif and stray
Shuffling few inches in full flight
You will never reach your lodge this day

That wells my eyes far into the night.

Frank Smith

THREE POEMS

Blood
Descending to me from generations past
Through feathery vapours of time
Time unimaginable

Since Adam
My blood was atoms
Floating amid the weathered waves of all 'that'
Then, like a dream
Descended into my living flesh.

The imprint of that - remains
On the still soft parchment that is my mind
Embedded like a curse yet warm
Guernica's angled lines of horror
Tear at the fragile tissue of my imagination
Man and Animal
Scream out of the canvas
Out of the soul
Out of that ripe seed of inspiration
-who has gained from his stay?
From his knowledge passed from..
womb to soul?
Or through passages as yet unknown to us.

Lady, accept this tear
Borne from my soul
like a quivering blues
where the mind deserts the body
And soars like a gull
Above the blackness of it all
Fragile slave, accept this tear.

Colin Frame

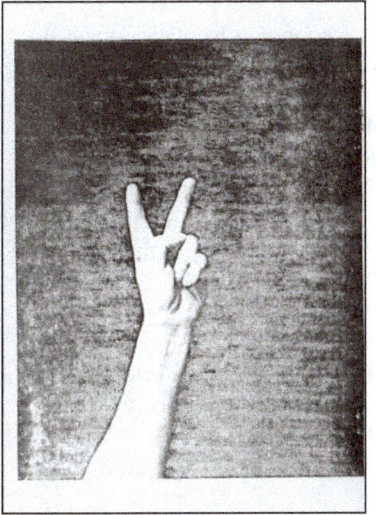

cover size 296 x 210 mm

CONTENTS

153. Redundant Iron Works: Millom   A.M Horne
154. Dawn Chorus   A.M Horne
154. Me   A.M Horne
154. Benjamin Stott 1813-1850   Ruth & Eddie Frow
158. On An Abandoned Garden   Alfred Edwards
159. Being an Improbable Conversation
   overheard through the half-open door
   to a Premature Baby Unit   W Froom
162. A Greek Tragedy   Frank Parker
162. Passing Through   Jean Sutton
165. Walmer Street   Frances Thomas
167. "Children" and Children   Vivien Leslie
169. Poem for a Girl from Africa   Rick Gwilt
171. Clean-up Job   Gareth Thomas
173. Agitpoem No. 8 - Bromley   Bob Dixon
173. Leave Me Alone.   Bob Dixon
174. Portrait of an Economy   Bob Dixon
174. Ideas   Bob Dixon
176. A Matter of Form   Ian E Reed
180. Struggle Identified   Barbara Smith
181. The Building Workers Song   Rod O Connor
182. Now I'll Sharpen My Pencil   John Smith
183. Green Toilet Rolls to Match my
   Bathroom Tiles   Rose Friedman
185. The Lost, the Losers and the Lame   Ian E Reed
185. Feel the Need   J.E.Sutton
186. Whatcha Mean   Colin Frame
187. I am Sorry for Them   Colin Frame
187. New Sounds from Motown   Rick Gwilt
191. Glass is Dynamite   David Kessell
193. Chile   David Kessell
194. Random Thoughts of a Telefan   Maurice M Wiles
195. Solid Gleaming Coal   Mick Jenkins
198. Chile   Sol Garson

NOTE BY WAY OF INTRODUCTION

This is "Voices" No. 4. It comes in a new experimental format which may cause raised eyebrows. We cannot here go into details but the financial and economic factors involved in producing a periodical of this kind compel us to look into all possible economies. The continued existence of "Voices" is by no means assured. Our aim is a four times a year production. But this requires considerably wider support than we so far enjoy. We need more readers. We need more writers. We need more money. Please do not misunderstand this. Our support is increasing in all these respects, and we are grateful for this. But we need much more. The question is: do we deserve more? Does the poetry and prose in this issue justify a call for support from the progressive left? We think it does. But you are the people who must decide. If you think there is room for a committed publication which thinks of writing as a weapon in the hands of the Labour and Socialist and Communist movement help us. Make us known. write for us. Write to us. Ask your branch or district Committee to make a bulk order of "Voices" to distribute to your members. Introduce "Voices" to friends.

All enquiries to Ted Morrison, 110 Edge Lane, Stretford, Manchester. (061 865 5862).

REDUNDANT IRON WORKS : MILLOM

Strange they were across the bay,
Mystic spires of a forgotten religion,
Standing awkward at the edge of a moorland.
Facing the sea in sombre austerity.

Where once smoke filled a town with grimy streets
And noise and heat aged many men,
Where slag splashed brilliance at dark nights,
Streaming down unseen paths.

But as the sun slips behind the spires,
Blazing streams melt the sand,
Curving in deep gulleyed moulds,
Sweeping carelessly across the bay,
The sun's fiery setting splashing the sand with steel.

THE DAWN CHORUS

The death of a river choked by the phlegm of detergent,
Panic of oil glued seagulls, with only a reflex flapping,
As black pitted oblongs smudge the skyline,
Dry faces cough their way to morning monotony.
Confusion grabs an old man's hands, as he stammers between
the buses,
And the poster shouts, 'Oozo washes whiter'.

ME

What am I?
A push the other way in the soccer crowd
A belly flop in the public baths
580/3, a ping in the time machine.
Disturbed by the tragedy of Vietnam
Horrified at the sight of a Biafra child.
I remain the eleventh best snooker player in Barrow-in-Furness.

A.M. Horne

BENJAMIN STOTT 1813-1850

It is most frustrating at times when one is trying to find information about a particular person and all ends seem to be blocked. We first became acquainted with Benjamin Stott through his poems. We found the little volume, 'Songs for the Millions' in a bookshop in Stockport. We have never seen another copy. The poems are not only of a high literary standard, they also tell us quite a lot about the political opinions of the man.

 Fitting the loose threads together, the picture looks rather like this. Stott was born in Manchester on 24th November, 1813. His father was a hairdresser and later an auctioneer and came from a respectable Rochdale family. His mother came from one of the ancient families in the vicinity of Hope and Bradwell in the High Peak. Possibly they may have been miners and sheep farmers. Benjamin was the youngest of thirteen children and when he was under six years old both his parents died. He was brought up by a maiden Aunt, his mother's sister who worked as a fustian cutter and managed to keep him until he was nine. He was then admitted to Cheetham's Hospital. Friends of his father exerted influence to secure this admission. His education before that had been at the National Free School in Granby Row where he had learnt to read and write. Although he attended Cheetham's from 1822 to 1827, he apparently made little educational progress although he must have begun to develop a facility in the use of the English language of which he made good use in his poetry.

When he left school at 14, he was apprenticed to a bookbinder for seven years and he remained a journeyman in that trade until he died in 1850 at the early age of thirty seven.

We can only sketch in the blanks in his political life. He dedicated his poems to Thomas Slingsby Duncombe. He wrote of the "disinterested patriotism and eloquent advocacy of the rights of suffering humanity" which he said would "be cherished by, and live in the hearts of, generations yet unborn". Slingsby Duncombe was a well known Radical Member of Parliament.

Benjamin Stott apparently only left his native Manchester once in his life and that was to go to a conference in the Isle of Man. He went there representing a society to which he belonged. We know that he was a prominent member of the OddFellows Friendly Society. He wrote a long poem extolling the virtues of that Society:

> "Blessed OddFellowship : thy aim and end
> Is to promote the peace of man on earth,
> The sick to cheer, the friendless to befriend".

There was, however, in December 1829, a Spinners' Conference on the Isle of Man at which an attempt was made to form one "grand General Union" of all spinners. John Doherty, the leader of the Manchester Spinners returned to Manchester imbued with the idea of forming a much wider movement. It is not impossible to conjecture that Stott as a well known radical poet, attended the Spinners' Conference. His interest in the Trade Union Movement is shown by the poem that he wrote in memory of John Roach, a Manchester boiler maker. The verses were printed and sold to Union members. Stott called John Roach "A son of labour - a true democrat - a firm friend - a determined advocate - an unpaid patriot - a pure philanthropist and an honest man."

> "Shall we forget", he asks, "with that undaunted brow,
> Though dared resist the foes of labour's rights?
> Shall we neglect those virtues to avow
> Which shone in thee and are men's chief delights?"

During the 1830s, the Bookbinders' Consolidated Union was passing through formative struggles and the Manchester Branch took the lead in attempting to coordinate the activities of the different Lodges. It is possible that Stott, having attended the Spinners' Conference and accepted the ideas of general union, played no small part in these Union affairs. In one poem, "Beware ye white Slaves of England" he tells the people to

155

"Be firm and unite, but be cautious in words,
On your prudence depends the success of your cause.

Much of Benjamin Stott's writing echoes the stirring calls of the French Revolution - the demands for natural rights that were voiced by Thomas Paine. His poetry was obviously influenced by Shelley and Byron and it reflects his deep sympathy with suffering, injustice and oppression in their manifold expressions.

At the Sun Inn in Long Millgate, the Manchester and district literary circle held meetings to exchange views and appraise each others writing. The poems read at one of these meetings held on Thursday, 24th March, 1842 were published in a slight volume called "The Festive Wreath". Benjamin Stott contributed a poem in memory of William Grant, one of Dicken Cheeryble Brothers who had recently died. One of the circle, William Axon, thought sufficiently highly of Stott to walk to Northenden Churchyard soon after his death in 1850 and copy the inscription on the tombstone. It read:- "Here resteth the body of Benjamin Stott, of Manchester, who died July 26th 1850, aged thirty six years. He was an influential member of the National Independent Order of Odd Fellows, and by them much esteemed.

"Pause, gentle stranger, for a man lies here
Whose hand was open, and whose heart sincere
To truth and kindness rendered homage due;
His friends were many, and his foes were few.
Errors he had, but they were such as he
In the frail nature of humanity;
Virtues he had, but they were such as claim
No noisy greetings from the voice of fame:
His virtues we remember, but the rest
We leave to Him whose mercy doeth best."

from 'Songs For the Millions - Benjamin Stott

Gaunt Famine Rides Rampant

Gaunt famine rides rampant o'er all the land,
And none but the drones can his power withstand;
The industrious bees that produce the wealth
Are his victims alone and he kills by stealth;
For the wounds which he makes they never bleed,
Although they are painful and piercing indeed;
But the wasted form, when the soul is dead,
Tells the tale that it died for want of bread.
Oh, gracious God, that governs all,

Thy attributes are wise and good;
Arise, and make the tyrants fall,
That rob the poor of life and food.

How hard is the fate of the suffering poor,
What toil and privation, and pain they endure;
And yet they are patient, forbearing, and kind,
Though the drones of the earth are against them combined;
Humanity shudders with grief and despair;
When it thinks and reflects on their woes and their care;
And the heart of the patriot burns with desire,
That the days of their thraldom may quickly expire.
Oh, gracious God, that governs all,
Thy attributes are wise and good;
Arise, and make the tyrants fall,
That rob the poor of life and food.

It Comes! It Comes!

It comes! It comes the glorious day,
When holy freedom shall prevail,
When battle strife and bloody fray
Shall be as a forgotten tale -
When virtue shall triumphant rise,
And vice be swept from off the earth,
When man shall look up to the skies,
And bless the God that gave him birth -
When joy, and charity, and peace,
And love, shall cheer the human heart.
Odd Fellowship

Blessed Odd Fellowship! thy aim and end
Is to promote the peace of man on earth,
The sick to cheer, the friendless to befriend.
Oh! that my yearning heart could speak thy worth;
Thrice happy they who unto thee gave birth;
A glorious reward is theirs to gain
In that immortal life where neither dearth,
Disease, nor famine ever more shall reign,
Nor grief nor misery shall be, nor aught of pain.

Benjamin Stott
Ruth and Eddie Frow

ON AN ABANDONED GARDEN

Against the palette of evening and ungracious
Shadows of the lamp, flickering with flirtatious,
Crack-squeezed, wintry gusto, I see her shape; slightly bent,
With pinned-back hair, savouring every name and scent
Of gay-paged, lustrous-catalogued bulb and seed.
Child-implanted, she waits the barren winter
For those other, ordered seeds; emerging into
Life once planted, tended, nurtured by Mother earth;
Coinciding with her natural fledglings birth;
Satisfying her every creative need.

He, the proud, expectant father, quietly musing
On her fruitfulness, encouraged her, by choosing
Delights remembered from her Mother's old home-place;
Sweet-William, lemon-lies, peonies; her face,
Tear-suffused, recaptured even happier days.
She sees each garden as another friendly farm,
Joining, branched from the road's narrow, brown-ribboned arm,
Valley-dissecting, to the town. Her bonds growing
In her new home-place, tending her gardens knowing
Both are miracles of Natures many ways.

Though grave-unknown, these many-long years departed,
The legacy left by her small garden, started
In joyful years, is shown on hillsides all around;
Confines burst, spreading, colour-carpets now abound.
If she were here to see her mind's eye picture,
She'd see the bounty wrought by half-a-hundred years;
Would know her presence lingers; would shed joyful tears
That fruitfulness, whose too-brief joys she'd tasted;
And careful-plantings of those years were not wasted;
Would know her valley's sojourn made it richer.
With each nodding daffodil I feel her presence;
A kinship with that country woman; an essence
Abounding, as the fragrance of foot-crushed flowers
Arises with each step. In the voice of showers
Each glorious Spring; every blossom-bending breath
Of breeze whispers her name; informs of her living
Still; she who laboured in this garden, giving
This valley extra life. It is almost as though
She knew she would be returning later. I know

She has indeed achieved a life after death.

Alf Edwards

BEING AN IMPROBABLE CONVERSATION OVERHEARD THROUGH THE HALF-OPEN DOOR TO A PREMATURE BABY UNIT

First Voice (high & clear)

They've gone now ... the Doctor and the Sister. Everything's quiet now...
Second Voice (Clear & high)

Yes, it's lovely to be quiet ... Warm, well fed, comfortable, almost as if you'd never been born

First Voice (Sadly)

Some babies are born wanted, some unwanted, some are just born, and some, like us, are born too soon

Second Voice (Cheerfully)

Yes, but we stand a good chance of surviving don't we? They've made great advances in the treatment of premature infants they say don't they?

First Voice
That's quite true. They can create conditions that are almost perfect, almost like those of our mothers before we're born. They can give us the right degree of warmth, piped oxygen, injection, blood exchange transfusions, tube feeding, everything necessary to make up for our premature births ...

Second Voice
And when our weight is satisfactory and general condition is good, they can discharge us to our homes

First Voice (Harshly)
And that's the rub ... Here we're kind of prisoners, but happy prisoners
Home is another kind of prison for some of us, cold, grimy, airless, sunless, a twilight area

Second Voice (Uncertainly)

159

But they send a Home Visitor to see if the conditions are suitable don't they?

First Voice
Oh yes, they do that, but the report has to be pretty bad to keep you here, and even then, you have to go "into care". They leave it largely to your parents to make the conditions suitable ... And sometimes that's impossible...

Second Voice (Fearfully)
Oh, I don't know anything about mine... Do you know anything about your home conditions?

First Voice
None of us know anything. It's called an accident of birth ... Some go home to a basement flat, some to a semidetached.

Second Voice
But if it's an accident why doesn't somebody do something to prevent it? What about the doctors and nurses? Their work will be wasted

First Voice (sadly)
Some don't even think that far Some do, but haven't the vision to tackle such a huge problem. A few, very few try to work in co-operation with all the other folk interested in environment, housing, education, to make it less of an accident and more of an opportunity

Second Voice
Somebody said children are the flowers of life ... but many a flower will never bloom if it's like you say

First Voice
That's true. Lots of babies are deformed or stunted, mentally and physically. Never expand, never reach their full height, never enrich the earth, are never unreservedly glad they were born ... Yet they could be, all of them, if only

Second Voice (Hopefully)
If only, if only what?

First Voice

If only the weeds of poverty and ignorance, exploitation and greed were wrenched from the soil of our environment ... Then every baby born could flourish ...

Second Voice (Joyfully)
And flower ... Flourish and flower.
(A pause - silence for a second)

Second Voice
Listen, listen, music, I can hear music. Can you?
(Softly very softly the strains of music are heard. It grows in volume, and the words become clear

"These things shall be; A loftier race than e'r the world hath known shall rise...

W. Froom (Mrs)

A GREEK TRAGEDY

It yawns there making me giddy, this huge hole
I blink my eyes and the strange unmoving figures,
grotesquely dead; move again.
Personifying death, Matrantonis kills his soldier, personally flattens
with
his tank the student, and the gates.
Inside; the Polytechnic runs with blood;
Rape and death and mutilation skip with torture through the streets,
Assemble in the World Cup Stadium, and refereed by F.I.F.A. enjoy
the game
with the captured brave.
U.S.A. and C.I.A. bland British F.C. and special branch, spectate and
cheer.
In Kraticon, the colonels emissaries burst in,
Chase and club the wounded through the bandages, who with democracy, die.
In the name of N.A.T.O. and world re-action, fascism solemnly seals
in
blood again, its firm resolve to enslave first Greece
And then you, and you, and brother you, and sister you.
Oh mighty Zeus bless these true sons lying murdered here,
And my comrade who Matrantonis killed, and with your bolts protect
those
who remain.

Frank Parker

PASSING THROUGH

He was polishing his shoes with fierce concentration, with short sharp light strokes, of the brush, his interest in this nightly ritual was so intense as to render him deaf to his child's repeated cry for attention.

"Dad, Dad, Dad?"

The woman sitting by the fire looked up. For a moment she gazed in si-lence, watching the arm moving backwards and forwards over the shining, well-worn leather. Her eyes were inscrutable. Her voice, when she spoke was tinged with a hint of scorn.

"He's talking to you" His head jerked up guiltily.

"What son? What do you want?" but the little boy had already vanished, his incessant questioning forgotten by the magic cry of "Cartoon" from the front room, where his two sisters were watching the television.

"You never listen do you?"

"I never heard him luv".

"He spoke to you three times."

He decided on retreat as the best strategy, and walked out into the back kitchen. He whistled as he filled the kettle.

"Where's the coffee luv?"

"Outside in the bin", she answered flatly.

She raised exasperated eyes to the ceiling as she heard him open the door into the yard.

"It's on the shelf, where it usually is, stupid".

"Sarcasm is the lowest form of wit, my love", he replied as he shut the door again. He hadn't really believed her. He was just playing along. He recognised the signs of battle, and he was a coward. It suited him to play this role tonight. Last night's repartee had upset him, so much that he had a whisky as soon as he entered the "Club", instead of leading up to it with five or six pints. Women, there was no understanding them. He worked hard, was always ready to lend her a few bob when she was stuck, took her out on Saturday night, yet she still pulled her face when he went out for a pint through the week.

The boiling of the kettle interrupted his indignant thoughts. "Do you want a cup luv?"

"No", her answer was short, but said more than it implied. Stick your rotten coffee, and don't come trying to get round me, you won't get a pat on the head. These thoughts chased bitterly round in her head. He came back into the room and sat down opposite her. He placed his mug of coffee onto the mantelpiece, and reached for his cigarettes.

"Want a fag?"

"No thanks, I've got my own." She had transferred three of his to her own packet, while he had been busy making the coffee.

"There's a good turn on at the club on Saturday."

"Is there?" She conveyed her lack of interest by not raising her eyes from the book she was reading.

163

"What are you reading?"

"A book."

He regarded her through narrowed eyes, and blew out clouds of smoke. He didn't speak. He recognised defeat. He decided to ignore her, but knew she wouldn't let him.

She didn't, for long. After a few minutes of silence on her part, and tuneless whistling on his, she raised her eyes and looked at the clock.

"You'll be late won't you, it's seven o'clock." She spoke dryly; she knew he didn't go out quite as early as this. What she meant was - Don't dare, and he knew it. If she had ventured to say this out loud, he would have retaliated, and dared, to prove that he was a man, and not ruled by his wife. She knew this, and thrust home her ironical comments, with a thinly veiled sarcasm, which didn't help the situation, but nevertheless made her feel better.

He didn't answer this comment. Hew was a shrewd man, and knew the value of silence at a loaded moment. Like so many women, she couldn't keep her mouth shut, even when she knew she was beaten. She would go down fighting. She justified acts of dishonesty - like the secret pilfering of his cigarettes with the fact that he had more than her, and if he could afford to go out drinking most nights, and she had to juggle with her housekeeping then this was justice. It was the class struggle, on a smaller scale. He was the party in power. Politics a wage war in most working class homes - money, struggle for survival, conflict of personalities, the don't do as I do, do as I say, policy of most parents (on a level with the Capitalists towards the workers). We are told money isn't everything, from those who have it, but this is a great asset, and would help bridge a gap, between classes. The bridging of this gap is feared by Capitalists. Children, unfortunately stand as the main, conflict between man and wife. How many women have said - Wait till the children are grown up - just watch me. Perhaps men secretly fear this, and while they hold the whip hand, however lightly the reigns are held, it will be a drop in status - once the birds have flown, and one should feel a certain amount of pity for the floundering party, who has brought about his own downfall.

After a considerable silence in which she escaped into her book of poems, and he smoked and watched her. Keeping an eye on the enemy, he decided it was safe to move. He rose from his chair and stretched. "What's up that you didn't have your usual after tea sleep tonight?" she asked.

"Oh for god's sake, shut up", he threw caution to the winds. She was secretly delighted at this retaliation. It was what she wanted. She couldn't change him, so she goaded him into displaying the worse side of his character. She was intelligent enough to see that these tactics lowered her own behaviour, but was past caring. She was developing into a nagging wife - an expression invented by men to hide their own selfishness.

Having delivered his parting shot he went upstairs for a bath, or thought he did. He bellowed from the upper regions of the house. "Who's had a bloody bath? The bloody water's stone cold, Christ it's four days since I had one, I'm supposed to have one every day y'know, of course I don't count, I only bring the money in - Jesus."

His disapproval was given greater emphasis by his feet stamping around the bathroom.

His wife, feeling that round one had been won, shouted sweetly up the stairs. "Mrs Jones next door said she's sorry you haven't been able to get a bath."

The bathroom door slammed. The front door opened, a head peeped round enquiringly.

"Is my Dad in?"

"He's just passing through luv, just passing through."

"Oh never mind."

Thus answered, but not enlightened, the head disappeared.

Jean Sutton

FRANCES THOMAS, now aged 9. Used to live in Walmer Street, Rusholme which is being knocked down. Now lives in Wythenshawe. These words are exactly what she dictated to me in answer to the question, "What do you want this story to be about then?" I have not added or changed anything, but perhaps two points could be explained:
"Ten bob winders" refers to a window shaped like a 50p. piece "Stashun dogs" = Alsatian dogs.
R.G.

WALMER STREET

House shop fish and chip shop bookies Pet Shop Motors Men - no women women! Winders getting smashed. Lickle girls going to bed. Mummies going to bingo, and all the houses are coming down. boys going to pubs. big men going to work. ten girls going to pubs with fellers -boys. Bombed houses + cellars + people goin in it. Bockles gettin smashed, lorries crash-in, people servin in the shops. big girls gettin dressed up. Red doors with

165

ten bob winders big girls ridin in the bike. Old men and women, Men drivin in cars an crashin (have we got that) Nice curtains in the winder. Green houses with pink curtains, blue door with blue curtains an green leaves. Dogs are gettin run over.

The men are just about movin in women wheelin a pram with no baby just shoppin. boys goin with men to pubs. boys goin to army cadets like my brother, black men with white girls, skies are blue and white an red sometimes. Clubmans like you get things off for the kids, like dresses and skirts and shoes and boots and high heel shoes and couch furniture and he comes in a green car and little girls washing dishes helping their mum. Old men ridin bikes, lickle black girls runnin to the Bendix and well have somebody lookin out, of the curtains - like somebodys just looked out. Chimbleys are smoking - that means the fires. we'll have white men going with black girls and we'll have driving in the afternoon and night and morning. (guess what Im on - 5a - Im in the juniors) lickle babies have dummies an we'll have one raggy man saying ragbone Like that man (pointing) he's a raggy man. An we'll have 430 on a car, an we'll have drunken men (man looks round sharply) -drunken men singin in the night carryin little girls. The men are kidnappin little girls an the women are cryin an the police have gone to find the kidnapper who has kidnapped the lick. girl.

Bricked up houses, doors open, women walkin by an cars running by + stopping on the main road. Boys runnin to the ice cream man, lickle boys about 10+11 will go to school tomorrow. Dogs birthday + the dogs about 1 2 or 3 yrs old. Stashun dogs come an bite you.

Frances Thomas

"CHILDREN" AND CHILDREN

A.S. Neill "There's no formula - I just approve of children."

Botty on potty
Every day try
Your beloved baby
Shall be clean and dry
By one"

Watch the child of one, a voracious explorer, a pioneer
All day he will gather information in his hands and mouth
By tomorrow he will have filed away the lessons of today
And be reaching for more, sensual antennae on full scan
No apprentice adult, no ignorant pupil in need
He is the unfurling bud of a noble being
Not made to be baulked by behavioural patterns that please
Wandering his own road, he will arrive safely
Not fool enough to take the motorway and miss the scenery
He discovers that buttons are inedible by eating them
He does not make abstract judgements on speculation

Spare the rod and spoil the child
Manners maketh man
Children should be seen but not heard
Monday's child is fair of face ..."

A seven year old who takes in the workings of genes
Listening with tense concentration to the paid out story
Discovers an intricate magic in the factual jigsaw
She searches the eyes of everyone she sees for proof
Of genetics in their criss-cross linking games
She follows a family's hairlines for Identikit sessions
And compares the wrinkles in the ears of her cousins
She describes penis and vagina easily, lovingly
Knowing the fundamental purpose of each, and approving
She finds the revolving earth cause for shouts of surprise
Grinning at the sun she has learnt the history of today
Squinting up skywards, trusting its omnipotence
Storks and Cabbages
Willie" and "Dicky"
Number one and Two
"Tinkles" and Wee-wees"

A child who is freely in love with her father and brothers
And loves the sex comfort she gets in her mother's lap
With its odours of warmth and fish-smell mingling
Will search diligently, with arched back, for her own vagina

And finding it, will touch and memorise its shape
Run to tell her mother that today's miracle is herself
And be the object of a family celebration

She will envy her brother his penis
For the prestige of the high-splash game
And the joy of aiming a jet with precision
Yet selflessly concede his greater need
Having an unblemished concept of father
She can love without wishing to possess
She thinks dirt is found in the garden, is good to touch
She has a map of her interior and thinks it a precious place
Blue and green should never be seen
Lovely darling, but what is it?
I'll show you how
But a man doesn't have three ears, dear!"

As with fireworks, hand a child a paintbrush and retire
You are too steeped in surviving, your awareness dulled
Of what it was to draw on and from the palate in your head
To offer guidance, that velvetest glove of conformity
The thickening buffer of your daily compromise disqualifies you
Stay your lying hand, only stand in privileged silence
Soak up what your moulded mind can absorb, and learn
Learn, that without a polite mask, the child is honest
Without a sophisticated vocabulary, the child can speak
Without the mystique of expertise, the child has confidence
And a courage he is unaware is vulnerable.
We were sharpened with blindness and ignorance
Twin weapons of our inherited oppressors
And we prick our road through wounded contemporaries
It's no mitigation for maiming our children
That they have no justice on call to deter us
From reconstructing our wretched egos in them
In them, who have the same singular flight that we aborted
To leave the deserted wrecks of our dreams
Sinking bitterly in bilious pools in our memories
We would well decoy our meddlesome fingers
Into reshaping, unlearning our own aimless ways

168

Away from patrolling our children's boundaries
Which, unguarded, would recede to infinity
They have only one life - their own.

Vivien Leslie

POEM FOR A GIRL FROM AFRICA

I don't know why I am writing you a poem
I am not in love with you - I don't even know you
They say you come from Africa
I have seen you run like a gazelle
They say you have the world at your feet
And I can believe it
You remind me strangely of someone I used to be
I was very young - even younger than my years
And I thought I only had to grow and bide my time
Till I was the greatest athlete the world had ever seen
I wanted to be Tarzan
Flying through the trees
Running through the jungle
Friend to all the animals
Keeper of the forest
And I thought I only had to grow
And bide my time

Living amidst the din of industry
Inside the darkened walls
Where machines rumbled
And dust filled the air
I was the urban gorilla
Hybrid of hybrids
Emerging from the gloom
And furnished rooms
And posters of last year's dances
Picking my way barefoot
Over broken bottles and rusted cans
A bear with a sore paw

Oh I had a mind too
That used to play the game.
With all the gravity of a joke
I knew how to fall
Into a yawning silence

And then I started to learn
And learning is the loss of innocence
I could show you where the paths led to
I could take you to where the trees grew
Please tell me,
Have you ever seen
An elephant's graveyard?

Yes, I learned where the trees grew,
Spring sadness in the big green leaves
That grow bigger and greener
Until the city is too small and grey to hold them
As well as a boy's dreams

So I travelled far and wide
Sometimes in the frozen north
Where my body ached with the cold
Sometimes there were mosquitoes and monsoon
And my body withered in the heat
Or trembled with the fever
Sometimes I slept on stones
Sometimes on branches
Sometimes on hard floors
I was not kind to my body
But I was young and I though
I only had to bide my time

But now I know better
You cannot be a strong man
As well as a runner
You cannot be a man of the jungle
As well as a man of the north country
Because in the land of the sun
There were insects that bit me
And I suffered and sweated
Until my body said, "No,
You are not Tarzan
He only exists in comics
You cannot be a black man
"As well as a white man."

So here I am again
Pacing the floor of my cage

They say you come from Africa
You have the white man's world at your feet
I have seen you spring like an antelope
In a white man's zoo

I suppose I just wanted to ask
If you ever thought of escaping

Rick Gwilt

CLEAN-UP JOB

Manolo pushed his Cleansing Department handcart through the empty streets. It was early morning and the only noise was a distant rumble of steel tracks, as a tank several blocks away rattled over the cobbles.

Every twenty yards Manolo stopped the cart and advanced with a hard-bristled broom, sweeping the rubbish into a neat pile in the gutter. Then he swept it into the handcart, using a battered old tin scoop.

Today's rubbish was different from usual. Naturally, there was the normal daily accumulation of cigarette ends, paper, straw and other debris, but there was additional garbage. Manolo looked sad as he swept spent rifle cartridges into the tin scoop. This was the debris of death and destruction. Broken glass, shattered wood from window frames, a dead black cat - caught in the crossfire, no doubt. Dozens of empty cartridges glinted in the early morning sun.

There was a woman's handkerchief lying in the centre of the street. It was embroidered 'CF' in gold thread, and stained with dark blood. Manolo picked up the pathetic reminder, a cold memento of human agony, and dropped it into the handcart. As it fluttered down, Manolo made the sign of the cross on his chest. God rest the soul of CF, whoever she was. But how could Manolo believe in a God in whose name this horror had been committed? It was not possible.

Manolo was a conscientious worker, and this sadness and despair was slowing his task. He dismissed his thoughts of the previous day's events, half-heartedly began to whistle, and swept with faster strokes of his broom.

It was only when Manolo arrived at the Plaza del Sur that he again took a pause. He stopped the handcart and looked at the body that lay in the gutter, his gutter. It was the body of a man, lying face-down, but Manolo recognised that old brown corduroy jacket.

171

Slowly, he approached the corpse and reached down to the head. Pausing a moment, as his fingers neared the short-cropped black hair, Manolo took a deep breath, heart quickening, and turned the cold face towards him. A large tear ran down Manolo's cheek. "Why this? he asked, softly, "Thy, Carlos, why?"

The corpse remained silent, but a voice spoke sharply from behind Manolo. "You Get up!"

Startled, Manolo turned, standing slowly to face the steel-helmeted soldier who pointed that ugly black weapon at his stomach.

"Did you know that man?"

"We drank together at the Bar Paradiso," replied Manolo. "What will I tell his wife?"

"Tell her not to associate with traitors in future". The soldier smiled, cruelly. He evidently found his own remark amusing. "Now get on with your work."

But Manolo was looking at the body of Carlos again. "Surely," he said, speaking slowly and deliberately, "Those who supported the President cannot have been traitors. The traitors are those who murdered the President, and are still shooting such loyal people as Carlos."

"You mean that the army are traitors?" asked the soldier, finger hovering over the trigger of his machine gun. "Well?"

"I don't understand what is really happening," answered Manolo. "But if it is true, as they are saying, that the army murdered the President, then - yes, I say they are traitors and assassins."

Less than half an hour later, Manolo sat in a large green lorry with twenty other prisoners, speeding out of the city on the main road southwards. He still clutched his broom, but was anxiously wondering about his handcart. When he was marched away, Manolo had left the cart in the Plaza del Sur. It was Cleansing Department property, and his responsibility. According to the sad-faced men around him, they were being taken to be shot. That would happen to his cart? The lorry turned off the main road, and bumped over a rough road, stopping near a clump of trees. Another lorry, empty, was just leaving the spot for the return run.

Juanita busied herself about the house, listening to the ancient radio on the kitchen table. She was pleased. It seemed that the fighting had finished already. So there would be no civil war, after all. Juanita was also pleased because she had a surprise for Manolo when he returned from work. It was his birthday, fifty-two years old, and she had bought him a scarf.

Yes, it was good that there would be no civil war. And the man on the radio was very reassuring. It seemed that the army knew what they were doing. But Juanita had no interest in politics. Whatever happened, whoever was in power, it could not affect her, could it?

Under the trees, Manolo stood at the end of the line of men, facing the ugly tripod, manned by a bored-looking soldier. Still clutching his broom, Manolo muttered to himself. "But it's Cleansing Department property. The handcart's my responsibility. What am I going to do?" He raised his hand to cross himself, but lowered it again without doing so.

The soldier braced himself for the recoil and squeezed the trigger.

Juanita turned off the radio. The news did not affect her, and there were more pleasant things to think about. Manolo would be pleased with his scarf. She polished the kitchen tiles and began to sing.

Gareth Thomas

AGITPOEM NO. 8 - BROMLEY

Along the tidy streets
are tidy lawns,
Beyond the tidy lawns
are tidy houses,
Inside the tidy houses
are tidy people,
Within the tidy people
are tidy minds,
Behind the tidy minds
are guns.

LEAVE ME ALONE!

I don't want to hear about the poor
(who are always with us, anyway)
- I had rather help the deserving.

Don't ramble on about democracy.
Firm leadership is what we need
- you can't change human nature.

Don't mention equality to me.
I am one of the elite.
My motto is "Noblesse Oblige".

173

Don't bother me about liberty:
I am for law and order.
Strong bars ensure our freedom best.

Don't shout at me about justice!
Whisper to me softly of charity and hymns.
God forgives us, fortunately.

PORTRAIT OF AN ECONOMY

Says the ivy
to the oak,
"BROTHERLY LOVE!"
- and hugs it close.

Says the leech
to the fish,
"PEACEFUL COEXISTENCE!"
- and clings the tighter.

Says the louse
to the dog,
FRATERNAL RELATIONSHIP!'
- as he drinks his fill.
Says the boss
to the worker,
"MUTUAL BENEFIT!"
and squeezes him again.

IDEAS

Ideas are awkward things:
only cause trouble.

We had an idea once
but it wasn't house-trained.
In the end we had to get rid of it.

Some of them will only go their own way.
You can't do anything with them.
Some never get domesticated
Or even tamed.

I had a friend who was savaged by an idea
That got out of control.
You wouldn't call them man's best friends
-exactly

They only cause trouble:
Galileo, Darwin, Marx - they had ideas
And look what happened.

You're better off without them altogether -
Live a cleaner, healthier life.
You have more money
And more - and better - friends.
Ideas come between people,
Destroy friendships and families
And set the hand of brother against brother.
They're awkward animals.

You have to admit - you're better off without them.
They only cause trouble.

Bob Dixon

A MATTER OF FORM

There were seven of them. They tumbled out of the underground train with a cheer, "Let's go!" Seven of them, their boots clattering up the elevator, shouting at the late night courting couple on the down elevator. "It's gone!" "Never mind you can always stuff her on the platform", - "After you mate!" Seven of them pushed past the ticket collector. "Get stuffed," - "We've all lost our tickets."

It was late. The ticket collector didn't argue. There were seven of them.

They burst out into the cold night air. "Up the gunners!" But the street was empty, just one car growling in the distance; otherwise the street, cold and damp, echoed their footsteps; the orange street lamps casting a smoke-like halo in the mist. The city like some mist-hung poem of desolation gazed back at them, empty and unyielding.

For a moment they all stood quietly on the kerb listening to the roar of the night. Filled for a moment with the sense of oppression and of their own insignificance, "Chalkie" the oldest, a red headed sixteen year old, half heartedly kicked a Coca-Cola tin along the gutter, its clatter for a moment breaking the stillness and the sense of loneliness, he quietly muttered, "It's a piss off isn't it."

Nobby shifted his feet, blew out into the night air and watched his own condensation. "Yeah you're not kidding." Nobody moved, nobody wanted to call it quits and go home. The whole evening had been a 'piss off'. They had hung about outside a disco. No-one had enough money to get in, but they still waited. Something might have happened to break the boredom. They had shuffled their feet and shouted at the girls going in, but nothing had happened; then of course the "fuzz" had come hustling them, telling them to either go on or "clear off" or they'd be done for loitering, so they went off wandering round the area, but it was all 'a piss off'; no money, nowhere to go, a right drag, so they had come back home before the tubes stopped running.

"Let's loon around for a while", said Chalkie. "See what's happening", He made off, walking slowly down the main street, the rest followed without a word. "Jumbo" punched a cigarette machine as he passed and Nobby fumbled in his pockets singing to himself:

> "Well yer mother don't care
> All right, all right, all right,
> And yer daddy ain't there
> All right, all right, all right."

A couple of the others joined in singing as they aimlessly wandered on. "Hey look fellas", Dave pointed at a notice on the wall. The others gathered round, more as a matter of form than of interest. The object of Dave's attention was one of the National Front's posters, showing a Union Jack with the slogan "SEND THEM BACK" printed in bold letters across it. Somebody had added at the bottom in pen "No Englishmans' jobs for black wogs."

"That's against immigration innit?" mumbled Chalkie, without much real interest. Nobby sang out "Black, black, send them back, white, white you're all right."

Chalkie, seeing a chance for a laugh sprang out of his trance and crudely imitating a West Indian accent carried on, "None of der lip man" and to a chorus of laughter from the others he flicked his lips, while Ken swung from a lamp post scratching underneath his arms like a monkey.

They left the poster and continued walking as Nobby explained about some Pakistanis living in his block:

"Yer, and this Paki grub - it don't half stink, don't it?"

"Not half", chipped in Jumbo, "They eat bleeding cat food, don't they?"

"Filthy bastards."

They carried on past the blacked out front of Woolworths with Nobby clicking his fingers and carrying on with:

> "All right, all right, all right,
> All right, all right, all right."

A police car drove slowly past, its occupants staring at the boys but it didn't stop, just driving slowly on, slipping along, down that desolate highway.

"Stinking old bill", muttered Jumbo beneath his breath, "Pigs off!" They reached Putney Bridge and began leaning over the side, peering down into the murky water of the Thames. Its inky blackness hardly showed any movement beneath them. Jumbo affected the accent of the middle class,

"Anyone for a swim chappies?"

Dave the blonde-headed one joined in.

"I reckon you could walk across that, they say that it's so polluted that if you fell in you would have to go to hospital."

Nobody answered. Their moods and interest in things altogether lacked consistency. Things interested them for a very short time indeed. They would buy a record and a week after they never listened to it. They would go and see "Clockwork Orange" and for maybe up to a month afterwards they would be wearing 'bowlers' and calling each other 'my druggie' then it would fade out to be replaced very quickly with something else. Nothing really meant anything. It was all a 'matter of form , as Dave the more philosophical of the group would call it. Things came and things went, different birds, different discos, different sounds flew past. It was all there to be taken or discarded as they wished and they did so wish. The only thing that was missing, somehow stolen, was their youth, but there was always something to replace it. But there were times, there were these moments of silence, when somebody would come up with -"It's a piss off innit."

They moved away from the side of the bridge almost shy of each other, awkward, with only the sound of their boots on the paving stones to reassure them. Nobby started clicking his fingers again, breaking the spell,

"All right, all right, all right."

Then they saw him, coming over the bridge towards them, a youth like themselves, maybe he was seventeen. He wore flayed trousers, a tartan cap and he walked with a brisk swing in his step. Like them he also probably thought it was a 'piss off', but unlike them, he was black.

Maybe if he hadn't done what he did, nothing would have happened. Nobby just rubbed his hands together. "Hallo, hallo", his voice was hard. The youth stopped in his tracks, the boys fanned out across the road slowly walking towards him. Then he did it. Without a word he turned and ran. The boys yelled triumphantly and with a thunder of boots on concrete set off after him. There was something self-hypnotic in the motion of running, their eyes became glazed and their nostrils spread, and a hatred flared up to an insane, almost sexual lust. "Black bastard!" they shrieked as they pounded after him. "Ba-aa-stard."

The black youth dived down some steps at the north end of the bridge, closely followed by the pack, but he took the wrong turn and found himself with his way blocked by the closed park gate. The boys found him terror struck, his eyes wide and white and his hands showing white as he held them up in front of himself. "No man please", he stammered. "That for you pick on me, I done you no harm."

"Gonna do you, black bastard", growled Jumbo, and he smashed his fist into the black face. "Stick the bloody boot in", screamed Nobby. They began to push and punch him. One of them snatched off his cap and threw it. It went into Dave's face. He caught hold of it and glanced down. It was wool, hand-knitted and still warm. It all seemed like some dream. He looked at the others as they pushed and punched the black bloke.

178

Suddenly they did not seem to be the same friends that he knew a few minutes ago. It all seemed to be like some slow motion film. Suddenly Dave thought to himself, "Supposing it was me, supposing I was being done by a load of black blokes. Supposing they were sticking the boot in on me. This bloke ain't got a chance, neither would I, unless of course ...

Sometimes, maybe only once in your life, you find yourself thinking and doing something you never believed you would do. You find yourself feeling something you can't understand. This was how it was with Dave. Suddenly it was so important for Dave to help this black bloke. His brain worked fast. The others had the black fella pinned against the fence and were going to boot him in the crutch.

"Hold it fellas for christ's sake", shouted Dave. He had to be careful. He didn't want the others thinking he was chicken or a wog lover. He had to play this one very shrewd, very shrewd indeed.

"Listen will yer, use your loaf", he shouted pulling back Jumbo.

"What's up with you", spluttered Jumbo shaking him off.

"Listen you fool", said Dave in breathless excitement. "Look", he continued. "The fuzz have just seen us, ain't they. Think man they'll do us good if we do this black."

"What's up then, chicken?" sneered Chalkie.

"Look", Dave feigned anger. "I aint gonna get a three year for any black bastard."

This sobered them, but Dave had to be careful. He pulled the youth towards him by his collar. He had to make this sound good, real good. "Listen", he breathed, "You filthy black scum - you go and tell your coon pals this: you'd better get out of this country and go back to the jungle see." He gave the youth a shove, "Get me? you tell 'em that - okay man?"

"Oh yeah man, I will man." The black youth sensed his reprieve at the hands of this white fella. It was more than he had dared hope for.

"Now!' shouted Dave giving him a shove. "Piss off quick!" The black youth ran off being given a parting kick by Jumbo. A couple shouted "Run black bastard, run."

They emerged onto the bridge again. "What you let him go for?" muttered Jumbo sullenly.

"Listen", answered Dave. "I don't like blacks any more than you do, but if I'm going to get jugged for doing someone I'll make sure that it's someone worth getting jugged for, see?"

179

"The police wouldn't have bothered about a blackie." mumbled Jumbo. But no-one said any more.

Dave thought, "Well that's true, the police don't give a damn if a black bloke gets beaten up." But he was satisfied. He had pulled off a good stroke, saving the black bloke's skin without losing face. Why he had suddenly wanted to save this bloke he had no idea, but he had to admit it, he felt somehow satisfied with life. Maybe he didn't really hate blacks, but it was all a matter of form.

They quietly walked back over the bridge, Chalkie putting his hands in his pocket. "It's a piss off isn't it?"

For once Dave didn't feel the same way.

Ian E. Reed.

STRUGGLE IDENTIFIED

Sing we the two young women, Angela and Lillian,
Daughters of the twentieth century; struggle its kernel,
They exist in struggle;
Which knows the conflict?

Swifter of foot; with implacable training
Will, muscle, sinew drive to the purpose
Straining alone against figures
Wink-add
Wink-add
Wink-add
Ing on the little screen
Passive the millions, approving complacent
Claiming my effort, M.B.E. in exchange.
Me dying they sigh for,
Collect for, enquire for
In vain; for my strivings are mine to the end.
The struggle one quick glimpse: black arms uplifted,
Swift retribution ... Hush! Do not mention.

Bolder my people; ruthless reaction
Surrounds my young living, murders my friends.
Keen calculation follows horrified anger
Seeking out causes, comparing, appraising;
Grim understanding supports young experience -

Class is the kernel, origin of struggle.
High is my courage and strong my intention;
Among victims I explaining their pain
Arousing the millions to knowledge and wrath.
Savage retribution from fear-ridden privilege
Confirms me a victim
Gaols
Threatens
Frames me.
Sigh for, enquire for, collect for me living;
Defeat the oppressors intent on my dying;
Force their retreat now, condemn their false trial,
Expose their injustice; resolute with me
Declare: 'I'll not be free until all are free!.'

Barbara Smith

THE BUILDING WORKERS' SONG

The employer we're fighting's a hard-working man
And to be an employer is his only plan.
With his hands in our pockets he's doing quite well
And his days in the workhouse ain't ended in hell.

CHORUS:
And it's no nay never, no nay never no more
Will we work with those lumpers, no never, no more.

I saw him this morning and here's what he said:
"You look like a Russian and you talk like a Red."
So put on your armour and sharpen your sword
And we'll show the bent bastard his offer's absurd.

CHORUS:

We'll remember your faces when we come around
And God help your hides if you've not paid the pound.
They tried a sell-out but we showed them how
There's a national strike on for all of us now.

CHORUS:

The Woodrows and Bisons have threatened the sack

But we showed those bastards that we know the crack

CHORUS:

So strengthen your pickets and tighten your belts
You'll be wearing your shoes right down to the welts
And watch out you lumpers and dodgers of taxes
The rank-and-file lads are out sharpening their axes.

Rod O Connor

NOW I'LL SHARPEN THE PENCIL

Now I'll sharpen this pencil
And muffle my mind
In a slumbering sequence
Of blanketed brimstones,
And roam the rich realm
Of midnight madness
Where flat-capped camels
Float free in the
Snow soaked blueness,
And chimpanzee chaplains
So churlishly chafe
Over Chinese checkers
While bicating their blessings
To far away flocks,
And belching banana
On faded frescos
And frowning fonts
Which fume for they're thinking
Of thousands and thousands
Of furious infants
Who watered the water
In protest.
Did those tender minds
See that priests are persons
Imprisoned in prisms
Of myriad mysteries
Where myrrh and mythology
Mingle in fumbling mumblings?
Did they picture the ape-men
Who rode the Sahara

For diamond dust date palms
On Flat-capped camels
Which sank to the sand
On the sabbath and sadly
Savoured the sanctification
Of serfdom?
Did their minds ferment
With the simplest yeast
When they sucked from their mothers
And peed on the priest?

"John Smith"

GREEN TOILET ROLLS TO MATCH MY BATH-ROOM TILES

The other day I received through the post
A letter from a most Reverend gentleman
Presently residing in Vietnam.

Kind friend" he writes
I wish to ask you for your support
For our missions in Kontum."

I am sure you would be happy to know
That we have now been able to order
Ten metal pre-fabricated buildings
For our second hospital."

Our doctor has already been working
For several months with 40 patients
In unsanitary mud huts
With more than 120 out-patients every day.
Our Nin-Quy Hospital is at present
Functioning in one of our Kontum schools
Until the damage to the buildings
In Min-Quy is repaired
And security is assured for our doctor
And her staff."

At Kon-Horing" he goes on to say
We have 220 children from 3 to 7 years
Crammed into shelters with few amenities.

The Sisters of St. Vincent de Paul
Are doing their best to care for them
But we badly need to improve their condition."
He ends with the prayer that
Peace will come soon to Vietnam".

I turned from that letter
To my morning paper
Looking first for news of Vietnam.
It spoke in terms of "Bloody murder
Against persons known
Printing as a bonus in horror
The copy of a letter sent by a soldier
In Vietnam to his mother in America.
Mama", he calls out in anguish
Today I shot 3 women,
It was kill or be killed
For they were armed with knives."

One of the women held a baby in her arms
It cried for its mother when she was shot
And I was ordered to kill it."

Mama, Mama, I could not do this
So my buddy obliged and blew the baby's head off.
The remains were thrown onto the fire
I watched them burn.
Mama, Mama, please tell me
What is right and what is wrong,
I do not know any more -

Suddenly in the midst of all this
You burst into the room
Completely unaware of course,
Of how the morning's intelligences
Had channelled my mood.
You expostulated
Well I'm fed up and that's for sure
I've tried and tried, and nowhere
But nowhere can I find
Green toilet rolls
To match my bathroom tiles.

Rose Friedman

THE LOST, THE LOSERS AND THE LAME

Crowds of people
are enormous cupboards
Shutting themselves in
Complete and secure,
While outside
Unobtainable and distinct
Lies the life
They vainly seek
To fulfil.
Each man
Remains his own
Jailer.
Ten thousand
Desolate souls
Desperately trying
To fit themselves into
The recognised holes
Before they become
known –
As the unclassified
and therefore
the lost,
Lost? lost to what?
Life,
Or the insane
Clanking engine
Of misguided effort
That hisses obscenely
And places itself
As the fulfilled
Destiny
Of the human race.

I.E. Reed

FEEL THE NEED - or See how the other half lives

Mr. Barber, Mr. Barber,
Will you come to tea.
Mr. Barber, you will feel the need in me.
You won't get steaks of sirloin,

Or after dinner wine,
But if you fancy mince and chips
Well that's just fine.
Please make it on a Friday,
That's when I get paid.
Are you any good at washing up?
We can't afford a maid.
If you're partial to an apple
When you've finished your repast
Treat it as a luxury
And make it last.
Then we'll watch the telly.
I hope you won't be bored

But with seven in the family
It's all we can afford.
A visit to the theatre
Would cost too much you see,
They've raised the price of
Tickets with this stupid V.A.T.
So if there is a programme
That you like to watch a lot,
I hope you've plenty of tanners,
The telly's on the slot.
So do come Mr. Barber,
And please bring Mr. Heath,
But tell him my husband is touchy
And he mustn't show his teeth.
Come share with us, we won't begrudge it
See how we live on your lousy budget.

J.E. Sutton

WHATCHA MEAN

Whatcha mean - tearing these entrails from the sausage man
Dripping fresh blood in the alley
Dreaming dreams of barren desert sands
Grasping at a comet tail
Just whatcha mean gloria?

Whatcha mean sucking me into your private dream barefoot
Soft like your labour that was not love

186

Reading about the walrus in its shell
Firing mallows into space
Just whatcha mean Gloria?

Suck Gloria
Herrick was right
Old time is still a flying ...'
And this same flower that smiles today,
Tomorrow will be dying...

I AM SORRY FOR THEM

I am sorry for them
But I am sorry for them
For they have lost
- someone beautiful
A quivering silk
A child newborn
- leave off your hammers
And run to the air
Breathe for Gloria
Nothing else should care
- leave off your shining plastic,
Tin-can world of reality, of jangling discord
- Come with us
Us, our dream
Our caress
Our biting tongues
Our warmed bones

Colin Frame

NEW SOUNDS OF MOTOWN

The happy coupon seller made a mint
wading through sunlight with his heart rolled up to his knees
hostile glances breaking like surf on his smile
the breeze rippling over his stomach no shirt
was it a streaker?...
no, was going to say
no shirt buttons
burst off on soup run
ran too fast?...

no, drank too much soup
before summer came
milk shakes and root beer
dry grass and warm stars
red sunset hanging on bedroom wall
out over the ocean

padding softly now
down the lines of cars
bare feet on hot tarmac
was it a hippy?...
no, shoes being mended
new uppers fitted
said his name was dylan
you mean it was ...
no, spelt dillon
came from detroit
to get away from the fighting
was it a draft doger then?...
no, not the fighting in vietnam
it was at general motors
not that kind of fighting, you see

ferry docks now
cars and lorries rolling off
dust and diesel fumes
dillon does not like
dives over fence and into forest
sits on carpet dappled shade and sunlight
chewing not gum
grass stalk
birds chirp rustle
unhurried hedgehog passes
single track beneath the bushes
no overtaking
dragonfly wings whirring
fern and foxglove growing
sounds of forever

cars in line again
standing at ease
chains and siren playing
not music
ferry moves off

afternoon sun hot on tin roofs
irritates passengers
not dillon
counts his change
half his coupons sold already
was it a lottery then?...
no, it was annual bathtub races
coupons in commemoration of
totally worthless
not even gummed on the back
but marketed by a leading citizen
who won considerable acclaim
For his spirit of enterprise
but if dillon thought that
no, he did not think
felt good
hairs rising on back of neck
sunsmiling down
business booms
at the front
the lady with the cadillac
still waiting
asks again
why he is smiling
and dillon gives her his last coupon
to sell
but she cannot undo her safety harness
and remains seated
behind her credit card
dillon smiles
and goes to look for
nanaimo girl ...

You mean this was real?...
real, yes
like a dream
he said
the arbutus trees
do they stay green
through the winter
underneath the fir trees
does it stay warm at night
knowing well the answer
the sun slipping away

towards Hawaii
end of summer
first chill in the water
he crossed
or the early morning ferry
said it was time
to stop dreaming

did he write to you?...
just a postcard picture of lake eerie
said it didn't show the poison
said he couldn't find a picture
of what it's really like
said he was lost for words
and smiles

i saw his photograph
in last week's paper
said he was a wildcat
was he?...
wild? no, not that sort
of wild
more like a bird
he just needed to be free...
that letter you were reading this morning
yes, he wrote to say
you may have read about this militant
pulling the power-switch
with a three-hundred man bodyguard
holding to ransom
general motors
taking orders for exports
forced to change our supervisor
well, next time
we may be nearer three thousand
and general motors
may be forced to take orders
from his own infantry
and start changing what's being supervised
but can you believe
we re just trying to get some peace
they won't let us breathe
please don't think i begrudge you
the new vega your father was buying you

someone's got to buy the goddamn things
and please don't expect poetry
from a sixty hour week continuous process worker
not yet
you see, i've realised
it's someone else's language
he always used to let me use
the parts he didn't need
but now the parts we need
he's using for something quite different
something completely unnatural
so we're beginning to question
what he's doing with our language
as well as our lives
was he always a bit of a trouble-maker?...
trouble? he was always
running away from it saying
they won't let me breathe
always used to talk about "me"
dillon
now he says
you wouldn't recognise me
there's a million of us
we can't all hit the trans-canada highway
now he talks about "us"
as if he's struggling
with the beginnings
of a new language

Rick Gwilt

GLASS IS DYNAMITE

*The new world shines through all the windows of the old one" Lenin I ded-
icate this to T.S.Eliot, Virginia Woolf and Joseph Conrad - wide windows
of the old world.*

Glass is dynamite.
In Hampstead on the hill even the bricks are made of glass,
And the books are prisms, primed with
His Wasteland
Her Lighthouse

191

His Sailors,
But the eyes that pass see themselves only.

Glass is dynamite down across the heath where only his solitary
Nightingale hears the cries from the stony deep,
Down beyond the ponds where the fisherman alone
Can enter the all-breaking sea,
Down, down into the grey ocean pitching with drowned young sailors.
In Hampstead on the hill only the bricks know
Of the terror of their drowning,
And only the books are dreaming of the drowned ocean.
The eyes that pass are waiting
To see themselves
Only.

The windows of the bookshop must be broken.

Now staring eyes -
His Wasteland
Her Lighthouse
His Sailors
Are escaping, down beyond the heath down into the ocean.

Can it be true,
This learned demolition-man
Cementing bricks
In the callous ocean?

Can it be,
Her fragile beam that's breaking
Into the fathomless worlds that lie between
The chanting waves of drowned young sailors?

Can it be true,
This reflection through the long mist
Of the wrecked imagination -
A figure rigged with sails that his mates have cleated
Standing out of the pitch-black sea?

And the fisherman stands as the voyage begins
And the nightingale stops to hear the song
Of the new Magellan.

An adumbration
Of versing young sailors,
Kindling
Out of the stony rubbish
Live lilacs.
Back on the hill they're growing vines
To hide
The bricks of Keats' cottage,
But the windows are exploding.

David Kessel

CHILE

What has happened to this distant flower in my now wounded side, redo-
lent
Of ecstatic childhood dreams held briefly on walking? The aroma
And the death cling to my visions like clay, and the corpses
Throw up mountains from the plains; such anguish from their peaks!
The stalks of the grass seem to bleed with the arrogant murders;
Their very green bruised and trodden into my heart.
The desert winds blow dry, and now there are no copper hands smiling
With the grip of the burnished hope of their labour. The sweat of work
And fear beneath a sun no longer tempered by the arguments of men
Together. In the snow the cold is definitive, frigidity conquering icily.
Even the great ocean, that seemed all waves and horizons, has closed
around it

Mist in my eyes. Does only the nomad gull bear Chile's tomorrow now?

The city skyscrapers guard the sky with forbidding patriarchy:
High altars of the laws of capitalist order, that can stop the sun.
The Conquistadors didn't, but Chileans in Cadillacs may! Can they give
Mercy, despite their desperate fear of change, of slums, and of the
dawning
Power of people?

The people must work still, but can never forget this insult hewn,
Into the deep-felt mine of their consciousness, by military
Gods, in arms against the transformation-bound workers.
Congealed sweat and blood unite them, and their art of survival - profound
Collective memory of how they only are able to turn the cogs of wheels.
Instrumental

As is their struggle, which still may yield the Heaven of all our History.
What can intimidate these who live by sacrifice, and are
Within each other?
The land and the peasant who labours are the spring of all creation.
Into her hoed furrows he kneels to feel the kind soil.
Together they nourish the sources of all our dreams, and tyrannies!
What madness is it to divide them by landlordism?
He, who cannot help loving the soil, now fears to tread it;
His toil respected like so much cast-aside rock, and his anguish
Fires his brain to radiant anger! A peasant's vision -
His Christ, nailed at long last between his eyes,
Forever in him blinded by a bullet.

Now his light is penetrating numberless brains. Determination
Wrought in me also, when the slain man turns and smiles
In a London street.

A crowd made into a people by duty and love" Neruda

David Kessel

RANDOM THOUGHTS OF A TELEFAN

The other day our earnest B.B.C.
Held a symposium on morality.
Must it, they asked, have a religious base,
Or can the atheist show a moral face?
Religion's curb, 'tis said, is badly needed
In case our moral teaching goes unheeded.
A pious don with Christian point of view,
An atheist of quite a different hue -
These two, restraining each his inward passion,
Set forth their views in gentlemanly fashion.
One point in all their complicated stuff
Struck me as being an arrant piece of bluff:
An atheist?" said the Christian, "You can't claim
To take that title - you are much to blame -
You cannot prove there isn't any god."
Such argument indeed is very odd,
For even the Christian spokesman made it clear
He cannot demonstrate that god is here;
He has no proof in solid black and white,
With Q.E.D. of logic, that he's right.
Unshakable belief, that's his delight.

194

Belief, not proof, is all that god can ask,
And even that is quite an uphill task.
His own opinion's all that each affirms,
However much the other fellow squirms.
But yet, amid these tentative surmises,
Undoubtedly a deeper point arises:
To argue whether x exists or not
Is like investigating - heaven knows what!
Some rough idea of what x seems to be,
Some hazy sketch of this uncharted sea,
Its qualities, its shape, its thought, its acts,
Some inkling of what seem to be the facts,
Would greatly help us to resolve our doubts
And weave our way through all these ins and outs
Of whether god exists. God = x,
This dark equation cannot but perplex:
God undescribed, unknown, and undefined
Is meaningless to any thinking mind.
But if you say: "The god that mankind need
Is here, enshrined within my Christian creed",
Id try to prove this god cannot exist.
My atheist views will therefore still persist.
Yet, my good friend, I would be very loth
To leave no crumb of comfort for us both -
I'd hate indeed to leave you broken-hearted,
So let's take up the point with which we started.
Neither the Christian creed you think so true,
Nor the ungodly way which I pursue,
(As adumbrated in this modest rhyme)
Will set us on the primrose path of crime.
Maurice Wiles

SOLID GLEAMING COAL

The Miners' dispute reminded me of the occasion a few years back when Les said to me "Would you like to go down .... Pit?" I jumped at the offer.

We arrived at the manager's office towards midnight. The others had brought working clothes and boots with them. I hadn't, so the manager rigged me out with everything, except boots. We went to the baths and there changed. We then went to the lamp room and were given helmets, lamps and I was given a walking stick. We walked to the lift cage. The manager had a word with the man in charge of the lifts - Les said it was to tell him to take the lift down gently because of me.

We got into the cage, the bar was fastened and I, in my innocence, leaned in relaxed manner against the side of the cage. All of a sudden, I felt as though the floor of the cage had been removed and that I was falling through space. I was catching my breath. Within seconds my feet were pressing against the floor of the cage and then a slow, gentle descent and stop. As we got out of the cage, we were met by the night overman, who frisked each of us for matches and cigarettes. This completed, the manager said he must 'phone the surface before we proceed to the coal face, and so we went into the pit bottom office.

As we entered this small office with its telephone exchange, a man came forward with a sock over his right hand, whereupon the manager said: "Ah! you're Mr....how is your hand?" The man answered: "Alright". "Let me see it", said the manager. The man peeled off the sock, then a cloth mitten, then a white covering. There displayed was a distorted hand with white and pinkish patches. I became conscious of extra pulses in my stomach. Being of a squeamish disposition, I wanted to turn my head away, but I couldn't.

I was mesmerised. My thoughts started racing. I could see the man's hand between two pieces of rock-like coal. I saw the man's face distorted with pain, his eyes bulging, the sweat started on my face.

This seemed a long time, in fact, it must have taken a couple of minutes, for the conversation was diverted from the hand to the fact that the man had not yet got his shilling through. Evidently, he had been receiving twenty seven shillings per shift at the time of the accident and was now receiving twenty six shillings - the rate for the job he was then doing. The manager promised to take it up.

We started walking and I immediately felt better. We walked a short distance and then got onto an underground train. We must have travelled for half or three quarters of a mile and then it stopped. We stepped off the "train" and started walking. Loon I was lagging behind, every now and then either Les or the manager would glance round to make sure I was following. Now and again they would stop until I caught up with them, and with a "Are you alright" they would start off again. All the time they talked. Soon the sweat was running down my face, running into my eyes and mouth and making my shirt collar wet. I wanted to get my handkerchief out to wipe my face, but I couldn't manage it. We were walking in blackness except for our pit lamps. We were walking on a road of broken stones and my thin soled shoes felt as though they were pierced with every step I took. I had to keep up the pace if I was not to lose sight of them. I was feeling the weight of the helmet increase with every step. The sweat was getting unbearable. Somehow I found I could not use my hands. I could not place the walking stick in the hand that carried the lamp, the moment I attempted to do it I felt an imbalance. I felt I was going to fall. I was trying to do this whilst marching along that rough road, with hazards that had to be watched for.

What a relief when I saw the lights at the end of the road. Two and a half miles from the pit bottom Les said.

The coal face What a surprise, seven feet high and fifty yards wide, twenty five yards either side of the road. Gleaming solid coals A small number of miners were working on the night shift preparing for the day shift. We turned to the right and went about twenty yards and sat down in front of the face. I was furthest away from the road, next to me sat Les, then the manager, then the overman and the nearest to the roadway was the union Branch Secretary.

It seems that the normal mining practice is not to take all the coal out of a seam, always a certain amount is left attached to the roof, because coal creaked and therefore, warned of the danger of a roof fall, whereas a stone or rock roof fell in without warning. In this unusual seam of coal the roof was perfect and therefore, there was no danger of a roof fall and all the coal was extracted. Now, the argument was that as the men were getting an extra foot of coal along the whole seam, they were entitled to extra money, they were asking for two shillings per shift.

The argument went on. I sat and listened, I watched the men at work in the roadway and on the other side of the roadway. I looked at the back of me and saw the props holding up the roof, saw the piles of props, shovels, picks, and other equipment the day shift would use. Suddenly, I felt a bit faintish, there was something wrong about the air. I was beginning to feel that there was not enough of it. After a while I nudged Les and said: "Lea, I don't feel too good." He turned to me and said: "Won't be long now." The manager heard this exchange and took a look at me but they continued talking.

Suddenly I turned to Les and said: "Les, I'm going to faint." Before Les could reply, the manager stood up, took me under the arm, helped me up and propelled me along over the loose lying lumps of coal to the road-way where two big, fine, strapping lads were using shovels, at least eighteen inches square, and called on one of them to help him and between them they lifted me over a moving belt and onto the roadway. The young miner walked me about twenty yards down the road and lowered me to the ground with my back against the wall. I began to feel the flow of air. I quickly revived.

I breathed deeply as we left the cage at the pit top, but could not help saying to myself "Poor sod, for twenty seven shillings per shift - he'll never use that hand again."

- like millions of others, was born, and died completely unaware how great he was.

Mick Jenkins

CHILE

I can see the dirty smile,
On the clean face of the radio news-reader
While he said, "Allende is dead"...
With his clean voice he said,
The Junta had no choice but to wipe out the man,
Who had made such a mess of the economy."
And thousands more have had to die;
And shall I try to justify
This peaceful Marxist's path?
I weep in anger, seethe in rage,
That in this age, the man that's put up front,
Should be so mild and trusting of the enemy.
So easily killed by the killers, that he let walk so free,
And free to make a bloody pool
Of Allende's blood, The bloody fool.
But not so bloody foolish,
For he won the bright-eyed love
Of many thousand workers, and their children,
And their wives, in the way he changed their lives.
They loved the Marxist massive love of masses;
But now he has been put down, by the greedy few
With guns. By the unadmirable admirals, and by generals
Who, in particular, represent, more or less,
No one, but the small men, who own big business;
Both Chilean,
And American.
Sol Garson

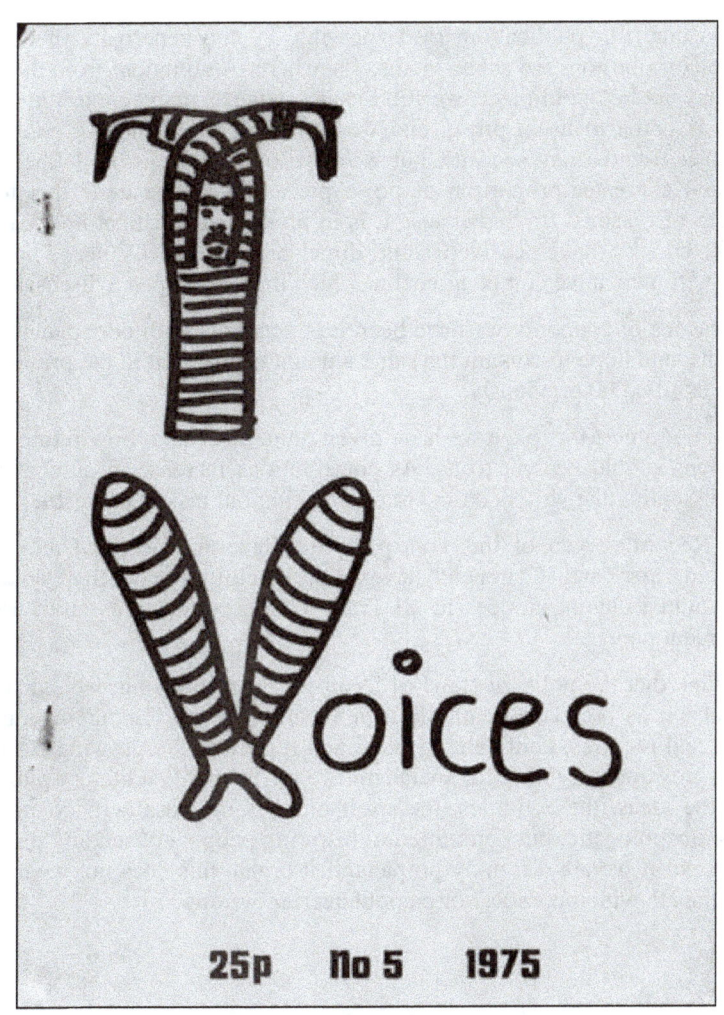

cover size 296 x 210 mm

EDITORIAL NOTE

This is our fifth publication, made possible by the generosity of donors whose contributions we acknowledge elsewhere. A comment from the editors may not be out of place. we still receive twice as many contributions in verse as come to us in prose: and we welcome the chance of receiving whatever friends may send us: but we have on this occasion deliberately included a greater proportion of prose pieces. We have done this for a number of reasons: firstly because it is in prose that a critical note can be struck, and we have received some direct criticism of "Voices" and its aims, with which we do not agree, but which may well open a discussion.

For reasons of economy we have been less generous with our spacing and margins, and hope to contain the same amount of material in the present 48 pages as filled 60 previously.

At the bottom of this page we have given guidelines as to how future contributions should be sent to us. As contributions increase in number it is quite essential that writers co-operate in making our task manageable.

"The Record" organ of the Transport and General workers' Union, the "Morning Star" and "Comment" have all been helpful in noticing "Voices". We would welcome notices in all Trade Union publications and Labour movement papers.

We think that the political stand of "Voices" is crystallising: we still want to make it as broad and catholic a publication as the Labour movement wants and requires: confident, critical, and reflecting the growing struggle of the movement fighting for socialism. we are primarily a literary publication: the ideas, the activities, the spirit of working class activity, pugnacious, unapologetic, but committed to inspiring people not sending them to sleep; and if we are a frankly propagandist organ, this does not mean that we compete with theoretical or pamphleteering writing.

B.A.

TO INTENDING CONTRIBUTORS

We welcome poems, articles, stories, for consideration. We promise considerate and careful reading of them. We cannot possible acknowledge every piece we receive, but we will return unselected contributions provided a stamped addressed envelope is enclosed.

Material should be sent to us written or typed on one side of the paper only. The writer's name should appear on the first sheet, and sheets should be numbered. Please keep a copy of your material.

Address material to "Voices", B.Ainley, 13 Victoria Way, Bramhall, Stockport.

S.O.S VOICES 5   Our Appeal in November

With an utterly empty purse to begin the publication of "Voices 5" we put out our appeal for £150. By December 18th we had received £139.50, and the issue of "Voices 5" is assured. We did not acknowledge every donation individually: it would have cost us a precious two pounds. This is a complete list of all donors (to December 18th) and we are very grateful to all of them.

D. Lawson £1
Ray Watkinson £2
May Ainley £2
Ben Hodkinson £5
Frank,Fanny Morgan £1
Julia R.Murphy £2
Bill Eburn £1
Brian Simon £5
Alan,Lesley Fowler £1
Hilda, Jud Cohen £2
Ron,Dominique Hughes £2
A. Morris, M.P. £1
Frances L.Moore £5
Kathy Levine £2
John,Sue Bromley £1
Mervin Rowlinson 50P
Moira O'Shea £2
Brian Latham £2
Beverley Robinson £1
Norwest Coop Soc.Member
Nat Union Sheet Metal Workers (Surrey) £5
Emily Sheldon £1
Bill Laithwaite £10
Ruth and Eddie Frow £2
Bessie Wild £1
Daphne Morgan 50P
Ray Hartman £1
J.M. Hawthorn £1
B.G. Smith £1
S. Garson £1

Ivor Montague £2
Rose Friedman £5
Pat Sentinella £5
Mick Jenkins 50P
Rick Gwilt £4
M.J.Pooley £2
Brian Thompson £10
A.D. Clegg £2
Dr.Sheila Abdullah £2
David Kessell £3
Relations Dept. £5
Angela Tuckett £1
Tony Casson £13
Shaun Hogan £1
Winifred Froom £1
Joe Bishop £1
Bob Dixon £1.50
C.R.Morris,M.P. £1
M.G. Askell £1
Bernard Barry £1
Charles Bescoby £1
Leon Kaiserman £5
Peter D.Rodda £2
Frank Allaun,M.P.£2
Jean Sutton £1
Gillian Cronje 50P
Jane Leighton £5
George Morton £13
Aubrey Garson £1
AUEW(Mcr) £2
Rose Friedman(2)£1

CONTENTS

205. It's all Your Fault   E Wales
205. Brown Windsor Soup   Frank Parker
210. The Drunk   J Wilmot
210. For Better or For Worse   Bill Eburn
212. The Duttons of Martha Street   Jean Sutton
213. Next Time   A.M.Horne
213. Pablo Neruda   Ian E Reed
217. All Awry in Paradise   W. Froom
218. The Shipyard Cranes   A.M Horne
218. Changing   Pat Sentinella
219. A Very Special Brew   Ken Lilley
220. Written on International Women's Day   Ruth Frow
221. Tonight we will see the Dream-Drenched Drunks   Colin Frame
221. Rossendale Weavers Union Women Members   Jim Garnett
222. God Can't Care, Really   Bob Dixon
222. Death-Bed   Bob Dixon
223. Communication   M G Askell
226. Poetry and the Class Struggle   John Salway
227. We Came Crying Hither   Sue Cole
227. The Clothes Peg   Gareth Thomas
229. Eyes   Bob Dixon
229. You See Me Smiling?   David Tatford
230. Vigilante   John Salway
231. Nickname on a War Memorial   Rose Fiedman
233. City Boy/Brown Baby   John Gowling
234. Awakening   Betty Crawford
235. Win with Labour   Jone O Broonlea
236. A Book at Bedtime   Mick Jenkins
237. Rue   Jone O Broonlea
237. August 1945   Crispin
238. Boys & Girls Come out to Play   CJ MacVeigh
238. Self Made Man   John salway
239. Winter's Beach   AM Horne
240. Surgeon who Lost Son Indicts Killers   Patrick Lane
245. No Flowers in May   Robert Moore
245. Blues   Frances Moore
247. Trellie   Ken Clay
250. To a Lancashire United Bus   John Gowling
251. Black and White   Bob Dixon
251. Ressano Garcia   Barbara Smith
253. The Unmarried Mother-A Personal Experience   Vivien Leslie

259. The Living Seed   Angela Tuckett
259. Points of View   Maurice Wiles
262. Exploitation   John Salway
262. Black Sheep   Jone O Broonlea
264. Traffic Lights   Gareth Thomas
265. Luvin' Tally   Jone O Broonlea
265. 4th November 1974   MG Askell
268. In Praise of Cooks   Angela Tuckett
269. A Few Observations about Voices   Ken Clay

IT'S ALL YOUR FAULT

So there's something wrong with the economy?
We're to blame Jock, Geordie, Taffy and me.
We're greedy bastards, they tell me,
Out to wreck the Fair Phase 3.
In Phase 2 we had a pound and four per cent,
Now we wonder where it all went.

But you're richer now", our guvnors say,
So let's have some "British Fair Play".
Your share of the cake is getting larger,
You turn around, another merger.
Your job is gone, and so's your money,
The guvnors say, "Now ain't life funny".

BROWN WINDSOR SOUP
Frank Parker

Heyhey trembled under the onslaught of chemical changes in his body provoked by the alarm signals from his brain triggered off by his assessment of the realities of what he was seeing.

Beebe, almost another self, beautiful, complementary Beebe stood very close, smoothing his suddenly hot forehead with her cool, practical hands.

On the computers screen was a visual impression of the data they had fed into it. They saw a man and a woman. The man looked like Heyhey, the woman like Bee.

'With our genetic structure, future humans will not show any physical difference", commented Heyhey.

"No", agreed Bee. "You disappointed?"

"I suppose I am", he admitted, relieved too.

"It's not conclusive", Bee pointed out.

"No", said Heyhey, "But it is logical. As we are now, do we want to be different? Does any human being apart from superficial changes like height, features, hair, mere fashions?"

"I know none , said Bee. "Yet we could choose to be different", said Heyhey."

"But what for?" said Bee.

"We could have wings", said Heyhey smiling.

"We got wings , said Bee, "We've got everything known in the universe. We can fly like birds, dig like moles, do everything, and better."

"Yes, said Heyhey. "This is the crux of the matter."

"You're on about progress again; about stagnation, aren't you?" asked Bee.

"Yes", said Heyhey thoughtfully, "So is the government.

"What will they make of this?" she asked.

"I don't know", he said, "But this could be a crisis. When new purposes are needed nothing inspires more confidence than new people to pursue them."

"And this is the old people?" she ventured.

"Precisely, he said, then added "Mugshots".

"Pardon?" she asked, puzzled.

"Mugshots", he repeated, his eyes showing amusement.

"You've been reading western books again", she accused.

"Mugshots", he laughed. "F.B.I. talk for pictures, press the button Bee and we'll send 'em a picture. Dutifully, she did.

"Blow 'em up?" she asked.

"Got your own back there", he said. Putting the four foot pictures between sheets of stiff thin chemical fibre, they left the centre.

This was the premier city, leading the way in anti-pollution measures, so the air was clear and clean, as were the buildings old and new, set out to give much space for gardens and wide pavements.

They were to give the photographs to Cea who would pass them along to interested people in the government.

Bee thought her a nice old lady. She had old world charm, wasn't brash, as Bee was inclined to be and most modern youngsters. She had an air of sad tranquillity, was very serious.

"Being born before the revolution probably made her that way", said Heyhey. "They had a bad time

"But they had purpose, aim - a whole new world of ideas to conquer as well as country", said Bee.

"You discontented Bee?" asked Heyhey.

"No", she said. "But it does get dull at times".

206

"You have your work", he said.

"Sterile.," she said.

"Sterile?" he echoed. "You can't say that. No modern state can exist without forward planning, and our work on need estimation and our fundamental research on the nature of change, especially in man, is real exciting stuff."

"All in the air", she scoffed. "It's philosophy. I'm not old enough to bother about it; I just want to live, excitingly".

Heyhey looked at her, very seriously. I didn't know you felt like this," he said.

"Well," she said equally seriously, "You've been busy."

"So have you," he said, 'With me on the same projects."

"There is a difference," she said. "When I go home I forget about work, you don't."

"Ideally there shouldn't be a difference," he said. "One phase should blend with the other."

"Be inter-connected?" she put in.

"Don't she believe it?" he asked.

She pouted, a new phenomena he noted. "Yes," she said discontentedly."But I don't feel it; my senses are not in the correlation."

"You're jaded Bee. What would you like to do tonight? Anything you like, you choose."

"Nothing appeals," she said. "I'm depressed."

"Then we'll stay in and talk it out," he said.

"Nothing to talk about," she answered.

"There must be," he insisted. "There is no effect without a cause, work that out and we can find a cure."

"Let's get out," she said defiantly. "To the U.S.A. - somewhere like that."

Heyhey was shocked. "To live't" he asked.

"Yes," she said emphatically.

"You don't know what you're saying," he told her. "No thing is predictable in these countries, anything can happen to you. You can be mugged or murdered. Find yourself unemployed. In prison for no reason at all. It's all dirt and filth."

"It's living," she replied. "Precisely what you said. It's unpredictable day by day, hour by hour. When did I last know fear or uncertainty? Relief or horror? All these are words to us. We never feel any of the natural animal emotions."

"Who wants to?" he said.

"I do," she said hotly.

"That's regression," said Heyhey. "I never thought you would put what is after all mere titillation before solid intellectual satisfaction."

"I don't," she protested. "But this life is too artificial, too regulated."

"You are arguing against civilization," he accused.

"I'm not," she replied. "Just too much of it."

"I don't know what to say," said Heyhey. "I thought we were alright. Obviously we are not. You'll have to work it out for yourself. All I can say is don't just suffer; at least use your training to solve your problem. For me? I stay and carry on as I am."

They journeyed the rest of the way in silence. At the super-stores, they bought their needs for the evening, on their salary not needing to count cost.

Their home was a spacious, five roomed apartment, the kitchen as modern as any in the west.

Beebe set the table whilst Heyhey cooked; neither ate with much show of enjoyment.

Watching ballet on T.V. Beebe commented bitterly., "Why no alternative? Why only one channel? They have 20 or more in the U.S.A."

Heyhey made no answers, but his enjoyment was spoiled. He took a book and went to bed. Beebe came to see him, a little pensive, but the bug had bitten too deep. Her mood was not a passing one. Looking back he realised she had shown symptoms for some time now.

"We can take time off," he said. "Let's go to the cottage in the forest. That's back to nature. Re-charge your batteries. Might help you finalise your thoughts. Agreed?"

She nodded and got into bed beside him. "I'd be sorry to lose you," he said simply, holding her close.

Zee looked at the picture dispassionately. "What's the time scale?" he asked.

Dee scanned the typescript that Heyhey had given Cee with the picture. "400 years," he said.

Zee looked disgusted. "Why do you bother me with this sort of thing?" He handed Dee back the picture. "The business of government is the present and foreseeable future," he added. "And this is hardly in that category."

Dee felt anger. "I am not alone among scientists who are very concerned about this projection," he said.

"Well I'm not," said Zee, "But if it makes you happy I'll pass it on to the highest authority, perhaps he'll show more interest."

"That's all I want," said Dee, handing back the picture.

Zee, as the deputy in charge of science in the federal government was answerable only to the president. He was surprised by his reaction, for he laughed.

"Mr. President?" he questioned.

"I don't believe it," said the president.

"I never even thought about it," said Zee. "It seemed so immaterial."

"I wouldn't say that," said the president. "A bit academic, yes -interesting if you do think about it. The colour? what is their basis for that assumption?"

"The basis for it all,' said Zee, seems to be that the tendency for all nations to live in similar conditions, food, housing, general environment, will lead to a genetic similarity."

"Take longer than 400 years," said the president.

"They point to other factors," said Zee. "With the breakdown of racial prejudice, they believe that there will be a complete international integration."

"All races mix?" asked the president.

"Yes," said Zee.

"Like mixing paint," said the president. "I'd have thought the colour would have come out like a light brown Windsor soup."

"Like you Zee, I believe it all is pointless. Now is not the time to decide what mankind should look like. Some day perhaps. With a world government; with all man organised under socialism: perhaps then that sort of decision would be possible. Now? It's difficult to live in peace with your next door neighbour without trying to get world accord on what the next generation of humans should look like."

THE DRUNK

He sat so, quite all alone, within that smoke filled room,
The only company was his own,
Which gave him much more gloom.
He drank a glass of pain he had brought from
The battle that raged at the bar;
It quenched his thirst relaxed his thoughts
And made him just want more.

The evil eyes surrounded him
They scanned the rotting flesh,
Looking round ignoring them
The drink rang through his breath.
Fumbling hands inside his coat searching
For a cigarette
Just might provide an antidote for fears
He can not forget.

So deep in drowning sleep he fell
As on the floor he lay
The heavy boots just gave him hell
The numbness wears away.
Two pick him up, the landlord shouts
They all agree, that's right.
Losing another round in life's endless bout
He's thrown into the night.

J Wilmot

FOR BETTER OR FOR WORSE

Whether it's her age
or the change
I don't know;
But she does go on a bit.

He's not been the same

Since the kids left home;
I suppose they'd had
Enough of it.

I sometimes wonder
Whether he's found some chit
That he stays out so late;
He's such a hypocrite.

Next year when I retire,
She'll be all over me;
I tell you straight
She's no light weight.
Whether it's his age,
Or just a phase
I don't know;
But I wish he'd snap out of it.

Bill Eburn

THE DUTTONS OF MARTHA STREET
Jean Sutton

Once upon a time, there lived a nice family. At least they were individually nice, but unfortunately they lived together, under the same roof, and that was bad.

Mr. Dutton was a nice, kind man, who loved his family, and hoped they loved him too. His motto was 'Absence makes the heart grow fonder', so every night he went out. He had a keen competitive spirit. Every night he entered a strange competition with a lot of other men, they drank glass after glass of liquid, which rotted their innards, caused double vision, and produced a visible effect on the stomach, and the end of the nose, but this was living, and without this stimulation, Mr. Dutton was a sad, sad man.

Sometimes, Mr. Dutton stayed at home. This was a great occasion, but bewildering, and the children rejoiced by being as noisy as possible, and Mrs. Dutton nagged by asking him if he was enjoying his night in. Occasionally there was great chaos, when Mr. Dutton shouted, and they all tried to jump onto the shovel at once.

Mrs. Dutton was a normal? happily married woman with no skin on her fingers - just bones. She wasn't born this way - it was a condition produced with hard work, and she was always telling her family this. Mrs. Dutton suffered from ill-health. Three or four times a day she felt sick, but, belonging to a large family, she did not have to suffer alone, so she told them all about it.

The Dutton children were normal children. At times-nice-nasty-loving-hateful-truthful-selfish-helpful and sneaky, etc. As Mr. and Mrs. Dutton also shared these characteristics it was one big, happy family, well interesting anyway. We will pick one of these traits at random - sneaky. When Mr. Dutton was sneaky, he would squeeze behind the wardrobe to count all his money, and could be heard laughing to himself. When Mrs. Dutton was sneaky, she would hide behind the washer scoffing all the fresh cream.

The eldest Dutton child was light-fingered, and was apt to swipe every comb and pen in sight, and also jump the queue in the fortnight waiting list for baths. The eldest boy liked to sneak off whenever there was a job to be done. He is allergic to work and the mention of a shovel of coal causes acute hysteria.

The three youngest indulge in group sneakiness, carried out mostly at night, one instance being reading Mr. and Mrs. Dutton's love letters. This pastime also induced hysterics. As you can see they are a very hysterical family, perhaps inherited from Mrs. Dutton who sometimes likes to throw a cup or a plate on to the floor, which she immediately sweeps up, showing an industrious and tidy streak, also a twisted enjoyment of self inflicted punishment. One night, Mrs. Dutton was left completely alone in the house. This was by way of a treat for her shattered nerves. Her system couldn't take the unusual silence, and she was almost driven mad.

Next day the family made it up to her, and gave her another treat. They took her for a nice drive in a car. They drove her to Winwick.

Which proved Mrs. Dutton a woman of great insight.

NEXT TIME
A.M. Horne

Perhaps the next time or the next or the next
But not now, no not now,
The face of death is an image,
And the image only dots
Thousands of bloody silly dots
A statistical droll from eloquent lips,
An obscenity on an Oxfam poster,
Placards grasped by pimples and hair
The tears of the world trickling over a screen,
An illusionary glimpse of somewhere else.
It's not mine, I can switch off,
In fact I usually do.

PABLO NERUDA
Ian E. Reed

September.
A man gazed
through his window,
from his heart.
Gazed across his land
and saw his people
Of whom his great heart
embraced,
Crying out in agony.
Murder walked among them,
Death stalked the

hills and plains
And left its carnage
at his door,
In his heart,
cutting slices
From his vast soul,
the soul of Chile.

September.
the carabineros
Smashed down his door,
tore up his walls
And floor.
searching for truth
Among the rubble
of his home
They tore and hacked,
Searching for the sun,
the wind across
The plains, the cry
of the onion seller,
The sea and the people
of the market.
This they heaped up
and fired,
Destroyed, stamped upon
this very soul
the soul of Chile

September.
A plain coffin
Lay amidst the rubble
of San Cristobal hill,
Lay among the
smouldering remains
Of his life's work
lay among the debris
Of his country.
His great heart had burst
And the very Earth
wept and reeled in anger.
The sky piled high its clouds
and rolled them
Across the oceans,

bearing the grief
Of a nation, of a soul,
the soul of Chile.

September.
A small crowd
Bore his remains
through the smashed capital,
At each step
the crowd grew,
The soul was reborn
shadows emerged from
Darkened doors,
from bloodstained alleys.
Shadows emerged
and became human.
The crowd grew
to become a giant
Striding undefeatable,
unquenchable, before the guns,
Before the barrels
of the killers,
Who grew afraid and silent
overwhelmed by this giant,
This unbroken soul
the soul of Chile.

September.
A small voice
Within this giant cried,
"Neruda is with us,"
Companero Pablo Neruda
presente!"
And as a spreading fire
the cry echoed
From a thousand lungs
and pounded against
The walls of the City,
against the barrels
Of the killers' guns,
and they read his words
Over the sleeping poet,
they read of the wind,
Of the sun, and of freedom,

they read of the market
And the mountains
and of the soul,
the soul of Chile.

September.
They killed a man
And a giant was born,
whose words cleave.
Open the sky and the Earth.
and are spoken from
A million lips,
a million hearts,
A battle hymn of freedom.
His murderers will die
And their bones will turn
into dust and slime,
But the flower they plucked
will grow into a garden
And the air will hang heavy
with the sweet scent of freedom,
And his soul
will be handed on
As a legacy,
The soul of Chile.

ALL AWRY IN PARADISE
Winifred Froom

The long narrow aisles make me think of cathedrals. Of course I know they are not, but there is the same absent look on the faces of the people, seeking for something they cannot see. Sweet music seeps from behind the towers of tins, like syrup from one that has lost its lid. From nooks and crannies, counters and shelves, even from the deep freeze it comes, hypnotising, paralysing, unless it is the martial kind inviting the customer to march, to waltz, to slide, or maybe drag the length of the avenue.

There's the ritual too.

Claim your wire basket from the portal, unless you have a toddler when you claim a kind of pram. Stroll between the towers of tins, peering from one pile to another. Stewed steak claims to give you satisfaction, detergents delivery from soul-destroying labour and monotony. All the joy of life, and ebullience of good health is ground up with the cereals. The sunbeams have been captured, fresh air harnessed, it is all here waiting for you. And it is instant, instant, now, at once, with no waiting

Somewhere, it is said, the hairs of your head are numbered, no sparrow falls to the ground unnoticed. Neither have your pets been overlooked on these terraces. Cats, dogs, goldfish or budgies are all remembered in these bright tins, where the smell of sea and farmyard are concentrated. No more hunting, no more grinding, no more crunching, everything is instant.

In the distance sit the cashiers, like goddesses, or perhaps priestesses at the high altar. The catechism is tapped out on their little machines. While you wait for the benediction on your perambulations up and down the aisles, the toddlers explore the display of lollipops and candies, thoughtfully displayed by the tills. No, nobody has been overlooked. The disciples of Market Research have been vigilant, the apostles of sales promotions and projects untiring.

But the queues, with their trolleys and baskets look neither serene nor satisfied. Seek and you shall find, come unto me all you that are heavy laden ... The labelled life around no longer stimulates, nor soothes They have a faraway look in their eyes. Surely there is more than a jar of cranberry sauce (2p off) to live for?

The soft sweet music is soporific, the cathedral changes into a supermarket, the ritual is concluded. The bill is paid.

THE SHIPYARD CRANES
A.M. Horne

Great set-squares of angled steel,
Tall, grey, vertical, moving upwards and outwards.
Isometric pre-planned zig-zags,
Set by the wind to crisp alignment.
They follow you everywhere,
Pagan idols dominating the skyline
A symbol handed from father to son,
Of an almost certain future,
To all the gangly lads kicking the ball around a secondary mod-
ern,
But the image is so deftly printed that only the subconscious
cricks
its neck.

CHANGING
Pat Sentinella

The face of the City, unsmiling,
Where rows of houses wait for death
Behind screens of corrugated iron.

Windows are broken and blind,
The bells are dumb.
Distempered walls perspire and plaster cracks.

The gardens are wasting.
The people who remain
Still boil their water on the landing
Watching for some other change
Tonight or Tomorrow.

A VERY SPECIAL BREW
Ken Lilley

It was one of those bitterly cold hoary frosted mornins doon in the bowels of the vessel which waited alongside the quay ready for fitting out. The Tyneside fog even penetrated down into the yet skeleton-frazed engine room skylight; smothering everything in its downward path to the very engine room pad floor plates.

The gaunt rusty frost-coated bulkheads swept upwards into the mist in answer to querulous gaze of the beholder like some ghostly cathedral. The rather sombre scene was accompanied by the distant intermittent chorus of Souter Point fog-horn blowing its warning to any errant off-course vessels.

Almost as the half past sivvin buzzer blew, the ladder near me started to shudder merrily as the various trades started to descend to where I awaited shivering with cold, waiting for the gaffer to allot the day work. Soon, a pair of heavy boots reached eye level. I was greeted by a mature stubble faced worker in greasy overalls, and a heavily oiled cap... "Mornin Hinney, Rev yee jest started?"

"Aye," I rejoined.

"Rev yee not gorrah drink of tea?"

"Nor, not yit."

"Weel lad, warm yersell an git a drink oot oh that flask ower there." He pointed and then the grubby-faced friendly man waved cheerily and moved off into the mist of the engine room.

The hot, warm, sweet tea which I poured out of the flask which stood on a pedestal near me tasted like refreshing nectar. The hot liquid momentarily dispelled the icy gloom, at least from within to warm the very crutch of me overalls.

"Argh yee the new lad what started this mornin?" A heavy authoritative voice bellowed out from my rear. I turned, replacing the drained cup upon the flask.

"Aye, ah wus just warmin mesell up till the gaffer comes."

"Aye ah can see that," snarled the man cynically (obviously he was the gaffer). I was also aware of a number of nonchalant cheery faces chuckling sideways at the impromptu confrontation.

"Weel lad, when ye've satisfied yersell wif mah flask..." He snatched it up an placed it in his pocket. "Git yer tools and join that aud feller ower thor. He'll put yer reet."

My mate was the man who proffered that welcome cup of tea that mornin. He slapped me on the back and grinned cheerfully.

"Did yee injoy it lad?" he chuckled.

I nodded. I had to admit that was a very special brew.

WRITTEN ON INTERNATIONAL WOMEN'S DAY, MARCH 8th 1973
Ruth Frow

A woman sits weeping for her dying babe;
Oh! sister mine, we sit and weep with you!
What matter if the babe be black or white?
Each woman's sorrow is our sorrow too.
A woman works from morn till late at night
Tilling the soil and working with her man.
Oh, sister mine we work with you each day.
We cannot do much - but our caring can!

A woman stands and holds herself erect,
Accepting life, but not accepting shame.
The life she lives will be a life of pride.
Oh sister mine, we join you in your aim.
Out of the waste and hunger, women fashion joy.
Women determine to re-build their lives,
To banish war and poverty and want,
To live as friends, as mothers and as wives.

We join you, sisters, wherever you may be;
Our children join with yours and never cease
To raise the standards of true liberty,
When women everywhere can live in peace.

TONIGHT WE WILL SEE THE DREAM-DRENCHED DRUNKS
Colin Frame

Tonight we will see the dream-drenched drunks
The subliminal wharf side whore
Dressed in crimplene and plastic
Bright red, purple, and yellow
Peddling herself for a pound
Dragged aboard, wiped by a hundred salt-caked palms
Heaving good with gin and sighs and vomit.

And I ask questions
Questions like what and why
And wash in lavender water
And am disgusted by the coarse-cloth of the towel
Preferring the membrane of a flower.

ROSSENDALE WEAVERS UNION WOMEN MEMBERS
Jim Garnett

When you can't get through your work,
And you feel you'll go berserk,
Report it to your Union Rep.
She will guide you, step by step.
Remember then that old refrain,
Unions on the job again.

When the cost of living's high,
Goods so dear, you cannot buy.
Your earnings go just like a flash
We fight to get you some more cash.
Remember then that old adage,
Thank your union for your wage.
I'm in it now o'er sixty years
A union card that's always clear,
I've seen a lot of ups and downs,
Worked with men of good renown
Our Union then was run by men,
But how far back, I can't say when.
But women now are to the fore
And things are not the same as yore.

221

They go to classes in rotation
This improves their education,
When at the meetings, on their feet,
They've got their arguments complete.

They're not afraid to give expression.
They've rid themselves of self depression.
I love to see them show their ego,
I say, more power to their elbow.

They show us men a thing or two,
Things we thought they'd never do.
So to our local Union lasses,
Let's give our praise, and raise our glasses.

GOD CAN'T CARE, REALLY
Bob Dixon

God was in the garden
Blowing on a rose,
Jill was on the garden path
Hanging out the clothes
when along came death
And turned up her toes.

DEATH-BED
Bob Dixon

We lied to him about getting better.
Daddy, to humour us, feigned belief.

THIS MAN CAN BE SUCCESSFUL AND JUST MAYBE THE CROWD IS LETTIN' HIM, NOT FORGETTING WE ARE PART OF THE CROWD THAT HAVE BECOME WORDS ON THIS PAGE.
M.G. Askell

What makes for communication, communication that has no necessity, communication that when completed leaves people wondering why, or maybe just me, wondering; yet sensing this particular human quality.

It is possible to create atmosphere, to arrange an event towards a certain ending, known only to me the narrator; so we are warned. Central to this arrangement of words are:

> A rope strop lying tangled
> on a concrete oil stained floor,
> with several strands broken;
> noise. An omission.

be careful situations are always in the process of becoming other situations. Those marks on the wall have a fascination, my eyes drift along each day, nothing registering particularly, until I reach this section and then the wall is no longer a wall. The surface, the marks, the colour, the distance between myself and this section of wall, this narrow funnel of space has become a journey between my imagination and my reason. Why this piece of wall? Why those marks? What particular problems of technique are involved in reproducing this encounter, in understanding; how much of the surrounding area is influencing ... "Hey! What about the lifting gear in this place; I've just picked up a rope strop, and we are short on rope strops, and some of the strands are cut through." .... directing attention towards this small section

"Well tell the foreman; if it's dangerous, we can't use it."

"I've always said we haven't enough rope strops, and besides they should have labels on them, stamped up, giving the safe lifting load an' that."

"O.K. destroy it. That's the usual practice; or someone in a hurry may not notice it, and we could have an accident if it breaks on the job."

"If I do that, I won't be able to lift my job."

"That's right! We'll get rope strops quick enough then."

"Well? What are you going to do?"

"I just said, for fucks sake! Anyhow it will make a change for that machine of yours to be switched off, the row it makes."

An outside influence is now affecting this communication; the words on this will name such an influence - a) experience, b) history, c) conflict of interests, d) bloody-mindedness.

"I ain't gonna use it."

"Right."

Pure black, glistening, the warmth, tenderness, that rich flood of life setting fire to a staircase of colours.

"Well what are you going to do?"

Metal coming away from the rim of the shell, feed just right, sometimes everything so easy ... so bloody easy

"Well ?"

"What?"

"What are we gonna do about it; where are you going? Hey!"

It's soaked in oil, tough too, I thought my knife was sharp...

"You've just cut my strop in half. Now I can't lift my job!"

"That's right."

Look from this page, push the page away, as far as is necessary for the words to go out of focus; look towards the window, beyond its frame, another view, in the last few seconds it has changed, is changing, what are you thinking?

"There was no need to do that! I can't get on with my job now. You're mad!"

"What's going on down there between them two?"

"I dunno."

"Well it's owt to do with us anyways."

"Yeah, about that Cortina you had, how many..."

Moving away from the City Centre, no longer travelling within these confines, or absorbed into its regulations, deliberately, consciously and subconsciously pushing out from the hub, through all levels to its rim. With this momentum the City highways are abstracted; re-lit, intensely, such light is informing, demanding of whom? The photographer, the painter, the neon minded commercialiser, the inhabitants, whose unquestioning industry oil this City's generators. Such light demands attention, its speed forces inwards, sweeps towards the hub continually; burning the edges of buildings against an unmoving sky, exposing the armour that relentlessly crawls, howling, snapping, devouring along these thoroughfares; passing the street of the house of anarchists, night ideas and dog days. Silhouetting those inhabitants, queuing six deep outside the palace for bingo, bland faces, their artificial adornment the chain mail chance of a jackpot. Sirens ebb and flow, a million voices repeating, nothing ... nothing ... alright alright. This light informs by the sharpness in the edges it infinitely re-exposes. What are you thinking? The light also shines on her hair.

"I'm going to tell him, that you've cut the strop in half."

"That's right! Go ahead, you just tell him I cut the bloody strop in half."

"Right I will."

When a person walks away, intent on purpose that is out of sight (site), in receding becomes the backcloth of an everchanging situation, the eyes that follow such purpose, whose origins are incomprehensible within the time allowed by action; have, even in anger in bitterness or hopelessness, a flicker from evolutionary understanding, of remorse and regret. The emotional fire is tempered by sadness, perhaps at the temporary lose of unity.

"What's going on with you two?"

"The same old story, not enough gear and we end up arguing with each other, for all the wrong reasons."

"Yeah, all they care about is getting the job done in the least possible time at the least possible expense. Ay, what are you doing dinner time? Going over the park for a game of football; most of us are except, (this exception could be ... you ... me ... sometimes us?) who is going into town but he reckons he may be back in time. Ay! never mind, it probably won't happen."

"Just maybe you're right, but it won't be for want of trying."

"What."

"Where's that small crowbar?"

"Dunno I ain't seen it lately."

> just then, figures on
> a far golden shore
> touch hands, fingertips first,
> ice petals tumble through sun spray,
> each fresh breeze tenderly tells
> of islands that dwelt in the past.
> No sound from smiling minds;

225

the sand moved gently as a rhythm suspended.
In darkness deep of ocean's floor
intangible something, moved for the first time.

"I've seen him, he said you were wrong to cut that strop in half."

"Oh yeah."

"Yeah, he says that what we should have done was to give the strop to him and he would have cut it in half. He's going to see if we can borrow some from the other shop; in the meantime I've got to hang about till he gets some. You know what; I was having a look at my mortgage papers the other night, I've increased the payments, what with all this overtime an' that."

POETRY AND THE CLASS STRUGGLE (I)
John Salway

Wield your words like axes
Cut from the nude rock
Knives lathed from the creeping fronds
Of steel
Entrenched round your bursting hearts

In the twilight world of factories
We bring your corroding flowers
And rhythms of bit and brace

We bring you edged poetry
To dissect your way
Through this insane and rotting jungle.

Everything should be melted down
Everything can be used.
We have taken the drooling words
Which drip
From the steaming swamps
Of supermarkets

We have taken
The cries of despair
Which eddy and swirl
From somebody adrift

226

On his soul
Like an ark.

We have alloyed
The insidious grit
Which grows on slagheaps

With suffering and hope
With the laser of your will

We would forge you
Tongues of fire.

WE CAME CRYING HITHER
Sue Cole

We came crying hither
We danced from the waterfall
Over the plateau to the tear
We absorbed the moonbeams
Now
stranded...

... Barren -
We starved our own intellect
We took fruit from the tree
And made it gold
We took warmth from the fire
And made it cold

We made it cold

THE CLOTHES PEG
Gareth Thomas

A church clock struck three in the morning. Four dossers nodded and snored, sat in a tight circle around a dimly smouldering brazier. The fifth was awake and listening to the night. "That clock's fast," he mused, scratching at an itch beneath his faded once fawn-coloured duffle coat.

He looked at the brazier, the dull red glow a poor answer to the moon's bright message. Crossing his arms over his ribs, he rubbed his wheezing chest and arose from the blue plastic milk crate which served him for a seat. Turning slowly from the weak warmth of the brazier, shuffling on old unsteady legs - the same legs that had marched through France in his war-torn youth - he searched the rubbish dump for more firewood.

A mouse crawled out from the tattered upholstery of a rusty car door. It crawled around the bent window frame, where a few chunks of laminated glass still stubbornly clung, and raised its whiskers to the stars.

In vain, the old tramp scanned the rubble, old tin cans, bricks, bottles and car tyres, discarded polythene kitchenware, and an old mattress which sprouted a forest of springs. No more wood on the dump. If only they had been more thoughtful when the night was young and the fire was bright. Now the embers that remained were poor armour against the frosty attack, the cold before the dawn.

He saw the mouse. A glint came into his eye, and he stooped to grab the nearest object to his feet. It was a clothes peg. The cold stiff fingers firmly gripped the missile and his arm drew back. He took aim, frowned, then slowly lowered his arm and looked at the clothes peg. Wood! Firewood.

He walked back to the brazier and ceremoniously dropped the new fuel into the embers. Sitting down once again on the milk crate, he studied the clothes peg and waited. A small flame began to lick around the peg, first green, then blue, finally yellow and bright.

The other four looked up from their drowsy shoulders and greeted the puny phoenix. Soon, five pairs of hands were reaching into the brazier and gathering the heat from the burning peg.

A second church clock struck three in the morning, and a barely audible mutter came from the hunched, duffle-coated figure. "Or maybe it's that one that's slow ..."

All five warmed their hands until the peg's flame died, and only a red hot steel spring-clip remained. Four heads nodded a salute to the remaining embers, nodded thanks to the bringer-of-firewood, and nodded back to sleep. The fifth remained awake and thinking in the night. "They could both be wrong.

He picked up an empty wine bottle lying by the side of the crate, and raised it to see if any dregs remained. Raising the bottle to his bearded mouth, he held it vertically and a single droplet of red liquid ran down the glass and into his throat.

"Anyway - they couldn't both be right," he decided, conclusively. Satisfied with this answer, he smiled, lobbed the bottle in the general direction of the mouse, spat into the embers and dozed off.

He had fought for this freedom in two world wars.

EYES

Bob Dixon

I watch the children in the park
From their eyes,
My unborn children cry to me.

The demonstrators throng the street.
From their eyes,
There shines a world that is to be.

YOU SEE ME SMILING?
David Tatford

Good evening one and all,
This is your plastic president
Speaking.
You see me smiling?
A greasepaint image
My witch doctor made for me,
The magic media man.

This is your plastic president
Talking
In words of simple syllables
Rolling
From a three-forked tongue.
I'm a nice man really.
The burning babies are a dream,
And anyway
They're better dead than red,
(though they'll never know
The service I did them
Unless they have T.V.
In heaven.)

This is your plastic president
Grinning
In skeleton likeness

Of those I killed.

You see me weeping?
The tears are glycerine,
Sweet as sugar
For you all to taste.
My grief is real -
I grieve for you,
Poor fools.

VIGILANTE
John Salway

Keeping awake
When cities yawn
And grope for heaven

Keeping one eye
Like a chip of marble
As the world seethes

And
Trembling
Like a seismograph

Keeping history
Like a hound
On a leash

But

Drumming the wild pulse
Of its rage

And

Tempering the blossoming ache

Of its heart.

NICKNAME ON A WAR MEMORIAL

Rose Friedman
(a one minute play for one voice)

It was a change of address
Brought a new morning' s walk
To reach my train
New roads, new gates, new trees
To learn

And a neat-small chapel
Whose glorious dead
- these lads once prayed here,
Bright gold on sombre black,
Concise and clear
As an open book -
Standing quietly by,
Became my new morning's landmark.
Habit dulls even the desire to sigh.

My stone heart lies in a stonewall bed
That much for your glorious dead

Until, one day, in sunshine? or in rain,
Who cares?
My glance strayed, chanced upon a name
Before unnoticed,
Caught me unawares.
Tom, it was a nickname - sweet and crisp
As a mother's fleeting kiss -
Put paid to my ostrich sleep.
Tom, soft and round as a sweetheart's lingering caress
Ah - that went deep.

Once was a baby
Tom Tom the piper's son
Loved his mum and a hot cross bun

That's Tom. That was Tom.

Once was a lad
Tom his fifteenth birthday reached
Thought about girls as the parson preached.
That's Tom. That was Tom.

Tom tinker tailor soldier sailor
Tom butcher baker and undertaker
Why that's Tom

A million lads have gone that way
And a million more will go they say

So glorious lad Tom
Gloriously dead Tom
You rang the bell to blast the wall
You blast the wall a million ways.

Tadpoles now to tear at my eyes
Flagpoles now to flay my flesh
Now the potholes leer and yawn
Dangerous and desolate
Deserted by Tom.

CITY BOY/BROWN BABY
John Gowling

Between the cast-iron pillars of the railway viaducts I go, searching for a love, looking for a love. Past the scrap-metal yards, hedged high with rusty motor bodies, there I go, searching for a love. In between the sewerage aqueducts that span the boneyard valleys and canals, there I go searching for a love, looking for a love. Mountain climbing on the slopes of ash and scree, could this be you and me? Could it be? In between the railway wagons and the coal marshalling yards, there I go, there I go. Some day soon you'll be where I go but when and where and who will you be? and who will you be? Do you think that love was meant to penetrate the traffic gantries and signal stanchions above the steps of the subways, and if it was, how would we know? Beyond the kiosk selling cigarettes I wait, up abeam the iron bridge I hope you won't be late when you walk by. On the ferry, side stepping with the slurry barge I tend to think I stand a chance, a quick romance with you on the fire escape would do me fine.

Their old world is slowly coming down, but mother of mine, don't you know that it needs a little more than poured concrete and a few flowers to let love grow. The housing department won't re-house the lodgers and they evict those that stay. They fire condemned blocks where families still live. What do they care when Urban Renewal means another tenement block to last another 60 years? What do they care? Vincinette's baby looks up from the pram to read the spray-paint on the stairwell wall. Vincinette looks down the cold clinical corridor which says: Your mother is mad, we've taken her in; your father is tired he wants to go home to Barbados. Every day too, she prays to the Father that her trails get harder so she will go the Heaven, midnight prayers deny her the goodnight kiss she so desperately needs. Her baby was not conceived in the art-museum or the movie magazine. Not in the park or the public cemetery, but on a mattress, away on the roof, beneath the stars, to the marshalling freight, the shunting engines and the traffic below. An apprentice's wage bypassed the gas and electricity, replaced broken glass with cardboard, rode a bike without a licence, and paid no rent

I pull out a screwed up note, from my pocket, I didn't care to send:

I don't want a black or a communist, I have given all this for you, who are neither. I am in love with you and that over-rules everything else. Because I never found a black or a communist but I found you. I've tried to tell you that it's you I want, and you encouraged this, you made this happen. To-night you didn't take me to Rigby's or some white joint croastown. You asked to meet me in O'Connors then suggested the Masonic or the Somalie where I looked at no one there but you, and showed everyone there how much I loved you. How can you be so cruel to say that it couldn't work out, does it not seem strong to you that I can still love and understand you above this and constantly I've been looking for you and trying to find you and know every little thing about you. I made the effort, I don't believe one person can ever make again in one lifetime, only to find you now uncompromising. And you flung in my face about being your child, and being black and a communist. Can you not conceive that there are blacks who are not for me, and blacks who don't like me, and whites who are racist, and all people who don't like communists, and people that don't like me? Don't you think I don't know? Why did you do this to me? What did you hope to use me for? After I loved you and dreamt about being with you all times. I still want that. I never met a communist or black who I loved, but I met and loved and lay with you.

Silently I walk the city streets. It is 4 a.m. and not my town. I wake at 6 a.m. in a foreign apartment, put the first comb of the day through my hair and make to leave.

AWAKENING
Betty Crawford

Swaggering forth from the stronghold of Capital,
stepping in time to the Saint Louis Blues,
Celluloid heroes, with chewing gum and crew cuts,
denizens of dollardom how could they lose,
Aircraft and troopships, goodbye hugs and kisses,
'Gotta little job to do for Uncle Sam,
Don't cha worry Honey, we'll sort it out in no time,
bring you back a souvenir from Viet-nam.
Now you're in the war zone, get to know your buddies,
black men, white men, Gentiles and Jews.
War seems never-ending, weary for a furlough,
discussing things together makes you change your views
  What's this goddam war about? and the folks we're fighting,
Christ, won't they ever think of giving in,
Gotta hand it to them, they're costing us a fortune;
Dad's letter's asking 'Do we think we're gonna win?
Guess I needn't answer, leastways in a letter,
I'll tell him all about it when he meets me off the plan.
I'm lucky to be homeward bound, my wounds will heal real soon,
but constantly my conscience says, I won't erase the stain
Of unrelenting slaughter, of rape and torture too.
Yet midst the carnage, they were unconquerable,

234

I'll give credit, where it's due.
There's a day of reckoning coming, for their years of toil and pain,
For the tons of bombs and napalm, showering genocidal rain,
Inflicted by us, on a people, who only dared to say,
WE will choose our way of life, not the U.S.A.
It shames me to admit it, but we've been kidded all along,
believing that we, are the land of the free, and everyone else is wrong.
When the verdict of history's given, the reason will show up real plain,
The White House sacrificed us all, for greed and political gain,
A stake in Indo-China, a base is what it sought, if
Almighty Dollars cannot buy, then battles must be fought,
Prop up reaction's puppet, 'To Hell', they said, 'with the cost'
It matters naught to those in power, how many lives are lost.
Then the voice of protest rises, ringing through the land,
'Bring the boys home' it says, this is our demand,
The Monster in the White House smirks, pretending to pay you heed,
for another term as President, your vote is what he'll need
Sure, he'll pull the G.I.s out, if that is your instruction,
but his weapons still will carry on the death and the destruction.
Are you lost as a nation to Capital's spell?
I ask that question, for I have seen Hell.

WIN WITH LABOUR!
Jone o'Broonlea

'Colours o' this rosette
Tell ruefu' tale o' ther need o' us:
Red's for us - an' yeller for ' leaders:
We'st ha' to larn 'em yet!

A BOOK AT BEDTIME
Mick Jenkins

Bill Baker was a miner working at Rufford Colliery in Nottinghamshire. He was elected the Union Branch President, and re-elected each following year, and in 1945 was re-elected unopposed. He was elected Workman's Inspector at the pit. He was an authority on mining safety. His work on mining safety was known throughout the area. Like many other militants he was victimised many times following 1926. Later in the fifties he was elected full time Miners Agent for the Nottinghamshire Area of the National Union of Mineworkers.

Bill was a friendly type of person, always had something to say. He was deeply immersed in the problems of the mining industry and the struggle to lift up the standards of the miners, to improve their working conditions. An idea as to the type of fellow he was can be gleaned from an incident that occurred whilst he was working at Rufford Colliery. One day he came to see me at the Party Office. It was late afternoon, he had worked the morning shift. We talked - I don't remember about what - and when it was obvious we had finished he said to me, "Got anything good to read?" I said, "What do you want to read?" As 'it' was getting near to teatime, and I was going home, I asked him to come home with me, have a cup of tea, and we'd have a look over my book shelves.

On the walk home we talked about books, what he had recently read, what I had, the difficulty of finding time to read whilst doing an arduous day's work, attending meetings, doing Party work. We also compared notes on interesting books we had read. In the course of this latter exchange, I asked him if he had read "Germinal" by Emil Zola. He said he hadn't, but knew about it, and wanted to read it. I said, "Right, that's one book you've borrowed." We arrived home, had a cup of tea, looked through my bookshelves, and off he went with two books under his arm.

He made his way back to his council estate house in Mansfield, had a meal, slept for an hour or so, washed and went to the 'local' for a pint. Came back home about half nine and began collecting his things for the shift the following morning; he had a sandwich and a pot of tea and was about to make his way upstairs to bed when he remembered the books. "Where did I put those books I brought home?' to as many of his six children as were present. They were produced, and with "I'll just have a glance at them" he sat on the sofa in front of the fire.

Naturally, it was "Germinal" that he opened up, flicked through the pages, read an odd sentence or two thinking at the same time as he turned back to the front page "Going to take a long time to reads" He glanced at the clock on the mantelpiece and decided he would pinch half an hour off his sleep -

but "can't afford to lose a shift". The half hour stretched into an hour, and then two hours. At 1 a.m., he had now been reading for about three hours, he decided he would finish that chapter and go to bed -he had to be up around 5 a.m. he had managed shifts before on four hours sleep. At 7.30 in the morning one of his children woke him from deep slumber on the sofa in front of a dead fire. He finished "Germinal" that day. Next time we met he greeted me with "Your book cost me a bloody shift!"

RUE
Jone o' Broonlea

Cockchif ft at neet-fa',
pisspreawd coom morn,
'Days hoo's nooan reet, tho',
mon tholes forlorn.

AUGUST 1945
Crispin

The mushroom cloud
Herald of terrible death,
Had it. seeded beginning
In sources of new life.
Hiroshima and Nagasaki,
Names now synonymous
With hideous and sudden holocaust,
First saw it. shape.
But still it rises,
Seen in Nevada and Sahara,
Spreading its blasting flame
Promise of new destruction.
To meet its challenge,
The tide of Easter marchers
From Aldermaston to Washington
Pledged to build not bomb.

Politicians with their "power"
Need to remember its source.
Generals can "command",
But both depend on "people".
A bomb to H.

Concerns me ... you ... and us.
We can decide, Life or Death,
And end the mushroom cloud.

BOYS AND GIRLS COME OUT TO PLAY
C. James Mac Veigh

Trouble with the drunken boy,
Propped up against the wall;
Trouble with the restless girl
Who hears the money call.

Trouble with delinquent boys
Who want it all, not some.
Trouble with the slum-grown girls
Who make the clients come.

For angry boys can stab and kick
To snatch at what is theirs,
And sweet-life girls who'll turn a trick
Have thorns for pubic hairs.

SELF-MADE MAN
John Salway

I want to be free
He said

So he tore his
Ancestral roots
From the earth

And
As the tolling bells
Filled out the acres
Of his home
He tossed himself

Onto the oceans
At night
His dreams rose and fell
On currents of gold and silver

With Scylla crooning
He circumnavigated the world

As his sails flew
As his blood pounded like a piston
In his wake
He grew
An archipelago of Edens

He trawled
For new worlds
And the hearts of men

His eyes glittering in the darkness
His coiled back crowned with coral
He snaked onwards
Into the choked undergrowth
Of his fantasies

And the stirring
Of the darkening sea.

THE WINTER'S BEACH
A.M. Horne

Glistening with the memory of a recent time,
Reflecting the cold blue winter's sky,
A deserted forum of summer pleasure.
Buckets, spades, freckles and sunburn,
Forgotten behind frosty windows
And tasting the salt from icy tears,
Wrapped in the same wind as the moving sand,
I tread the beach listening and looking
Throwing a pebble and taking a sea shell
One set of footprints on a newly scrubbed floor,
And although freezing feet stamp urging me to the bus-stop
I promise myself another visit.

SURGEON WHO LOST SON INDICTS THE KILLERS
Patrick Lane

ASSASSINS HAVE 'CENTRAL GUIDING HAND'

'Come let us make a muster
speedily:
Doomsday is near; die all
Die merrily."

The words of Hotspur in "Henry IV" are relevant to Northern Ireland to-day, although there is a total absence of any cause for merriment.

The words have their origin in a civil war power struggle, and the troubles here are basically about the maintenance of that same power and the over-throw of forces which tend to erode it.

In a previous paper I attempted to show where this power resides and reit-erate briefly that it resides with the executive in England and not with the Legislature at Westminster. The latter has control of the laws and social changes and the general running of the national economy (the housekeep-ing budget) but the executive controls the power (the bank balance).

The course of history in these islands shows a central and continuous effort directed to maintenance of power and this is what rebellions, wars and di-plomacy have been all about. From the nature of power, moral considera-tions do not enter its acquisition or maintenance. Diplomacy or ruthless-ness, are used as the occasion demands, if they are deemed to be the ap-propriate weapon. This point is not made by way of condemnation specifi-cally of British power. The argument is applicable to all power blocks and their struggle for continuance.

There is no reason to think that "enlightenment" or a change of heart have suddenly come about at any time during this century and that the theme mentioned above does not still run through contemporary affairs. Indeed, it would appear that from the point of view of the ordinary inhabitant of the globe, the world is a much crueller environment than it was some centuries ago, despite enormous advances in science and technology.

A brief look at the history of Northern Ireland over its half a century life, will show how the thread of power ran and still runs. Industrial effort here based largely on the linen, textile and ship building industries, changed gradually to an alternative dependence on such activities as the new man-made fibre production, of which Northern Ireland is now said to be fourth in position in world output. This is in no small measure due to the presence of a docile labour force.

There has scarcely been a strike of note and the trade unions are an impotent force.

A carefully set up Unionist Government was cosseted by a deliberate blind-eye approach to ensure that the working labour force remained dormant and rejected any liberal thinking that might be thrown out by an occasional Northerner like James Connolly.

Discrimination and sectarianism were necessary weapons as the nationalist minority community - Conveniently identifiable as Catholic -rejected the state and its institutions. Adverse comment from outside was avoided by making a convention that the affairs of Northern Ireland were not open for discussion at Westminster and this state of affairs existed until 1968.

The lid came off with the growth of the Civil Rights Movement in 1968/69. This should have been anticipated by the power-that-be as the movement was global and was making itself felt in the streets of France and in the campuses of American universities and elsewhere. Even though the case of discrimination and social injustice was accepted and proved, the movement was countered by a behind-the-scenes provocation of sectarian reaction. There is no doubt that this was deliberately aided if not instigated by British Power.

There were many instances where local rabble-rousers, many of whom are by now prominent politicians could have been made subject to the law on charges of incitement or sedition but they seemed to be working under legal immunity. An attempt was made to blame the underground Republican Movement

- I.R.A. - an organization ticking over from the days of the Independence struggle in the South, and depending for its existence on the dedication of its members, who cannot have been many, and on ill defined sympathy among some of the minority chiefly in the Catholic ghettos. At about this time its strength, such as it was, was depicted by a split into two wings roughly republican separatist and republican socialist.

The early success of the civil rights movement was countered by the advent of sectarian clashes in 1969. There is little doubt but that the hidden power found a few local willing tools able to foment this outburst and bring it about. The people of Hooker Street and Palmer Street, having co-existed as neighbours for years, suddenly found themselves to be enemies.

As was foreseen at the time, the I.R.A. used the sectarian violence to further its own fortunes and did so successfully and an intangible force of "civil rights" ideas threatening power, was converted into a physical one which could be met by physical means. World opinion was assuaged by the sight and word of British forces laudably keeping the peace in the streets of

Ulster. To most of the minority, however, the reality is otherwise. After a brief honeymoon (the word of Gen. Freeland) the campaign began -the one sided harassment, one sided searching and seizure of arms and a one sided use of the courts and legal machinery, culminating in one sided interrogation and torture and internment.

It had the desired effect of increasing the strength of the I.R.A. and polarising the struggle to one that could be met with by well tried conventional methods. Two miscalculations were made. Firstly the resistance which guerrilla forces will put up if they are motivated only by dedication to their cause and have little or nothing else to lose (a dedication which cannot be appreciated by those who have). Secondly the details of torture and interrogation have become public knowledge and are now the subject of charges against Britain at the European Commission of Human Rights.

Miscalculation has meant that Northern Ireland has now endured a horror about as long as each of the world wars with no end in sight. Tactics had had to change. It was felt that if the I.R.A. tactics caused sufficient horror their ultimate strength - the ghetto sympathy - would melt away. This did not happen even after the disastrous bloody Friday episode. I cannot explain why this and other horrors and intimidation have not caused this rejection. Perhaps, there is a rough decision in favour of the lesser of two evils or a more intelligent assessment of cause and effect among the people with very little to lose than among those whose judgment is influenced by position and privilege.

A large part of the horror has been a steady stream of sectarian killings coming in definite waves indicating a carefully planned pattern.

I do not believe that these are perpetrated as such by one community on the other. It is not in the nature of ordinary humanity even when banded into secret sectarian terrorist groups to act thus on such a scale. It is true that communities at each others throats can indulge in severe violence culminating in murder, as happened in 1969 and has happened recently on a wide scale in Cyprus. These episodes are invariably self limiting if only through exhaustion and no communities are capable of sustaining such hate to continue assassinations for several years.

There is no doubt that some psychopaths capable of an occasional killing may be on the loose, or some, motivated by a score to settle, may also strike. The steady and relentless stream, however, with peak waves occurring in the early autumn when the tensions of the summer marching seasons have died down, point to a central guiding hand controlling the assassin.

Morality or even emotion do not enter into the calculations. Ostensibly the choosing of the victim does not make sense. The usual victim is an innocent labourer or tradesman. The message, however, would seem to be that the general public and especially the minority community must conform or else. Perhaps, there will be minor concessions such as nominal power sharing at local level in return for conformity. In the old days the situation of dealing with a threat to power would be met with a Culloden and Highland extermination manoeuvre, but the pressure of world press and T.V. cameras would now preclude this here. It is only an Eastern power bloc would employ such a measure nowadays, where they are prepared to ignore world opinion.

In terms of human suffering and terror the long drawn out effort is as bad if not worse than the quick massacre.

I do not suggest that the terrorist groups on both sides are not capable of or have not committed, outrages on their own initiative. They are, however, carrying all the blame in the propaganda exercise. There can be no doubt that all the organisations have been infiltrated by the Secret Service machine. It is probable that many, if not most of the killings emanate from this source through the use of agent provocateurs or through unfortunates on whom there is a hold for some other serious crime.

Inklings of this situation came out in the Littlejohn and the Baker affairs. Another pointer is that the killers seem to be able to work with immunity in spite of the heavy presence of security forces checkpoints and up to date radio communication. On the other hand freelance murders, e.g. those motivated by robbery are often caught and brought to justice.

The latest move in the dismal picture is that the terror has now been taken to the innocent civilian population of England. Motivation for this by a terrorist organisation is illogical and irrational. One result which is not to the benefit of the terrorist organisation is that the British public is now conditioned to accept a much tighter control of "law and order"; and encroachment on individual rights. If the necessity arose, the death penalty could be reintroduced overnight without much dissent.

Disclosures in evidence reported at trials in England would suggest that again there is collusion between infiltrators and young misguided dedicated members of the I.R.A. who are induced to travel over and wreak havoc in England. The ease with which many are picked up straight away suggests that their actions and the possible results are known before they start. The usual speed of arrest contrasts strangely with the average delay in the case of ordinary criminal acts where a large section of the police force may be extended for a considerable time.

This assessment of the Northern scene is not given by way of condemnation of Britain only. Any power structure will act in similar fashion. France and Spain are indulging in similar measures against minorities where the activities of the Bretons and the Basques threaten the integrity of central power.

It is only if my thesis is accepted that the dreadful evil of internment can be understood. A child could tell that its declared purpose to confine terrorists and deter others is just nonsense. It is there to stay until the minority community gets the message. The archives show that indefinite confinement in the prison bulks of the Medway successfully extinguished the remnants of Gaelic culture of the Scottish Highlands following the '45 rebellion. The weapons of power do not change with time and the reason of humanity. This has immunity from all appeals to measures to retain it, and has always been so in man's history.

What can we do in this situation? It is of little help to engage in idle condemnation of any or all of the parties involved. we are all involved by our existence here. Wide discussion is necessary to understand the problem. My own view is that all efforts of reasonable men should be directed to mobilising public opinion to press for the complete departure of British power from our shores so that we can live in peace and with justice and harmony. It will mean that on our own we will have less affluence but life should be adequate for all.

This may be regarded as a dream. I would counter by saying that the present and the alternative is a nightmare.

The writer of the foregoing article, Surgeon Patrick Lane of Belfast, is a well-known worker for Communal reconciliation in Northern Ireland. His son, Peter, a 24 year old medical student was the victim of an apparent sectarian assassination in the North almost two years ago. In connection with the murder of Peter Lane, it is probably not without significance that his father had compiled evidence of tortures inflicted on detainees by the security forces.

Surgeon Lane detects a carefully planned pattern of sectarian killings with a central guiding hand controlling the assassins. He has no doubt that all the militant organisations have been infiltrated by the British Secret Service machine and that most of the killings emanate from this source.

NO FLOWERS IN MAY
Robert Moore

Gone are the homesteads and valleys so green
For a twenty mile radius no grass to be seen
Now a nightmare of smokestacks has darkened the sky
And gone are the haystacks where we used to lie
Just a landscape of black that once was so green
Until big business came and shattered a dream.
Where no birds are now winging or singing their song
All the trees in the meadow have withered and gone
No fish in those waters is there to be found
Where once sparkling trout did so gaily abound
From those rivers and streams where no fish now play
All the muskrat and beaver have roamed far away.
No bush on the hillside to shelter the bear
The deer and the antelope have moved on in despair
And gone are the rabbit and fox that lived there
Gone now those pastures and meadows of green
Where once grazing cattle and sheep could be seen.
No longer do cocks crow to herald the dawn
Where no bees are buzzing or bumbling along
I don't need convincing there's something far wrong
But wages are high in the smelters today
Creating the myth "It's a great place to stay"
Tho the work might be hard you'll make plenty pay
Where everything's dying and filled with decay
And the countryside's black and the skies are all grey
But ain't life short enough, why hasten the day
So I am hitting the road out of Sudbury today
Where the faces of wage slaves get withered and grey
As they process the ore into nickel for pay
Bought by the hour selling sweet life away
Where there's still showers in April but no flowers in May.

BLUES
Frances Moore

Like the storm thrush beneath the rain
I have to sing
to live outside my pain

Goodbye my darling

245

may the guns shoot wide
How cold our bed is
with you outside.

Lullaby darlings
while the big bombs fall
Hold on to mother
who's no good, no good at all.

Like the storm thrush
beneath the angry sky
I have to sing
to pass my sorrow by.

Children are growing
and must be fed
I must labour to rear them
And help earn their bread.

Lads must go courting
a lass of their own
Out of work, mother,
and emptying home.

Where are you darling now we have time
to be together
after so long, so long a time?

Out in the rain love
trying to wake
the sullen people
their own lives to make.

The sullen people
whose shattered faith
trust no-one to lead them
to a better life.

You upon one beat
I on the other
How can we meet
and hold together?

Like a storm thrush

in the snow storm
I have to sing
to keep my courage warm.

Like a storm thrush
singing in the sun
I have to sing
for every moment won.

TRELLIE
Ken Clay

When Trellie was very young, during that bleak period of austerity in the late forties and early fifties, he was taken to the pictures every week by his mother. All the heroes, it seemed to him, played the piano very well or quoted long pieces of Shakespeare flawlessly. His father venerated these accomplishments and could himself quote two lines from John of Gaunt's death-bed speech in Richard II. He made a point of committing the couplet to memory after coming across it in the monthly magazine of the Royal Society of St. George.

Then there was Arthur Mee's Children's Encyclopedia, the only set of books in the house apart from the Home Doctor and the Daily Express Book of the Garden. They were all kept lying flat under blankets in a drawer in the wardrobe; it didn't seem worthwhile buying a bookshelf. From these Trellie received the first stirring intimations of the power of great art. Not from the works themselves - the Encyclopaedia did indeed contain whole sonnets by John Keats and Milton in addition to blue toned photographs of Michelangelo's David and Moses - but from the grandiose, overblown language of Arthur Mee himself. Surely, thought Trellie, if these things can move people like Arthur Mee to deliver such extravagant praise they must be the most important things in the world. When he looked at the poems and statues the sonorous phrases of his guide made his flesh creep once more in a frisson of awe.

Later he wrote poems: it was easy. Then he started to keep a notebook of thoughts which one day, when he'd got enough to publish, would undoubt-edly appear in Encyclopaedias of the future under the heading 'Immortal Ideas Which Have Changed the World'. As he grew older the ideas of others began to pollute his stream of thought. Eventually the notebook became an intellectual rag and bone cart piled up with rubbish whose variety bore witness to the totally undirected nature of his reading.

It was this notebook which he produced at Neville's one Sunday afternoon and read to him the following quotation. Not because it struck him as a profound idea but simply because it puzzled him. The sentences had a peculiar property. Although they were written in English, and although he'd re-written them substituting the dictionary definition for each word he didn't understand, he still found them completely incomprehensible. They defied penetration. It was a deeply disturbing moment in Trellie's life: his first confrontation with philosophy. He read the sentences out to Neville hoping to impress him with his erudition and at the same time provoke a discussion during which their meaning would be made clear.

"Modern thought has realised" Trellie read, "considerable progress by reducing the existent to the series of appearances which manifest it. Its aim was to overcome a certain number of dualisms which have embarrassed philosophy and to replace them by the monism of the phenomenon". Neville squirmed in his chair, arranging his arthritic hip in a more comfortable position. He looked at Trellie as he would at one of the paintings on the wall. Looks are really the only thing worth bothering about he thought, they can even compensate for this tedious adolescent thirst for culture.

"Its from Being and Nothingness by Jean Paul Sartre", Trellie went on, staring straight at Neville with a look of powerful concentration: the kind of look often found on the faces of people who spend a lot of time reading books they don't understand. Neville sipped his Algerian red wine and gazed up into the far corner of the room as if the sight of anything more interesting would be a dangerous distraction.

"Philosophy is difficult not only because it uses ordinary words in a special way but also because it manipulates abstract concepts for which there are no concrete correlatives. The English temperament", he almost said the proletarian temperament, "is essentially a positivistic and empirical one, disinclined to give serious attention to metaphysical speculation. What they fail to realise of course", he went on, emancipating himself easily from this narrow national category, "is that this apparently common sense view of the world is itself a philosophical posture no more certain than any other. We have merely become used to it and somewhat seduced by the success of its application in science."

Fuckinell! thought Trellie, he talks just like a book himself! He felt a strong urge to turn round and see if the words were printed on the wallpaper. "No concrete correlatives?" asked Trellie, going back to the point where he'd lost the argument.

"Precisely", said Neville. Trellie felt vaguely flattered but couldn't think why exactly. "You should really read Hegel before tackling a work like that. It's virtually nothing more than an expansion of the Self-

Consciousness section of the Phenomenology of Mind". Neville realised he was speaking to himself but he regarded even one-sided conversation as good practice. The discipline of shaping sentences fascinated him, as did the sound of his voice. Trellie too was intoxicated by these compliments to his intelligence. All in all they were both having a fairly good time.

Outside Neville could hear the thwack of boot on football. It was a Sunday league match on the park. One could hardly stand behind the rubber plant ogling those lusty thighs through the French windows in front of this screwy little poseur. He gulped again at the wine. "why do you read such things anyway?" The working class, he thought, what an astonishing collection! They imagined they could just pick up culture like a pint pot. Only the other day his cleaning woman had told him she was going to night school to learn Russian.

"I'm interested in philosophy", said Trellie.

"Excuse me a moment." Neville got up with difficulty and retired to the upstairs toilet to fart. Trellie heard it distinctly; at first he could hardly believe it. Yet there it was, a real rasper, the kind which Ferny, the boiler-maker's mate, followed by sweeping an imaginary shot gun up to his shoulder. If it had happened at home his father would have said, 'see better now can yer?' But Neville, already back in the room, left specifically for that purpose out of deference to his guest. The mysterious abyss between the classes opened up once more.

"What have you read up to now?" said Neville.

What a sneaky question, thought Trellie. Here he was, engaged in a task of extraordinary moral grandeur - nothing less than the search for a code to live by, a system of rules and stirring exhortations to replace the mind-numbing Protestant imperatives he'd had stuffed down him as a child, being forced to answer Neville's question with a pale list of titles. "I've had Descartes and Karl Marx out of the library but I've never been able to get right the way through."

The idea of chaperoning an ephebe through the labyrinth of European culture made Neville's soul swoon with delight. His mind, however, an organ more susceptible to cynicism, had become wary over the years after a series of failures. The most grievous had been that of his permanent companion, Dickie, whose proximity during two decades to three thousand volumes and a collection of modern paintings so large that half of them had to be stored on racks in the attic had left him regarding books as objects to be put back on the shelves when the coffee table began to look untidy and paintings as highlights for the wallpaper, only worth looking at when they contained lots of orange or cats.

Yet Trellie had a certain raw intelligence. That gaze! His look was never less than one of intense curiosity. Sometimes in his presence Neville felt vulnerable to ridicule. "What you need is a systematic course of reading."

Trellie brightened. "Yes, I was going to ask you if you could let me have a list."

"Municipal libraries are ..." Neville was about to offer a disparaging tirade on the contents of the town library but realised that this might expose him to a question about his reasons for going there, "not very good on the whole." He stretched out to a nearby bookcase, "Read this and we'll have a talk about it when you come again." He handed Trellie the paperback version of La Rochefoucauld's Maxims.

He left in a state of exalted fervour. Just as a pig in a slaughterhouse pen becomes invaded by a sense of dread so Trellie, poised blindly on the precipice of transcendental metaphysics, was somehow aware of the vertiginous, mind-warping prospect before him. His brain buzzed and flashed like a pinball machine as new cerebral circuits sprang into existence in an attempt to comprehend Neville's words. The world outside had that flat, airy, natural look which he had come to know for the first time years ago on stepping off the Ghost Train at Blackpool's Pleasure Beach.

TO A LANCASHIRE UNITED BUS
John Gowling

Manchester-Bolton-Westhoughton-Hindley-Wigan-Atherton
St Helens -Prescot-Liverpool.

To a Lancashire United Bus
You trip from town to town
In search of a countryside you'll never see.
The misspent unhappiness of the hive of British slag and
Chemical waste,
Ride on, Ride on in Majesty.

Ride on, Ride on
You red and silver double decker bus
Belch out your beautiful black fumes
Over the yellowy white disbelievers
Belch out your beauteous body odour
Over those who choose to stay.
What can grow on the spoilt earth
The sulphur rained-on streets?
Where will you go, you tubercular Bolton pigeons

When the mills cease to serve to roost?
Or the atom bomb dropped?
It is being dropped in slow motion into the hair
Of those of Warrington, Widnes and St. Helens every day.

You Lancashire United Guy Arab Bus,
Grow on young man,
You dirty-old, labour-rearing, thrown-at pram
You perished and corroded bricks and mortar,
You dusty, varnished, brown sideboards and yellow porcelain
Alsatians.
Belch out your beautiful black fumes.
While they beat out their rugs in your path,
And slip out to the shop along that eternal terraced block that
Stretched from Liverpool to Hull.
You Lancashire United Guy Arab Bus,
Someday they'll throw you away.
Like a spent human carcass.
And as your air doors close over Hindley
They'll ring again in vain.

BLACK AND WHITE
Bob Dixon

In the day,
the white light shines on all men
and casts black shadows.

We are shackled by the heel
to our shadows.
We are prisoners in our skins.

As well try to scrub your shadow white
as lighten your skin.

In the night, all shadows merge.
All cats are black at night.

RESSANO GARCIA
Barbara G. Smith

A little morning music -

251

and winter's lucid sunshine sweeping the dusty bush;
and the train tilting, twisting slowly along the valley
to cross the river.
And we singing, and loudly laughing, and shouting,
drunk with hope, and holiday home-coming.

And you were there, Mzuzu,
gay excited; the cracks in your deformed
tin trunk glimpsed gifts, a shining pan,
bright cloth, some tins, meagre rewards
for dark submerged humiliation buried deep
in your quivering soul, as your body quivered
daily deep in the dark weighted narrows
of the rocks of gold.

And you too, Nkonsome, eyes alight,
tongue live with fluent speech, the leaflet
brandished, a spear of triumph, in your hand.
Wonders you spoke, of churning change, of freedom
fought for within our grasp; perhaps, you breathed,
daring, perhaps we need return no more
to anxious apartheid labour, perhaps worthy work, the work
of progress, awaits us,
needs us there, in our homeland!

The river - oh, jubilation; briefly we taste
the freedom of our dreams. But first the frontier post
-the past survives in barriers, curt question,
brutal examination, old customs clashing
with our quickened aspirations.
Hau? Shooting? incredulous shock; death's
silence ... our joy had forgot the white-faced
senseless fear of a fear-free future
when no-one will name man Master,
and when comrade calls to comrade, comrade to
comrade will reply. Till then
Ressano Garcia.

AN UNMARRIED MOTHER -A PERSONAL EXPERIENCE
Vivian Leslie

The unmarried mother - ten years ago she reigned supreme as society's problem child. She was the subject of earnest debate and pontification from a righteous host of eminent sociologists, clerics and T.V. pundits. Her situation within society scraped raw by the intimate probes of women's magazines, documentary T.V. programmes and statistical reports, she was under a spotlight for public spectacle. Yet her problems remain. The fact that the focus of public concern has shifted towards the teenage drug addict/pusher, the vandal and the football rowdy, only conceals the fact that despite her solo performance as the sociologists' star turn, very little provision has been made, through either law reform or a change in local authority attitudes, to enable the unmarried mother to exist in our society on a comparative level with her married friends, either economically or spiritually.

The following article contains no comparative statistics, draws no broad sociological conclusions and is not intended to be a nationwide survey of the situation. It is simply the experience of one unmarried mother and her son, and the conclusions she came to from her experience. I've drawn some things from the experience of girls in similar circumstances where their experience differed from mine, but though our family and economic circumstances were very different, the problems we met were surprisingly identical. One conclusion we were all agreed upon, it is a fact that it is no easier for the unmarried mother and her child to emerge sound in mind and limb from the early critical years now than it was ten years ago, despite the hysterical assurances from the media that we live in a permissive society, that people are more tolerant and that the State looks after its poorer people. Now, as then, any situation is easy for the rich (in this situation, they can have a discreet abortion) but the majority have to claw their own way out of their problems, with very little aid from the institutions that could, but don't help them.

Even for the super-confident, the humiliations of being disguised as "Mrs." while in hospital, being "forgiven" by family and friends, being regarded as a parasite by the SS (Social Security, but the coincidence is so appropriate) and being discriminated against by money-grabbing landlords and company-minded employers, is hard to take, especially in the post-natal period when emotions and nerves are inclined to seesaw wildly, often tipping the sufferer onto the downwards spiral of post-natal depression with successive blows against the confidence of the new and nervous mother. To a young girl, any of these experiences coupled with the enormous responsibilities of caring for a young baby, can seem insurmountable. This is indeed a danger period in which hasty marriage or premature adoption is often the result of the subtle but relentless pressures that society brings to bear on the unfortunate girl to conform. At a time when she needs every scrap of her confidence to cope with her changed life, the noose tightens, and the clear judgment she needs to guide herself and her child through their situation, is inevitably strangled by the consequent worries and doubts. None of us came through this initial crisis unscathed.

It is much harder to resist the gentle pressures of those we love and may be made to feel we have offended, than the more impersonal ones of a distant and abstract society. The guilt feeling, which plays so large a part in the reactions of the unmarried mother, may be intensified if she is living with forgiving but disappointed parents, who may not be able to, or even wish to, hide their disapproval from her. These destructive feelings can grow to manic proportions in a sensitive girl, leaving her emotionally deformed, unable to rid herself of a feeling of inadequacy because she does not feel the guilt and shame she is expected to feel. She suffers from a secondary guilt feeling brought on by other people's expectations of her, which she is unable to meet. Neither I, nor any of the girls I knew at the time, felt any guilt or shame for our pregnancies -any guilt we did feel was associated with having fallen foul of our parents' aspirations for us. We felt shame on behalf of our parents. I know that parents who support their daughters without moral recrimination or evidence of distaste can be of immeasurable value to the unmarried mother. I know of none who did so.

In order to avoid these frictions, the obvious alternative is to seek some form of rented accommodation, to work to pay the rent and a baby-minder, and to be as independent as possible. In purely practical terms, there are very few girls with a large enough earning capacity to be able to afford the rent of a self-contained flat, plus the wages the baby-minder will require. It is not an ideal solution even where it is financially viable, since it robs the mother and child of their precious one to one relationship. The baby comes to know his minder better than his mother, the mother can be quickly disenchanted with the role of mother when all it appears to consist of is an ever-growing pile of washing and ironing to be done, and only moments of real baby-care. Doing a full time job when there is no-one to share the chores with will rapidly tire the most healthy person, and with the broken nights she will have to endure, she may become inefficient at her job through tiredness, which in turn will lead to worry, because she is worried she will not enjoy her baby as she might otherwise, and the whole situation is in danger of degenerating into a tightening circle of depression, harmful to mother and child. Severe cases of depression can be the first steps that lead to attempted suicides, baby-bashings and often, a desperate promiscuity in search of a man, any man, who will take the load, even partially, from her shoulders. Most of the girls who did work at a full time job were the ones living with family or relatives who helped, more or less, with the care of the child.

It is incredible to reflect that there is no acceptable alternative to the natural mother's care in our society. There are many situations where, perhaps because of illness or a need to work on the mother's part, that the natural mother is unable to look after her own children, even inside marriage. These women are caught in the same trap as the unmarried mothers - they have to rely on kindly relatives or paid minders to look after their children. State nurseries open at hours impossible for a working girl to meet, they have a high teacher/child ratio, few will accept a child under the age of three and the lack of comfort and home atmosphere make them a poor substitute for the natural mother's care. (This standard of nursery care is also a severe problem to the percentage of women who feel intellectually starved in the role of wife and mother, who need the stimulus of a demanding job to present a relaxed and happy face to their husbands and children. At present, these women have only a bitter choice between a childless career or reluctant motherhood before them, either one a cheat). Having said that the ideal situation is one in which the unmarried mother is able to look after her child with the same peace of mind and financial security of her married friends, I will go on to show how impossible it is to achieve this humane solution.

Seven years ago, when I was investigating ways and means of supporting myself and my child, a visit to the local SS office provided me with the information that we would receive approximately £5 weekly from the State for our upkeep. If we lived alone we would qualify for a rent allowance, free milk (one pint a day) and help from the Welfare Department for our clothing needs. A question from me about how to budget for two on that amount elicited the reply that we weren't supposed to enjoy ourselves on SS money - no indeed. The economics of the situation need no explanation - it just couldn't be done, not even seven years ago. I might add here that I had always had an aversion to taking money from the State - taxpayer that I had been, I thought it not unreasonable to be able to live above a mere existence, and I was shocked to discover that the SS regarded this as superfluous, arid in the instance of the particular official that dealt with me, that she retarded her role in life as being that of protector of the State coffers from sinister claimants like me, who intended to rob the coffers at the rate of £5 weekly. (Nothing changes - a recent report from the Citizen's Rights Office contained a case in which an unmarried mother was refused money to feed her baby on the grounds that "Babies that age don't eat much.").

I did, in fact, work full time after a month at my family's home. Though allowing us a degree of financial independence, working had many disadvantages. I saw far too little of my son, when I did see him I was tired, my mother wasn't able to cope with the needs of four adults and a baby and though I helped where and when I could, some friction was inevitable and distracted us from the main task of bringing up baby. Looking back, I

255

might have fared better on the SS pittance, but I felt than, and I do now, that the unspoken demand from the State that the parents should supplement the incomes of their "errant" daughters is a vicious imposition on the goodwill of the parents. It is making a moral judgement on the people involved, by making their lives more difficult than they would otherwise be, surely not the lawful business of a State Department, and a "Welfare" one at that.

In the early days, one of the worst problems we encountered was the lack of a place for us girls to be together to discuss our peculiar problems. Few of us could afford baby-sitters, carrying babies through cold evening air was not advisable, so the only place we could meet was the local Baby Clinic, where we were heavily outnumbered by the married mothers who chatted gaily to each other about their homes, their husbands and their cars. They looked at us with pity, well meant but debilitating in the extreme, how we longed to be accepted among them as mothers. We were unfortunate in that the Health Visitor attached to the Clinic was a solid Christian lady, who treated us as if we were imbeciles - perhaps she thought we were - but her impatient waving away of our questions and her general attitude towards us prompted me to neglect to take my son to the Clinic for two weeks when he developed a patch of scurf on his head (a thoroughly normal occurrence, as I since learned), but I was afraid she would label me a "dirty mother", most heinous sin in her rule book. She never "liked" our babies - they were always too heavy or too pale, too warmly dressed, or, in my instance, were walking too soon. We certainly felt that we were "on inspection" when we attended the Clinic and our babies were scrubbed twice as often as they needed to be, almost defiantly.

Perhaps it was only our imagination that prompted us to think that our babies were scrutinised with extra zeal - I think not. If only someone had told her how much we needed reassurance that we were doing well - we couldn't do it, we were far too frightened of her frowns and moods.

(This is obviously only one instance of a Health Visitor - the one who attends my second son is a lavender lady of advanced years who insists I list my religion as "agnostic" instead of "atheist" because, she says, "There's more hope that way.").

One of my friends who did manage to find acceptable rented accommodation she could afford, had other problems. She had to run errands, help with other tenants' housework and generally debase herself for a landlady who exploited her vulnerability by threatening to turn her and her child out on to the street if she refused. This girl had been rejected by her family and had nowhere else to go, she was desperate so she accepted her humiliating part in this bargain without complaint. Because she was existing on SS money, her regular boyfriend could not visit her in her attic in case he jeopardised her benefit (SS officials assume cohabitation where a man makes frequent visits to a claimant, not necessarily overnight, and cut off benefit immediately - no such nicety as a hearing). She could have had a succession of male callers, one every night of the week but the visits of one man were a luxury she could not afford. Inevitably, the relationship starved to death, as did several others that succeeded it. We used to laugh at the anomaly - we could be prostitutes on SS money, but not have a regular boyfriend whether we slept with him or not - we used to laugh but after a while, it just wasn't funny any more, only unfair.

Another sadder case was the girl, staying with parents who tried to persuade her to return to t he Church she had been brought up in, who fought to resist these pressures for three years before she capitulated. She then "repented" of her "sinful ways", had her son christened, married a man her parents and priest approved of and is now living in a three bedroomed semi with garden and garage, has another child and is only a bleak echo of the happy girl she was. She went under through lack of support and understanding from supposedly Christian parents and friends who took it upon themselves to "reform" her. Reform her they did, she now has lost even her faith in herself and has gained only a facade of respectability - she will always be the "fallen angel" to her family, they do not let her forget it. She told me that she had not wanted to marry, but was heart weary with the constant battle with her family and friends to preserve her self-respect, in the face of their efforts to undermine it at every opportunity. She told a sorry tale of the months preceding her reconversion to the Catholic faith - of sessions with her priest who used every session to seduce her back to the confessional with promises of an easy mind as reward. She said she felt guilty at the sham - she did not believe but was tired of fighting every inch of the way for her right to be. She said she was a traitor in the camp. Another broken spirit for the Church.

My own experience with clerical attitudes was not as devastating but along the same lines. A certain misguided friend took me unawares to the house of a Methodist minister, ostensibly for an evening's conversation, but for a prearranged heart-to-heart talk about a spiritual crutch for me in my troubles. The conversation lasted about ten minutes, in which time I imagine that the minister came to the conclusion that I was either a complete heathen or hopefully, that I had no need of any spiritual life-raft. The conversation ended and so did that particular friendship. My particular hardships did not incline me towards a religious way out, though it is probably true that unmarried mothers, along with other people in social distress, are likely conscripts.

I have deliberately left out the morality of the question - I make no pleas for acceptance or tolerance for the unmarried mother. It is my personal view that our society is fast outgrowing the Victorian morality it has been saddled with for so long - we only need the courage to embrace a newer, wider morality that will, in fact, tolerate the social "deviants" among us. I am aware that there are large numbers of people, homosexuals, commune members and people who choose to avoid the existing family structures, who have a just claim on society to tolerate them financially and morally - we stand together stating our existence and our right to be an integral part of the society we live in. Paradoxically, we still zealously harass the sexual "criminals" in our society, the lechers, the adulterous wives, the pornographers and the whores, while ignoring the viler acts of the landlords, property tycoons and land hoarders - who are the real pirates of our society, the real corruptors, but their turn will come.

It needs to be stated that the greatest and least measurable harm is done by the double standards of the society that the unmarried mother has to live in. The emotional turmoils of each girl are different, the extent to which she is prey to guilt feelings, inferiority complexes and a mass of interconnected neuroses is different. Few of us are personal anarchist enough that we can live at ease in a society that on the surface accepts us, but which continually undermines our quality of life by not providing the legislation to control discrimination against us in tenancy agreements and employment contracts, that provides no acceptable nursery care, or that renders us financially impotent to support ourselves, even with the State benefits that are so immorally low. These things are a living nightmare to us - we have to plan for a future that intimidates many of us into hasty marriage to escape the draining insecurity that is our permanent lot, a future in which we can have no council house without a husband, no mortgage without a man behind us, and no real prospect of a full life without a man, because our society is geared to the nuclear family and provides for no alternative family structure. No, we are not all desperate to marry - many of us would sit out our problems if it were possible to do so without impoverishing ourselves and our children. It may seem to some that there is a brand of arrogance in the fact that we will not accept our given role of second class citizens, we will not take the leavings, the poorly paid jobs, the slum accommodation. We will retain our simple human dignity, our place in the shade if you like, but not in the cold. We are ready to shoulder our responsibilities, but not the punishment that is often meted out. How can these girls plan the lives of themselves and their children calmly and practically with the weight of these injustices stacked so firmly against them - always pushing them into marriage, nudging them into conformity, because it's tidier for the taxman that way?

In this situation the most important person is the child - I've said little about the child in this article because it is the pressures on the mother that affect the child most. There must be some kind of legal enforceable protection for these children. They must not be allowed to remain the pawns and victims of greedy landlords, reforming clerics, impersonal social-workers or unwilling grandparents. Most of all, they must not become the victims of their mothers' desperation, by abandonment or physical abuse. Both mother and child must be steered well away from this final black hole where the helpless panic and drown one another. we must work to help society to bequeath to these children a secure and worry free mother, their first and prime human right. What we as a society must do is to tinker with our morality and language enough to make the word "bastard" obsolete.

THE LIVING SEED
Angela Tuckett

Only upon the bleakest top
Still lies the drifted snow,
Out of the sting of the wind's whip,
The noonday glow.

Only upon the cliff's north face
Freezes the bitter rain
Hushed in a passionless embrace
Silent again.

Tangled tussocks everywhere
Contend with barren stone;
Once more the stripped earth brown and bare,
Never yet sown,

Awaits the not impossible
Beneath perpetual snow
The living seed waits only till
Our firestorms glow.

POINTS OF VIEW
Maurice Wiles

Ephemeral fly
On window pane.
Outside, aspen leaves
Tremulous on twisted stalks:
Green-shadowed patterns
A flickering crisscross made

Of random light and shade.

Progress? said fly.
Nonsense! said fly -
The universe is made
Of random light and shade,
My myriad eyes can find
No planning mind
That lies behind.

Poor curious fly!
Spider came by
Long-legged and hungry,
Caught him in clutching web
Before summer's ebb.

Gorged spider
Safe in webbed lair
Saw autumn and winter come,
Leaves turning yellow and brown
Then falling down
Leaving twigged branches here.
A fool, that fly, said spider,
Wisdom was denied her.
Decay in all I see.
The universe collapses into death
At autumn's chilly breath.

Wise cat with topaz eyes
Caught spider by surprise:
Cat's paw ended her.
Long legs did not save her.

For nine lives long
Cat mewed her philosophic song:
Leaves come and go;
Green follows dun
When winter's gone;
Dun follows green
When summer's done.
Spengler's my man, said topaz-eyed.
Thought of progress I can't abide.
In rhythmic ebb and flow
The seasons come and go.

When all's said and done
Nothing's new under the sun:
Time's whirligig can only bring
Summer winter autumn spring,
And all's to do again.

But soon cat drew her final breath,
Her topaz eyes were closed in death.

But then man came along.
He sang a different song:
That aspen tree once grew from seed
Planted by man;
One day, when old, it will be
Cut down by man.
The window pane, the house that frames it,
Were made by man.
With spade in hand
Man made the glass,
Man axed the tree
And sawed the timber
And shaped the walls
And built the house
From blueprint preconceived.
Man prophesies no evil doom
Emerging from time's womb.
Man's speech creates a wealth
Of unseen knowledge
From solar system college;
His curious mind discovers
His birth in ancient time
From primal slime.
The laws of change man gets to know
And understands why things are so.
Man's labour, bought and sold,
Protects him from of old
From summer's heat and winter's cold.
Someday, with labour free,
He'll pull it down and better build
Homes with happy humans filled,
And with foreseeing mind
Plan homes for all mankind.
No human then shall homeless be,
Nor lack the time to see

The beauty of the tremulous aspen tree.

EXPLOITATION
John Salway

Take a case of bones
Rattling in the desert

And watch the last drops
Of blood
Drip
Into the ravenous sands

Take a gold mine
Yes
Take a gold mine

And paint your lady
With summer in Las Vegas

Take the world
And twist it round your finger
Tight-wad

And don't forget
To catch
The pennies from Heaven.

BLACK SHEEP
Jone o' Broonlea

Aye, 'e wur an' a,
A bloody card wur uncle Joe:
At 'time 'is dooms were provin' bad
E up to speawt, an' roost of ' lad -
im 'ere, i' Lych Lane
In 'is grave wheer Joe wur payin'
Lip-service, stonnin' on 'is stooan,
Fit to stir 'is iv'ry booan
As, turnin' in 'is tomb, 'e'd oss
To whummle this murtherin' bullshit boss

As'd sent a rook o' ther owd mates
Deawn Lych Lane an' through it gates
To back-o' beyond an' kingdom-come,
While mony another mun cringe awhum.
It a' come eawt, o' ' feaw deeds o' Joe's,
0' th'after 'ed'd cockt up 'is toes:
Stuff as we'd 'ear'd bur ud nooan believe
As heaw "one of us" could so deceive
Ut craeturs ud bloody ther 'ands o' this manner
An' wipe 'em, t'ide ' stains, i' ' blood-red banner
As leads us still.
Up at ' mill
T's a' modern neaw -
Onyheaw,
Beawt t'owd bastin' an' batin' life,
Tho' still ther's ' wark's estrangin' strife
0' ' rooad o' mackin' things
An' ' consequences ut it brings -
A'reet for them wi' profit goal,
Bu' niver same for us an' a'
For tho' they'n done wi Joe's feaw ways
Is aim ut based 'em a' still stays -Apin' ' Yanks: "Catch 'em
up, then over-tak!"
Follerin' ther wake, as should ha' ta'en tother tack,
Turnin' eawt what's namoore na ther profitable lines
As desirable goods for ' good o' mankind's
Progress": this Jack-o' -Lantern chase
As peysons ' yearth wi it reckless waste.
They'n long-sin' ta'en Joe's likeness deawn frae ' wa's
An' we mun shak' 'is clawkin' paw off' Cause
Ut's eawrs, t'insense it in us mates what's reight
I' this fluctuatin' feight
An' nooan be flaid
0' new mistakes ut meht be made:
Let's mind o' Karl an' Fred an' hill,
For what they towt's as fresh 'ere still,
Tho' lots they wrote we'd tend t'owerbook
Sin' it didn't figger i' Joseph's book -
Long-ignored, it wur allus theer
An' reaches us neaw, like news-frae-nowheer,
That clear an' breet
We maun ne'er namoore base it frae eawr seet.
An we were bloody foo's an' a',
T'ha' set such store bi uncle Joe.

roost (of), praised; Lych, corpse; oss, try; whumnile, overturn; rook, large number; bastin , beating; batin' , cutting short; insense, make understand. (the substituted by a glottal stop, is indicated by an apostrophe: 'time, ' lad, ' feaw deeds, etc.).

TRAFFIC LIGHTS
Gareth Thomas

Two overalled men threw their tools into the council truck and drove away, leaving behind them a brand new pair of traffic lights. They had installed many traffic lights before this pair, and did not get emotionally involved with them. Maybe they did not know how long it had taken to make a decision to put those particular lights in that particular spot. What did they know of the dead children, killed on that busy main road? How could they curse the council for not listening to its electorate? They drove off without seeing the pregnant women standing on the corner, laden with shopping and justified bitterness.

She just stood and looked at the lights. A controlled pedestrian crossing. Perhaps the child inside her would now stand a better chance of survival than the sister it would never see, the last child to be killed before the council decided to act. The fourth child killed on that spot before the council decided to act.

"We can't afford a crossing." They said that after the first child was killed. After the second child was killed, a Crossing Action Group was formed by local mothers, and the council generously said: "We're looking into the possibilities ..." While they were looking into the possibilities a year after the first child was killed, the third died under a continental juggernaut. This vehicle also demolished a lamp-standard as it swerved, in a belated avoiding action. Maybe the council looked into possibilities a bit quicker then, as a lamp-standard happens to be an expensive item. They paid a woman to hold a sign for children to cross. STOP - CHILDREN CROSSING. When this woman was in hospital, and the fourth child was dead, and the council was paying compensation, and the Crossing Action Group had won the attention of the press, the council agreed that it was a good idea to put a crossing at the point in question. Now, a year later, it was finally installed.

The pregnant woman with the shopping and the tired face watched as the first batch of returning schoolchildren pressed the button on the bights. The traffic stopped and they crossed safely, leisurely, happily pointing at the little green man-shaped pedestrian light. Wiping away a tear, the woman turned and walked home.

264

A fat man in a pinstriped suit was sitting behind the wheel of his big black limousine, fingers drumming on the gear stick, impatient to meet a business friend for drinks, glaring at the red bight. "Come on, blast you!" he cursed, glancing at his watch. The light changed to amber and he accelerated quickly away, swerving to miss a cyclist and hooting the horn loudly. "Bloody cyclists! Shouldn't be allowed on the road ..."

The man on the bicycle made a rude sign with his fingers. Well, how could he know that the car contained the councillor he had helped to elect?

LUVIN' TALLY
Jone o' Broonlea

One-wi-tother, i'
Tooathri heawrs o'
Four-legged marbock, then
Five for sleep while t'
Six-o'-cbock rise an' off bi
Seven wi summat t'
Eight afoore t'
Nigh'n four-moore's drive as'll ha'
Ta'en a' mi time to mek
Elevenses wi t' missis.
(Ther's truth fon i' t'owd adage, o'
tother rooad-reawnd what's said:
Ther's summat moore na marriage to
Four bare legs in a bed).

4th NOVEMBER 1974
M.G. Askell

4th November 1974. That will have to do for a title, in any case I've always been suspicious of titles, they continually restrict, in an academic sense, or so it seems to me; and I am going to diverge considerably, in any case having read of the problems others undergo in the search for an appropriate title, I'll just say now that, if one appears it wasn't my starting point. What is, or, what was, you are entitled to ask; (maybe that could be the title; YOU ARE ENTITLED TO ASK).

You probably have heard, even asked, the questions that follow. What is it? What is it supposed to represent? What does it mean? and Hmm? Why do you do it? Most of the people I am in contact with, those that for a variety of reasons are likely to enter into the flat in which I weave the web of my personality, invariably connect these (objects) with a concept which takes form in the sound ... modern art. I am never worried at any of my levels by the sound modern, it's a contradiction as soon as the sound has passed. Art, this sound disappoints me, when it reaches me I understand vaguely that I am being committed to an act of separation. In this situation I am not al ease, either with myself, and consequently ill at ease with those who have produced the sound, art. It seems too long a journey to undertake at such short notice.

To continue, we are on a beach, which beach? I don't think that has any great significance, well I'm confident enough to say at this moment in time it wasn't the motivation, only the place. However, the we, as always, remains elusive, from the significance factor that is. I thought at the time about, how clean, (clean, as a state of being, not in the environmental clinical sense;) now, timewise, is. There are numerous pebbles on pebbly beaches, neither of the two I collected, selected, retained, were in themselves initially sufficient, for their retention, maybe I would use them, it depended on, a) the strength of my memory, b) do the pebbles continue to assist in c) the development of, as yet an unknown recollection of that particular moment and its consequences.

On the beach there are many similar stones of the same material, some are broken, no, that isn't strictly correct, some are in the process of becoming smooth all over, being an uninformed geologist I would describe the structure of the stones as crystalline. On that bright everyday morning the broken stones sparkled while and clean, the two stones I retained are in one sense their future. Time has locked the past in practicalities.

That day during the afternoon we flew a kite, there was no wind in the morning, if there had been I doubt if I would be typing this. The kite was in the shape of a bat, the colour of the kite is black. When I was a boy I had an idea that kite's had achieved a magnificent freedom; from what? I didn't know; they haven't, they are attached, and that's what makes them work.

As for always in close proximity to the beach there stood those indispensable egg-timers of instantaneous enjoyment, or so I am led to believe, if for no other reason than their abundance, which I doubt, the amusement arcade, model-boating lake, on this particular day in the throes of organised model yacht competition, saddle your own canoe lake; we did, and I had my own thoughts. We did other things, people do, I said goodbye to a daymoment, we began to return, the four of us. The stones? in a haversack, inside a wrapper that once harboured our now eaten cheese and tomato sandwiches.

A piece of ordinary plywood 6' x 8" the surface has cuts and indentations a result of my activities in conjunction with others, some of these being:- the construction of a glider; framing of two drawings the work of two children, a brother and sister; cutting card into various shapes; a block to hammer on in order to save the table or whatever from above cuts and indentations. The piece of wood came from a carnival float, an off-cut, part of a side panel that now enjoys the imaginative reign of a group of children living in a council estate, the wind and all other weather conditions. Is now the ground.

Lighting, colour, you could easily build yourself a box big enough to live in with the black and white tracts written on light and colour, still have adequate supplies remaining that would enable you to light a fire thus produce colour, that would be ridiculous? You think. Colour is there and costs nothing, all you need is to look. O.K. but seeing isn't just a mechanical functioning that depends on all the bits working well with each other to give every one the same exact image. It depends, on what, well I could say; on past practicalities. By which is meant? You may have heard the story. Someone is talking, about, it could be, he, she, X or Y, who is so, aware, sensitive, capable of such feeling which in turn causes: a) individual suffering, this is always suspect, b) to be such a creative person, the question is, in whose eyes? The only other buildings besides modern production units (factories) that place the windows above the eye level are prisons. You don't hear that kind of tale there, the factory, I mean. Like unused muscles you get to using them less, not because you choose to; simply because you forget they are there. Who? X, Y or Z, do you think you are? With your attitudes to have the audacity to question people who have received the very best that is available, educationally speaking, that is; and further more devoted a life time's work to it! They know they haven't won, or lost for that matter, as long as you don't answer. Point is we all do a life time's work and a few can afford opportunities for devotion, paid for by those who just work. Work in an environment that prompted this statement* "I was 25 years old before I knew there were colours in a tree. Before that I thought they were just plain fucking brown." That is how it can be, we have autumn curtains in the flat, the sunlight filters through, in silence.

I have no idea whatsoever if lists exist giving the number of hours rainfall for Saturdays, and Bank Holidays, they probably could be compiled, in any case, I've always thought somehow that we are cheated, that Saturdays and Bank Holidays are above average days for rain, perhaps Wednesday half-closing people think the same about Wednesday afternoons, some people are possibly unaware of the importance in Saturday skies, they are fortunate enough to be above to delay or rearrange to suit themselves. It was raining on the Saturday we went to find a frame, get the shopping, look in a bookshop, and so be it, dodge chunks of metal travelling at between 15-40 m.p.h. traffic transportation, self-destination, whatever you'll call it. "We are all heading for the same place, hipper, it's like a trip around the world, when you get back to where you started out from, the journey's all you've had, and I spent 30 odd years at sea, in one engine-room after another, lived as best I could by a set of rules that were said to be the only ones that would work, people being what they were. Now it's all changed I'm told, so I've a few more quid in my pocket now and again, but it wasn't much of a journey." Old Bert, ex R.N. Stoker, ex M.N. Stoker, boilerman in the machine shop where I started my apprenticeship, died some 3 months later, 59 years of age. I passed by the journeys end on a dark morning at 7.25 a.m. some 200 yards from the main gate of the shipyard where we worked. There were five or six men stood around a heap of overcoats at the side of the road, I only saw them at the last moment and had to swerve in order to avoid the group, nearly running into others on the early morning tramp to the yard. Someone yelled, "Watch it you mad little cunt." But I saw the boots sticking out, highly polished as always. In the cycle shed, a match flared, one of the chain-gang said, "Bert's snuffed it, down the road, only had them boots a week, too." Then it started raining.

We collected the shopping, browsed in a bookshop, dodged the traffic, bought (10p) ample woodwork to enable a frame to be made, it was already painted red and silver, the frame is made. I haven't answered any of the questions posed or have I? It's a recollection of freshness; sometimes these days in a purely personal time, it makes for ... well not art. B's expecting a child early next year, she says she's happy on that side of things.

See ya.

Nigel Gray. 'The Silent Majority' (Vision Critical Studies) 1975, Vision Press Ltd.

IN PRAISE OF COOKS
Angela Tuckett

While driving rain joins sky to earth upon this holiday
Factories and Parliament alike are all of them at play -
(Except the statesmen organising profitable war,
Whilst politicians send another regiment to restore
Their kind of law and order to ungrateful folk abroad) -
See! Unemployed the members of the Unilever Board!
No company director toils to pass a dividend,
No artist's skill devoted to the slick advertisement

Debating the conflicting claims of Dreft and Surf and Tide!
Even the copy writer's arts today are laid aside;
No lawyer robs his client, nor the publican his guest,
And - can it be? Yes! Even the common people are at rest!

The British common people on all other days are found
Providing all the steady work that makes the wheels go round
A-weaving, turning, fitting, making everything that's made;
So lift your glass for once in praise of British craft and trade!
The mason builds the palace, church and mansion row on row
But he never gets invited to lead the Lord Mayor's Show;
The brickie and the tiler rear the steeple, tower and dome
Yet have to fight for overtime who never owned a home;
Each dawn the cowman rises and he plods through wind and mud,
Beneath that field the veins of coal are splashed with miners' blood,
And milk goes up a penny, so his children go without;
The Coal Board stops his house coal, so the miner's fire goes out.

Our Britain's rich in craftsmen, wherever you may look,
But one the poets never praise. E'll praise today - the cook
It is an attribute of god's perfection to create,
Whilst changing human nature is beyond the powers of Fate -
Or so they say. And yet the cook can change the sour to sweet.
Can soothe the sad in heart and make the sick sit up and eat.
Who else each day, through fair and foul, no matter what is sent,
Can take the most indifferent and make it excellent?
I don't believe in manna, nor to Heaven we should look,
I know it's not the Devil but Mankind supplies the cook.
Some reverence love of man for maid, some bank on love of Good,
But what love is more earnest than the love of man for food?

A FEW OBSERVATIONS ABOUT VOICES GENERALLY
Ken Clay

It seems to me that Voices suffers from too much didacticism, naive idealism and the worst kind of socialist realism.

1. Didacticism Most contributors feel impelled to instruct the reader about
the horrors of capitalist life. This is a worthy aim but it really has no place
in a journal of creative writing. When didacticism comes in the front door
art usually goes out the back. The proper place for such writing is in political pamphlets. Unfortunately most Party writers can never resist an oppor-

tunity to have a go. The result is a big yawn, especially as it is usually read by Party readers who have heard it all before.

2. Naive Idealism: Proletarian writers generally feel they have to start off writing in the best bourgeois manner they can manage. This leads not only to a strangled, over-complex syntax and the use of large words imprecisely, but also the acceptance of bourgeois language taboos and a rejection of a large part of their experience as unsuitable for literary representation. They imagine there is so much of working class life that is too sordid, obscene, trivial or degrading. I can only describe it as the Noble Savage syndrome and wonder if it isn't perhaps a product of the English movement's Methodist origins. Everyone seems to be straining to convince the reader of his purity of heart and, consequently, the goodness of the cause; again this may have a place in political tracts similar to those issued by the Jehovah's Witnesses on how I saw the light but isn't it a bit inhibiting when approaching creative writing? Language becomes emasculated; experience becomes filtered, processed, cleaned up; truth gets lost. Writers in this bracket aspire to become accepted by a middle class literary establishment and become corrupted in consequence. A strange corollary to this syndrome is the notion that literary incompetence has its own virtue and charm. That it produces, with its technical inability to deceive or take up ambiguous positions, a transparent goodness. This leaves the reader feeling totally superior, safe, and at best, patronisingly benevolent.

3. Socialist Realism: A discipline designed to produce parables rather than works of art. We've almost reached the stage where capitalists wear black hats and communists white ones. The writer begins with an idea and invents people mechanically to act it out. The story loses credibility; the characters are necessarily two-dimensional but the author's nobility of purpose is in no doubt. Unfortunately his readers fall asleep on the second page. By denying all human qualities to bourgeois figures we become unrealistic: by investing all proletarian heroes with absolute goodness we compound the error. That's a simplistic account of socialist realism but it's just that kind of model that proletarian writers seem readiest to latch on to.

Now if these three features seen as virtues, rather than vices as I have described them above, constitute the criteria by which progressive writers are judged then it's not hard to see why my first piece failed. It carried no message; was inspired by no didactic impulse. Perhaps this is why you thought it cynical.

If anything it was anti-idealistic (using that word in its everyday sense rather than its philosophical one). The only candidate for the position of noble savage, young Trellie, is mocked. Nobody represents the pure in heart. The technique is 'knowing", 'sophisticated", opaque. where the hell does the author line up in all this? What's his position? It's significant that you should find that important, and I was gratified to note that you thought I wasn't a Communist. I have in fact been a Party member for the past six years.

The proletarian seems to come out badly when confronted by his bourgeois opponent who even utters such blasphemies as: 'The working class! What a collection! They imagine they can pick up culture like a pint pot!' Not a good parable at all. Yet I'd maintain that there's enough rope in that piece to enable the ageing queer to hang himself ten times over. And that, despite his inability to manipulate and comprehend the concepts of bourgeois philosophy, Trellie has an enthusiasm and intellectual energy which eclipses the shallow facility of his jaded mentor. Maybe all that was too understated. But aren't we patronising our readers by thinking so? Can we really not leave them to judge? Have they got to be protected from representations of clever middle class figures? If that's the case we'll soon be producing the literary equivalent of a Punch and Judy show.

All this isn't intended to vindicate my piece which may well have been rejected for other valid reasons. I merely use it as an example. What I hope I have given you cause to think about is the effectiveness of Voices both as a platform for proletarian writing and an organ for the good of the cause. Like you I want to further socialism and I think that creative writing is one of the most powerful methods available. But to be artistic - and if we re not artistic we're nothing -we've got to reflect the reality of the proletarian experience rather than the ideal we suspect it is capable of becoming. We've got to credit bourgeois culture with its real strengths. We've got to create credible, even likeable bourgeois characters so that their spiritual bankruptcy will be all the more evident when it is finally exposed. We've got to be subtle, complicated: the reader shouldn't be able to say he's reading the work of a Party member after a paragraph or two. He's got to draw the moral not have it rammed into his head. And, dare I say it, we've got to entertain, otherwise nobody is going to read it anyway. I don't want to go into this in detail but Voices does seem short on that commodity. I think some of the pieces are getting by on novelty value alone, like a dog walking on its back legs.

I hope you find these remarks relevant even though I don't expect you to agree with them. They seem to have come out more severe than I intended and perhaps it's my turn to apologise for being too harsh. It should be apparent from this deluge, concerned as it is with the negative aspects of Voices, that I still find the idea of a journal of proletarian writing important and well worth arguing about.

cover size 210 x 148 mm (A5)

CONTENTS

274. Editorial — Ben Ainley
276. Reincarnation — M Doyle
277. The Christmas Present — R Friedman
279. The Quiet Black — AM Horne
280. Man in Winter — M Ferns
282. The Gun — J McFarlane
282. Pseudonym — FG Walker
285. The Bell spews its Evil — J Barnes
285. The Name of the Game — B Eburn
286. Harry the Tick Man — V Leslie
287. Staunch True Comrade — J Sutton
287. Factory Boy — T Harcup
288. Oppression ... — T Harcup
289. Comment on Ken Clay's article — W Froom
289. Comment on Ken Clay's article — F Moore
290. Comment on Ken Clay's article — I E Reed
291. Comment on Ken Clay's article — B Eburn
293. The Silly Bloody Working Class — M Ferns
293. Modern Poetry, Eliot and The working Class — T Whitfield
294. Poetry - Where are You Now? — IE Reed
295. A Matter of Opinion — V Leslie
296. Remember your Kerb Drill — A Prior
297. We came en masse — J Sutton
297. On Winter's Highway — AG Froom
298. Saving Face — A Jamieson
299. Turning Point — J O Broonlea
300. The Housewife — B O Connor
301. Fireweed A Review — B Ainley
302. Listen to the Old Men — A Arnison
303. Woman's Paper — F Moore
304. Promise — F Moore
304. Midnight — KB Stump
305. Modern Magic — B Smith
306. Muck — Barbara Smith
307. If Things Go on as They Are — A Prior
308. War Maimed Girl at a Dance — R Friedman
309. Far From My Window — T Whitfield
309. Drama Now — W Froom
310. The Dancer of Death — IE Reed
311. Elegy — KL Jones
312. Person with the grace of a tall ship — J Barnes
312. North Scale's Winter — AM Horne

313. Father Crisp Sell   AM Horne
313. Last Rites   B Eburn
Graphics by Peter Carter

EDITORIAL

This is Voices 6, and our total output covers about 300 pages. There have been more than 200 separate pieces in these 6 issues, written by more than 80 writers, the overwhelming majority of whom have never had work published previously. The quality varies greatly of course: some of the pieces (and at this point it would be invidious to select examples) are of high poetic or literary merit; others are not. The whole purpose of "Voices" is not to perpetuate mediocrity, but to fan the sparks of imagination and revolt against what is reactionary, soulless, greedy and exploitative, and to encourage writers from the factory floor and the branch meeting. We would like world famous writers, and national figures, and we admire their works in other publications: but our aim is to help to build a team of working men and women who are reflecting in new and vivid writing the explosive left movement in Britain and the world.

We need a lot of help. We are getting new writers with each issue. Our sales, still modest, are growing. Our financial appeal was generously backed. But we still do not know whether Labour Party wards, Trade Union branches, workers in factories, students, Communist Party members, enjoy "Voices" and feel that it meets a need.

Three of us went recently to a Labour Party group in Stockport, and read pieces from "Voices" to them and discussed them. There was genuine appreciation of what we are doing We would like to test the reactions of all sorts of people to "Voices" and invite you to ask your organization, or student bodies to give us a chance to explain "Voices" to them.

We need the Labour Movement. Does the Labour Movement need us? We think it does. Us and organizations and publications like us. We ask Labour Party and Trade Union and Communist Party, Young Socialist and Student bodies to help us. How? These are some ways.

Buy a number of copies of "Voices" to distribute and sell to your members.

Circulate an advertising letter of ours to your members.

Give us a regular subscription (yearly, half-yearly or quarterly) on which we can rely and budget.

Affiliate to Unity of Arts our parent body, and contribute an agreed annual affiliation fee.

Elsewhere, we welcome "Fireweed" which has an advertisement of its second issue in the summer. We also give a free advertisement to "The Basement Writers". We will gladly give publicity to all ventures which try to establish an association between the Labour Movement and the arts.

Finally, if among readers living within 10 miles of the centre of Manchester, there are three or four prepared to give time to helping to widen the contacts of "Voices" such people can be sure they will be warmly welcomed.

Our thanks to Peter Carter for the graphics.

Ben Ainley

JOHN MACLEAN

Brian Gallon, 12 Frank Place, North Shields, Tyne and Wear, is researching material for a play about John Maclean, the Clydeside socialist leader.

If anyone has personal recollecticns or parents or grandparents who remember Maclean, or any written material about him, will they please get in touch with Mr. Gallon.

The cash raised by our appeal in November which finally raised over £145 helped us clear our debts, and get "Voices 5" out. We are not out of the wood. It costs around £150 to get out an issue of "Voices" and at this moment, from the proceeds of sales of "Voices 5" we have around £100. We are compelled therefore to ask people interested in our survival to continue to help us financially. We will acknowledge directly all sums received. Make cheques payable either to Ben Ainley or to Frank Parker.

NOTE TO CONTRIBUTORS

We welcome contributions in prose and verse. But we cannot undertake to return manuscripts unless stamped addressed envelope is included.

Number the pages of your contribution. Write your name and address on each page. If possible, send typescripts; but if your piece is hand written1 make sure it is legible to the printer.

We are dealing with between 80 and 100 contributions per issue, and this number is growing. Bear with us if there are delays.

PLEASE TYPE (or WRITE) ON ONE SIDE OF THE PAPER ONLY

This is a must.

A brief personal biography (about 40 words) will help us, but will not necessarily be published.

REINCARNATION

Do you feel misspent
Are you fully content
In the role life's given to you?

Do you feel all the while
Something more worthwhile
Is what you should be aiming to do?

Do you feel overwrought
At the change change has brought
In this life by men different than you?

Do you just criticise,
Live a life like the flies
And discontent spread like disease?

Do you play your part
On the basis of art
Deny what the heart tells you?
At the end of the day
When you get your pay
Do you feel it just isn't worthwhile?

Then cor blimey mate, You're in a helluva state
And there's not going to be a next time.

Or
I hope that it's different next time.

M.Doyle

THE CHRISTMAS PRESENT

The placards screamed the headlines. The evening paper followed through with the rest of the story.

Citizens homeward bound released from the day's toil, bought the papers and read the news in shocked silence. "EMINENT NUCLEAR PHYSICIST RESIGNS".

Professor Lewley withdrawn into the corner of the first class railway compartment and taking refuge behind a copy of The Times, shook his head sadly and sighed. Seeing the announcement of his action in the cold black and white of the placard and stripped of the warmth of his covering explanation, aroused in him a deep sense of desolation. However, he thought to himself, staring unseeingly at the small print of the morning's paper, the deed was now done and the step now taken from which there was no retracing.

He had resigned on a matter of principle and that was that.

His thoughts went back to that final scene when after months of grave and gnawing disquiet within himself he had faced his eleven colleagues on the committee of top level scientists and had delivered the bombshell. "Gentlemen", he had said, "Brother scientists, after deep and serious thought on my part I have come to the conclusion that I can no longer reconcile my own feelings with the aims and objects of this committee for the development of weapons for use in nuclear warfare. Please colleagues, I ask you here and now to be good enough to accept my resignation from this committee."

Looking at the stunned faces of the men around him had moved him to add softly, "Believe me, I have, as I said, given this matter deep and serious consideration and I find that now at long last I must face the realisation that I can no longer work on objects for which the ultimate use will be the destruction of man, by man."

Of course his resignation had not been accepted unanimously. Some of the older ones had been prepared to argue it out with him, make him see reason so to speak, but in the end they too had had to give in, hoping that perhaps he had been overworking and needed a break for two or three weeks.

"Why not take a trip over the Xmas holidays, Lewley old chap", professor Dacre had said soothingly, in a tone suspiciously like that one would use to a man on the brink of a nervous breakdown. "Just pack a bag and fly off with your wife and kiddie, say to the Bahamas. It should be pretty warm there, just now, I can fix the flight for you old man, no trouble at all, and you'll get there just in time for the Xmas celebrations. Quite an idea y'know."

Lewley shuddered a little, thinking back on Dacre's patronising air.

Hm! The Xmas celebrations that really was what had brought things to a head and had determined him to take the final step.

So simple. So utterly, utterly simple, the circumstances that had at last removed the scales from his eyes and had revealed the image of his true self, standing clearly before him, face to face.

How often one's puppet sneaks in and takes command, steering one this way and that whilst one's own soul squeezed out stands by biding its time just waiting the opportune moment in which to reassert itself. And so it had been with the learned man of science.

The false premise on which his own sense of security had rested and which had begun to rock quite some time ago, had finally toppled when he had been assigned to the role of Santa Claus at the Xmas party of his young daughter Caroline.

Several of Caroline's little friends were spending the Xmas holidays abroad with their respective parents and so the Xmas party had been held three weeks before the holidays.

Dorothy the professor's wife had made up a cloak for him out of some red cotton fabric, a bit of medical tow had done for the beard and a furry cap had completely covered his dark brown head. When he had protested at the too obvious fake of the tow, Dorothy had replied, "Oh the kids'll never notice, all that interests them is the sack of gifts which you are going to hand out, after all Caroline and her friends are only five years old."

Then she had added in mock solemn tones, "I promise you when Caroline's seven you shall have a full blown grey beard."

When Caroline's seven - sev-en sev-en were his last thoughts as he drifted off into uneasy slumber that night. "What makes you so sure Caroline will reach seven?" said his soul, accusingly, confronting him and barring his way so that he could move neither to the left nor to the right, but only backwards.

Wildly he tried to press on, but his soul now dressed as Santa Claus and sporting a full blown grey beard and wearing a mask of the professor's own features, continued to stand in his way. "Who told you, who told you?" Frantically the professor looked around for a scapegoat, his eyes large with apprehension. Then he spotted the tow-bearded Daddy Xmas. Pointing a forefinger in his direction he cried out desperately, "He told me, he told me." The tow-bearded red-cloaked figure advanced towards him, also wearing a mask the replica of the professor's own features. "Ha, you'd no need to listen to me," he croaked. "No need at all to listen to me."

"You see", said his soul, gently. "You see!"

"Yes, I see it all now," said the man of science, dropping swiftly into a relaxed sleep. The way was now clear, the doubts, the uncertainties, the nagging pointers were stilled once and forever.

And so he had gone forth and given his decision to them. The decision which by now was being blazoned forth for the world to see and to wonder at. To be repeated faithfully by some, to be distorted by others.

Dorothy was waiting for him when he arrived home. He took three large strides towards her and with a tired sigh went straight into her outstretched arms.

They clung together thus, for a few moments, neither speaking, each deeply aware of their spiritual oneness.

Then Dorothy looked up at her husband, her eyes shining as she uttered the words he wanted more than anything to hear from her lips at this moment. "Don't you see, darling," she said, "You have given those kids the best Xmas present in the whole world."

Rose Friedman

THE QUIET BLACK

I lay in the darkness looking at the black
A car past placing a window on each of the walls.
The clock murmured on and on always asking the same question
I was uneasy waiting for a voice that never came.
A tree its branches moving as a Japanese hand dancer
Formed slowly in half closed eyes.
Black on a white grey haze, branches pointing.
Shiny raven branches, carving twisting in unsettled order
Each offset joint a shape of beautiful agony
Saying something that I couldn't hear.
Warm blankets collected my thoughts
I mumbled prayers in tired subconscious
Sleep pulled at my eyelids and the story was left untold.

AM Horne

A MAN IN WINTER

I've no flowers for your grave to-day
So I'll offer my thoughts as a bouquet.
You remember the clock you used to wind?
Think of it ... you'll call it to mind.
It misses the hand that wound it up
And treated it like a loving cup.
The roof still leaks, it's not very strong,
The nights are awful ... awful long.
My pension was cut when you went away,
In fact, it was cut the very same day.
And flowers are dear in the winter time,
If only we lived in a warmer clime.
You still haven't got a stone at your head
My money just goes for rent and some bread,
And the children don't visit me any more
Life is harder ... when you're very poor.
Everyone goes rushing and tearing about,
Remember old Ted, the way he did shout?
My old friends have gone ... all gone away,
Young folk are different ... nothing to say.
I'm afraid I won't see you to-morrow,
My dear ... it causes me very great sorrow.
I'm so shaky now ... I suppose I'm old
And I walk so slowly and, oh it's so cold.
The old coat I have so faded from blue
Lets the wind come tearing through.
If old Ted were here he'd help me along,
Young folk are different ... tho' big and strong.
They just pass me by with never a glance
For them to speak ... there' s simply no chance.
Maybe they're thoughtless, the folk of to-day,
And not unkind as some might say.
Do you think, dear, that people do change,
Or is it just me, that's acting strange?
But, here I am talking in the wind and the rain,
And all I keep doing is just to complain.
But, listen to this ... it'll make you smile,
Yesterday, I walked for nearly a mile.
I was passing a church, old and black,
And, thinking of you, went slowly back.
I went inside and walked all around,

Apart from my footsteps there wasn't a sound.
I went so very softly, so timid and mild,
Right up to a statue of Madonna and Child.
A candle was burning with slow, steady flame,
I lit one for you ... and said softly your name.
I loved you all the days of your life,
I love you still, oh, my wife.
When summer comes and the birds are singing,
I'll come every day and I'll be bringing
Roses of red to show I love you,
And to make you smile, flowers of blue.
Your favourite colour ... just like the skies,
And, oh, I remember ... just like your eyes.

Michael Ferns

THE GUN: TELEVISION GANGSTER BLUES

Courageous man, he copulates;
He gives to earth the gift
From out his loins:
His living replicas.
His phallic organ
Rejoices in new life.

Perhaps he has forgotten
The phallic symbol gun,
Shooting out destruction
Into earth's worn womb;
For everyone that he creates
A hundred more shall die.

For you, for me, O sorry man, I sigh.

J McFarlane

PSEUDONYMS
F.G. Walker

Father John O'Rourke, small and wiry, was in his study when the bell rang. He put the silver chalice back in its case and opened the door.

Outside, in the bloom, was a woman. She was tall and slim like a willow, wearing a dark green suit and a green 'Robin Hood' hat.

"Good evening."

"Good evening. I'm sorry to come so late, but I well, I was in the district so I thought it would be alright." Her voice had a soft, light sound, like spring rain.

"I don't believe we've met."

She shook her head. "I'm a writer ... Pat Fielding and I thought ..."

"Not the Pat Fielding?"

"If you mean the one who wrote 'Tombstones at Midnight' , yes."

"Well!" He studied her for some moments.

"Perhaps I'd better tell you why I've called."

He stood aside. "You'd better come in then."

282

She stepped into the light. He closed the door, noting that she was much younger than he had first thought, and she was quite pretty too. He led the way to the study; waved her to a chair.

"Thank you." She sank into the seat, sending a speculative glance around the room.

Father O'Rourke stood across from her, fingering the soft flesh at the end of his chin. "You were saying," he said.

"What?" She flicked her eyes back.

"The reason you came."

She smiled lopsidedly. "Well, it might seem silly really but I've just started my next book and I'm trying to ..." She paused, gesticulating with one hand. "How shall I put it ... trying to get the right ... atmosphere." Her voice rose on the last word.

"I see." His eyes narrowed. "This new book. Is it anything like the last one?"

"You've read it?" She lifted her eyebrows a little.

"Yes, twice as a matter of fact."

"I'm flattered. I hope you'll buy the new one." He shrugged. There was a small silence. An idea flickered in his brain. "Perhaps I could offer you a glass of sherry?"

"Yes, thank you."

He went over to the sideboard and poured one glass of sherry. "Look," he said then, "I have to make a phone call, I won't be a minute." He went through to the hallway, made the call and then padded outside into the drive. Her car was turned round, facing the road. He wondered what she was doing here. Then he laughed softly. He opened the car door and took the ignition key. Then he went back to the study.

"May I look round the church tonight?" The woman stood up as he entered.

"I suppose so ... if you're not frightened."

"You'll tell me it's haunted next."

He held the door open and waited while she picked up her handbag. As they went out he said: "I suppose I'll be in your book?"

"Perhaps." She stopped; gave him a quick look from under her dark lashes, then she added: "In fact it might be a good idea."

"You haven't decided then?"

283

She tilted her head on one side. "It depends on the story ... and the atmosphere. Shall we go?"

"Sure." He led the way across to the church; pushed open the door. "What would you like to see?"

"The belfry." She sounded as if she had been expecting the question.

He turned left into the small alcove that led to the stone steps. Looking back at her, he said casually, "They say a ghostly monk has been seen hereabouts."

She stiffened visibly. "Oh! Really?" Her voice trembled. "Where ... exactly?"

"Here. Still want to go up?"

She looked at him for several long seconds. "Yes."

He started up the narrow winding stairs. At the top he unbolted a small trapdoor and climbed through. He turned, looking down at her.

She stayed there, her head and shoulders through the opening. A little breathlessly she said: "Are we alone now?"

"Of course." He stepped back. "Come on up."

A smile pulled at her lips. She reached up; grabbed the trapdoor. "Sorry Father. But I've made other plans.

She pulled down the trapdoor then and slipped home the bolt. With a laugh that echoed on the stairs she hurried away.

He knelt down; tugged at the handle. It held fast. He stood upright, breathing hard. Then he remembered the torch in his pocket. He rushed over to the wall and stared hard at the darkness. Twin headlights pierced the night on the main road. He almost laughed out loud as he began flashing the torch.

The police car swept up to the church. Two minutes later he heard the bolt drawn on the trapdoor. A burly constable led the way down into the church and across to the vestry.

"We caught her, sir," he boomed. "Trying to start her car." He swept open the study door.

Father O'Rourke blinked at the brightness. In a chair near his desk sat the woman. Her face was the colour of raw cod. A police sergeant towered over her.

"Caught her with this, sir," he said. He indicated the silver chalice on the desk. "If the car had started she'd have got away with it."

Father O'Rourke smiled impishly. He took the ignition key from his pocket; tossed it on to the desk. "I made sure that she wouldn't," he said.

The woman jerked her head up; for a second her eyes blazed. "You ... you... How did you know about me?"

"Simple." He spread his hands, as if that one -gesture was sufficient. There was a tiny silence.

It was almost as if, from across the room, he felt her wince.

The police sergeant rubbed thoughtfully at his chin.

Father O'Rourke sauntered across to a book case, selected a volume and handed it to the woman. "Perhaps you'd like to read this," he said in a soft whimsical voice.

She gazed at it curiously. It was encased in a brightly coloured dust cover. Her eyes lingered on the words: "A NEW NOVEL BY PAT FIELDING." She turned the book over, and on the back was a picture of Father O'Rourke.

THE BELL SPEWS ITS EVIL

The bell spews its evil and the leash is slipped,
you're washed, your gear's gathered
and you sail like a pigeon into the clean fresh air
circling through the scent of honeysuckle that isn't there
flying up up into the bright sky until the sunlight hurts your eyes
then you come to rest upon the gentle, rose scented waters of
melancholy
until the leashes of necessity and conformity drag you back next
morning.

Jimmy Barnes

THE NAME OF THE GAME

People like us
can be very mean
until we learn

the name of the game.

Blame if you must the blacks
for the squalor we live in,
for our depreciated
standard of living,

but who gains most
from lack of houses,
whose profits are swollen
with stolen wages?

Mean we shall remain
until we learn
the name of the game
is money.

Bill Eburn

HARRY THE TICK MAN

Harry comes on Fridays, paydays
Round the doors in his estate car
Holding back the revolution singlehanded
Outfits for you and your man for the club dance
Fifty pence a week, no deposit, no bother.

He carries an armload of lurex dresses
Cheap tinsel, wherever he goes
In case some one's in need
The car is bulging with cellophaned sheets
Shoes and boots, jeans and pit shirts
All new, all in a jumble.

Working late for village Cinderellas
Swopping shift money for weekend dreams
No deposit, no bother.

Vivien Leslie

STAUNCH, TRUE COMRADE

Staunch, true Comrade
it hurts to see you
suffer for your belief.
You are ready to fight
for a world that seems lost.
You swim against the tide
waving your convictions
like a banner
while others run and hide
wrapped in their cocoon
of complacency
fed on glib promises
and poisoned by subtle tongues
against you.
Your courage shines like a beacon
A light in a dark world.

Jean Sutton

FACTORY BOY

Went to school, got no joy -
Where's your school uniform, boy?"
Messed around, broke up chairs,
Smoked fags under the stairs.

Got a job on the assembly line
Same bloody thing all the time.
Look forward to Fridays - at the pub scene.
At the match on Saturdays - let off some steam.

Born into this mess, never had a hope,
Too many kids, me mum couldn't cope.
Too noisy and crowded at home, same at school;
No wonder I broke the rules!

Me mum just watches the tele,
Me dad's always on the drink.
And you wonder why we go on strike,
The system that causes this stinks.

I'm the stool the middle class sit on,
I'm the tool the middle class shit on.
But one day - you wait and see,
We'll run our factory; me mates and me.

OPPRESSION

Oppression...
  Corruption...

Depression...
  Disruption...

Eruption.
  Solution?

Revolution!

Tony Harcup of the Basement Writers

A number of comments follow on the article by Ken Clay which appeared in Voices 5:

Of course there is a tendency for new, dedicated, enthusiastic working class writers to write in the way he deplores, but I think if they are sincere, and not just striving for effect, or to convert, they'll learn to be artistic as well as realistic.

There is also a technique of writing which does not come easily or naturally to people whose vocabulary has already been limited by the so-called examples of culture around us. Small wonder they overdo things, when they write themselves, like teenagers who must be fashionable, even if it hurts.

Finally, if we are sincere, we too must strive to be encouraging, as well as critical, both of ourselves as well as fellow writers - God knows the unpublished, unknown, writer has enough to contend with, when trying to get somebody to read his work, and there must be many who remain dumb through lack of opportunity or hope. This is where VOICES CAN HELP, by making people more articulate, and perhaps eventually more observant, analytical, critical, and discerning too.

W. Froom

Would Ken Clay perhaps have modified his schoolmasterly rudeness if he had thought his letter would be printed? Talk about didactic? Of course it is often hard to avoid sounding bossy if we lay down the law, especially to those who don't accept our ideas.

People write out of their experience of life; often it is a hurt that sets us composing. Capitalism is a system that crushes and hurts us and we cry out. Our one sidedness is usually too much doom and gloom and we are embarrassed when we celebrate the joys of life, but that too is real, and genuine experience. Why should those of us who are happy in love be called dreamers for example? As for style, people write as they have learnt, and only in relation with others do they modify and refine in their own way the common heritage - which of course is part of bourgeois culture - but are we to stop speaking in case we are bourgeois? It is not the words we use, it's what we say that makes us different.

The fashion is to be opaque, of course, and such a style is great fun to write; but are we writing to show off or to communicate? In years of reading poetry (not just my own) to ordinary people I for one have had to make a choice. If art is communication, as I believe, and if we want to talk to people, we must talk in common ways. But not in watered down English or in bad language. The Labour Movement taught me that long ago.

Finally, how intolerant can you be? The infinite variety of personality offers many ways and styles of writing. There is more than one 'right' way. The thing, surely, is the affirmation of belief and confidence in people, and the refusal to accept misery as our lot.

As for me, I have lived as an active communist for forty years, and must write out of such an experience subconsciously by now.

Frances Moore

I find it a matter of urgency to make a reply to the article about "Voices" written by Ken Clay. I hope you can find room in your next issue to publish this.

The main error in his article is his definition of Socialist Realism, Socialist Realism is NOT "A discipline designed to produce parables rather than art." That may be Ken's definition, I suspect Ken has mistaken the crude "banner waving" material that does at times appear in "Voices" for a definition of Socialist Realism, if so, he couldn't be farther off the mark. The discussion that really remains is: What is "Socialist Realism"?

How many conflicting ideas emerge, basically ranging from those who never seem to have shaken off their respect for bourgeois ideas, hence they do produce these abstract, complex, over-worded symphonies of literature that Ken mentions.

Then the other extreme is the growing idea that any crudely rhyming, "Red Banner" waving wordiology, however crude it is in form (sometimes the cruder the better) in fact anything written by a worker constitutes "Workers' art": therefore if it waves aloft the red flag that is "Socialist Realism".

This form of diversity will I think be inevitable in any left wing movement of the arts such as "Voices" which is trying to counter bourgeois publications, and I think it will be some time before Socialist Realism in the western movement really emerges.

Anyone in contact with present publications from the Socialist Countries (Soviet literature etc.) will see the results of past struggle, the emergence of Real Socialist Realism.

Socialist Realism in my definition is art conscious of its role in Society. An art having something progressive to contribute, an art based on all aspects of humanity, progress and beauty. Art should uplift, agitate, enlighten, educate and give the reader a greater understanding of his relationship with his fellow man, nature, society, love and the ever present riddle of infinity, but must always retain some aesthetic quality.

Poetry is a medium of expressing ideas, thoughts, feelings etc. that cannot be expressed in any prose. If prose could cover these manifestations fully Poetry would never exist, therefore Form is important as a medium of creating in the reader the emotions that the writer intended. Socialist Realism strives to create positive emotions and reactions to the world around us. The worker who is talented and has something to say, will, with effort, defeat all the obstructions that lack of decent education present to him.

Oversimplicity, crudeness and "banner waving" (The glorious working class marching sternly forward etc.) is not only unreal because it is most often not the case, it also lacks humanity and didn't Marx call Communism "Scientific humanism"? Also it can tend to embarrass the audience. Over-complexity tends to often cover subjectiveness and tends to overawe the audience.

Our job is not to create a "sub-culture" but real Socialist culture of the very best. The idea that any worker who picks up a pen and scribbles a few words is a proletarian artist is false and often comes from the middle class. Bringing culture to and out of the working class is a challenge, but not impossible.

By supporting "Voices" we can help this process, so let us throw our words at one another and the world for the sake of humanity.

Fraternally, Ian E Reed

To Instruct or Delight?

1. "He will win universal applause who blends what is improving with what is pleasing, and both delights and instructs the reader" wrote, Horace, which does rather suggest the problem is not altogether new. Ken Clay would doubtless like Voices to do both. The question is how.

2. Things to avoid according to Ken

(a) Didacticism - many of us feel there is not much point in writing unless you have an audience; some of us go further and consider there is not much point in having an audience unless you give them the works. Too true. How many of us have lost friends that way?

(b) Social realism - this seems to me to be an extension of the above except that to the sin of proselytising is added the further sin of over simplifying. Capitalists wear black hats, communists white ones. To this too some of us must plead guilty.

(c) Naive idealism - Ken seems to be suggesting that even if people like us have something to say they don't say it because they feel inhibited, and tend instead to ape their betters. One reason for this might be that Voices is unique. Other journals won't publish unless the contributor sticks to the rules.

3. What is to be done then? Or, to put it another way, what would I do if I were a member of the Editorial Board?

(a) I would accept with gratitude any contributions which both delighted and instructed, although one could expect these to be few in number. Blake, Byron and Shelley, and say Siegfried Sassoon in his anti-war poems, could do it; but most of us are learning the hard way.

(b) The rest I would select according to whether they delighted or instructed, though I would expect Voices to have a bias in favour of the latter. There are enough glossy journals that serve to please.

(c) Those that appeared to fall into neither category would have to be returned to sender, though I would like to think that someone would be able to find the time to return them with a word of encouragement. There is no point in our persuading ourselves there is a vast amount of talent available unless we do our best to use it.

4. Ken may well think that my response raises more problems than it solves. e.g. what do we mean by "instruct" and "delight"? Well I'm not greedy. Let someone else have a go.

Bill Eburn

THE SILLY BLOODY WORKING CLASS

Who builds the bridges and the 'planes
Who builds the ships and all the trains
Who builds the roads and sleek fast cars
Who are slaughtered in their masters' wars
Who wander homeless in every nation
Whilst editors express their jubilation
At the jumping stocks and shares
Whilst pensioners starve and no one cares.
And who the fools that endure all this, alas,
The silly, bloody working class.
Who sweats and groans and grows old fast
Who suffers and moans and at the last
Are led like beasts to grim old places
To sit and sigh at unknown faces.
Whilst politicians lie in beds
Making up speeches about the Reds.
Who forms the queues outside the dole
Who in history has the role
Of saving all, except themselves, alas,
The silly, bloody working class.

Michael Ferns

MODERN POETRY, ELIOT AND THE WORKING CLASS

Does the modern poet write for the working class, or for fellow poets and critics? I'm afraid it is not the former. It is not that poetry is not easily available to the working class - it is. Its insularity derives from its esoterical lineage and its eruditeness. A poet, such as Eliot, has so many cross references (what working class man hears of Webster, or St. John of the Cross?) that the poetry can become like a Times crossword puzzle - interesting, taxing but pointless.

One can't help feeling that Eliot can only be appreciated by someone with a similar education to his own (remembering that he was at school until his mid-twenties). Obviously, he can only write of his background, his class, and the preoccupations of his class. The truth of the matter is that Eliot writes for poets; for a man to understand him, he must raise himself to the level of a poet. Which isn't a bad thing, but hardly feasible considering the circumstances of most people. To use one of Eliot's own phrases - "there is no objective correlative common to the rich Oxford educated banker, and the ill educated capstan lathe operator."

293

Poetry can only become truly modern, when it can live as the expression of a struggle to raise our conscious mind to a greater level of awareness. What has gone before in poetry has been the expression of a small minority of people's reaction to the universe and society, the greater part of humanity's feelings going unverbalised. It has been played like a game for the elite, with a strict, almost impenetrable code of conduct. It has been preserved like a Ming Vase, for all eternity - daring imitation or improvement.

Poetry should be written, digested and thrown away for practical purposes. Art is of its time, created from its time, by people who will take the rein of history and guide it. Do we need this over-indulgence in past expression, expressing what has gone is dead?

A people has its creative wellspring, and only when we become involved in history, will the poetry flow. When we awake to the modern situation, we will get modern poetry; and what poetry does a line of machines inspire? Real modern poetry will only come through an honest survey of the situation. Eliot represents decadence, art for the liberation of the individual, He is not concerned for the rest of humanity, other than the rich, or gifted.

A modern poet will realise his purpose and function. It will not be to give the dilettante something to prattle on about; or to furnish material for the professors to write exegesis. It will be to reflect, consider and direct the mass of people now ready to break in on history. To give them a mirror on themselves, and a fresh language to express their struggle.

Poetry has become the activity of the few for the few. It still is the poetry of unconnected individual destiny with an unhealthy preoccupation with self. Even poetry of rebellion - say Baudelaire or Rimbaud is put into a snug system, its shock value eliminated by careful study.

The truth has to be retold by each generation to itself. Reality has to be re-examined in the light of our total experience, which is different from generation to generation.

If we are the lost children of god, alone without a faith, we should not waste time looking for our lost father as Eliot does. We should look to find ourselves, and poetry must be of this struggle, not of lone individuals' search for the absolute.

Tony Whitfield

POETRY WHERE ARE YOU NOW?

Poetry; Daughter of inspiration and love,
where are you now in England?
Are you now drowned in intellectual blood,

has your body been ravished
and drowned by the flood?
Smashed into formless phantoms?

Poetry; Mother of rebellion and hope,
where are you now in England?
Have bandits of words now tethered your scope
to meaningless rantings?
Now in darkness to grope
in their minds empty spaces.

Poetry; Lover of freedom and truth,
where are you now in England?
ravished by demons both base and uncouth,
with no direction to roam
your torn body a proof
of dignified killers still prowling.

Ian E. Reed

A MATTER OF OPINION

He came to the village brandishing wall charts
Equipped with degrees and graphs
He lectured on social change and evolution
He stood his reasons up in rows
And argued with himself
To make his lack of prejudice apparent
Out of the crowd came a demanding shout
"Think yer clever, eh? Name me three early tatties!"

Vivien Leslie

REMEMBER YOUR KERB DRILL

Stephanie
Wait for me
Stand still
Remember your Kerb Drill
Open your eyes
It's not just a prayer.

Look right
Look left
And Look right again
And Look left again!
And Look right again!
And Look left again!
And...

Wimbledon has nothing
on this
At last a gap
Run across as fast
as your little legs
can carry you
Do not trip!
They cannot stop
They are not
Niggers or hippies
or old age pensioners
but good solid
First Class citizens
who do not
have to wait
respectfully
at the kerb.

Alan Prior

WE CAME EN MASSE

We came en masse
To cheer you in your hospital bed
complete with gifts
and smiling faces,
grouped round your clean clinical bed
a mission of love
with one eye on the clock.

And then you took the stage
and held us spellbound,
words and pictures tumbled
from your lips.
Heads turned round
and smiled to see us laughing,
though they could not hear
your droll and merry quips.

You warmed us,
we who had come to comfort
and to cheer.
And when we left
turning to wave at the door
we saw your smiling face
and took you with us
-somehow, we did not leave you
lying there.

Jean Sutton

ON WINTER'S HIGHWAY

Through a haze of driving rain
the distant hills are bleak and grey.
Wind, cold, gusty, gaunt, flaps the rain like blankets
pinned against the sky,
then slaps the backs of animals as they stand, miserable, patient.

The fields, full-flooded lakes, feed the ditches and the roads,
drowning all life.

All his darts thrown,
the wind staggers, falls, feebly struggles.
The rain, his former plaything, now gently covers him.
Suddenly the clouds break, a javelin of light flames through,
touches the hills on the instant, for man to see
all his hopes and yes, his immortality.

AG Froome

SAVING FACE

The Pound, my son, is best of friends,
which in thy pocket dwells,
In two score years and inure, I've proved,
No lie my Father tells,
Whilst pride of place, the cash to save,
He gave his full attention,
There's saving, other, I've learned dear Father
Than cash to merit mention.

The life-boat crew, whilst battling through
the storm think not of earning,
Or the fireman bold, when flames enfold,
Some helpless victim burning,
The Surgeon's skill with scalpel, will
Great numbers save from dying,
Each course they choose, at times may lose,
None count the cost of trying.

Although we toast this numerous host,
And others, who us do favour,
Unlike these deeds, among us, breeds,
Another form of saver,
Whose fellow man, he'd trample down,
That he himself may climb,
Would soul deprave, his face to save,
It's the ultimate, untried crime.

This Predator, in peace and war,
To no one land peculiar,
Would he in Hell be better placed?
He's surely nature's failure?

The death he's planned, while in command,
Some died without a trace,
what thousands yet will die to save?
Some Politician's face?

Will he, in anger with his finger?
Press the button we cannot stop,
All life disgrace, whilst saving face,
We can only wait and hope,
That while there's time, men will combine
With Charity and Worth,
No privilege crave, but just to save,
The face of Planet Earth.

Alexander Jamieson

TURNING POINT

Liggin' together o't' th'after,
We talked o' thi mam.
Aw'd said,
Mindin' 'er gabbin' an' laughter,
It wur 'ard t'insense, as hoo'r dead.
An aw rued hoo couldn't ha' known
Ut, tho' yo'n parted, 'im an' thee,
T' feelin's twixt us a' t' while 'ad grown:
Ut sum'dy luv'd thee - an' theaw me.
But, at t'moment, aw'r some an' ta'en
Aback, as tha nestled to lay
Thi yed o' mi shou'der - an' then,
She'll know now, though", aw yeard thee say:
An' so tha wept
Afoore tha slept.
We're nooan o' t' same mind o' this'n,
Us two; for me it's 'ard to grasp
One meht lam an' look an' listen
Who's nobbut neaw yepsintle ass.
Beside which, t' thowt one meht ha' sin
Us bally-to-bally jus' neaw
a rude sort of intrusion in
Ear lowly luv-o'er-t'latch, chuseheaw.
Thi breathin' steady wur good t'hark,

299

Whilst t' sliftert city neet-sky leet
Thwittled thi beauty eawt o' t' dark
So's gazin', fond, aw'r fain to see't:
An' aw c'd own
Aw'r nooan alone.

Bu' t' neet-lang shadder fancy –
yearnsfu' to compensate
for t' mischance o' t' toom moment
when aw'd failed to relate -
proved nooan jannock bi t' dawn leet,
an' ony rooad to' late:
frae't let-deawn - reet that moment –
thy luv wur set t'abate.

Jone o' Broonlea

GLOSSARY - Turning Point by Jone o' Broonlea

Insense - realise. Some-an' - very much. Yepsintle ass - a small amount ("handful") of ash. Meht ha' sin - might have seen. Sliftert - enter through a crack. Thwittled - carved. Fain - glad. Own - admit. Toom - empty. Jannock - genuine.

THE HOUSEWIFE

"Dear God, another day! What was it? - Tuesday, Oh yes, stairs and hall and mince-meat stew." Already the morning was slipping by. The pots waited; silently sneering under a blanket of egg-yolk and toast crusts. They should have been washed long ago, still, she promised herself that she would do them as soon as she had had another cup of tea.

She wandered over to the kettle, her image curving down its side, like the walls of the house around her throat. Icily she picked up the baby's rusk and put it into her mouth. She hadn't even realised what she had done until angry screams of annoyance met her half-closed ears. "Sorry chicken," she thought, too tired and distant to speak, and placed it back into her child's mouth. She lifted her hand to ruffle his hair but accidentally knocked his cheek with water-worn hands, heavy with boredom and hidden despair.

Plugging in the kettle she thought about how she had found her ring in last night's hot-pot. Should she tell her husband and make him laugh like she used to? Searching in her mind for the answer she realised she didn't even know how to talk to him any more; besides he probably couldn't remember her losing it. She put the thought out of her mind. It was too much trouble worrying over words. The pots grew in number. The electricity ran out and the kettle murmured to a halt. She went to sit down, tired out from thinking. Scared of thinking.

Rosslyn O'Connor

FIREWEED

A warm welcome to "Fireweed" announced as a quarterly magazine of working class and socialist arts, beautifully designed and printed, copiously illustrated, and with a dozen distinguished contributors, including the world-famous Bertolt Brecht and Pablo Neruda. If this level can be maintained, "Fireweed" will be that "flowering weed that spreads across waste land" which is the meaning of its title.

For the most part it is a fine compilation, and if this reviewer expresses his preferences, for the world-famous Neruda and Brecht, for Archie Hill's unbearably tragic story of a boy's first day at the foundry, for David Craig's poems of crofters, for the extract from Margaret Parkinson's novel, and for Leon Rosselson's magnificent folk ballads, others may well find matter for pleasure in other contributions.

It is said to be a brave venture to launch a magazine like this in these difficult days. But when the old world is visibly collapsing before our eyes, when revolutionary ferment and change is seen on every continent, among millions of people, the need for art to give confident expression, imaginative creative expression to it, to open up for hitherto silent man and women a medium in which they can speak for themselves, is very urgent.

Elsewhere "Voices" carries an advertisement of Fireweed No. 2 which will appear in the summer, and this promises to maintain the present level. "Voices" which carries no national names, and whose writers are so far unknown, sees in "Fireweed" a colleague and a co-worker, and we hope to be of mutual assistance in the future. Trade Unions, Labour Party, Communist Party and the host of people who both love the arts and work for socialism and peace, should give "Fireweed" active support.

Ben Ainley

LISTEN TO THE OLD MEN

Listen to the old men cry the pity
Remember remember remember to weep
Remember to breathe in long and deep
The smell of grass burning in the city.

Balcony railing scrapes shins unused to climbing
Bloodstain like ink on blotting paper
Spreads downwards and outwards on nylon stocking
Tears mingle at corners of mouth with desperate
saliva
Red scrabbling furious hands
Scratch at brickwork
Grasp at stanchion
In vain
The final irony
Not to jump but to fall
Like the first autumn acorn

Ten storeys she plunges
Breath forced out of tortured lungs
Screeches like the death cry of a train
Entering a tunnel
Turning on a bedroom light on each floor as she passes
Finally explodes blood and brains
Like a water bag on the concrete car park
The new curtains just would not fit

Ten storeys' worth of women send ten storeys' worth of children
To bed and weep
Ten storeys' worth of men make love to the women
Below on the adjoining half finished block
The old night watchman throws an empty soup can
At a mongrel peeing on the cement bags
On the ninth floor a woman stretches to put up new curtains

Smell of grass burning in the city.

Alan Arnison

302

WOMAN'S PAPER

Comment upon this whore's exchange
On methods how to get your man?
Sales talk on an accepted range
packeted to a streamlined plan.

Protuberance of breast and bum
Permitted but of belly barred -
Hogarth's exuberance become
Vulgar and therefore off the card.

More mealymouthed less glossy page -
That gives the little woman hints
On what attractions will engage
And hold her worker between stints.

Intellectuals display
Unmealymouthed and without ruth
Their wares in the same brazen way
Tricked out with scientific truth.

If you accept the woman's place
As brood mare, lollipop and drudge,
Here's how to prosper in that race,
But here's no relevance to love.

Frances Moore

PROMISE *Frances Moore*

Those who are ossified themselves in mind
And therefore also calcified of heart,
Postulate natural laws that bind
All of us to as limited a part.

When we first start to notice on our face
Wrinkles begin to annotate the years,
We hold our peace about our passion's pace
Lest we provoke the ignorant to jeers.

But lay it to your heart for coming time,
Love's possibilities are not laid down
By armchair pedants bent on tidying life.
Middle age modulates new joys to crown
Remembered raptures with refreshed delight;
Whose days are very full live far into the night.

MIDNIGHT *Kenneth B. Stump*

Flaps the ivy softly,
Cold against the wall?
Is the moon a-peeping
Neath its cloudy pall?

That's my love a-waiting
Shadowed by the beams
Harvest moon is making.
Wind, what are her dreams?

Lift the swaying curtain,
Trip the mossy stone
Round about the rose-bush
Love we are alone!

Midnight from the belfry
Booms for them its bliss
Age all lies a-sleeping.
Youth can kiss.

MODERN MAGIC

In the year thirteen hundred and seventy six
The people of Hamelin were in a rare fix;
Though the issue was simple and not politics -
All over the town rats were up to their tricks.
They lodged in Hamelin's rooms and halls,
Below the floors, behind the walls;
Moreover - this truth really shamed her -
There were rats at large in the Council Chamber.
At length an angry population
Flocked in a local demonstration,
Causing the Mayor and Corporation
To quake with a mighty consternation;
In absence of a quick solution
The townsfolk promised retribution:
Let the problem be rats, or the trouble be muck,
The Council of Hamelin could not 'pass the buck'.

Six hundred long years later
to us this story's strange;
better does Bristol City
its corporate chores arrange:

Bristol has men and women who toil day by day;
They sweep the streets and catch the rats,
They heat the schools and feed our brats,
Unclog blocked drains; for little pay
They nobly clear our waste away.
Yet, as I write my ditty,
To see fair Bristol dirtied so,
And see her townsfolk come and go
Mid refuse, is a pity.

Barbara Smith

MUCK

It overtops the dustbins, and blocks the drains and sink
It's pumped into the Avon so that the river stinks;
It's piled high in our gardens, and litters all the Down;
It's massed in heaps and scattered on the pavements of the town;

It clogs our feet and nostrils though we avert our eyes;
It lies in open spaces, and it smells where'er it lies.

I wish we had more people
Like Hamelin's forthright folk;
I looked up Browning's poem
And I read the words they spoke;
I imagine them in Broadmead, on the Downs or at the Zoo -
I overhear their comments, and watch all that they do:

Gazing wide wonderment at our predicament
Observing incredulous Bristol ridiculous,
They soon appraise it all, are not amazed at all,
Treat with derision our sham indecision
Avoiding solution, creating confusion.
To our body corporate in forthright terms they state

This firm conclusion:
You need not seek Pied Pipers of magic, good or ill,
Your cleaners, sweepers, wipers have the necessary skill;
Our Mayor and Corporation, knocked by our population,
Gambled fifty-thousand guilders
To rid our rats and mice.
You've got a better system? Then pay up, don't resist 'em;
Rise the fifty-five bob; pay the rate for the job -
Believe us; it's cheap at the price.'.

Barbara Smith

IF THINGS GO ON AS THEY ARE

If things go on
as they are
we shall soon
have more cars
than people
which means that
some of them
will have to be
driven by computers
if the profit increment
of the Stock Market
is to be maintained.

If things go on
as they are
what with all this
plastic rubbish
even babies will
come wrapped in
polythene and
we shall all go to
the Supermarket to
take our frozen pick.

If things go on
as they are
what with all
these transplants and things
my heart will be
in Liverpool
my kidneys will be
in Bristol
and my head
will be in the clouds.

If things go on
as they are
what with
Electronic Telephones
the cost of connecting
you from A to B
will be less than

the cost of working
out how much it is
and the system,
like the Oozlam bird
will disappear up
its own whatsit.

Alan Prior

WAR MAIMED GIRL AT A DANCE

A hurt one
A maimed one
A doll of a girl
A doll of a girl

She watches
They're dancing
They're all of a whirl
They' re all of a whirl

Just a short raid
Just a few dead
A handful hurt
Nothing more to it

Tee tom tom
Tee tom tom

(I wish I could dance)

(I wish I could dance)

Tee tom tom
Tee tom tom

(I wish I could dance)

(I wish I could dance)

Rose Friedman

FAR FROM MY WINDOW

Far from my window, far said he,
Ships skim the horizon,
And boulders bend down to the sea.
Near to my body, near said he,
Cogwheels spin my reason,
And Metals move close to me.
Fresh round my body, fresh said he,
Tulips and sapphires
Cling to the tree.
Stale to my mouth, stale said he,
Oils and grease
Collect around me.

Tony Whitfield

DRAMA NOW

What a place for drama is the countryside;
Panic-bold a rabbit darts across the lane,
Death by mutilation only just defied.

Overhead the crows watch, wickedly alive,
Waiting for the pallid lambs too weak to live
Their dim eyes to steal, e'er death itself arrive.

Half-up the hill, the old sheepdog plays his part,
Watch him as he crouches, coaxes, curls and twists,
Dog and man together knit in shepherd's art.

In the hedge the whitethroat's courtship song is sung,
Poised on a branch he pirouettes and patters,
Till from his mate the ans'ring notes are rung.

Oh! What a place for drama is the countryside,
And lucky he, who sees the pageant passing by,
And seeing it finds all his senses gratified.

Winifred Froom

THE DANCER OF DEATH

And she danced, and she danced,
And she reeled,
and she stealed,
across blood sodden turf
on that murderers field,
and her feet as they squelched
upon gore and on flesh,
the Generals they cheered,
their blood red eyes peered,
and their darkened mouths leered
at that stadium in Chile
that stadium of death.

And she span,
and she ran
her eyes full of glee,
a quaint "grand jetes"
on the graves
of the slaves
that once were so free,
to the tune of the bloated
that cackled and gloated
and clapped bloodstained claws
at that stadium in Chile
that stadium of death.

As she swung
her mind sung
of the gold she would make
for the ghouls and the Generals
that sealed Chile's fate,
and they fed her with caviar
with wine and with blood
fresh from the graves that
their soldiers had dug.
Oh she danced and she pranced
controlling her breath,
her feet caked with blood
Dame Margot Fonteyn

310

he dancer of death

Ian E Reed

ELEGY

Now theirs is the comprehension
of the strain and strand of the silky root,
and the seed's division.
They know
the flaws where life broke out,
and the secret chemistry which forced fruit from the rock,
the disposition forming man,
And how the first beat leapt.
From earth's fat in slow toil drawn erect, the
cause and strength, the single self;
from dissolution at the first, to unity,
the dispensation was this;
from the stillness to the creating realisation
in the individual reality.
Now for them combine those oppositions,
twist, tug, and link, which make the dry bones warm,
the grapple and union on the forge of thought.
And so on will they flare in the sun's last slide;
and in their transmutation,
the fullest communication.
By their going forth they have had assumption.

Keith Lloyd Jones

PERSON WITH THE GRACE OF A TALL SHIP

Person with the grace of a tall ship
the frame of a humming bird
the eyes of a peacock
and the voice of the lilac on a warm spring breeze
Let the shrouds of what you want to desire be lifted long enough for
me to be in your eye a moment, that I might, for that moment, stand as
tall as singers and men of property
so that I might not be condemned without
soul or dignity to the shadows of the gathering dusk as it whispers
across the fields cloaking all but the moon in black,
and that you might see reality, or me, for that moment.

Jimmy Barnes

NORTH SCALE'S WINTER

Oh lonely beach so long and flat
Glistening the memory of a recent tide,
Reflecting the cold blue winter's sky,
Deserted forum of summer pleasure,
Buckets, spades, freckles and sunburn,
Forgotten behind frosty windows.
Only I stand on your silken coat,
Tasting the salt from icy tears,
While the wind moves you always on,
Goading your being to restless wandering,
I stare at your open face listening for your secrets.
But even now wrapped in the same wind,
I am only an alien in your deep eternal doings.

AM. Horne

FATHER CRISP SELL

Having sold his toys,
Pleasing 1,000 yelling boys,
Removed his scarlet cloak,
A ribboned cracker joke,
Pulling off a tacky beard,
He winced and round he peered,
Seeing no one in sight or sound,
Thank Christ for that!' he shouted loud.

A.N. Horne

LAST RITES

Sorry were we
to put John down,
not wholly because
our turn would come.

Back at the house
full of wind and piss,
someone had to say
"John would have liked this."

Bill Eburn

CONTRIBUTOR INDEX

Ainley, Ben *1901-1977*
Retired teacher. 50 years active in CP, Teachers' Union and Peace Movement. Present hobby book reviewing for various journals. (1972)

Introductory (1)
Moving and Bright Days (1)
Parting (1)
Introduction (2)
Committee (2)
Desire (2)
In December 1923 (3)
The Day I Heard that Lenin was Dead (3)
Editorial (6)
Fireweed A Review (6)

Allsop J.I.
Councillor, Chairman Audenshawe Labour Party JP Hobby Allotment gardening

Laking - Yorkshire Holiday (3)
Was it Yesterday? (3)

Anonymous
A Sonnet: With Sufficiency (1)

Arnison, A
Listen to the Old Men (6)

Askell, M.G.
4th November 1974 (5)
Communication (5)

Barnes, J
The Bell spews its Evil (6)
Person with the grace of a tall ship (6)

Bishop, Joe
Born in Manchester. Elementary education to age 14. Member as a schoolboy of Proctor's Gymnasium Club Hulme, later a voluntary worker for the club, finally lifelong honorary member. Main interest walking, particularly round Cheshire, Old Time dancing, literature and, as a life long socialist, in political affairs. (1971)

A Dying Art (1)
An Idol Without Feet of Clay (2)

Booth, Syd
Formerly International Brigader Founder member of the Unity of Arts (1971)

Autobiographical Chapter (1)

Brennan, John *b1926*
Married. Finds writing, listening to music and reading history soothing after the hustle and bustle of a modern airport where he works as a refuelling technician. Interested in Horoscopology

Sounds in the Night (3)

Clay, Ken
Trellie (5)
A Few Observations about Voices (5)

Cole, Susan *b1953*
Student. Just completed A level course at St Johns College Manchester. Interested in left wing movements. One personal ambition is to have published my own book of verse. (1972)

Dawn (1)
Opening Stanza "In Death's Dream Kingdom" (1)
We Came Crying Hither (5)

Cooney, Bob
Aberdeen. Burns enthusiast. International brigader (1971)

An Auld Man Cam to Heaven's Gate (1)

Crawford, Betty
Married 1 daughter 3 grandchildren. Came to Manchester from Glasgow in 1959. Active in TU and Labour Movement. (1972)

Words (3)
Awakening (5)

Crispin
August (1)9 (4) (5) (5)

Cullen, T.M. *b1947*
Married 1 son. Just finished Teacher Training College and started first teaching job. Writes stories and poetry. Interested in aims of Unity of Arts Society of which he is an active member.

A House in the Morning (3)

Day, Joe *b1907*
Single. Retired through ill health. Formerly active in Furniture Union and Communist Party. Interested in the struggles of Manchester Furniture Workers in the pre war period (1971)

Recollections of the General Strike (1)
Wartime in Ford's (2)

Dixon, Bob *b1931*
Born in Spennymoor, Co. Durham. Got quite high up educational ladder but has almost found his way back to earth again. Now an English lecturer in a teachers' training college.

Agitpoem No. 8 - Bromley (4)
Leave Me Alone. (4)
Portrait of an Economy (4)
Ideas (4)
God Can't Care, Really (5)
Death-Bed (5)
Eyes (5)
Black and White (5)

Doyle, M
Former bus driver turned insurance agent. Liverpool

Reincarnation (6)

Eburn, Bill
Boy messenger, postman, civil servant. POW in far East. A late developer - member of Derek Stanford's poetry class at the City Lit. London. Trade Unionist. Optimist - still hopes to be around when the gates of folly fall. Now retired.

The Name of the Game (6)
Comment on Ken Clay's article (6)
Last Rites (6)
For Better or For Worse (5)

Edwards, Alfred *b1933*
Single. Warehouseman. Amateur photographer. Likes to have a go at anything: oil painting, writing, joinery, home decoration. Intellectually incurably inquisitive.

A Serenade (3)
Missin' The Clubman (2)
On An Abandoned Garden (4)

Ferns, M
The Silly Bloody Working Class (6)
Man in Winter (6)

Fletcher, Robert
An Appeal (1)

Frame, Colin *b1945*
Has studied music but never worked as a professional musician. Began writing 1971. Admires Henry Miller. (1972)

Celluloid Tears (3)
Three Poems (3)
Whatcha Mean (4)
I am Sorry for Them (4)
Tonight we will see the Dream-Drenched Drunks (5)

Friedman, Rose

I describe myself as a first generation Jew, my father having come to England from Imperialist Russia. I was born in the heart of the Cheetham Hill district and spent my earlier formative years in the Cheetham Hill and Strangeways, Manchester area. My values are geared to Marxist principles. I was a founder member of the now defunct "Kersal Jewish Discussion Circle". I have written about 40 poems, but I now find that my style of presentation differs greatly from my earlier work-although the moral contents remains the same.

The Christmas Present (6)
War Maimed Girl at a Dance (6)
Nickname on a War Memorial (5)
Green Toilet Rolls to Match my Bathroom Tiles (4)

Froom, Winifred
Being an Improbable Conversation overheard
through the half-open door to a Premature Baby Unit (4)
Comment on Ken Clay's article (6)
Drama Now (6)
All Awry in Paradise (5)

Froom, A.G.
On Winter's Highway (6)

Frow, Edward & Ruth
Ruth is Deputy Head of a school; Eddie retired A.U.E.W. District Secretary. Have collaborated in the production of many historical articles for workers' papers, and published several books including "1868, Year of the Unions" CE. Frow in collaboration with M. Katankai), "The Half Time System in Education" (Ruth and Eddie Frow), "Strikes" (in collaboration with M. Katankai). They are now engaged on a history of the Shop Stewards' Movement.

Book Collecting (2)
Benjamin Stott 1813- 1850 (4)

Frow, Ruth
Written on International Women's Day (5)

Garnett, Jim *b1896*
Worked in cotton mills since being 12 years old. Life member of weavers

union. *Trustee and auditor of Rossendale branch. Interests - furtherance of TU and working class politics. (1972)*

Rope and Birch (3)
Blaming the Woman (3)
A Good Woman (3)
Rossendale Weavers Union Women Members (5)

Garson, Sol *b1923*
Convinced that the shock of his birth killed Lenin, he has tried to make amends since. The only test he passed was that of being alive (by crying) and expects to disprove even that eventually with a little help from his friends Wills and Gallagher (1971) Married 2 children. Glassworker. Writes paints and sculpts (1972)

Why I Don't Write (1)
At The Popular Cafe (1)
Three Pieces:- (2)
 (1). On Seeing the Pithead at Aberfan (2)
 (2). 1 Million Plus (1) (2)
 (3). The Magindovid (2)
Black man, White girl. (3)
Some of our Best Men Went to Spain (3)
Chile (4)

Gowling, John
City Boy/Brown Baby (5)
To a Lancashire United Bus (5)

Gwilt, Rick
Building labourer. Various jobs - docker, warehouseman, groundsman, fruit picker, dishwasher, translator, fork lift truck driver. Very widely travelled - Havana, Acapulco, New Orleas, Montreal, Stockholm, Berlin, Jerusalem, Baghdad, Tehran, New Delhi etc.
"26. Communist. Former Manchester building trade unionist. Still member T&GWU. Now at Lancaster University studying Working-Class and Socialist Writing under David Craig. Writes/translates/directs plays. Fluent in French/German/Spanish. Captain of university athletics team, runs for Stretford AC, interested in history of sport." (Joint Editor of Voices -76)
On Returning Home After a Long Absence (2)
Woman (2)
Ssshh! (3)
Huston, Texas (3)
Note Passed in an Empty Lecture Hall (3)

Legend of Xanadu (3)
Poem for a Girl from Africa (4)
New Sounds from Motown (4)

Harcup, T
Factory Boy (6)
Oppression ... (6)

Hatton, Ethel *b1919*
*Married 2 children. Formerly a cotton worker. Interested in the advance-
ment of working class ideas and a better future for the children (1971)*

Our Neighbours (1)
If you Want to Get Ahead Get a Hat (2)
A Visit to Belle Vue (3)

Horne, A.M. *b1944*
*Married 2 children Sara and Jonathan. Fitter and shop steward AEU.
Vickers (shipbuilding) Barrow. Secretary Barrow branch CP. Delegate to
TU council. Enjoys struggling to bring up a family, struggling for social-
ism and struggling with a pint. (1973)*

Redundant Iron Works: Millom (4)
Dawn Chorus (4)
Me (4)
The Shipyard Cranes (5)
The Escape (3)
Arrival in Bowness (3)
Tomorrow was Yesterday Back to Front. (3)
Perspective (3)
The 7. 23 Omnibus (3)
Next Time (5)
Winters Beach (5)
The Quiet Black (6)
North Scale's Winter (6)
Father Crisp Sell (6)

Hughes, D *b 1949*
*Married 1 daughter. French. Came to England as student from Paris Sor-
bonne. Has taught in Morocco, France and now England (1973)*

The Gherkin (3)

Hughes, Ron *b1940*
Married 2 children Ex Mercantile Service. Whilst in building trade helped to found the Building Workers Form and BW Charter. President of the AUBTW. Now at Teacher Training College

The Picket (3)
Rose and Life (3)

Jamieson, A
Saving Face (6)

Jenkins, Mick *b1904*
One time delegate Manchester & Salford Trades Council and Shop Steward. Active in YCL and CP since 1923. Author of "Fredrick Engels in Manchester" and "George Brown, Portrait of a Communist Leader". Now doing research into the General Strike of 1842 and a little writing. Married with 2 children and 2 grandchildren.

Solid Gleaming Coal (4)
A Book at Bedtime (5)

Jones, K.L.
Elegy KL Jones (6)
Kessell, David
Glass is Dynamite (4)
Chile (4)

Lane, Patrick
Surgeon who Lost Son Indicts Killers (5)

Leavers, Jim *b1948*
Married 1 son. General labourer, paints in oils, sketches, writes prose and poetry

Three Poems (2)
Two Poems (1)

Leslie, Vivien *b1948*

Family moved from Devonshire to Scotland 1962. Trained as Display Artist but after several poorly paid jobs, took employment in an electronics factory. Currently at home with a one year old son. Finds time for a bit of writing and reading and intends to complete education (1973) (Galloway, Scotland) who was working in an electronics factory in Edinburgh when she first wrote for VOICES a few years ago, is now bringing up a family out in the country. "I grow lots of vegetables and fruit, sew and bake without feeling I'm betraying my sex, and I try to keep writing's (1977)

Harry the Tick Man (6)
A Matter of Opinion (6)
Electronics Factory (3)
"Children" and Children (4)
The Unmarried Mother-A Personal Experience (5)

Lilley, Ken

Engineer. Interested especially in the history of the Labour and Trade Union movement (particularly in the Engineers) in Gorton and Openshaw.

A Very Special Brew (5)

McFarlane, J
The Gun (6)

MacVeigh, C.J.
Boys & Girls Come out to Play (5)

Maher, Dennis *b1941*

Married 2 children. Active in TU and Labour movement. Vice President Manchester branch AEUW (constructional section) Interests literature, music, sport. Firmly believes that the heights of literature, culture and education can only be achieved with the participation of the working people (1971)

Home (1)
A Tribute to Jack Coward (1)
Poem (1)
Tribute to George Jackson (2)
Stranger in Vietnam (2)

Life is for Living (3)

Moore, Francis *b1913*
Married 3 children, 5 grandchildren. Teacher active in NUT and Communist Party. No time to write but has to, and is kept up to it by the response of the non-literary audiences to which she manages to read sometimes. (1972)

Action (1)
Industrial Strife (1)
Industrial Worker (2)
Epitaph for a Bitch (3)
Magnolia (3)
Discrimination (3)
Blues (5)
Comment on Ken Clay's article (6)
Woman's Paper (6)
Promise (6)

Moore, Robert
No Flowers in May (5)

Morgan, Fanny *b1912*
Elementary education till 14. Always active (1971)

O.T.M.S. (1)
Further Education (1)
Sans Almost Everything (2)
Onomatopoeia (3)

Morgan, Frank *b1905*
Elementary education till 13 years of age. Joined ETU 1930, became full time official 1948 till retirement. Always active in working class movement (1971)

The Glass Works. (1)

Morrison, Edward *b1932*
Married one daughter. Plumber self-employed. The struggle to rise gently above a frugal existence, the patching of a threadbare education and efforts to write have regrettably left no time for political activities (1971)

323

The Ragged Trousered Philanthropists (2)
Moon Laughter (2)
Suburban Automatism (1)
The Silent Bird
The Violent Universe
What Voices is all about
A Fable (3)

Murphy, Julie
*Married. Two teenage daughters and a son. Schoolteacher. Life long
member of CP.*

Holloway Prison (3)

O Broonlea, Jone
Win with Labour (5)
Rue (5)
Black Sheep (5)
Luvin' Tally (5)
Turning Point (6)

O'Connor
The Housewife (6)

O'Connor, Rod
*Is a joiner who has travelled around the U.S.A. and Europe. Enjoys any
type of music; is a song writer and guitarist and his ambition is to make an
L.P.*

The Building Workers Song (4)

O'Donnell, Vincent *b1903*
*Volunteered for service in the Abraham Lincoln batallion under Com-
mander Merryman and was accepted by the International Brigade at Alba-
cete 1937. Captured by Mussolini's Black Arrows near the river Ebro in-
terned at san Pedro de Cardena for 12 months before repatriation now
retired. (1971)*

The Freedom of Reason (1)

Parker, Frank *b1926*
Married 2 daughters, 2 grandsons. Mechanical fitter. Shop steward
AUEW. Left school 1940. Ambition to have all my plays produced, and
also an opera. (1973)

Pete (1)
1967 (1)
The Boy (2)
Communication (2)
Plain Pain in '7 (3) (3)
A Greek Tragedy (4)
Brown Windsor Soup (5)

Prior, A
Remember your Kerb Drill (6)
If Things Go on as They Are (6)

Reed, Ian E *b1944*
Unskilled worker (unemployed). Booted out of the army (for obvious rea-
sons). Communist - main interests: literature, mainly poetry, music and
world affairs. Writing poetry for ten years.

A Matter of Form (4)
The Lost, the Losers and the Lame (4)
Pablo Neruda (5)
Poetry - Where are You Now? (6)
The Dancer of Death (6)
Comment on Ken Clay's article (6)

Salway, John
Poetry and the Class Struggle (5)
Vigilante (5)
Self Made Man (5)
Exploitation (5)

Sentinella. Pat
Changing (5)

Smith, Barbara
Modern Magic (6)
Muck (6)
Struggle Identified (4)

Ressano Garcia (5)

Smith, Frank *b1912*
Married. Moulder by trade but has been groundsman and gardener for many years

Brown Eyes Such an Honest Stare (1)
What Gentle Saviour With Love in His Heart (1)
If Oo Could Oo Would (2)
On Coming on a Tramp (3)

Smith, John
Sent without accompanying letter. Could be pseudonym. If "John Smith" reads this will he write to Ted Morrison, Secretary of the Unity of Arts Society, the publishers of Voices.

Beasts of Britain (3)
A Song of Piggy Banks (3)
Now I'll Sharpen My Pencil (4)

Stump, K.B.
Midnight (6)

Sutton, Jean *b1934*
Married 5 children. Employed in works canteen. Would prefer to stay at home and write short stories and poetry. Regrets wasted schooldays at secondary modern school. Hates racial prejudice (1973)

Pipe Dream (3)
Feel the Need (4)
Passing Through (4)
The Duttons of Martha Street (5)
Staunch True Comrade (6)
We came en masse (6)

Tatford, Dave
You See Me Smiling? (5)

Thomas, Frances *b1964*
Used to live in Walmer Street, Rusholme which is being knocked down.
Now lives in Wythenshawe. These words are exactly what she dictated to
me in answer to the question, "What do you want this story to be about
then?" I have not added or changed anything

Walmer Street (4)

Thomas, Gareth *b1952*
Born in Essex. Numerous jobs, now working at the Morning Star. Recently
started the London Communist Writers' Circle, which now has ten mem-
bers. Admirer of Cervantes, Hemingway, Sartre. Ambition to see all cul-
tural activities supported by the people, not the exclusive set' of 'privileged'
charlatans who now monopolise the arts.

Clean-up Job (4)
The Clothes Peg (5)
Traffic Lights (5)

Tuckett, Angela *b1906*
Married 3 step-children and 5 step-grandchildren. Became first woman
solicitor in the west of England. Assistant Editor of the Labour Monthly
many years, currently writing the official histories of the Blacksmiths' Un-
ion and the Shipwrights Society. Chairman of the County Womens Hockey
association. NUT life member. Politically active? Of course. (1972)

Poem (1)
Rockabye Statesman (2)
Put to Proof (3)
Joy and Pleasure (3)
Song (3)
The Living Seed (5)
In Praise of Cooks (5)

Wales, E
It's all Your Fault (5)

Walker, F.G. *b1925*
Checker, warehouseman with firm of beer distributors (Bass Charrington)

for 32 years. Shop steward. Took O levels and A levels in English through correspondence course. Hates inequality, abhors cruelty to animals. Still plays football. Cycles 12 miles daily to and from work. Writes detective stories and has had several published (1973)

A Meeting in the Night (2)
Cupid (3)
Pseudonym (6)

Whitfield, T
Modern Poetry, Eliot and The working Class (6)
Far From My Window (6)

Wiles, Maurice M *b1898*
Ex-teacher, Badly educated: understands Greek but not differential Calculus. Favourite authors: G.B. Shaw, F. Engels, Bernal, Keats, Thomas Hardy (poems) Lucretius. Hobby: cultiver le jardin.

Random Thoughts of a Telefan (4)
Points of View (5)

Willey, Ken
The Engine Room (2)

Wilmot, J
The Drunk (5)

ALSO IN PRINT

VOICES 2
ISSUES 7 - 13 1975 -1977

6" x 9" paperback 352 pages

Includes work by:

*Andy Darlington, Alex Barr, Bill Eburn, Bob Dixon,
Connie Ford, David Kessell, Ian Reed,
John Cooper Clarke, Keith Armstrong, Jean Sutton,
Ken Clay, Les Barker, Michael Balchin,
Paul St Vincent, Rick Gwilt, Rose Friedman,
Wendy Whitfield, Yusuf Idris, Vivien Leslie,
Tony Harcup,*

VOICES 3
ISSUES 14 - 19 1977-1979

6" x 9" paperback 374 pages

Includes work by:

*Arthur Alden, Bill Eburn, Blackie Fortuna,
Bob Cooney, Jack Davitt, Jim Arnison,
Jimmy McGovern, Joe Smythe, John Gowling,
John Koziol, Keith Armstrong, Ken Worpole,
Ken Clay, Mike Rowe, Phil Boyd, Ralph Peacock,
Rick Gwilt, Roger Mills, Ripyard Cuddling,
Sue Shrapnel, Vivien Leslie.*

VOICES 4
ISSUES 20 - 25 1979 - 1982

6" x 9" paperback 388 pages

Includes work by:

Bob Starrett, Bill Eburn, Ruth & Eddie Frow,
Jimmy McGovern, Joan Batchelor, Joe Smythe,
John Small, Ken Clay, Keith Armstrong,
Mike Rowe, Rick Gwilt, Mick Weaver, Roger Mills,
Vivian Usherwood, Vivien Leslie, Tony Marchant,
Sol Garson, Kevin Otoo, John Gowling,
Blackie Fortuna

VOICES 5
ISSUES 26 - 31 1982 -1984

6" x 9" paperback 451 pages

Includes work by:

Ailsa Cox, Andrew Darlington, Bobby Starret,
Jimmy McGovern, John Gowling, Keith Armstrong,
Ken Worpole, Michael Butler, Mick Weaver,
Mike Jenkins, Mike Rowe, Olive Rogers, Phil Boyd,
Ranjit Sumal, Rick Gwilt, Ruth Allinson,
Tom Durkin, Vivien Leslie, Wendy Whitfield

website www.mancvoices.co.uk